To Booby Buddha,

All the best,

Bill Cedie.

_____

Whoosh!

Charlie Spuds

By Bill Leckie

A London Press book

Copyright 2004 Bill Leckie

The moral right of the author has been asserted.

A CIP catalogue record for the book
is available from the British Library.

ISBN 0-9544636-9-2

London Press
108 Westcott Crescent,
Hanwell,
London, W7 1WR

0871 218 0214

www.thelondonpress.co.uk

Printed and bound by Antony Rowe Ltd, Eastbourne

Thanks for help and inspiration are massively due to...

Des McKeown, George Rowe, John McVeigh, Andy Smith, Mark Wilson, Brian Crawford, Colin McKinnon, Jamie McKenzie, Allan Moore, Jimmy Thomson, Gerry McKenna, Ally McMillan and Neville Neville.

Christine Bruce for the proof-reading.

Cheers also to Steve Wolstencroft for loads, to Scott Bowden, Graeme Provan, Garry Ollason and Keith Campbell.

Plus, of course, undying gratitude to my soulmate Melanie, without whom I would be nothing.

Oh, and apologies to mum for the sweary-words...

For Kenny, the Guv'nor

Charlie Spuds, *n*: Football dressing room term for one who has ideas above his station and expresses them in an arrogant way.

Charlie Spuds, alternative *n*: Big, bad, bastard who doesn't react well to having bags stuffed with cash nicked off him.

11.10pm, Tuesday

"SO what's yer plan, fannybaws?"

"Dump ma bag on the bed then dump ma guts in the bog."

"Just remember an' dae it that way round, eh? Mind if Ah watch telly – there's English highlights on."

"Fire away, Ah could be some time in here."

"Gie's a shout if ye want a hand wi' the paperwork. Anythin' decent tae read?"

"Thought ye were watchin' telly? Honest, Screech, ye're hyperactive."

"Thanks, Dr Weston, Ah'm well capable o' doing two things at once – which it sounds as if you are as well. You crappin' a bowlin' ball?"

"Feels like it. There's Viz and Q in ma bag or a Spike Milligan. Help yersel'. Screech? Ye found them? Schreech!"

"Westy..?"

****

"WELL?"

"He's sortin' it."

"How?"

"Flight tickets. Have them by the mornin'. Naewhere we could get tae this time o' night anyway."

"Where we goin'?"

"Does it matter as long as we GTF pronto?"

"Ah still say we got clocked."

"Aye, we heard ye. But what if we were? What could they dae? They'd never know who we were. Fuck them."

****

"THE boss is gonnae kill us, Rhino."

"How? It wisnae our fault."

1

"Ah mean, when we go in an' tell him we don't have a Scooby where it is."

"So whit's he wantin', Tam? For us tae shout the odds, get everybody talkin'? The polis would be on our backs before ye could say blag."

"You tell him that, then."

"Aye, right. We'll get the bastards, don't worry. An' anyway, chances are he'll have had a sniff fae somebody on the phone. Anybody that knows anythin'll want tae tell Charlie Spuds."

"Jesus, an' will thae twats get it when he finds them!"

"Nae money in the world's worth that pain."

****

"WESTY? You deaf in there?"

"What?"

"Did you pack this bag yersel'?"

"How, what are ye? British Airways check-in?"

"If Ah was, Ah'd be callin' security, son."

"How come?"

"How *come*? Let's just say it's a little more full than usual. Ye hear me? Ah said yer bag's - oh, there ye are."

"Ah heard ye, Ah was just pullin' ma kegs up. Honest, if that wee bastard Chunky's done a shi-."

"He hasnae. Look."

"*Fuuuuu*-ckin' hell..!"

****

"*ANYWAY, nae point worryin' for now. We'll sort it first thing.*"

"*Sort it? Ye mean sneak out the country without what we were meant tae be sneakin' out wi'?*"

"*Will you fuck up? Yer bottle goin', is it?*"

"*Bollocks it is – but we should a' be in Spain by now. Loaded and pished. But we're in this shitehole instead, skint and fucked.*"

2

"Shut it, you two. It's been one long fuck-up, it's naebody's fault. It happened. Let's just forget it and get out before they suss where we are."

****

"SORRY, boss."

"Don't worry, boys, I understand. Panic'll get us nowhere. You were right not to shout it about."

"Thanks, boss. You got any leads?"

"Zip. Yet. But they'll come, then we'll be on them. We'll get back what's ours and they'll get what's theirs, big time."

"Cheeky bastards willnae know what's hit them."

****

"THIS, ma boy, is utterly unbelievable."

"Like Ah mentioned before, fuuuuuu-ckin' hell!"

"Ye know what's happened here, don't ye?"

"Ah think so."

"An' ye know what we've got tae dae, eh?"

"Aye...."

****

"WE'VE got tae get some sleep."

****

"We've got tae find these people an' quick."

****

"We've got tae phone the boys an' get them in tae see this!"

3

Monday

HE put the phone down and blew out through pursed lips until his lungs must have looked like burst Mitres.

"What? What's up?"

"It's the morra."

"The morra?"

"The morra."

The four of them sat silent until one breathed: "Jeeee-sus..."

Silence again. Clock ticking on the kitchen wall. Boiled kettle clicking off. A siren on the street. All four wishing someone would say something. Eventually someone did.

"Look, heids up. We've planned this for months and we only get the one crack at it. If we're gonnae be brickin' it we might as well no' bother. Lose our bottle and we lose the lot."

"OK. So he's a hundred per cent sure it's the morra?"

"Hundred an' ten. He knows the deal if he sells us a dummy."

"An' he's sure they won't be mob-handed?"

"Definite. Yer man wants the deal done low-key, face-tae-face. Just him and two minders-"

"Who?"

"Tam Robinson and big Rhino McAllister. His main men."

"Rhino's a monster."

"Aye, but it's like the joke about telling the boy that wants tae mind yer motor ye've got a rottweilers in the back seat – and the boy says: 'Can it put fires oot?' He's only any good if gets his mitts on ye."

"Or clocks ye and gets ye later."

"No chance. Stop worryin', man, it's nae sweat. They'll be at the warehouse, the other mob trap wi' the dosh, diddly-dee, the

4

gear gets handed over, other mob splits, easy-peasy, him an' the minders walk calmly tae the motor carryin' a coupla bags an' drive away, diddly-doo. Our guy says that's how he did it last time."

"What if the other mob bring a squad, take the money AN' the gear?"

"No chance. They widnae dare turn yer man over. Who would? There'd be mayhem. That's why he does it himsel', broadcasts a signal that he's no' tae be messed wi'."

"So let's go through the plan again."

"Aw, shite - how many times..?"

"Haw, button it! Ye cannae plan too carefully, ye know that fae way back."

"Aye, but we're no' in the Army now."

"Still on manoeuvres, though, eh? Still a team. One fucks up, we a' fuck up."

"If you say so. A'right, get yer wee drawin' wi' the pins in it oot again, then."

He rolled a piece of wallpaper across the table, a crude map sketched on the back and little coloured tacks dotted here and there.

"Right. So yer man and his boys drive in through the gate here, 15.45 hours-."

"Why there anyway? Miles away fae his territory, innit?"

"Exactly the point. Never does it on his ain doorstep. OK? So they park, walk back tae the warehouse - round the side door, no' the front. Other mob's due at four. They'll drive up close to the front door, be in and out in five tops an' Bob's yer auntie's live-in lover. Yer man won't make them wait till he counts the dough, they know the drill if they short-change him. Same goes the other way wi' the gear. Once the other mob goes, we're on. Clock yer man and his monkeys comin' oot, wait till their backs are totally turned to us, then-."

"Bang!"

"Correcticus! They're sparko in the alley, outa sight. Never seen us, never heard us. We take the bag – he says they always use big

5

fitba' kitbags, ten-a-penny an' incognito as ye like – and we're outa there. By the time anybody finds them we'll be 200 miles away giein' it yee-hah."

"Sounds easy right enough, but are we dead sure the minders won't check out the area before it goes down? Or that they willnae have a couple of spotters up where we're gonnae be?"

"Trust me, he swears they never leave their gaffer's side. He won't use spotters because of the whole low-key thing. An' even if they DID do a sweep round just in case, we've hidden fae Argies commandos in Port Stanley, we can surely lie low when a paira nightclub bouncers come tramplin' through the undergrowth."

"So we get there at – what? – three? Come in across the disused factory site behind, up the banking, get down in the grass an' wait?"

"Yep."

"Are we happy wi' oor van bein' round behind the warehouse? An' while we're at it, whit we daein' makin' a getaway in some heap called a Renault Kangaroo?"

"Kangoo, fudface. An' we've got one because it's as nondescript as any vehicle in history, which suits us perfectly. We're no' auditionin' for The Sweeney. We're no' skiddin' about in a '66 Jag. We dae a quiet job, we make a quiet exit. A'right?"

"S'pose."

"Good. So the Skippymobile'll be well outa anybody's vision. Remember, ye kid on ye're sleepin', right, so anybody gies ye a tug ye say ye're havin' a quick skive."

"Nae sweat."

"But it'll no' happen. Yer man's pullin' this in broad daylight, which tells ye he's confident naebody's gonnae tumble. Stay cool an' we're in Carlisle in two hours. Torch the van, fly out first thing in the mornin'."

"Then it's sun, sea an' shaggily-daggily-ding-dongs! Y Viva Espana for the A-Team! Just wan thing, though – are these guns gonnae dae the job right?"

6

"Listen, there's enough tranquillizer in there tae bring down three REAL rhinos. An' we've got spares if by chance one o'them disnae go down first time. They'll wake up half an hour later wi' sore heids, sore arses an' no' a Scooby what happened. Nae blood, nae murders, just the perfect diversion."

"Plus, they willnae fancy goin' tae the cops tae report losin' 250 grand they'd only just picked up in a heroin deal."

"That's why it's perfect."

"Skoosh case."

"Cannae fail."

"Fuck..."

7.30pm, Boston Bar, Springburn

CHARLIE SPUDS put the phone down ever so gently, sat back in his leather chair, crossed his legs, steepled his fingers under his chin.

"That it sorted, gaffer?"

"It is, Rhino."

"What time they be there?"

"As planned, Rhino, as planned."

"Ye don't think they'll try an' turn us ower us, boss?"

"Like the man said, Tam - war, what is it good for? Absolutely nothing."

"Ah don't get ye."

"Maybe not, Tam, but they do. An' that's what matters. They won't try and turn us over. They wouldn't dare. They're on our territory, so they'll be in and out and gone and it'll be job done. Nope, this is looking nice, boys. Very nice."

8.05pm, Ochilview Park, Stenhousemuir.

INVERCLYDE THISTLE v OCHIL UNITED
Tuesday April 8
Meet at park 4pm for 4.15 <u>prompt</u> departure
No pre-match meal arranged. Club tracksuits.

Squad

Kevin Oates
Harri Baum

Garry Ronald
Barry Ronald
Jimmy Donaldson
Francis Albert
Rowland George
Danny Campbell

Giovanni Wilson
Jamie Kennedy
Martin Boothroyd
Mark Gerrard
Ally McGonigall
Mark Weston
Stevie McCracken

Willie Walters
Frank O'Donnell
Gibby Johnston
Lee Allan
Crawford Brown

"LISTEN up. *Listen!* Haw, SHUT IT!"

The post-training dressing room babble gradually died away until the only noise was Shyness murdering Robbie Williams in the shower.

"Shyness! *Shyness!* HAW, McGONIGALL, PIPE DOWN!!"

"Sorry, gaffer!"

"Right, listen in. Good session the night, good tempo, ye're startin' to get what ye're told. Only taken since July, but miracles don't happen overnight, eh? Now, we all know what a huge week it is for this club. Three points at stake tomorrow night at Cappielow, then away straight after the game to the hotel."

"Aye, the wife's delighted, gaffer."

"She will be when the bonus comes in, Porridge."

"He'll drap his."

"Shut it, Chunky, ya fud."

"A'right, a'right. Ah know yer families'll miss ye for a few nights. But how often will any of us get this chance again? A Scottish Cup semi wi' Glasgow City at Hampden? Forty-odd thousand there and live on the telly? Aberdeen or Hearts waitin' for the winner? Europe just 180 minutes away?"

He gave that last one a few seconds to sink in with them.

"Aye, that's right. Us, two games fae EUROPE. That's how big this is, boys. It's HUGE. The club've done right by us, lettin' us go away to prepare right. We've got the run o' the facilities at the hotel and use o' the park at Greenock Juniors for trainin' every day. City themselves won't prepare any better."

"Or run up as big a bar tab, eh Taxi?"

"Well, there's nae chance that you'll buy a beer, Donaldson."

"Aye, well that's a point. Wednesday mornin' we'll have a half-hour loosen off then you're free till a right hard session on Thursday. Do what you want in between – golf, swim, sleep, have a few beers even. No curfews. We're treatin' you like grown-ups, but that means you have to act like grown-ups. This is the biggest week some of you will ever know in football, maybe in yer lives. Don't cock it up for the sake of a bevvy. OK? Francis, you're in charge. It's on your head."

"That's how Ah'm baldy, gaffer. Ah had an afro before you made me captain."

"Ye can always trust Blue Eyes, gaffer. We'll a' be in bed before eleven."

"Aye, but we're trainin' at ten, Gio. Anyway, that's miles away yet. For now – an' Ah know this is hard – forget Saturday. We need these three points at Cappielow. We're four behind them wi' a game in hand, so two wins an' we're second top wi' four to play. It's in our hands. Let's win this one THEN get ready for the semi."

"Ah think Ah've got one already just thinkin' about it!"

Tuesday

4.05pm, Denny, Stirlingshire

INSIDE an echoey, empty, warehouse, Charlie Spuds stood up from behind a square, formica-topped table and held out a right hand knuckle-dusted with a sovereign ring, another with a large ruby in the middle and a third with the initials CK.

The leather-coated black man on the other side of the table had stood throughout the meeting. He kept his hands in his coat pockets for a second, then pulled the right one out and extended it. Charlie Spuds shook it firmly and smiled politely.

"Nice to do business gents. You'll excuse us if we don't see you to the door. No offence."

"Just so long as there's no guard of honour waiting outside it for us, guy."

"Aw, come on. That's no way to think about a trusted business partner who's invited you all the way from Manchester. There's no one around but us three and you three and we'll not be leaving until your vehicle is well clear of the premises. Fair enough?"

"Suppose. So we'll be off, then. Speak to us again some time."

"We'll do lunch. Now, safe home."

"You too."

4.18pm, Ochilview Park, Stenhousemuir.

TOM HAGEN looked at his watch then back at Taxi Allen as the pint-sized winger sprinted round the corner towards the bus. When he was just about level with the door he told Jackie to drive off. The boys watched their mate drop his holdall and stand there, hands on hips, jaw gaping, afternoon sun illuminating his big sticky-out ears.

11

The bus was out halfway down Tryst Road before the gaffer told Jackie to stop and punched a number on his mobile.

"If ye're no' on board in six seconds ye're drapped for tonight AND Saturday."

He made it in five point seven.

The gaffer never even looked in the winger's direction as he barked: "Let's get this nursery outin' on the road, Jackie."

4.31pm, A803, Stirlingshire.

"HE clocked us!"

"For the millionth time, he didnae!"

"He fuckin' did – he turned and he clocked us!"

"That's pish – he was on his way doon fae ma pellet up his jacksie, he just fell awkward, he couldnae have seen nothin'."

"Ah'm tellin' ye, he fuckin' saw us – we're dead men!"

"Any chance you two bawbags could shut the fuck up? Ah've had this for the last 20 fuckin' minutes, Ah'm tryin' tae drive along a country road as normal as possible and every bastard that's passin' can see youse screamin' at each other in the back seat."

"Aye - rap it back there. He saw fuck all. An' even if Ah'm wrong, what DID he see? We were ten yards away, up on a hill, camouflaged. He'd need tae have laser vision tae know who'd pinged them."

"Well, Ah still think-"

"SHUT THE FUCK UP AND LET ME FUCKIN' DRIVE!"

"Belt up an' watch the road, fuckwit!"

"Who you callin' a fuckwit? Ah'll take yer heid aff!"

"Road, ya boaby, road! Yer headin' for a junction! We're comin' ontae a dual fuckin' carriageway!"

"It's thae wankers, they're burstin' ma hump."

"Ah thought that was just a plook on the backa yer neck!"

"Right, ya prick, that's it-!"

"Naw! BUS!"

"Fuck it!"

"SHIIIIIIITE!!! HAUD OAN!!"

JACKIE MITCHELL'S reactions were sharp for 61. He clocked in the wing mirror that nothing was belting up the outside lane, jerked the wheel, avoided a head-on with the white van screeching across the give way onto the southbound A80. He yelled for the guys to get down, cover their heads.

Then the dull thump, the squealing like a fork across a greasy plate, the smash of glass, the shouts. Followed by an awful silence while they tried to work out if they were alive or dead.

Jackie leaned forward on the wheel, eyes closed, breathing hard. Didn't feel like he was hurt. Got up and faced into the bus, standing behind the gaffer who was already scanning beyond the ashen faces of the directors to see how his players were. Guys were picking themselves up off the aisle, one or two holding bumped heads. No one seemed badly hurt. He said he'd go and check the damage outside. Bill the kitman said he'd go too, he'd seen some bags spill onto the road.

Blue Eyes did his skipper bit, made sure no one had broken bones or burst eyes, then followed the pair of them off.

The van had hit the back end of the bus and spun off, ending up facing into the traffic. Cars were starting to slow up behind the accident, hazard lights blinking.

"Thank God the road's quiet," said Blue Eyes. "That could have been horrible."

The luggage hold door had opened on impact. Holdalls and hampers were all over the road. Looked like it had flipped up and caught the van, forcing its back doors open. The van's whole passenger side was dented and scraped. Jackie, Bill and Blue Eyes looked at it until they were pretty sure it wasn't going to do the U.S. cop show thing and blow up then nodded to each other to go and see what was what.

They'd just taken their first steps towards it when the passenger door flew open and a heavy-set man in camouflage gear stumbled out.

Waving a rifle.

All three instinctively ducked tight against the side of the bus. On board, the guys at the back hollered to the rest to come and see the drama. The gunman had run across the carriageway, leapt the central reservation and was standing on the northbound side, pointing the rifle at a woman in a silver Escort who was too transfixed to swerve out of the way. She screeched the brakes, but they were all sure she'd splatter him. Suddenly it wasn't a telly show they were watching, it was terrifying real life and death.

"Jesus!"

"Ah cannae look!"

"The guy's a maniac!"

She stopped no more than three feet short. The guy never blinked, just loped round to the driver's side, rifle still fixed on her chalk-white face, wild eyes almost burning through the windscreen. Then he was opening the door, hauling her out, getting in. She lay on the reservation, screaming her lungs out. He battered the horn.

CHARLIE SPUDS couldn't possibly have heard a van and a bus crash six miles away, but right at that moment something woke him with a start.

He had a terrible pain in the arse. But not half as bad as the one he'd have when he realised what had happened to him.

As the dried ice cleared and his head spun a little slower, his eyes began to focus. All he could see was a wall with a crack running up the pebbledash. That and gravel. Then he realised he was lying on the ground.

Then he remembered where and a wave of anger went through him like a bad curry.

He tried to push himself up to a sitting position and his head swam again. He made it at the second attempt, closing his eyes to stop himself fainting as blood hurtled to his brain.

But the pain in the arse nearly made him keel over anyway.

He lifted his left buttock, reached round and fumbled, felt feathers, a stem. Pulled.

"Fuck!"

It was a dart. A short, slim dart like the ones tribesmen fired from blowpipes. He put his hand to his backside again, checked for blood. There seemed to be none.

By now it all seemed to be pumping into his temples.

He opened his eyes, blinked against the sunshine. Didn't have a clue what time it was. Looked at his watch but couldn't focus on the numbers yet. Looked at the dart again, half in fury and half disbelief and stuck it in his jacket pocket. Then his ears tuned in to the groaning behind him and he turned, hell of an uncomfortably.

"Tam! Rhino!"

His head throbbed at the sound of his own voice. The two bodies sprawled next to him started to stir.

"Wha-? What the f-?"

"Tam, Rhino, get up! C'mon, fuck sake! Get a grip o' yer pants!"

Tam got up first, one hand against the wall to steady himself. He looked at Charlie Spuds, confused, like a toddler wakened from a deep sleep. He looked down at Rhino, then back up at his boss. Then they both looked down as Rhino let out a long, low moan. He too tried to get up, but his arms buckled in the press-up position and Tam had to reach forward and grab him. They collapsed in a heap together. Rhino boaked and some of it splashed onto Tam's black trousers.

Charlie Spuds put his head in his hands, partly because it weighed a ton but mostly in anger and confusion. The full enormity of what had happened was coming together. Somehow felt it was happening to someone else, but the picture was forming all the same.

15

They were shaking hands on the deal. He was getting a bad vibe from the other lot's attitude as they took the briefcase and left. They were giving them a few minutes to get clear, then Tam was nodding the all-clear, Rhino had the bag and they were off.

They were outside, Spuds was locking the door and pulling down the shutter, Tam and Rhino were waiting for him. And then … and then … nothing.

Until he woke up with that terrible pain in the arse.

"Boss, the bag's away."

"Ye don't say?"

"How in the name – Ah mean, how did they-?"

"Feel yer arse, Tam."

So Tam felt his arse and pulled out a dart. Rhino reached round behind himself and pulled out a third.

"The cheeky bastards!"

"They drugged us?"

"Cheeky bastards!"

Spuds struggled to his feet and told the other two to do the same. Rhino looked at his dart, held it between thumb and foreigner like a ciggie, then threw it hard against the warehouse wall. Then they all just stood there, dusty and shaky and disorientated, wondering what had hit them.

And who.

Spuds brushed down his black pinstripe suit with the flat of his hands, straightened his yellow silk tie, smoothed his greying hair. Took a long, calming breath. Then he looked down at his two dishevelled henchmen and pointed his left thumb and forefinger like a gun.

"Gentlemen? Someone is going to die for this."

THEY'D almost been able to hear other's hearts beat inside their shirts. They'd cruised the job, sweet as you like. A team, just like old times. Then the van had filled with adrenaline that poisoned their minds like someone had hooked them up to the exhaust. And they'd lost it. In every way. The springs had gone boing on a clockwork operation and poked them right in the eyes.

"You better hope we get outa this, ya twat."

"Shut yer f-!"

"That's him set! Go! Go! GO!"

They leapt from the van, everything such a blur now they didn't even see the three terrified guys in tracksuits trying to make a bus suck them in, nor all those pairs of goggle-eyes glued to their getaway. They just had to get in that Escort and beat it or they were finished. They'd almost made it when they remembered they'd forgotten the one passenger that really mattered.

"The money - get the fuckin' money oot the motor!"

"Fuck it!"

But when he raced back to the battered van the money wasn't there. Must have got flung out the back doors in the crash. He hadn't even noticed all the other bags strewn across the tarmac. Don't panic, though, stay cool. The one he wanted was very distinctive, a bright red Reebok with blue and gold trim.

Just like that one there.

And just like the one lying three feet away from it.

The bastards were identical. An' he could hardly open them up to see which had money in it and which didn't.

He heard the horn honk. Again. Again. Angrier each time.

"JESUS CHRIST, MOVE IT! GET THE BAG, YA DICK!"

Think, think fast. Angle it came out at, where would it land? There, it would have landed right there. That was it, no doubt about it. Thank fuck. Grabbed the bag, got it on his shoulder and ran like fuck. Threw it onto their laps in the back, dashed round and in the front. Smoke belched off tyres. Offski.

"What the fuck were you daein'?"

"Gettin' the bag – it fell oot the motor!"

17

"What? Wi' the ones aff the bus?"

"Aye, but-."

"Tell me we've got the right one! Please tell me!"

"Course we have, open it an'-."

"FUUUUUUCCCCCKKKKKKK!!"

"WHAT?"

"A shellsuit. Some night-oot gear. Shoes. Books. A Walkman. But nae wall-tae-wall used notes tae be seen, ya- ya – ya FANNY!"

"We should kill you right now, fuckface."

11.20pm, Room 312, Glenbank Hotel

"SO whit's the big panic? You two hoofs comin' out the closet at long last?"

"Naw, Chunkster. Even more shockin' than that. Everybody got a good view o' the bag? Good – now, remember the scenes in Pulp Fiction when Samuel L Jackson opens a case an' there's a blindin' gold light and whoever sees what's inside is, like, totally awestruck? But the audience never gets to see what causes a' this awe?"

"Aye...?"

"Well, this is a bit like that. Except this time ye DO get tae see what it is. Ready? Eyes down..."

He unzipped the holdall and pulled the flaps apart.

"Jesus, Mary and Joseph!"

"Ma thoughts entirely, Reverend."

"So how much is there?"

"God knows, we're too busy hyper-ventilatin' tae count it."

"So does this mean-?"

"Aye, Gio, it means that somewhere out there a gang of armed robbers are frantically tryin' tae find a fence who'll launder young Westy's rancid y-fronts."

"They'll go *mental*."

"Ye think?"

"They'll come after us, nae danger. What the fuck dae we dae?"

"Jimmy's right – fuck gettin' involved wi' thae loonies!"

"So what we gonnae *dae*?"

"Ah'll tell ye what we're gonnae dae. We'll – hang on, Westy, somebody at the door. Stash the bag in the wardrobe before Ah get it. Could be anybody."

"OPEN UP, DUGBAWS, THIS IS YER CAPTAIN SPEAKIN'!"

"Come in, Blue Eyes, quick. Gaffer about?"

"In the bar wi' Bibs and the chairman. What's a' the racket in here? Ye can hear it right down the corridor."

"This. Show the man, Westy."

Westy pulled the bag from the wardrobe and opened it again. Blue Eyes recoiled like something had leapt out and hit him between the eyes.

"Jesus wept! Where did that come -? Hang on, is that what Ah think it is?"

"If ye think it's ma pocket money, no. But if ye're thinkin' it's what thae nice men in the white van thought they'd taken away in the hijacked motor, ye'd be dead right."

"How much?"

"Havnae counted it yet. But mair than fifty quid."

"Blue Eyes, we've got to hand it over to the police."

"Aye, Ah might have known you'd read the sermon, Father Rowland."

"Shut it, Chunky. He's right. They'll be lookin' for this money right now. We're in big shit if we don't turn it in."

"Ye'd think so, skip. But can we stick on Ceefax for a moment?"

"Why? Cheap holidays tae Rio?"

"Naw, ya dick. We were watchin' it in the room when these two shouted us in. Page 106, ah think it was. Oooo-kaaaaaaay – slow as a week in the jail, this shite is – aye, there it is. POLICE BAFFLED BY GETAWAY WITH NO ROBBERY. Read on, boys – remember what the gaffer said after him and the chairman spoke tae Plod? The polis hadnae been investigatin' any robbery, so they couldnae work out where the guys who smashed intae us had come from or where they were goin'. Now, we a' told Plod we saw the neds do a

19

runner, we saw them take what they thought was their loot, but NAEBODY has reported anythin' being stolen! See?"

"Chunky, correct me if Ah'm wrong here, but are you suggestin' Westy just keeps this rather large amount of cash an' we act as if nothin' has happened?"

"Well, how no', Bluey? Think about it – the bad guys realise they've left the bag wi' us, but they'll be certain the polis have picked it up at the scene and if not that we've done the decent thing and handed it in. The polis, though, think the bag the bad guys have is the one fae the robbery. But that's where the trail ends, because whoever was robbed hasn't felt the need to tell Mr Plod. That means Mr Plod doesn't even know how much was taken, never mind where from. And no one but us has a clue where the money actually is."

"Ye've given this a bit though, eh, Chunks?"

"Just a tad. And is it just me or is what transpires from all this quite lucky for us?"

"No, Chunky, it's not. It's dishonest. Whether someone's reported it or not, these are the proceeds of a robbery and we have a duty to give them back."

"Fuck sake, Ginge – gie's a break. This is ma fantasy here, Ah'm just throwin' it out tae ma pals so they can enjoy it for a few minutes. Ah know we have to hand it back, but you don't have tae say it. Ah mean, we know deep down there's nae Santa, but we don't say it."

"There's nae Santa?"

"Tell ye later, Gibby. Meantime, Ah never thought Ah'd say this, but Ginge is right."

"Aye, you shatter ma fantasy as well, Willie."

"Sorry, Chunks. But we're takin' a hell o' a risk even standin' about here lookin' at the money. The polis are bound tae ask why it took us tae nearly midnight tae ring them."

"Haud on, that bit's easy. Ah didnae open ma bag until we got in the room. Ah never needed anythin' before. That's the truth."

"An' we just happened tae be here when ye did. Just took a while tae get over the shock before we did our civic duty, eh?"

"So how come naebody's on the phone yet? No' even you, Ginge? Willie? Blue Eyes? What ye sayin', skipper?"

"Blue Eyes?"

"Ah hear ye. Look, Westy, is there any way ye could have checked in an' hit the sack without openin' the bag?"

"Well, Ah was knackered when Ah got here. Ah mean, that was a right hard game. An' Ah was carryin' ma toilet bag, so it was teeth brushed, kit aff an' beddy-byes."

"So conceivably, we could *all* go beddy-byes none the wiser an' find out about the money in the mornin' once the situation vis-à-vis the polis, the robbers an' the mystery victim has become clearer?"

"Mibbes..."

"Sounds fair."

"I'm still not sure..."

"OK, Ginge, respect to that. Pick the phone up right now, dial 9 for an outside line than three more if ye really want tae ease yer conscience. No one'll hold a grudge. Right, boys? Chunky?"

"Course not. It was only a fantasy, eh? On ye go, Ginge."

"Well – well, I should, but Blue Eyes might be right there. We're tired. We're wound up from the game-."

"You're no', ye sat in the stand."

"-and leaving it till morning's not the worst plan. Saves the police tramping all over the hotel and getting the gaffer annoyed, eh? It can't do any harm, can it?"

"That's the boy. Just nobody talk in their sleep, eh?"

The Boston Bar, Springburn

CHARLIE SPUDS'S head was still full of cotton wool, the backside of his trousers stuffed with lumps of it. But what hurt most of all was his pride. It stung like he'd been attacked by a dozen jellyfish - except that jellyfish poison was neutralised by being pissed on, while the knowledge of how badly *he'd* been pissed on from a great height that afternoon only made the pain worse.

Had somebody grassed? Mibbes, mibbes not. Mibbes when the other mob had made that crack about the guard of honour they'd had their own little surprise waiting outside for him. It was the risk he always ran doing things so low-key. Maybe they'd reckoned he was getting soft. If so, they'd soon find out they'd been well wrong.

But if there *was* a grass, a rat under the floorboards? Oh dear. He'd be sorely, sorely disappointed. He'd out them and they'd tell him who they'd grassed to, no worries. And once he'd dealt with that end of it, he'd personally send a message to anyone who thought they could profit from stiffing Charlie Spuds.

He'd had that nickname since Ian McGill gave him it when they were in Primary Five. Hadn't said it in a Charlie Big Potatoes, He-Fancies-Himself-Rotten sort of way. He just had a head like a King Edward. He flushed the wee rat's head down the bog for that – just to help wash the blood off. But for some reason the handle stuck with his closest mates.

And so, as he graduated from playground protection racket organiser to running a gang of shipyard apprentices nicking and selling everything from toolkits to grand pianos, then to moneylender to bookie-cum-bare-knuckle-fight-promoter to respected giver to charity and big-time drug dealer, Charlie Kerr had become known to friend and foe as Charlie Spuds.

Woe betide anyone who heard the label and laughed.

He shouted at whoever was at the door to come in and regretted it immediately as once again his ears rang from the sound of his own voice. Rhino and Tam squinted in the gloom of a room lit by a single standard lamp behind their gaffer's antique leather chair. The low glow turned him into a silhouette, feet up on the walnut desk, hands behind head.

"So?"

"Hee-haw, boss. Nobody saw anythin', nobody heard anythin'. We've been well turned over."

"Not what Ah want to hear."

"Sorry, boss, but that's the truth. An' we couldnae really be too visible in case the wrong ears heard, could we? We're headin' back out the now tae chap some mair doors, slap a few faces if we need tae-."

"No. Get some rest, but be back on the case first light, understood? We'll sort it, don't worry. Some shitebag will pay for this."

Same time, Flat 16/4, McLean Court, Dundee

"YOU asleep?"

"Sleep? Ah cannae sleep – Ah'm too worried about what we're gonnae dae about the money."

"Find out where they fitba' wankers are an' get it back!"

"Aye, right, Rambo – ye think they'll still have it? It'll be at some cop shop hours ago. If yer man still hasnae reported it, CID'll have divvied it up among themsel' an' it's case closed, baroomp-ching!"

"Aye, an' the only way the fitba' wankers would still have it is if the polis are usin' them as bait so we'll charge in. Nah, we're fucked."

"Fucked twice if yer man tumbles us. Nae money AN' deid – that's a shite day's work by anybody's standards."

"He'll no' tumble us. Who'll grass?"

"Who'll grass? Your grass'll grass once his share doesnae turn up!"

"Aye, an' risk getting' his legs broken for turnin' Charlie Spuds over? Get a life, man!"

"That's pish and you know it!"

"Everybody calm down. We're a' tired, let's get our heads round this in the mornin'. We'll sort it, don't worry. We've two hundred and fifty thousand reasons tae sort it."

23

Wednesday

1.10am, Room 316, Glenbank Hotel

"**WILLIE?** You awake?"

"Naw, but Ah was getting' up tae answer some dobber shoutin' ma name anyway, so don't worry about it."

"Ah cannae sleep for thinkin' about that money. What d'ye think we should do?"

"In the real world? Gie it back first thing in the mornin'."

"But..?"

"As much as he's generally a halfwit, Ah see Chunky's point. If naebody knows where it is, why no' keep it and spend it? Who'd gonnae know the difference, know'mean?"

"But what if thae loonies that stole it come after us?"

"We'll blame Screech an' Westy an' let them take the kneecappin', OK? Now go tae sleep, man. Some o' us had a game last night."

"Ah cannae sleep. You got anythin' tae read?"

"Just the programme fae the game."

"Surprise, surprise – just happens that the only readin' material in the room's the thing wi' your big write-up in it?"

"Quality, son, quality. It's lyin' next tae the telly. Just try and no' make too much noise when yer lips move readin' it, OK?"

Gibby Johnson got up, took the glossy A5 magazine with Thistle News in blue on the cover, flopped back onto his bed and flicked through until he came to his pal's grinning mugshot:

24

MEET MY MATES

ON SATURDAY at Hampden we'll all be behind giantkillers Ochil United as they carry the Diddy League flag against mighty Glasgow City in the Scottish Cup semis at Hampden Park - but tonight we wish them all the WORST as they come to Cappielow looking for vital Diddy League championship points.

Among their squad will be one of THE great lower division character … larger-than-life striker **WILLIE WALTERS.** *So who better to take us on a guided tour of the United dressing room in a special Meet My Mates?*

KEVIN OATES: Our keeper's nickname is Porridge for obvious reasons, but the way he looks the morning after nights out it should be Quaker! Loves a bet and a beer and fits in the odd clean sheet. Age? Between 29 and 104.

HARRI BAUM: How we landed a teenage German back-up keeper is a mystery. Officially, it's something to do with a student exchange and there's talk about him being a Bayern Munich youth team superstar. Nickname? Hairy Bum.

GARRY/BARRY RONALD: One's the right back, one's the left back. But take their numbers off and I'm lost. Such identical twins they're even as thick as each other. Dad Ronald is our club secretary and sister Mhairi is receptionist at Ochilview.

FRANCIS ALBERT: The captain. The big cheese. Numbero Uno. The head honcho. The baldiest git in football. The son of mad Sinatra fans, he's United's karaoke king - and while old Blue Eyes is at the back, we always sing when we're winning. Sorry!

JIMMY DONALDSON: They call him The Shadow. Why? Imagine being his room-mate, waking in early dawn with light creeping through the curtains - and seeing a 6ft 4in silhouette doing something that's sure to ruin his eyesight.

DANNY CAMPBELL: The lads shouldn't still call him Lambchop — I mean, it WAS only ONE sheep. Had to be patient recently thanks to the Ronalds, but patience is his middle name. That's parents for you.

ROWLAND GEORGE: The Ginger God of our subs' bench plays football as a distraction in between counting his share of the family fortune. About 17 minutes of first team football in seven years, but we're nice to him in case we're in his will.

LEE ALLAN: Ah, those ears - it's a miracle he still goes up the wing so fast considering the drag factor. But the truth is he's NOT nicknamed Taxi because of his Dumbo-stylee lugs. It's because he was conceived in the back of one.

STEVEN McCRACKEN: Most ironic nickname at the club? Chopper. Anyone who thinks he's our resident hatchet man has plainly never seen Mr Nice play. The Trevor Brooking of Scottish football. Favourite curse? 'Flipping heck'!

GIOVANNI WILSON: Jet-black hair, stubble, swarthy skin and smouldering eyes. He just HAS to be our midfield Enforcer. Er, no. He couldn't fight sleep, but he CAN pass a ball when he isn't checking himself in the mirror he keeps down his socks.

MARK WESTON: Every day is Valentine's Day for our Mr Romantic. Been dating Kirsten since they were foetuses and everything he does, he does for her. The fact that he does hee-haw most of the time is neither here nor there.

JAMIE KENNEDY: If they gave Moan Of The Match awards, Chunky couldn't find a cabinet big enough. Call him a great ballwinner and he'll say: "No Ah'm no'." If he won the lottery he'd complain that the jackpot was too low the next week.

KENNY GERRARD: The Great Screech ploughs tirelessly up and down the right, though yet to touch the ball. More tattoos than Edinburgh Castle - the latest is under his oxter and says MUM. Nice tribute to the last deodorant he bought.

MARTIN BOOTHROYD: They don't call him Heed for nothing — like a wise man once said, it's like an orange on a toothpick. It's got its own weather system. Meets the ball on his forehead and it's still a foot above his eyelashes.

ALLY McGONIGALL: Walter Mitty's life was mundane compared to Shyness. His tan suggests Monaco, his gear screams Milan. Truth? He lives up a close in Partick, has a sunbed, a Next catalogue and a fantastic imagination.

FRANK O'DONNELL: Fud by nickname, fud by nature. Holds in perpetuity the World's Most Irritating Conversationalist title. Could send the air in an empty room to sleep. I dread matchday because it's the one time I can't get away from him.

CRAWFORD BROWN: Nickname? Craw. Not because of his name, because he looks like an extra out of The Birds. It's the hooky nose and the talons for fingers. And he eats worms for his pre-matcher while staring at women through the window.

GIBBY JOHNSON: My perfect best pal - loyal, discreet, generous and not good enough to take my place. We go back to our schooldays, where he spent five happy years in Primary Two. Many great times in football, though not with Ochil.

WILLIAM WALTERS: What can I say? Slim, fast, alert and in his prime. A striker very much in Scotland's plans for the future. Also one of the most handsome characters in football today, as well as the wittiest and most modest. Nickname? Sir.

"Cheeky tosser."

"Ah heard that, Johnson."

5.34am, Flat 16/4, McLean Court, Dundee

FOR a few beautiful seconds when he woke he was sure it had all been a nightmare, that it was actually only Tuesday morning and it was all still in front of them.

Then, like the horrors of drunken disgrace breaking through the fog of a hangover, it all came back. Piece by piece. Fuck up by fucking awful fuck-up.

And he closed his eyes and cursed as the truth seeped through his very bones.

They really had ambushed Glasgow's No1 hardman minutes after he'd done a major heroin deal. They really had shot Charlie Spuds and his two heaviest heavies with tranquiliser guns and robbed him of £250,000.

Then they really *had* lost the money.

Now it really *was* dawn on Wednesday and they were dead men.

He'd known hijacking the woman's motor had been stupid, but what other way out had there been? Hijack the fitba' team's bus? Take them all hostage?

There'd been no option but to act fast and think later. Five minutes up the A80 he'd got his head back together and formed a plan. Gave the order to come off at Stirling services, park up, spot two sets of wheels that looked like they were there for the day and quietly take them.

OK, they'd be caught on CCTV, but they'd already been clocked big time by half the teatime traffic in Central Scotland. All that mattered was getting away. Two in each motor, head for Dundee. He had a pal there, ex-Army, sound. That's where they were now, four of them in the spare room of his shitty high flat.

Hadn't given him any bull, he'd have put two-and-two together soon as the news came on. He wouldn't drop them in it, he was too far off his head 23 hours a day. A few bob for skank and he'd be their pal for life.

But what now? Where next? They should have been on a plane to Majorca an hour ago, well sorted. Though even then, it was dawning on him now that he didn't know what the fuck they'd have done once they got there.

Blown it, probably.

Got mouthy and let word drift back.

Ended up face down in a pool somewhere.

Yesterday, everything had seemed so simple. Now, it was all negative, seemed so obviously doomed to failure from the off. Black. No way out.

No, stay positive. Focus, like the old days. What would Charlie Spuds be thinking? That they had the dosh, of course. Until, of course, he rang a plod on the take and found out it'd been handed back – and after that he was screwed, because it wasn't like he could ask the cops to hand it over. He couldn't even admit to anyone who wasn't bent that he'd ever had it.

All that would even go partways towards making him feel better was finding out who'd taken it and nailing their noses to the Town Hall clock. Number one suspects would be ones he'd sold the drugs to. They'd have some big talking to do and chances were he'd make an example of one of them so the talk was also straight. They might even convince him they were innocent. He might even believe them.

And then? Dead end, hopefully. There was certainly nothing to put him onto them. Even off CCTV their faces wouldn't be known. No previous, no connections and the Army had never flashed their mugs about much, not with the kind of work they'd done. They'd been pros.

And by fuck, hadn't all their training come in handy yesterday?

Infiltrated half the terrorists in Belfast without dropping a stitch but couldn't hold onto a gym bag.

6.54am, Room 312, Glenbank Hotel

"TWO hundred an' fifty thousand pounds."

"A quarter of a bastard million."

"Arrabiatta's wages for a month."

"We've got tae gie it back."

"Course we have."

"Nae option."

"Ah cannae sleep."

"Me neither. Want tae look at it again?"

"Mair than porn..."

8.14am, McLean Court, Dundee

ANDY came in with the papers. Silly bastard should never have risked it, but there were too many other things going on to argue the toss. The biggest one being the fact that they were all over every single front page.

There were CCTV piccies right enough, but bugger all anyone could I.D. from them. Good news was the cops still hadn't a clue who'd been turned over, where, when or for how much.

All they knew was, four neds had hauled some bird out of an Escort and done one with a bag full of money.

Except, of course, that they hadn't. They'd taken the wrong bag. But that was the thing – it didn't say anywhere in any of the stories that the actual bag with the actual money in it had turned up. And hang on - how come they didn't know yet how much had been nicked? The fitba' tossers must have handed it back, surely?

He sat back like he'd been hit with a cattle prod.

"Fuck me!"

"What?"

"The cheeky bastards have kept it!"

"Who?"

"The Alexander Brothers - who d'ye think, chuffbucket? The fitba' tossers! They've got oor two fifty grand!"

"So? Let's go an' get it."

The rest were awake now as well.

"What's the noise about?"

"The cheeky fuckin' bastard fitba' tossers have kept our money. The polis still don't know we took the wrong bag or how much we got away wi'."

"Or didnae."

"Or didnae, smartarse. But they've still got it, boys."

"So let's go an' GET IT!"

"Just like that?"

"How no'?"

"What? We just drive up tae their Scottish Cup semi-final hideaway hotel, ding the reception bell an' ask tae speak tae the tosser wi' the holdall wi' £250,000 in it?"

"Aye, well..."

"We could kidnap one o' them an' get it back as a ransom."

"Aye, or we could always just walk intae the nearest polis station and haud that CCTV picture up against our coupons. Get real, man."

"So what's your plan, brains?"

"Ah don't fuckin' have one."

"Nice."

"Aye, but think about it. If we continue not to have a plan we could always forget it ever happened an' walk away. It could remain one o' the great unsolved crimes of modern times."

"What?!? An' let them keep it? Spend it? When it's OURS?"

"Spend it where, exactly? A buncha part-time fitba' players start runnin' round wi' cash hangin' out their pockets an' naebody bats a hingmy? Ye think the fact that they've got it willnae get back tae Spuds? That he'll no' be on them like a shot? He'd skin them alive. He'd burn their hooses, burn their fuckin' STADIUM. They'd no' last two minutes."

"So we just leave it?"

"Would ye rather go after it an' get huckled?"

"Fair shout. Just the one problem."

31

"What?"

"No' what - who. Your man on the inside, he's gonnae want his £10,000. Ah'd get ready for a call."

"Ah'll blank it."

"An' he'll shop us. Ye should put the phone aff."

"Cannae, Ah'm waitin' for a call fae that boy who's tryin' tae fix us a flight out. Anyway, Ah told ye already, Spuds would kill him as well as us if he shopped us."

"An' that's meant tae make me feel better? Ah don't gie a fuck about him, just me."

"What happened tae us? Maybe if we'd been us yesterday this widnae have happened."

"You tryin' tae blame me? Because Ah'll fuckin'-"

"Ye'll what? Come on, Ah'm just aboot ready for you, ya twat. Fuckin' wrang bag? Ah shoulda pushed you oot the motor an' left you tae the polis."

"Haw, you two! Pack this shite in! The question here isnae who's tae blame, it's can we walk away fae this an' live. Can we?"

"Aye, Ah think so."

"Me tae."

"We mibbes need tae get away further, but probably."

"Then let's keep thinkin' that way and keep walkin'."

9.20am, Glenbank Hotel

"OH-HO! Here comes Chopper McCracken, the man o' the moment!"

"What have Ah done?"

"Got yersel' a' over the back pages, superstar!"

"Let me see..."

Willie held up the *Scottish Sun* with the headline:

SHAKIN' STEVEN!
United goal hero tells of armed robbery terror

SHELLSHOCKED Steven McCracken handed little Ochil United a Hampden boost last night — hours after staring down the barrel of a ruthless gangster's gun.

The part-timer and his Diddy League mates cowered as robbers SMASHED into their team bus then HIJACKED a car to make their getaway from a daring hold-up.

But United showed incredible courage to play on in their vital promotion clash away to Inverclyde Thistle - and engineer McCracken threw a spanner in the home side's work with the only goal 12 minutes from time.

He said: "Seeing those armed robbers so close up was terrifying and we were all shaken up. The gaffer asked if any of us wanted to sit it out, but the game was too important. Fair play to everyone for coming through it."

"That's poetry, mate. Ye're a legend."

"Aye, except that he never stared down any barrel of any gun, did he? The twat was hidin' under his seat!"

"That's right, Fud, Ah was – you were hidin' behind me. Personally, Ah think the boy's summed up my performance perfectly. He should get an award."

"For what? Fiction?"

"Jealousy, Jimmy, pure jealousy."

"Anyway, never mind all that bollocks. What about the front page? Turn it over, Wills – see? MYSTERY OF ARMED HIJACK GANG – Cops hunt robbers AND victim."

"Your readin's comin' along nicely, Chunks."

"Thanks, William. An' ye'll agree Ah read the situation nicely last night. Naebody still knows nothin' about-."

"-what those guys did? That's right, Chunky. Anyway, are we all still up for that meeting in Screech's room after breakfast? The gaffer just wants me to make sure he knows what everyone's up to on their day off. OK wi' you lot?"

"Thought it was after trainin', Blue Eyes?"

"Ah, that's where I am the bringer of glad tidings. Such was the magnitude of our performance last night in the wake of our encounter with those gun-toting scallywags that we have been excused boots."

"Superb – so where's the gaffer now?"

"Him an' Bibs are watchin' City videos. Ah've just had a chat an' told him you'll all be good little boys today. So then, Screech's in – what? – 15? An' Chunks? See if ye can postpone the Town Crier audition till then, eh?"

"Funny guy."

CID Briefing Room, Central Scotland Police, Falkirk.

DI ANDY McKENZIE had never been so frustrated by a case. He'd investigated murders with no sign of a killer, hold-ups so quick and daring there wasn't a witness statement worth the paper it was printed on, disappearances that left him believing in alien abduction.

But never a £250,000 armed robbery without a clue about who'd been robbed.

The neds who'd pulled it weren't the problem. He'd get to them soon enough, within the day if everyone got their fingers out. This was a gang who'd cocked up so badly half the teatime traffic in Scotland had seen them. Their dabs were all over not just the van they'd used on the job, but the two cars they'd hoisted from Stirling Services as well. Their mugs were on CCTV from there too. They'd left a smellier trail than a slug with the runs and couldn't possibly hide for longer than a few hours more.

No, the problem for McKenzie was that he still had no idea who they'd turned over - or even for how much.

In fact, if it wasn't for the fact that four masked men carrying shooters had been seen running to a hijacked car with a bulging holdall, McKenzie would have no reason to believe there had been a crime at all. But what the hell else was in the bag to make them act like that? Were they hurrying home before their chips got cold?

He looked round the gaggle of tired, unshaven faces and sighed. Fourteen plods and tecs had been on the go all night and no one had turned up a shred of info worth a monkey's. Outwith the sightings of the gang, no one was saying anything because apparently no one had seen or heard anything. So make that no info worth three wise monkeys.

"Right, boys and girls - as much as I fear I know what the answer will be, anybody got anything fresh for me?"

Suddenly everyone was looking at their shoes. McKenzie shook his head.

"OK then, we'll do it the classroom way. Ronnie, where you at?"

DS Ronnie Black gave an apologetic shrug. "Pretty much where I told you last thing last night, boss. We've spoken to all the Ochil players and management, to the chairman and directors, the kitman, the bus driver and got the same descriptions all round - army combats, ski masks, three out of the four pulled up so their faces showed. We've spoken to the woman driver whose car was hijacked-."

"How is she?"

"Shaken up, couple of scratches, not kept in hospital overnight. She gave a pretty good description of the one who put her through it. There's an e-fit on the bulletin board behind you. About a dozen other drivers caught up in the traffic jam have also contacted us with info."

"A dozen? The road was chocca all the way back to the services!"

Black shrugged again. "Hard to track down any more if they don't come forward, unfortunately. Apart from all that, the scene of

35

crime boys have combed the Renault Kangoo and the woman's Escort and seem to have buckets of residuals."

"Which tells us that either these guys were amateurs-."

"Or supremely confident that they weren't going to be caught, boss."

"Correct. And I think the second. Anyone got any thoughts?"

Alison Gray, a young DC who McKenzie thought was heading for the top fast, coughed and piped up.

"Strikes me that they were confident for two reasons, Sir. One, that they have no form, which suggests they're a team put together for one job they had an inside track on. And two, because they know that whoever it was they rolled can't report the loss of however much it was to us."

"Give that girl a coconut! Those, Alison, are my thoughts entirely. So what we have to establish is this; who was doing something naughty enough to involve a whole shedload of naughty money somewhere in the Falkirk area sometime yesterday afternoon?"

"Why only the Falkirk area, Sir?"

McKenzie looked across to his left, where DC Ian Allan was leaning against a filing cabinet. Slow boy, but thorough. Probably knew the answer that was coming, but wanted to make sure his own assumption wasn't off the mark.

"Good question, Ian. And my answer would be that they were on a sliproad onto the A80 when the crash happened. A sliproad coming from the village of Haggs, just outside Bonnybridge. The A803 out of Falkirk through Bonnybridge to Haggs leads onto Kilsyth, Kirkintilloch and the north side of Glasgow. Had they pulled the job here in the town centre, in Stirling or any big town even further afield, they'd have been more likely to get on their toes a far quicker way than this one. Question is, where were they coming from? And, more importantly, WHO were they coming from?"

Again, the whole room looked at its shoes. Then, as if on cue, the door opened and in came a tall, muscular figure who would have made heads turn when he walked into any room, even if it hadn't been halfway through a meeting as important as this. DS Des Bradley's chiselled features wore a look that half suggested he'd run some distance to get there and half that he'd just been given some excellent news. As it turned out, both were true.

"Sorry, boss. Did you get the message that I'd be late?"

"I did. And you look like it was worth the effort getting here, so fire away. We could do with a wee lift right now."

"Hope I can give you it. Remember the tip four or five days back that a big drugs number was going down? Well, I've just spoken to two separate snouts who swear it's gone down and that was where the robbery happened."

"Interesting. So are we talking about the drug suppliers doing a double-dunt?"

"Don't think so, boss. And you probably wouldn't either when you hear who they think was at the selling end of the deal."

"Surprise me."

"Charlie Spuds."

The gangster's name caused the usual murmur it did when mentioned in most circles. DC Gray jumped in again.

"Makes sense. He's got a warehouse on an estate near Denny, eh? Did we not turn it over looking for bent gear a while back?"

"We did, Alison. If I remember he seemed to get wind and it was clean as the proverbial when we got there. Seems to happen a lot with Mr Charles Kerr."

The room let McKenzie's dig pass without further comment, but they were all thinking the same as their gaffer was. Kerr was a heavy, heavy man with a growing empire of moneylending, dope dealing and extortion hidden behind the clean-as-you-like front of chains of bookies, pubs and dry cleaners, a man with cops breathing down his neck 24/7 - and yet a man who never seemed to turn a hair about their attention. Each time they got close to nailing him - be it Glasgow cops, Central cops or Lothian & Borders cops - he seemed to be one step ahead. It was almost as if he had inside knowledge of when they were coming.

So many plods and tecs in all the forces touched by Charlie Kerr's spreading tentacles had been left with red necks after raiding his offices, boozers or lock-ups only to find the square root of hee-haw that being on his case had become one of their most hated duties. A ton or two of smack when they arrived to surprise him? Forget it, not even an aspirin. They never even had to batter doors down. Kerr always let them in personally, offered them tea and biscuits, made them squirm with his put-on politeness.

Almost as if? Of course he had inside knowledge of when they were coming. The bastard knew before they did.

And now at least a couple of them in that briefing room were about to draw the short straw and have to face the biggest humiliation yet. Asking him to admit he'd been robbed of money he wouldn't admit in a million years he'd ever laid his manicured hands on.

Des Bradley would be one of them for sure, it was his tip. The smart money would be on Alison Gray going along with him because she knew the lie of the land at his Denny branch.

DI McKenzie turned back to Bradley. "Any idea of how much?"

"I'm told a quarter of a million and I've no reason to doubt the source."

McKenzie gave a little whistle. "Nice bit of work by our demolition derby team. Now, if it was Charlie Spuds who they turned over, he'll obviously be keen to do our work for us, hunt them down and relieve them of the merchandise, so that makes it all the more crucial that we find them first. No point this turning into a murder enquiry as well. Ronnie? See me when we break up and you can co-ordinate that end of it. Those two cars they nicked must have turned up somewhere by now, even if they've been torched. I get the feeling finding these guys could be the easy bit. But I'd rather find them alive, squeeze a confession out of them about whether it was Spuds they robbed and kill two birds with one stone. This could be our chance to put the arm on Mr Kerr once and for all. Des? You find him and talk to him. By the time you go back upstairs, Bob Grieve should be on duty. Take him with you."

He saw the disappointment on Alison Gray's face. "And you, Alison, take DC Allan out to that warehouse and nose about. Knock doors, see if anyone saw anything, anything at all that might place that Renault Kangoo there. You know the drill, give the whole plot a good combing."

"Sir."

"Listen, it's a thankless task for all of us on this one. We're almost working backwards, because we know who did it, we know what they did, we just don't know who they did it to. That makes it hard, but that just means we do all the shitty jobs twice as thoroughly, OK? Someone, somewhere knows something that will clear up all the mystery."

"Is it worth someone going back to Ochil United, sir?"

"Doubt it, Des. They saw what they saw and that's that. If we strike out we might give it a crack, but I can't see the use. Let's get going for now on this lot - reconvene here at 5pm unless anyone's still on the road. If so, make sure you pass on a full update. We're on the clock and it's ticking fast. Right, beat it."

Room 312, Glenbank Hotel

"SO, this money. Are we tellin' the polis or not?"

"In other words, do we do the right thing – or gie it back."

"That's the Chunky we know an' love. Ye've slept on it, ye've read the papers, seen the TV news. The wee man's theory was right, naebody knows where this money is apart from us 20 lucky chappies."

"Nineteen."

"Mornin', Ginge."

"Sorry, I still don't want anything to do with this. It's totally immoral."

"Fair point. Anyone want to come back on that?"

"Aye, me."

"Craw?"

"Listen, whoever was robbed didnae report losin' £250,000, so they were obviously up tae somethin' as immoral as ye get. Whoever nicked it is fairly immoral by their very choice of profession, unless they took it to fund operations for sick children, in which case they sort of negated their charitable image by throwin' that poor lassie onto a central reservation an' blaggin' her motor. An' if the polis get it back an' still don't know whose it is, they'll split it among themselves, nae doubt."

"Nae doubt?"

"Well, OK, that last bit's conjecture based on an inherent dislike of the filth, but the rest makes perfect sense to me. We'd only be adding another tiny link of immorality to a long chain of the stuff."

"Tiny? We'd be the ones spending it!"

"We, Ginge? Ah thought you'd counted yersel' out the equation?"

"Slip of the tongue, Chunky. Fact is, there's no theory any of you can put up that will justify us keeping someone else's £250,000 just because it landed in this room by accident. I'm having no part in it."

"Ginge, Ah'm sorry to tell you this, but you are already ARE part of it. We ALL are. We've obstructed the course o' justice by hangin' on tae this dosh so long. An' Ah seem tae remember you knockin' back the option of phonin' the law last night, eh? So unless you're up for lettin' Screech and Westy take the rap on their Jack Jones?"

"Course not..."

"Good tae hear it. An' Ah'd hope ye'd think about me as well. You've no idea what Ah've gone through durin' the night thinkin' about what we should do. Ah'm the skipper. Ah'm the link wi' the management. If the gaffer even finds out we've discussed a scam like this Ah'm fucked. OK, so maybe Screech and Westy go too-."

"Thanks, Blue Eyes."

"Well, you've got the bag, boys. But who'd ever trust me again - in fitba' or business, Ah mean? Ah'm a financial adviser, for Christ's sake."

"So what's yer financial advice?"

"We keep it. All of us. Split it 20 ways an' everyone does what they want wi' it. Gie yours to charity, Ginge."

"Yeah, right - stolen money for Romanian orphans. Nice, Francis."

"Well, it's up tae you. But either we leave here wi' – *doodlydoodeedlydee* - twelve an' a half long each or we leave wi' nothin' and stick tae the Westy-only-opened-the-bag-after-brekky crap an' hope they send DI Fuckwit tae collect it."

"They're a' fuckwits."

"That's as may be, Craw, but still slightly irrelevant given the circumstances. Leavin' Ginge out, hands up who fancies the risk. Right - Porridge, Jimmy, Chunks – big surprise there, eh? – Screech? Westy? Craw? Chopper, Taxi, Fud, Shyness, Gio? Willie, Gibby, Lambchop – hey, Ah forgot you were there, ye've been that quiet -."

"Just listenin' tae a' the smartarses as usual."

"Aye, an' trouserin' bonuses aff us as usual tae, Campbell."

"Up yours, Shyness!"

"Guys, guys – sort it at playtime. Fact is, Lambsy, ye're in? Heed? You as well?"

"Yip."

"Harri? Good, son. An' me, of course."

"What about the twins? What you two sayin'?"

"Ah'm not sure-."

"Me neither-."

"Aw come on - it's easy money, boys!"

"Easy for you tae say, Screech. But our dad's the club secretary. Our sister's the receptionist. If we get caught, they lose their jobs as well. It's not just us."

"S'pose."

"Ach, take it, guys - it's 25K between ye. What ye on? One eighty each a week?"

"Look, Ah don't know about Barry, but Ah don't think-."

"Well, if Garry's not in, Ah'm not either."

"Aw for fuck's sake!"

Flat 16/4, McLean Court, Dundee

"WHAT d'ye reckon the bastards are daein' right now?"

"Countin' it out an' havin' a wank. Same as we'd be."

"Time o' their lives, the shites."

Room 312, Glenbank Hotel

"NAW!"

"AYE!!"

"NAW!!!"

"Can we no' have some time?"

"There's NAE time, for Christ's sake!"

"Everybody calm down!"

"Calm down? This is HUGE, Blue Eyes - fuckin' calm DOWN?!?"

"A'right, a'right - this is gettin' us nowhere. Everybody take a deep breath. What's the time?"

"Five past ten."

"Right, the gaffer knows we were meetin' up, but only so Ah got the checklist for where ye're headin' today. If we're in here shoutin' much longer someone'll hear and blab tae him, so let's sort this out once an' for all. Are we keepin' it or not?"

"Actually, Ah've got a plan that might be a decent compromise."

"You, Porridge? You've got a plan?"

"Don't sound so surprised. This isnae just a hat-rack, ma friends."

"So hit us."

"We bet it."

"We *bet* it?"

"Aye. Gie oursels a fightin' chance to get rich quick without walkin' round wi' it burnin' a hole in our pockets."

"Or consciences."

"Correct, Fudster. We hit the town right now an' put it on the game."

"Aw come on, City are 10/1 on, that's only £25,000 profit."

"Fuck OFF, Jimmy! Bet against United? Of a' the immoral things Ah've heard this mornin', that takes the Huntly & Palmer!"

"Aw, wait a minute – are you suggestin' we bet it on US tae beat CITY! Fuck me, Porridge, that's no' a compromise - that's a quarter million quid donation tae the Bookies' Benevolent Fund."

"You don't fancy us then?"

"An' you dae, Willie?"

"How no'? We've got this far. You an' Blue Eyes have been outstandin', even Porridge's done well."

"Cheers."

"Don't mention it, P. Listen, it's 11 against 11 on Saturday, if we don't believe we can win a two-horse race we might as well no' go tae the post."

"Aye, it's a two-horse race, but their horse is on a motorbike."

"Don't you start, Taxi. Put it this way, if we vote tae bet against Ochil United, Ah vote for phonin' the polis an' takin' our chances."

"I don't like gambling."

"FUCK UP, GINGE!!"

"Skip? What d'you say?"

"You boys are unreal, that's what Ah say. We find a bag wi' £250,000 in it an' decide tae bet it on us tae hump the biggest, richest, bestest team in Scotland at Hampden? We must be mental."

"And?"

"What odds are we?"

"Sixteens."

"So that's-?"

"Four million, Craw, four big millions."

"Somebody tell me again why we just don't split it twenty ways?"

"We could, Westy, but it depends if ye think havin' twelve an' a half grand in yer tail makes lookin' over yer shoulder from here tae eternity worthwhile."

"Aye, but are we no' just in danger o' givin' the lot away an' gettin' done in anyway? Ah mean, we a' know how hard this game's gonnae be. A quid on the lottery can win ye £4million without some gangland boss comin' after ye."

"True, Westy, but surely 16/1's better than 14million/1. That's the chances that ye'll have six balls on a Saturday night."

"As long as we've still got two each come Sunday, eh?"

"Don't even think it, Taxi."

"So, if we do it this way we have it in our powers tae win £4million?"

"Aye, PLUS the £250,000 stake back, which means we can anonymously hand it back tae the polis an' everybody's happy."

"Except the armed gang who stole it, of course, Porridge."

"Fuck."

"Double fuck."

"Aye, Ah forgot about them as well. Still think they'll come after us, Blue Eyes?"

"Mibbes. Chances are not. Ma guess is they're lyin' low somewhere tearin' each other tae bits for cockin' it up an' cannae afford tae show face here."

"An' the guy who lost it?"

"Still thinks the gang's got it. But if he's not reported it he must be well heavy, which means he must be connected, which means he could find out it was once with us. Which means-."

"We need tae move our arses."

"Got it in one. Ginge? Garry? Barry? You with us."

"No choice, really."

"If he's in, Ah'm in, so yeah."

"Much against my better judgement. So how's this masterplan going to work, then?"

The Boston Bar, Springburn

"AH, tea. Lovely. And caramel logs too! Janet, you're an angel."

"No problem, Mr Kerr."

"As ever, m'dear. Now, if you could make sure we're not disturbed, please. We've important police business to discuss."

Charlie Spuds had kept this smarmy bollocks up for what seemed to DS Des Bradley and DC Bob Grieve like hours. He'd greeted them in person at the Boston Bar, deep in the heart of darkest Springburn on Glasgow's tough North side, with the air of a landlord who spent every day pulling pints. Which was, of course, more bollocks. The two cops had shot each other a look that said: "He's had the wire again."

They both just wished they knew who among them - because it was definitely, no doubt about it, someone in the job - tapped the signals out so they could flush him or her away and make their jobs a damn sight easier. And Charlie Spuds knew that's how they felt, so he smarmed them all the more.

He'd shaken their hands, ushered them through to a little back lounge, made a big play of asking the barmaid to rustle up a brew. He even asked the cleaner if she'd be a darlin' and run out for some biscuits. Now he was taking an age to pour, to ask them what they took in it, to put the milk and sugar in for them, to make sure they took a biccy. Then he sat back, lifted his mug to his lips, took a sip, made an exaggerated *Aaaaaaah* sound with his eyes closed before finally looking at the pair of fed-up faces in front of him.

"So let me get this straight if you don't mind, gentlemen. You're asking me if I was robbed of £250,000 at any time yesterday, right? Right. Well, let me see, let me see - it's so hard to keep track of all the little things that happen in a busy day, don't you think? I mean, is it just me or do you two go home at night and tell the missus that nothing much went on, only to remember later on that your best pal had been fired or Sandra in the typing pool's pregnant? Or, in this case, that armed robbers have taken a quarter of a million pounds off you?"

"Look, Charlie-."

"Look at what, constable-?"

"Sergeant. Detective Sergeant Des Bradley."

"OK, so look at what, Des? It's a daft phrase, eh? I mean, I'm already looking. Shouldn't it be 'listen'?"

Bradley sighed and counted to ten inside. "What I'm trying to say, Charlie, is that there has been a £250,000 armed robbery which has not been reported by the victim, but that our information suggests that victim was you. Yes or no?"

"But why would anyone lose that much money and not inform the police? Surely you're the ideal people to investigate such an occurrence? What do you think, constable-?"

"DC Grieve, Bob Grieve."

"Well, Bob? What's your theory?"

"Er, well, that whoever was robbed was in the act of doing something illegal himself and therefore is in no position to get us involved."

Kerr put his mug down gently on the round table, sat forward and looked intently at the young, fair-haired officer. Grieve felt himself redden. Bradley bit his lip and wanted to punch the smug shite who was ripping the mince out of them.

"So, Bob - or can I call you DC Grieve? - by the very fact that you and your colleague are here asking me if I was the victim of this terrible crime, the reckoning must surely be that you suspect me of having been carrying out some illegal activity of my own. Which sort of changes me from victim to, well, perpetrator. And if that's the case, I'm afraid this is where we need to get Janet to bring a fourth tea mug in. For my lawyer. I mean, I'm not great on all this legal stuff and could maybe do with some expert help. Or maybe DS Bradley here will suggest that we continue this chat down at the station and my lawyer can meet us there? What d'you say?"

Bradley held his temper in check. "I say, Mr Kerr, that our information suggests you were robbed of £250,000 at around 4pm yesterday afternoon. Where were you at that time?"

"Here."

"Can anyone verify that."

"What do you think, DS Bradley?"

"Yeah, silly question. Course they can. They'd verify that you were having cucumber sandwiches with the Pope if you put the arm on them."

For the first time since he greeted them at the pub door, Charlie Spuds darkened visibly. He sat back, hands behind his head, eyes fixed on Bradley.

"That's not nice talk to a respectable man with no history of criminal activity, Mr Detective. Especially a respectable man who's invited you in for tea. I might have to ask you to leave now, unless that invite to the station is in fact to be forthcoming."

Bradley thought about it for a moment, then thought better of himself. Not worth the grief, son, not worth the grief. He stood up and DC Grieve took his cue to follow.

"OK, Mr Kerr, have it your way. We'll leave this for now. But we may well have to talk to you again soon. Very soon."

Spuds lightened again, as if the dark cloud had scudded past his eyes and exposed the sun.

"Lovely. I'll have the kettle on."

He waited until they'd left the pub then punched a number on his mobile.

"Alistair? Those two planks came round right enough. Aye, Bradley and Grieve, like you said. Hey, that Bradley fancies himself a bit, eh? What's his form? Yeah, well be a good Chief Inspector, find out and let me know. He could do with a wee message about future conduct, know'mean? Any more word on the soon-to-be-former armed robbers? Aye? That as exact as you can be? Ah well, better than a punch in the kidneys. Right, keep me posted. I might even defer a lump of that dosh you owe if you're a good lad. Later."

Then he rang a speed dial number. "Tam? You and Rhino bring the car round to the Boston. We're going to get the money back before this nonsense drags on any longer."

Flat 16/4, McLean Court, Dundee

HIS moby was ringing. The Great Escape, that was a laugh. Ringing and mocking, ringing and mocking.

"Answer it, for fuck's sake!"

"Dunno who it'll be."

"Aye ye dae, it's our man."

"Aye, a'right. Hello?"

"Where's ma money?"

"Who is this?"

"Don't piss about, where's ma money?"

"We've no' got it the now."

"Aye, right. Ah need that money. We had a deal. So gie's it."

"We've no' got it - it got lost."

"Fuck off!"

"Straight."

"Fuck OFF!"

"Look, honest. There's a problem. We'll sort it. Ye'll get it, nae hassle."

"Listen, Ah don't know yer game, but Ah'll cut tae the chase. Ah phone back in an hour, you cough the ten grand or Ah go straight tae the man."

"Ye widnae dare!"

"Fuckin' watch me."

"Hey, don't threaten - bastard! He's hung up!"

"Ring him back!"

"Nae number."

"We're fuckin' deid..."

Glenbank Hotel

SO Blue Eyes told Ginge how the masterplan would work. It was simple - 20 of them hitting as many branches of the big four bookies as they could as fast as they could and betting £250,000 on themselves to beat Glasgow City at 16/1.

At least, it sounded simple when they said it quick.

Porridge told them the main chains wouldn't take more than £500 on a single bet without phoning head office to check it was OK. And phone calls to head offices they didn't need.

Any smaller outfits would have to ring their head offices before they even took anything like £500, so they were out. But even the big chains would smell a rat when so few faces started laying so many decent-sized punts - especially when they eventually added up to a quarter of a million.

The first four £500s at the first branch at each of the four chains wouldn't make a ripple. But that was only two grand. Two hundred and forty-eight grand to go. Four hundred and ninety-six more bets, each one a slightly bigger stone skiffing across the pond.

The longer it took to turn it into a tidal wave of support for one of the biggest outsiders in semi-final history, the more chance of a coup being suspected and the book being shut. So they had to do this quick or not at all.

"Ye're lookin' worried, Fud."

"Ah'm wonderin' what happens if somebody just keeps their share."

"Fuck them."

"Very diplomatic, Blue Eyes."

"Nah, Ah mean it. It's a team thing. Everybody knows the score. The less money we collect if we win, the more it costs everybody t'pay the bad guy back. It's the same as on Saturday – if somebody doesnae pull his weight, the rest suffer. An' that doesnae happen wi' this team, does it?"

"S'pose not. So what if somebody bets it on City?"

"What ye lookin' at me for?"

"Sorry, Jimmy, force o' habit. Anyway, the answer is: Fuck them twice over. Anybody who even thinks that the game's up before we kick a ball's no use to us as a player or as a mate."

"Fair dos."

They got the Yellow Pages out and split the bookies into areas within easy reach by train. Greenock was the nearest station, they'd

49

taxi it to there and Willie and Gibby would comb that area. The rest would take the Glasgow train, Porridge, Shyness and Taxi getting off at Paisley then going on to do Renfrew as well.

At Glasgow Central, Blue Eyes would take Jimmy, Gio, Lambchop, Westy and the bookies novices – the twins, Ginge, young Harri, Craw and Chopper. The city had bookies every ten yards, so they'd work the centre first, jump on the subway to hit Partick, Hillhead and Paisley Road West then taxi it to the South Side and East End. Chunky, Screech, Fud and Heed knew Lanarkshire, so they'd go down to the Low Level platforms at Central and do Airdrie, Hamilton and Motherwell.

Then they made sure everyone knew how to fill out the slip:

Ochil United to beat
Glasgow City
@ 16/1
£500

"Simple enough, Yeah?"

"Yeah."

"Ah think even we'll remember that, skip."

"Good. Last thing we need is the staff rememberin' that diddy who had loose cash but nae brains an' then tae see him walkin' back in again."

And that was the thing – the guys hitting the smaller town centres would have to go back to the same branch a second time, a third, maybe more. They'd have to try and get a different teller each time and try to make sure they weren't clocked. The last thing they needed was being spotted even making what looked like a single bet on themselves for Saturday.

Plus, sooner or later someone in one of the branches of one of the chains would mention something to someone else and a light bulb would come on over their head and they'd ring another branch and then head office.

So it had to be quicker than quick or not at all.

As soon as they got to their destinations, they were to start hitting branches. Team members had to remember who'd served them and pass it on to the next guy. Then it was all about moving, moving, betting, betting.

Sweating.

Flat 16/4, McLean Court, Dundee

THE Great Escape again. He should have switched the fuckin' thing off. No, he should have smashed it into fuckin' bits – but the guy still hadn't phoned about the way out of the country, so he couldn't afford to be out of contact.

"What?"

"Time's up. Where's the money?"

"Ah told ye, we've no' got it. Listen, Ah'm sorry, but-."

"But fuck a'. Ah risked ma neck tae help you wankers, Ah see in the papers that ye've got the dosh but ye still rip me aff? That's shite patter, man!"

"Ah know it is, but it's the way it is. Gie me a day or two an' we'll turn up some new cash."

"Sure ye will. An' ye'll fuck aff wi' it. Listen, forget it – Ah told ye Ah was goin' tae the man an' Ah'm goin' tae the man. Fuck ye."

"Listen, there's nae need for-."

The phone went dead.

It might not be alone.

Glenbank Hotel

THE dosh had been in 50 bundles of £5,000, all in used £20 notes. The twins sat and made it into 20 piles of £12,500. Each player took one and stuffed money in every pocket, down waistbands, inside tracky tops. Then they went back to their rooms and changed for action.

Blue Eyes went to see the gaffer and told him the boys were off out. The gaffer said he wanted them back for dinner at six, then the night was their own again. Anyone late sitting down to eat was fined £50. Blue Eyes thought better of saying Big Fucking Wow.

Five minutes later, three seven-seater taxis rolled up and took them to Greenock Central.

At 11.16am, Willie walked into the first bookies of the day, wrote out a slip, sidled over to the counter and tried to look cool about placing £500 in Nelsons on Ochil United to beat Glasgow City at 16/1. The girl with Linda on the badge clipped to her blouse never cracked a light. Still, he was breathing a little quicker as he walked back outside to meet Gibby.

"A'right?"

"No sweat. Where next?"

"Ah'm goin' tae Hills round the corner. You?"

"Corals. Then the Tote. You come back tae this Ladbrokes next.

"How many branches did ye say we've got to go round?"

"Here and Port Glasgow? Fifteen, sixteen. So if we need to go into any more than once, let's pick the busiest ones. It'll no' take us long to get the job done."

"Then what?"

"Then, me old sausage, we go out an' get pished."

Springburn, Glasgow

CHARLIE SPUDS made him stand in front of the big desk for what felt like weeks. Rhino and Tam were sitting on two big leather armchairs in opposite corners of the office. They ignored him too. It was like he didn't exist.

This was starting to feel like a big, big mistake.

Finally, Charlie Spuds put his marbled black fountain pen down neatly beside the pad and looked up.

"So?"

"Er, so, - well, Ah'm sorry to disturb ye, Mr Kerr, but, eh-."

"Billy, isn't it?"

"B-Billy Andrews, Mr Kerr."

"Dearie me, Billy Andrews, that's some stutter ye've got there. Why don't ye take a deep breath, start again and speak clearly or maybe the boys there'll do some surgery on yer tonsils."

He concentrated really hard on not shitting himself.

"Sorry, Mr Kerr. It's just that Ah overheard talk about some money ye might have lost an'-."

"What money's that, Billy?"

"Er, Ah, er, Ah mean it was just some guy sayin' that he knew who'd taken whatever money it was an'-."

"And where was this?"

"The pub, last night."

"What pub?"

"The Cawdor."

"The Cawdor?"

"Aye."

"Who was on behind the bar?"

"Ah – Ah dunno any o' their names."

"But ye're far enough in that ye can earywig on the conversations of people who know about money Ah may or may not have lost without gettin' yer face marked for bein' nosey?"

"Naw, well, Ah mean Ah-."

Spuds raised a meaty hand and made a gentle shooshing sound. It made Andrews shudder.

"It's OK, Billy boy. Ah understand. Sometimes ye hear things even when ye don't mean to. It happens. All that matters is that you tell me what ye heard an' never mention it to another livin' soul. Deal?"

"Absolutely, Mr Kerr. No problem."

"So?"

"Er…"

"The name, Billy boy, the name."

"Ian Cowan."

"Who the fuck's he?"

"Ah – Ah dunno. They just said he had the money."

"Who's they?"

"Ah don't know them. They were just guys in the pub."

"Doesnae know much about anythin', this one, eh boys?"

"No' much at a', boss."

"Any idea how he could be educated?"

"Ah've always believed in short, sharp lessons, boss. We could take him for one the now if ye fancy."

"Aye, good shout. Education broadens the mind, Ah always say. So, Billy boy, how about you run along wi' these two members of the company teachin' staff an' come back when ye've passed a few exams."

"But – but – Mr Kerr, Ah only wanted tae help – ye know, help ye get yer money back."

"Well, try harder! Who the fuck's Ian Cowan? An', more to the point, where the fuck's Ian Cowan!"

"Ah – Ah -."

"Ding-a-ling, school's in-!"

"He's an ex-Army guy, Mr Kerr – commando, somethin' like that. Ah only didnae say because he's right hard, know? Ah hoped ye might know him an' Ah wouldnae get the blame when he found oot."

"Billy boy, first things first. Company loyalty. My employees think of their boss first and outside wankers a very distant last. And second, once Ah get to Mr Cowan, there's two chances he'll get tae blame you. None and fuck all. So. Where?"

"Ah've got – Ah managed tae see a fag packet wi' a number on it. A mobile, it looked like. Wrote it down for ye, Mr Kerr – there it's there."

"Tut, tut. Ah must say, the gentlemen in The Cawdor are gettin' most remiss. Not only do they let total strangers overhear their conversations about missin' money, they also leave cigarette packets lyin' around for those total strangers to copy vital numbers off. Still, that's their problem. Now, here's yours, Billy Boy."

Billy Andrews always knew he'd been taking a chance passing info to Cowan and his mates, but they'd been Forces buddies and that counted. Comrades forever, all that stuff. Even the thought

54

that he'd have to go to Carlisle and get his share from a railway station locker was no big deal. He knew – or thought he knew – they could be trusted. Plus, there was nothing to link him to any of it.

It was only when Cowan had told him they didn't have the dosh and then he'd read the paper that he started to get twitchy. Then the anger had set in and he wanted to get Cowan back for leaving him without a bean. He'd known that by going to Spuds he ran the risk of him putting two and two together, but had gambled that getting £250,000 back would have made the nobody who'd given him the tip an irrelevance once he'd given up what he knew.

What he never expected in his worst nightmare was that the boss would prove why he was the boss by working it all out in his head so quickly. And so accurately.

"Mr Kerr?"

"You're a lyin' wee shite, that's your problem. And a two-faced one at that. You sold me out to some cowboys for a few bob, they turned you over, so you thought you'd shop them to me and somehow be in ma good books. That turns ma stomach, it really does. Boys?"

"Bad enough that he grasses you, boss, but his ain mates..?"

"They're no' ma m-!"

That chillingly-gentle shooshing gesture again.

"Doesn't matter, Billy boy. They'll soon be yesterday's news. Same wi' the money. And you? You'll never have been news in your life. Of no interest to no bastard. And missed by no bastard."

Billy Andrews felt the heat of pee in his boxer shorts.

"Now, fuck off."

"F-f-?"

"You heard, ya stammerin' prick. You're a free man – if you can get through the door before Tam or Rhino here count tae 20 an' come after you. Ah'll start ye off, boys – one..."

Billy Andrews turned and bolted for the door, almost falling as the rug rucked beneath his feet. He heard them count.

"Two, three..."

Then he felt a hand on his shoulder and a fist in his back. As he slammed into the door face first and felt himself slide to the floor, he heard Charlie Spuds laughing.

"Oh – an' by the way, the thick bastards cannae count!"

Glenbank Hotel

BLUE EYES had given each of them a starting point and a meeting place after they'd put down the first £500. Then he'd talked them through their moves again and again.

"Walk in nice and casual, pick up a slip and a pen, take a few seconds to look at the prices on the screens, then fill it in and put it on. Don't make too much eye contact, but don't avoid their gaze either. Just act normal. You're all just punters with a few bob to burn."

Outside Central Station he'd wished them all good luck and told them everything would be cool. By tonight they'd all be laughing about it, he's said.

So ten minutes later, there he was – Rowland George, standing in a bookies for the first time in his life, with £12,500 in various pockets, ready to throw away all his principles because of some stupid stunt his stupid team-mates had dreamed up.

He didn't want to be there. He should have done more to talk them out of going through with it. But he hadn't, so now he was part of it, had to make the best of it he could. And he was actually quite chuffed with the solution he'd come up with to do just that.

11.40am, The Scottish Sun

PAUL ARTHUR stared his laptop out, going over and over his work. Changing and tidying, tinkering and tightening, chipping away at every wasted word. Never trusted the sub-editors to do it for him.

Some guys battered it out and if it was too long or there was the odd spelling mistake or factual error, who cared? The subs'd pick it up. That was their job.

Arthur was different. He'd been a sub for years before they let him loose and he'd seen too much dodgy copy come in to let his own standards slip. He'd ploughed though unreadable guff a million times, dredging out lines, sorting the lousy grammar, un-mixing metaphors and wondering how writers could live like that.

How could they pick up the paper next morning and see their stuff so heavily rewritten as to bear no resemblance to the original product and not get angry? Why didn't they vow it wouldn't happen next time, that if that was how the desk wanted it written that's how they'd write it? Of course, if their stuff was changed it always gave them a nice out with angry managers or players.

"Yeah, I'd be angry too, Jock, but it's not what I wrote. It was the desk. You know what it's like – they spin everything. What can I do?"

And any manager with any savvy would know it was an excuse so lame it would lose a three-legged race to a one-legged hamster - and would also look at the reporter and wonder where his self-respect was. Arthur often wondered that, too. He didn't like many other writers much - and it was pretty much mutual, because he never stopped letting them know where they were going wrong.

Meanwhile, the subs at the *Scottish Sun* knew he moaned to the gaffer at the way they treated his work and thought he was a pain in the arse for it. So they did their best to take out his favourite lines to annoy him, all of which made him paranoid about the quality of his finished pieces, which was why yet again he was going through one with the finest-toothed comb since Sherlock Holmes got nits.

The piece was for Saturday's cup semis pullout. City v Ochil United would be his 100th game of the season. A ton of action in 13 competitions at nearly 50 grounds across a dozen countries. Paul Arthur took great pride in how much football he saw in how many competitions, involving how many teams. What bugged him most about other top writers was how they slavishly covered the big Glasgow teams and Scotland yet still pontificated about the rotten state of the national game.

It'd been bad enough when Rangers and Celtic had played in Scotland, but now that they were part of the North Sea League there were reporters who never saw a domestic game all season yet STILL slagged their own country off.

It did his head in that they'd called for skint clubs to amalgamate or even shut down when they wouldn't go there if you laid them a trail of gin leading to a suitcase full of cash. He knew they laughed at him for spending Tuesday nights at Greenock or over at Stornaway. But it only made him go there more.

Especially when the Greed-Is-Good goons had taken over the old Scottish League and decided to amalgamate the three lower divisions into one and force through mergers no one wanted – well, no one except the goons themselves and his twat colleagues in the media who'd lobbied so long to see the back of clubs they'd never even seen the front of.

Arthur hated it when the gaffer sent him to cover Rangers or Celtic in Trondheim or Katowice or wherever the hell they were that week, but he went because he believed in covering all of football, not just the stuff he liked. And so, after ten months of watching everything from World Cup qualifiers and the Champions League right down to a Stirlingshire Cup-tie abandoned at half time when both linesmen got hypothermia, he was ready to pronounce his findings.

One last check and it'd be ready. Unsubbable. A beginning, a middle and an end, chiselled to fit perfectly into a five-page special. It had flow, it had passion, it had anger, it had humour. And the wankers would still find a way to cock it up:

MELVIN LAW and Tom Hagen will walk out of the Hampden tunnel at five to three today, side-by-side but a million miles apart.

One earns half a million a year, wears tailored Italian suits and handmade brogues, speaks five languages and has a supermodel wife.

The other's the manager of Glasgow City.

Nah, only kidding.

Truth is, when the bosses of the richest and one of the poorest clubs in Scotland lead their teams onto the pitch for the mother of David and father of Goliath of all cup semi-finals, a stranger wouldn't be able to tell the Prince from the Pauper.

Law, for all his money, is the least showy football bigwig I know. Sorry, poor phrase for a man with a world-famous hair weave. But you get the point. United's expensive blue club suit hangs uncomfortably on him, plus he insists on wearing brown shoes with it — and, of course, because he's the gaffer, everyone else has to go around looking uncoordinated.

The short, bulky Welshman looks uncomfortable in front of mikes or cameras, despite his legendary arrogance as a coach. Fact is, he's only truly comfortable on the training field, in a tracksuit, deploying his troops like the Pint-Sized Field Marshal he's come to be known as throughout the game.

And then there's Tom Hagen, a man whose style belongs at Stamford Bridge or the San Siro, not ramshackle Ochilview.

It's not that he wears expensive suits or even that he can pick shoes to go with his cheap ones. No, this is a man who could look good in a hessian sack, one of those swines who can carry anything off and appear cool.

I like Hagen. In fact, I like both today's managers. They're men with dignity, ability, who both love football to death in a beautifully old-fashioned way.

Law has not attempted to hide his distaste about the appalling Greed-Is-Good League. Like me, he called for years for a 16-team top division and was delighted when word came last season that we were getting one.

But what a kick in the danglies for him, for me, for all of us who wanted it when it was announced that those 16 teams would be chosen on a franchise basis.

What a waste. What a scandal. What a shower of clowns who run our game.

Yes, the standard's been decent at the highest level. Yes, eliminating the fear of the drop has meant more open football. But when rich men can BUY their way into the elite, it's time to pull down the shutters and go home.

What must they think in the Diddy League, that model 24-team set-up run so well by the hard-pressed EssEffEll, when they realise they're battling to win a title which will mean nothing unless they can come up with the £5million bond necessary as a down-payment for entry into Greed-Is-Good?

Even the name is evil. Greed-Is-Good. Only the slick-talking, Bollinger-swilling idiots at the head of Groovy Premier Elite Vibe plc could have lined up a sponsorship deal with what is — let's be honest — a high-class debt collecting agency.

I'd always hoped that one day if the Old Firm left we'd not only be rid of their vile religious baggage but we'd also have a league made more competitive than ever before by the relatively level financial playing field the rest would be on.

I should have known so much better.

The franchise system let rich men plug the gap left by Rangers and Celtic upping sticks and relocating to Amsterdam and Rome respectively. And the following generated by the instant success of the artificial clubs they spawned, Glasgow United and City, proves that we have learned nothing from 125-odd years of division.

I must have been naïve to think that when the Protestant and Catholic bigots followed their idols to Europe, many actually taking jobs in Holland and Italy, the air would smell sweeter around us. Instead, United have attracted the Jewish community, whose battle songs taunt the Moslems who sprung up in opposition at City.

Suddenly you were left hoping these two would also sod off to play in some plastic TV-led league elsewhere. But even if they did, it'd only mean Methodists and Mormons battling on the streets four times a season in their place.

Ochil United are on a real push for the title to go along with their semi-final place and there's no doubt theirs is a team with lovely balance, boundless energy and fantastic spirit.

Keeper Kevin Oates is big and strong, with old-fashioned shovel hands. The back four is tidy, with identical twins Garry and Barry Ronald flanking lanky, loping Jimmy Donaldson and the balding, elegant, karaoke-loving Francis "Blue Eyes" Albert.

The midfield four oscillates like the graphic equaliser on your hi-fi; the pint-sized Taxi

Allan, Giovanni Wilson — so swarthy he could be Italian and sometimes with enough arrogance on the ball to make it there - stocky ball-winner Jamie Kennedy and a handy goalscorer in Stevie McCracken.

Then, up front, such contradictions. The pipe-cleaner-thin yet short-fused Frank O'Donnell playing off barrel-chested, heavy-set, always-smiling Willie Walters.

It's a blend that might just come together just too late to win them the league. What a pity there's no chance of it taking them into the top flight, though.

Not while the goons are in charge.

There's a new stand at Ochilview to take capacity up to 8,500, the Tryst Road terrace re-stepped and roofed. Who cares that behind the other goal is fenced off for two six-a-side astroturf pitches? The board at what once was Stenhousemuir showed vision years ago in laying them as an income source and to give the players somewhere to train in the depths of winter.

It's a smashing little ground, full of history and atmosphere with a big, wide pitch that's improved year on year. I've seen countless cracking games there back to when I was eight watching St Mirren in the original Second Division.

Yet the lunatics who run the Greed-Is-Good asylum don't think it's good enough for their superstars to muddy their boots at. It all makes me hope — and Glasgow City fans can abuse me all they like for it — that United go out there today and do the impossible.

The day we allowed a few rich know-nothings to replace competitiveness with financial clout was the day Scottish football became an all-out war between the Haves and the Have Lots.

Ochil United are one of the Haves. They have passion, they have desire, they have ambition. They have ability. What they DON'T have is £5million kicking about to grease the right palms and the same again to build two new stands.

It stinks to high heaven that these are the ways into the big time today, not the number of points you rack up or the number of goals you score.

In this war, it's David v Goliath, pea-shooters against cruise missiles.

But a pea-shooter neatly aimed can give the big guy a right keeker. Let's pray EVERY Greed-Is-Good merchant gets one in the eye at Hampden.

BRILLIANT. He loved it. A boot put in here, an arm round the shoulder there. Well-paced, sculpted, ideal to walk into the space set aside for it. He'd still worry about it non-stop until it was in the paper.

And even then he wouldn't be happy.

MELVIN LAW wasn't happy either. He rarely was, because his entire life was one long search for perfection and that, by its very nature, meant he would remain unhappy until he found it and even if and when he did he would be soon be unhappy again at the thought of having nothing more to strive for.

To most other managers of hugely-successful, enormously wealthy football teams packed with highly-paid international stars, this week would have come as a welcome relief from the normal stresses and strains of the season.

Most weeks were about keeping Glasgow City ahead of arch-rivals United and thus by definition the rest of the Greed-Is-Good League. Either that or preparing for another fixture in the Midweek European Table Of Champions. Every time Glasgow City ran across the white line they were expected to win and thus when they did they rarely felt they were given the praise they were due and when they didn't the critics battered them from pillar to post.

But this week was different. They were three days away from a Scottish Cup semi-final against Diddy League part-timers Ochil United. They were massive odds-on favourites to win. Anyone who even suggested they wouldn't win had to be crazy. Not even the sternest anti-big-team campaigner could possibly predict anything but a resounding City win out of anything but sheer romantic folly.

And yet Melvin Law still wasn't happy. At training this morning, he'd prowled back and forth along the touchline like a caged tiger. His players looked relaxed, at ease with themselves. Yet with every sprint, every cross and volley, every kick of the seven-a-sides, he'd grown more and more irritated.

Because they were just too relaxed.

They were too at ease with themselves.

They were training too well.

It was as he'd watched Rozenkrantz sell Arrabiatta a beautiful dummy and pull the trigger to shoot at Salz, only for Fish to appear from nowhere and make a bone-crunching block, that the problem had hit him between his bespectacled eyes.

They were as confident of beating Ochil United as the rest of the country seemed to be. And that simply wouldn't do, really and truly it wouldn't. He expected at least some tiny hint of nerves before big games, to see at least one of them looking down in the mouth or sweating too much or mis-kicking in front of goal.

But no. It was all too - no, not perfect; perfect was how others might describe a session where men at the pinnacle of their profession all appeared to be on peak form at once, where every man did all that was asked of him not just with 100 per cent effort but with a sense of style and of enjoyment.

Not Melvin Law, though. Perfection for him was - well, he'd never know until he got it, would he? All he'd known as his squad laughed and joked and worked their tails off in the morning sunshine was that this wasn't it. They were too relaxed, which to him meant they were not taking Saturday seriously enough.

But how could he stop training and tell them that? How could he march on and tell the strikers to stop scoring so many goals, the keepers to stop saving so many other certs, the midfielders to stop tracking runs so diligently and the defenders to stop being so much of a damn unit?

They just wouldn't understand, would they? Because they just weren't on his wavelength, were they? If they understood the need to seek perfection they would be out there making mistakes at the thought of making mistakes on the day, thus cementing in their minds the necessity NOT to make them.

No one else seemed to see that the way Melvin Law did. No one else seemed to see much the way Melvin Law did.

Which was maybe the real reason why Melvin Law was so discontented. Maybe it wasn't everyone else, maybe it was him. That was a sobering thought and it wasn't the first time it had flitted into his mind, however briefly. Truth is, it bothered him that recently it was flitting in more and more often. Yet he refused to believe it, put it on hold and pressed Play on the video.

There wasn't much footage available of Ochil United. None of the TV stations bothered much with the Diddy League, so he'd had to make do with bits and bobs from their earlier cup rounds. He'd already watched every second dozens of times since the draw was made three weeks ago, but each time he seemed to look deeper and deeper into the screen, almost willing each frame to become 3-D, searching for something he could tell his players that would make them more nervous about Saturday and train with a bit less confidence.

Not that their confidence was misplaced, mind - deep down, Melvin Law thought they'd beat Ochil United the same as everyone else did. But once he admitted it out loud, even to himself, he and his team were in trouble. Always expect the worst and it won't seem quite so bad when you get it. Yes, it was a way of thinking that took the shine off of many of his best days in the game, because he'd usually been so pre-occupied with pessimism that victory brought only relief and not the explosion of ecstasy others seemed to enjoy.

Once the job was done on Saturday night, he'd go home and have a meal and a drink with Amanda and say very little. She'd know he was still thinking about the game and wouldn't push him to be more sociable. Later they'd sit together on the sofa and put on a video - maybe that afternoon's game, but more likely the one which would have been dropped off mid-evening of their next opponents.

The search for perfection never ended. Amanda understood that.

TOM HAGEN'S idea of perfection, meanwhile, was a mug of tea made just the way he liked it - bag dunked in and out for two-and-a-half minutes exactly, a level teaspoon of sugar, a splash of milk and then a tiny splash more. Medium brown, not dark tan. He hated baby tea, over-sweet tea, stewed tea.

Nothing else in his life got him as worked up as tea.

A bad brew first thing could spoil an entire morning. This morning he'd made himself a rotten one and was still bugged about it. Those stupid little hotel pots of UHT milk didn't help. Who invented those mantraps? You tugged away at the skittery little lip for ages then when it finally opened it splooshed onto your dressing gown. But no excuses, he was the one who'd forgotten to send down for real stuff, the one who'd lost track of time and dunked for nearly four minutes. Hands up, it was his own fault.

Well, his and Caroline's.

He couldn't concentrate on anything this morning for thinking of Caroline. She was the real reason he'd spoiled his tea, the real reason he'd cancelled training, not last night's win. He just couldn't get his head round football tactics for planning the ones he'd use that night.

Normally he lived for training, for the tinkering and tweaking that turned losing teams into winners. But the truth was that if he'd been out there that morning he wouldn't have spotted a subtle change waiting to be made if it'd come up to him waving a placard saying I'M A SUBTLE CHANGE WAITING TO BE MADE.

Tom Hagen was somewhere else, with someone else.

What's more, the change he was thinking about making wasn't subtle. It was massive, obvious, glaring – so massive, obvious and glaring he could only slap himself and wonder why it'd taken him so long to think of it.

He was going to ask Caroline to marry him again.

He ran the proposal over and over in his head, changing the inflection of the words here and there until it sounded just right. But who knew if any version would sound anything but crazy to her? Maybe she'd just laugh. Maybe she'd punch him. Jeezo, what if she said yes? It was torturing him, but not as much as the thought that none of this emotional equivalent of electrodes on the testicles would have been necessary if he hadn't let her go in the first place.

Why hadn't he tried harder?

Simple. Because he'd been assistant manager at Ibrox and he had no time for anything else but his ambition – even though Caroline could see better than anyone that his ambition was completely in vain. Because his ambition was to be manager and that was never going to happen.

By the time things turned rocky at home he'd been caretaker twice and each time results had gone fine but at the end of the day they'd taken on a big name who'd patted him on the head and told him he was invaluable. Maybe, but as what? A lapdog? Mr Nice to their Mr Nasty? The man the players trusted enough

67

to let things slip to so he could go running back to the gaffer with them?

Much later he'd realise all this to be true, but whenever Caroline told him at the time he'd thought she was mocking him. He'd show her. He'd bury himself deeper and deeper in his job until he'd make himself really invaluable.

And all he did was get in so deep he couldn't see he was wrecking his marriage.

In the end, she got tired waiting for him to come home and she left. He begged her to come back, promised he'd change. She did. He didn't. Second time round, he left. Moved into a flat a corner kick from the stadium and settled the divorce miles in her favour out of guilt.

Two months later they binned him because they felt the problems in his private life had stopped him concentrating fully on the job.

He'd done his best not to think about her and for a while it'd worked. Moved out of Glasgow, found a nice flat in Stirling, took over at Alloa then moved to United when the amalgamation came, worked hard as hell not to think about her, to let old wounds heal, to move on and come out the other end stronger.

It had taken six years, but he'd almost got her out of his system. Almost. Very, very nearly. Just about erased the last flickering memories from his mind.

Then she'd turned up at the quarter-final.

He'd been invited up to some hospitality room afterwards to meet some sponsors or other. And there she was, sitting at a table with folk from her bank as if she'd never been out of his life. The centre of attention as usual, making everyone laugh at some story or other. She looked fantastic.

He wondered if they were laughing at him.

Nah, she was never that nasty. How could anyone so beautiful have a bad bone in her body? He watched her toy with a strand of chestnut hair that contrasted spectacularly with her powder grey suit and suddenly he felt self-conscious of his paunch and his thinning thatch.

Then she caught him staring and gave him a smile that somehow seemed to say he was the very person she'd expected to see standing there. He saw her nod his way and mouth excuse me to the company. He was aware of himself shifting from foot to foot like a lovesick schoolboy who'd been held back 40 years.

He was shaking as she put her hand on his arm, kissed his cheek and gently asked, "How you doing, sweetheart?"

"OK," he heard himself reply, "fine."

"Fine? You just got that wee team of yours into the cup semi-final – and you're fine? You should be singing and dancing, Tom Hagen. That's your trouble, you never let yourself go."

Which only made him suck in his gut all the harder, because anyone could see he had let himself go. Hadn't seemed much point in preening himself without her to impress.

If only she knew how much he'd wanted to let go in the sense she meant, though, how much he'd wanted to grab her and kiss her and whirl her round the room and shout that at last he'd done it, done what he'd always wanted to.

But it would have been a lie, because he knew then what he really wanted was to have his wife back.

He took a furtive look at her left hand. No ring. Good sign.

He was about to ask to see her later when some SFA wallah tapped him on the shoulder and said the BBC were waiting for him on the touchline and could he come right now. He wanted to tell the telly to go to hell, but she nodded for him to go. She had that look again, the one that said she understood he had to work but that it made her want to spew.

I'll give you a call, he'd said. No you won't, she'd said.

He had, though. He'd called her first thing this morning and asked if she was free for dinner tonight. Her voice had dripped with sarcasm as she'd asked why he wasn't working. He said he'd given the boys the day off to relax. Good for you, she'd said, half in surprise and half in admiration. So, was she free? She was? Great! Where? Brilliant, brilliant. See you there.

And now he couldn't have been more nervous if he'd been taking the last penalty in the World Cup Final with the threat of a boxful of Andrex puppies being shot if he missed.

LAMBCHOP wasn't placing 25 bets like the rest. Running around bookies shops like a headless chicken on his day off? Bollocks to that. Nope, he'd made up his mind from the off to stake the lot on just four lines. Who cared that the shops made him wait a few minutes each time while they phoned head office? He was still finished in half an hour and had the afternoon to himself.

Four bets, £2,000 each, £8,000 in total on Glasgow City to win at 10/1 on. He'd make an £800 profit come Monday - and had £4,500 left right now for a wee spree round the shops. If the rest had any brains, that's what they'd have done as well. But no, not them, they were all on some fantasy trip about United pulling off the shock of the century and making them millions.

Wankers.

KIRSTEN REID couldn't believe it her phone rang and it was Mark saying he was waiting downstairs for her. Why wasn't he with the team? Was something wrong?

"Course not, honey, we got the afternoon off, so Ah thought we could spend lunchtime together."

"Brilliant - I'll grab my coat and tell the girls I'll be back in an hour."

"Cool. I've got a surprise for you."

THEY were on the subway, rattling towards Partick. Everything seemed to be going smooth as you like.

"No problems, boys?"

Blue Eyes grinned as they shook their heads.

"Superb - we're like a wee Ocean's Eleven, eh? Pullin' the big stunt right under their noses. Takin' the house before the house even knows it's bein' taken."

"You live in a fantasy world, Bluey."

"Aye, Jimmy, an' you should come for a holiday, ya miserable big shite."

"Whit's the matter wi' yer coupon anyway, JD? You get yer pocket picked while ye were checkin' yer reflection in a shop windae?"

"Up yours, Porridge. Ah'm just a wee bit uneasy, that's a'. Worried that this thing comes back an' bites us on the arse, eh?"

"How's it gonnae dae that? Listen, the bookies are takin' reasonably wee bets - by their standards, anyroad - on a 16/1 shot in a two-horse race. Now, by close o' play the night when it a' adds up, they might sniff a jobby in the cistern, but as far as each individual cashier in each individual shop goes, each punt is just another halfwit wi' mair money than sense tryin' tae chase the ace."

"Aye, but what if we pull this aff? What if we beat them an' then people find out it was us who had a' that money on? We could be in big keech then."

"Calm down, Jimmy. Look, anybody who's nervous about collectin' their dosh can always send a pal in an' gie them a wee drink for their trouble. Winnin' a bet's no' against the law."

"Naw, Blue Eyes, but usin' somebody else's money tae dae it is. Ah still cannae get away fae the feelin' that whoever's it is will come and try tae get it. Criminals have a tendency to be unreasonable like that."

"Fuck me, Jimmy, even Ginge isnae as big a blouse as you. Eh, Ginge?"

"Me? Cool as you like, skip. Enjoying every moment. The thrill of the chase and all that stuff."

"See? He's a cucumber."

"Aye, an' you're a lemon if ye cannae see he's bein' sarcastic."

"Actually, Jimmy, I'm not being sarcastic. This is more fun than I thought - I've been to eight bookies already and never had a moment's trouble. Porridge is right, they just seem to look at you as if you're the village idiot when you put £500 on something as outrageous as I've been doing."

"That's the spirit, son."

"ARE you winding me up, Mark?"

"Nope."

"But - but how you going to pay for it?"

"Cash. Been savin' win bonuses an' never touched ma last signin' on fee."

"Good God."

"So, d'ye like it?"

"Ah love it, babe!"

"An' it seems a lucky omen that the one they had in the window fits perfectly, eh? So, will we go for it?"

"It's up to you, babe."

"OK then, we go for it. We'll take it, thanks."

"And how would you like to pay, sir?"

"Cash, if that's OK."

"No problem, sir. That'll be five thousand eight hundred pounds."

"Sure - that's one, two, three, four, five, six thousand there. You OK, honey?"

"Just a bit shellshocked."

"Well, wait until we sit down for lunch an' Ah show ye what Ah got us earlier. For now, down to the offimcial bit."

"Oh my God, Mark – are you doin' what I think you're doin'? Get up, ye're so affrontin' me!"

"Hey, Ah've got tae do this right, honey. So Kirsten - will you do me the honour of becoming Mrs Mark Weston?"

"Of course I will, babe!"

And the shop girls all clapped.

LAMBCHOP ducked into a doorway as he saw Westy and the bird coming out of the jeweller's. Last thing he needed was one of the others spotting him - though now that he thought about it, what was Westy doing there?

It didn't need a genius to work out the answer to that one. He'd had no more intention of chucking £12,500 away on betting against Glasgow City than Lambchop himself had. He was splashing it on his bit of stuff instead. Good on the boy, he had more savvy than Lambchop had given him credit for. Why make a no-hope gamble that would be beaten in ten minutes when he could buy the love of his life something shiny and keep her sweet for years?

And if she ever binned him, he could always take it back and flog it.

Was he gone? Good. One last look around to make sure none of the others were about to appear out of the blue, then in he went.

"Good afternoon, sir."

Aye, er, it's about one of the watches in yer window, please. The one wi' the wee diamonds round the numbers..."

Flat 16/4, McLean Court, Dundee

IAN COWAN'S watch had seen better days in every sense. He'd bought it in Gib as a young private and it had seen action with him in Cyprus, Ulster, the Falklands, then his years undercover. That's when the four of them had got together. Others he'd known had come and gone, but the clowns he was sharing this stinking living room had always been there. Them and his watch.

He glanced at it now. Ten to one. Fuckin' hell, was that all? Felt like they'd been cooped up here for days, not 16 hours. He closed his eyes and willed sleep to carry him away for a while.

Then he heard The Great Escape again.

He hoped against hope it was the pal of a pal with their ticket out of this hole. But he knew even before he pressed the button that it wasn't.

"Hello?"

"Christ, ye're so thick ye can't even turn yer blower aff. Here was me tellin' the boys ye'd be impossible tae find as well. Ah mean, what use was a bloody mobile number? Ye could be anywhere, eh?"

He wasn't dumb enough to act like it and ask who was calling.

"We don't have it."

"Don't have what, m'friend?"

"Yer money. We lost it."

"Hold on a minute - Ah'm holdin' the phone away from my ear so the boys can hear ye say that again. Right? Fire away, m'friend."

"Ah said we lost yer money."

He heard them laughing, then the voice came back close to the mouthpiece again.

"Right, pal. Let's cut the jokes. Where's the money?"

"Honest, we lost it. We had it, our car crashed, the bag it was in got mixed up wi' bags fae some fitba' team. That's the last we saw o' it."

Even at the other end of a phone line, he felt the anger rise up in Charlie Spuds.

"An' you expect me to believe that? You get some weasel in ma firm to set me up for a shaftin', ye shoot me and ma boys wi' Horlicks an' fuck off wi' ma money an' then ye expect me to buy some shit that ye GAVE IT TAE SOME FUCKIN' FITBA' TEAM?!?"

His neck was pulsing now.

"Look, ye've nae idea how fucked up this a' is for us. D'ye think we'd still be hangin' about this fuckin' country if we still had the-."

"So ye're still in Scotland, then. That's somethin'-."

Cowan realised what a stupid slip it had been to make. He was going to make one last play, the big honesty number, then get off the phone quick as he could and get the lot of them to fuck out of there before it all came down on top. They'd knock over a bookie's or a post office and do one with whatever they laid their mitts on.

"Aye, well, there's nae point me tryin' tae bullshit ye, Mr Kerr. We turned ye over, fair dos, but Ah'm tellin' it like it is. The money went away wi' thae fitba' wankers. That's the God's honest – ye only have tae read the papers tae see where they're stayin' an' go get it back."

"Easy as that, eh? Well, tell ye what - how about YOU go an' get it back, seein' as how you're the ones who nicked it in the first place? How about Ah give you 48 hours tae put that 250 grand back in ma possession or Ah cut you an' yer wee pals into 250 thousand pieces?"

This was the moment when Ian Cowan made his biggest mistake. Never assume.

"Tae be fair, Mr Kerr, ye'd need tae find us first."

The others gave him the thumbs-up for that crack. He was handling the biggest hardman in Glasgow like a veteran.

"Aye, son, that's true. We would need tae find ye first. So it's just as well we're slightly less fucking dense than you are, eh?"

Someone knocked ever so gently on the front door and their hearts boomed like five kettle drums.

Then they heard Charlie Spuds's voice, except now it wasn't down the phone. It was coming through the letter box.

"OPEN UP, LITTLE PIGGIES, OR WE'LL HUFF AND WE'LL PUFF AND WE'LL BURN YOUR SCUMMY HOUSE DOWN!"

"Fuckin' -? Ah mean, how the fuck did they-?"

"Your man on the inside's done us right in!"

"How could he - he didnae know where we were either!"

"Well he's fuckin' found oot somehow, the bastard!"

"Little piggies, little pig-gies. The big bad wolf and his two big fuck-off grizzly bear chums are getting im-pa-tient. So open up before we risk typhoid by kicking the fucker in!"

"Is there a back way oot?"

"Can ye fly?"

"Don't get smart, ya junkie arsehole!"

"Ah'm just sayin' - fuck me, ye didnae say a' this was comin' ma way. Naw, there's nae way oot."

"Right, you open the door, then."

"Fuck off, this is your mess!"

"Shite! A'right, a'right - everybody grab yer tools an' get ready tae take the bastards oot, right? This is how we get out o' this mess. Keep the livin' room door ajar until Ah gie the signal, then let them have it. Just don't get me in the crossfire."

"Right."

"Locked an' loaded!"

Cowan tip-toed down the lobby, put the chain on the door and opened it a few inches. He'd hardly even focussed on the faces outside when the chain burst and the door smacked him in the face, bursting his nose. Charlie Spuds followed close behind and punched him between the eyes with a fist that must have had at least three rings on it under a soft leather glove. He staggered back against the lobby wall, knees buckling. He heard the sound of guns being cocked in the living room and hoped they still had steady aims all these years on.

"Gaffer, into the bog - they're carryin'!"

Spuds ducked behind a door to his right, eyes instantly watering at the stench. Rhino and Tam were already flattened into the alcove outside the toilet, clipping cartridges into pistols. Rhino motioned to Tam, who dashed up the narrow lobby and into a room on the left. He got his back to the door and breathed heavily. Charlie Spuds nodded to Rhino to shout the last warning.

"Mr Kerr's giein' ye a fightin' chance here. Put the water pistols down an' come out an' we'll talk about this like grown-ups."

Silence. Rhino looked down at Cowan and motioned with his gun for him to have a word. Cowan's eyes narrowed.

"Sit tight, boys. They're bluffin' - they cannae afford a scene any mair than we can."

The lobby rang with ear-splitting noise as Rhino shot him in the leg. Cowan screamed in pain and shock. In the living room, they looked at each other and made faces that asked what the fuck they should do next. No one was sure. Sit tight or start blamming? With every second their indecision was draining the life from them. Charlie Spuds knew that was how they'd be. Now it was his turn to do the talking.

"Right, lads, let's not turn this into The Alamo. Chuck whatever ye're carryin' out the door before anybody else gets hurt an' Ah promise ye'll be OK - a' we came for's our money, no' a battle. Though if ye want one, ye'll get it."

In the living room, they knew for certain now he wasn't bluffing. They put their guns on the floor and shoved them out of the door, one, two, then three.

Rhino looked down at the shaking, sweating, bleeding Cowan and asked if that was the lot. Cowan managed to nod. Rhino nodded to Tam, who spun, booted the living room door open and drew his pistol across four terrified faces.

"Down, the lot o'ye. Faces down, hands behind heads. Right, gaffer, in ye come."

Spuds never even looked at Cowan as he stepped over his sprawled body and walked slowly up the lobby. Rhino gave the wounded man a kick in the guts on his way past. Cowan vomited and wished for death.

JIMMY DONALDSON only had one reservation about lumping money on himself for the big game – that someone might recognise him. After 15 punts, he was gutted that not a soul had.

Seven and a half grand he'd laid now. Five to go. Then all it needed was one kick of the ball and he was made for life.

One million pounds. Just for scoring a goal.

He'd only taken a look at the coupon in the first shop so he didn't appear too keen to rush up and smack his cash down. And the second he'd seen the odds, he'd known he couldn't resist it.

There wasn't another Diddy League nobody with anything like the Champions League hit JD had for himself.

In the First Goalscorer column, Rozenkrantz was favourite at 5/1, then Jensen at sevens, Bothwell at 15/2, Brown eights, Van Hoffen tens. There wasn't a United player in the running until Willie at 25/1. Fud was 33/1, Craw 40/1 – he took the penalties – and so on further and further into long shot territory.

Then there he was. Jim Donaldson. Eightys.

His first thought was that Ladbrokes were cheeky bastards. He'd scored six already this season, for Christ's sake. Why couldn't he make it seven? So what if it was Glasgow City, that big poser Arrabiatta and all his poncey mates? If United got a corner or a free-kick, JD would be in there, head and shoulders above them all, SoulGlo gel glinting in the Hampden sun as tight curls met ball and bulleted it past the best keeper in Europe.

Who wants to be a millionaire? I do, matey boy, and if the right cross goes into the mixer I won't need to phone any friend to hit the jackpot. Thank you and goodnight. Goodbye lousy Larbert, aloha Hawaii.

If he didn't score and they lost, no one ever had to know about his little private wager. If he didn't score and they won? Hey, they were onto £200,000 each. He'd cough, they'd laugh and he'd waive his original 12 and a half. They'd know it was just big JD's way, like they always did.

Ten more bets now and he'd be set. Say bugger all on the way home and after that nobody'd be talking about this whole business anyway in case the wrong person was eary-wigging.

The way he saw it, he'd actually be under less pressure than the rest of them now. They'd all be sweating that every mistake they made could cost their mates £4million. All JD had to think about was himself and the fact that he was on one mammy and daddy of a bonus if a stray shot went in off his backside. He'd just play his own game.

And hope it turned out to be his last.

WESTY'S idea of no one knowing about his little romantic surprise had been just what it said on the tin. No one – as in no one - was to know. Kirsten's idea of no one knowing was to tell the whole world.

When he'd produced those tickets for a fortnight in Barbados she'd heard a voice somewhere in the distance telling her she had to keep schtum until after the semi-final, but it didn't really register. She was in a perfect little world of her own. The 1.5 carat solitaire? The proposal? The honeymoon? It was all she'd ever dreamed of, with the only guy she'd ever called a boyfriend. She felt incredible.

"Babe? D'ye hear me? Please, tell nobody. Not yer mum, not yer sister, not the priest at confession, nobody. It's really, really important that it stays quiet. OK?"

"Yes, Mark, of course. Anything. This is just so – so – wonderful. I love you so much, honey!"

"You too, babe. Now listen, Ah've got to get back to the hotel. Are you goin' t'be OK? Ye look pale."

"Ah'm just – just – overwhelmed. This is just amazing, amazing."

"So, not a word, eh?"

"Not a word, promise."

She wasn't even back at her desk before she was on the mobile.

"Mum? Mum, fantastic news – Mark's proposed! Yeah, a huge solitaire – went down on one knee in Mappin & Webb! And we're going to Barbados on honeymoon! Ah know! Isn't it? Just one thing, please don't say anythin' to anybody, eh? Mark's so made me promise. No, of course I'll tell Kim, she's my sister, for goodness sake! Bye!"

The girls in the office were gawping at the ring in the open box as she gabbled the good news to Kim. By which time her mum had phoned her mum, then Aunt Vera, then Margaret from the bingo, then gone round to the Co-op - even though she'd already been - just in case she bumped into anyone worth bragging to.

Kirsten made Kim swear she wouldn't tell anybody. Kim thought it wouldn't do any harm if she told the girls in her office. Or to phone her best pal Brenda. And her second-best pal Rhona. Who told her colleagues in the Daily Record advertising department. One of whom told her boyfriend on the news desk.

Who told his gaffer. Who loved the story.

Flat 16/4, McLean Court, Dundee

ON THE face of it, finding four experienced undercover operators in a country of five million people from a standing start had made looking for a needle in a haystack seem like spotting John Barnes at an NF rally.

But Charlie Spuds had a logical mind and, more importantly, pliable contacts. A word in the ear of the same Glasgow police superintendent with secret gambling debts who'd tipped him off about the cops coming to visit him that morning started a chain of internal calls from Strathclyde to Central to Tayside HQs that established where the hijacked car had been dumped, what replacements the four men had been filmed taking and where those replacements had, in turn, been abandoned.

After that, it was just a case of leg work and arm-twisting. Spuds, Rhino and Tam hit Dundee and looked up some faces. Only took an hour to narrow down where they might be. Another 30 minutes of pointed questions and they were standing outside the grotty high flat. And now here they were, standing right over the prostrate bodies of three of their prey - plus their terrified, drug-addled host - while the fourth lay shaking and groaning in a pool of his own blood and sick 15 feet down the lobby.

"So, gentlemen, am I to assume that hopeless twat out there was your leader-off? Because if so, woe fucking betide the rest of you. Bright as a blackout, that one – but the frightenin' thing is, he's Bamber Gascoigne beside you lot. Names!"

"A-Andy Collins."

"Is that A-Andy with two As or one? Don't answer, Ah might squash ye. You, snivellin' right at ma toes?"

"Sean McGinlay."

"You, Shakin' Stevens in the corner!"

"Tam Guthrie, but Ah've got fuck a' tae dae wi' it – they're just stayin' at ma-."

"Then ye've got everythin' to dae wi' it, m'friend. You, what's your name?"

"Brian McGlynn."

"Right then, we'll address this through Seany boy, shall we? He looks the most grown-up."

Spuds hitched up the knife-edge creases of his dark blue suit trousers and crouched over McGinlay. The ex-soldier was built like a heavyweight boxer, but lying there on the sticky carpet, hands behind his head, he looked helpless as a baby.

"Sean, you people took somethin' of mine. You know what it is, so let's not go through the embarrassin' rigmarole of denial. Now, Long John Silver out there tells me it's gone missin', correct? Nod once for yes, nod twice and Rhino there'll blow yer head off."

McGinlay nodded once.

"Good. Well, bad, Ah suppose. For you, anyway. Ah mean, Ah could tell you an' yer girlfriends right now tae get down tae Halfarse United's hotel an' get the money back by hook or by crook – but the flaw in that plan's that as crooks, you tossers make good pastry chefs. Yours, Sean, was the perfect crime. Except for the aforementioned fact of you bein' tossers. So what chance would there be o' you bringin' ma dough back? Two chances, Seany – none an' fuck all. Ah can see it now. Ye snatch it back dramatically, do a bolter than crash intae a school bus an' the weans end up spendin' 250 long on Monster Munch and E. Nah, Sean, this is a job for professionals. Or, more precisely, two jobs for professionals. Rhino? Tam?"

"Gaffer?"

"Do yer stuff, make it quick – and just for good luck, use their weapons."

Charlie Spuds walked from the room and once again stepped disdainfully over the now-comatose Cowan. He went back into the stinking bathroom and looked at himself in a smeared, cracked mirror. Then waited for the muffled cracks. One. Two. Three. Four. He stepped back out into the hall and watched his men walk towards him as if nothing had happened.

"Right, chaps, finish off Field-Marshal Montgomery here an' let's get the fuck out o' this shitehole."

Tam let Rhino do the honours. He put a bullet in Cowan's temple, placed his pistol in the dead man's left hand and they all walked nonchalantly away.

DI ANDY McKENZIE was almost in a trance thinking about the case when the phone on his desk startled him back to the real world.

"McKenzie."

"Boss? It's Alison. Listen, Ian and are just on our way in, but I thought you might like to know this soonest. It's about what we found at the warehouse."

"What?"

"A dart."

"A dart? What, as in Jocky Wilson?"

"No, as in Zulu warriors. Mental as it sounds, Spuds might just have been, well, tranquillized to get the money off him."

DI McKenzie couldn't stifle a laugh. "So we're looking for paras trained to bring down runaway elephants? Should narrow it down a bit. You got the dart in some sort of bag?"

"Tissue paper. Best I could do. Get forensics on it before I come to the briefing."

"Good girl. See you soon."

She cut the call off and cursed him for calling her a good girl.

4.20pm, West Nile Street, Glasgow

"GIOVANNIBAWS! A'right?"

"Craw."

"You spent yer wad, then?"

"Oo-er, missus - just done the last five ton. You?"

"Just going in here to finish aff. Wait two ticks for me, Ah don't know this place we're meetin' the rest o' them in."

82

"Ye mean the bar in Central Station? It's in Central Station, strangely enough."

"Ah. Right enough. Wait for me anyway."

Two minutes later

"SORTED? Good, let's go for a beer."

"So who's yer money on?"

"For what?"

"The one who didnae put their 12 and a half G on United to win."

"Ye think somebody'll have done us in?"

"Stick on, Gio. Human nature. Think about it – there's 20 guys out on the razz wi' mair money in their tails than they've ever seen before an' only one mission – tae lump it a' on themsels tae dae somethin' ridiculous. It stands tae reason that one o' them – at least one, by the way – will think: 'Bollocks tae that'."

"Craw, ye've got a very suspicious mind. But ye're probably right. So who?"

"Ten to one on Lambchop, the devious wanker. I've had mair loyal snotters."

"Fair shout. What about Jimmy? He was whinging about us puttin' it on United before we left the hotel, wasn't he?"

"Aye, but he's a' talk, eh? He's no' gonnae bet against us."

"Mibbes no' – but somebody will have. You have any hassles?"

"Nah, but Ah tell ye this – an' don't mention it tae the rest, right? – Ah was sorely tempted to put a dod on masel' for the first goal. Hundred an' fifty tae one, me!"

"Hey, don't think Ah didnae have a wee thought about it as well – though to be honest, Bobby Bothwell at 9/1 was a far better shout if ye wanted to make a few fly quid. Ah mean, if ye're assumin' we don't beat them, ye could have banked ten grand an' risked two an' a half at thae odds without battin' an eyelid."

"Except we're a' decent guys, so we didnae, did we?"

"Course not."

83

"Good show."

"Glad that's sorted."

"OK, Garry?"

"In the circumstances. Ah'm shakin', Barry. Did you enjoy any of that?"

"Not a second. You get any hassle?"

"Only from a woman in a Hill's shop who swore Ah'd just been in two minutes before an' put the same bet on."

"Told ye we should've worn different gear fae each other."

"Ye know what Ah hope?"

"That we lose?"

"Got it in one – what the hell are we goin' tae do wi' 200 grand each? How do we explain it tae dad and Mhairi?"

"Ah know. As much as Ah want to play in the final, Ah'd be in bits tryin' tae hide a' that money. The whole thing's wrong. We should never have done it."

"Aye, but we did. It was either that or we shopped the boys, because if we hadn't we'd still have been as involved as the rest. It's done now, let's just meet them and smile when they ask how we got on an' get back to preparin' for the game, eh?"

"Aye, we can work on imaginative ways of scorin' own goals if we're 1-0 up wi' a minute left."

"WHERE'S this boozer?"

"What? The one Blue Eyes said we were to meet in once we got inside Central Station? Have a guess, Chunks."

"Sorry, ma heid's mince. Anybody else totally shagged out wi' this whole thing?"

"Ye're no' kidding – Ah just kept waitin' for some eight foot security guard tae leap out and nab me for tryin' tae pull a flanker."

"Jesus, Fud, can you no' keep it in yer breeks for two minutes?"

84

"Piss off, Screech – ye know what Ah mean. It started out a buzz, but after a while ye just wanted tae-"

"Lump the fuckin' lot on Rozenkrantz for first goal an' go for a pint?"

"Subtle, Heed – though what's the bettin' somebody's done that, eh? Who d'ye think?"

"Lambchop!"

"Fuckin' Lambchop."

"Definitely that twat Campbell."

"Mibbes, but Ah'm worried about the twins – no' that they'll put it a' on a City player tae score first goal, but that they bottled it a' thegether an' blabbed tae some assistant or somebody that looked at them funny."

"Don't think it's no' crossed a' our minds, Heed."

"An' then there's Ginge as well, Chunky."

"Ah know – we put a lot o' pressure on thae guys tae handle somethin' totally new tae them."

"Makes ye wonder what we were thinkin' about in the first place."

"Fuck off, Chunky, it was your idea!"

"Aye, well you lot should've talked me round. Anyway there's the twins, so schtum."

BLUE EYES, Ginge, Hairy, Lambchop, Gio, Craw, Chopper and Jimmy were already sitting round a big corner couch when Garry, Barry and the four who'd come off the Low Level train walked in.

"Boys! Over here – how d'ye get on?"

"Top action."

"No sweat."

"Everybody else OK?"

Everyone nodded and smiled and looked calm as you like. Blue Eyes gave it the big captain bit.

"Ah've told the boys to go easy on the beer for now, lads – have a shandy of two so we're lookin' the part at dinner. Anybody fancies a batter, have it later. Heads down for now, eh?"

"No sweat, skipper. Anybody want anythin'? Naw? Cool."

"Heard anythin' fae the others, skip?"

"Seem to have done OK – Willie an' Gibby are already back at base an' we might see the Paisley squad on the train to Greenock. Is everybody definitely OK here? Seems a bit tense in here."

"Just tired, man."

"Knacked."

"Ma heid's burlin'."

"Mine as well – that was torture."

"Aye, there must be easier ways tae become millionaires."

"Lambchop? You're no' sayin' much."

"No' much tae say, Blue Eyes. Did what was tae be done, havin' a wee Guinness, lookin' forward tae the game the night."

"That's right – Ayrshire Cup Final, innit? Who's goin'?"

"Me, the twins, their da, Porridge, Ginge, Chopper. Hotel's givin' us a minibus for the night."

"Who else is daein' what?"

"Willie's got a squad sorted for some boozer in Largs – his nephew's playin' in a band."

"Sounds a good excuse for a yeehah. Who's in? Usual suspects?"

"Aye. You up for it?"

"Nah, yer old skipper's havin' a quiet night in front o' the telly."

"Take it the porn disnae show up as porn on the bill, then?"

"Is that a' you think about, Fud?"

"What? Hotel bills? Aye, they dae it for me every time. When we off?"

"Now, as it happens. Train's in five minutes, Platform 11. Try an' keep it down on there about what's been goin' on, though, eh? Ye know what walls have."

"Sausages?"

"Exactly."

Briefing Room, Central Scotland Police, Falkirk

"GAME of 501, anyone?"

They looked up from around the table as DI McKenzie walked in, finger and thumb of his right hand held up like he was throwing at a board. It was the first sign of a good mood from him since this robbery had happened.

Alison Gray felt pleased with herself. She'd sent the dart they'd found down the alley beside Spuds' warehouse for testing and it had turned up plenty. She waited for McKenzie to let her fill the rest in with the news.

"So, Ms William Tell, hit us."

"With pleasure, sir." She didn't hide the hint of sarcasm. "The lab confirms it is indeed a tranquillizer dart, as used to subdue animals in the wild. It was tipped with enough sedative to bring down a large mammal – anything up to an elephant - for ten minutes or so and a human for well over half an hour. Forensics also showed traces of polyester and wool, possibly from a pair of trousers, and while that is of no real good to us, the fingerprints found on the shaft of the dart may well be."

"Whose?"

"Neil McAllister. Also known as Rhino. Well-known as a henchman of one Charles Kerr, aka Mr Spuds. We've given Rhino a tug-."

"Lucky him, usually suspects just get questioned..."

McKenzie joined in the laughter, then quickly shushed them down. "Thank you, DS Bradley. Go on, Alison."

"Sir. Anyway, we went to see Rhino and - well, as you'd expect, he's blanked it."

"Blanked it how?"

"He says that, yes, he works for Charlie Kerr. Yes, he was at the Denny warehouse on Tuesday afternoon. And, yes, he even says he was knocked out with a dart just after locking up the premises at around 4pm."

"But?"

"Claims it was just neds, that it's the new craze with them - they nick the darts off vets and from the zoo, knock punters out and either rob them or just laugh at them while they're zonked."

"Was this Rhino robbed?"

"He says not. And before you ask, Sir, we did ask why he hadn't reported the incident. He says it was too much of a brass neck."

"So have we checked the line about kids knocking off darts from zoos and vets?"

"It didn't ring bells with either myself or Ian - er, DC Allan - but we checked anyway just in case. Cobblers, of course. No record of any thefts of this kind at all in the past three months anywhere in the Central Belt. And it seems too far-fetched to think that neds are going to the bother of having them stolen to order elsewhere and shipped in when they can just use a good old-fashioned chib to stick victims up."

"I'd say that's right. Which means young Rhino is at the madam. Question is, where do we take it? We're still no nearer knowing who fired the dart - or, darts, if Spuds and anyone else was also around at the time, as we suspect - in order to make off with that mysterious quarter of a mill. Any ideas? Des?"

"Well, as you'd expect, Spuds was all smiles and tea when we went round there. Says he was at The Boston Bar all Tuesday afternoon and that 12,569 independent witnesses will verify the fact. After that, we hit all the other big outfits that would deal in amounts that large, Sir."

"And?"

"Square root of sod all. Certainly doesn't seem to be any of them who turned Spuds over, if indeed it was Spuds who was turned over. Too much risk of a gangland war and none of them fancies that much, they made that pretty clear. As for Spuds pulling off something big, everyone's heard the same rumours as we got passed to us. But that's it. Rumours. Nothing more concrete, I'm afraid."

McKenzie rocked back in his chair, hands behind his head. He had a meeting with the Super in ten minutes and at least he had something of a picture to give him - even if they were painting by numbers with the most important colour missing. He rocked forward again and slapped his palms on the table.

"OK, so here's how it looks. Our commando pals get wind that Spuds is doing a big deal at the Denny place, they take the unusual but highly effective step of bringing him and his monkeys down with tranquillizer darts, they nick the money, they crash the getaway car, they hijack a second motor, they do a runner to a place unknown. Agreed? Good. Which leaves us with the same problem as we started the day with. Finding out where that place is. Once we find these daredevils, I reckon everything else will fall into place. Des? Phone CID at Tayside HQ when we get out of here, the last word was the field had been narrowed down to somewhere in Dundee. That's where the two cars hoisted from Stirling Services were found torched."

DS Bradley nodded. "Course, the only thing is like you said earlier, boss - Spuds might get there first. And if so, he'll most likely get his money back and silence the commandos for good."

"In which case there's next to bugger all chance of us ever actually confirming that there was ever a robbery in the first place, because Spuds will leave not a single fingerprint. He never does."

Alison Gray piped up. "Well, Sir, his sidekick did get careless with the dart."

"Aye." McKenzie laughed mirthlessly. "And you can imagine the merriment that caused in the camp. You know what? I'd almost rather Spuds got there first, Tayside got to clear up the mess and this whole shitty business died a death."

And they all reckoned he looked like he meant it.

5.05pm, Small Shoes Bar, St Vincent Street

EVERYBODY knew Marion Wallace. She'd been with Ladbrokes for 30-odd years and for most of them had been unofficial social convenor to Glasgow's betting shop community. But now it was her to turn to relax and let everyone else put on a party.

Marion was retiring. And it seemed every cashier and manager who wasn't still stuck behind a counter was already waiting to raise a glass to everyone's favourite person in the industry. The rest would follow as soon as the last winnings had been paid out on the last race.

Robbie Cheyne took a long slug from the neck of his Michelob and closed his eyes as the tension of the day began to ebb. Brenda McKay smiled at him as she stood at the bar, money clasped in her hand as she tried to attract the attention of staff more interested in checking their make-up in the mirror than serving customers.

"Busy one?"

"Mental. And weird."

"Weird as in..?"

"As in a wee pattern started emerging as the afternoon went on, bets coming in for Ochil United to win the semi on Saturday. Big bets, right up to the counter limit. Five hundred at a time."

"How many?"

"Not squillions. Ten, maybe?"

"Us too."

"Yeah?"

"We got the same. Every half hour or so? Sometimes the same guy putting more than one on?"

"God, Yeah. Hang on – Alan! Alan Robinson! C'mere!"

"A'right? What's happenin'?"

"Any odd bets today?"

"Nah – just a right few bob on Ochil United to win the semi on Saturday. Some people have got more money than sense, I suppose."

"Might not be as straightforward as that. Me and Brenda had the same in our shops. Let's ask about."

So they did. And everyone had the same tale. In isolation, a few grand here and there on a huge outsider was nothing unusual. A wee tip maybe, some inside knowledge. But over five, ten, 20, 40 branches? That was organised. That sounded more like a coup.

Managers started ringing their managers and letting them know. Those managers didn't want to jump to conclusions, but there really only was one to be drawn. Someone, somewhere knew something about Glasgow City that the bookies didn't. And that was never good news.

The first thought in situations like these would be to lay some of the money off in case the tip came good. But as all the chains had taken almost identical amounts on United, that would make no difference.

Yet as there was no evidence – yet – of any wrongdoing, they could hardly suspend betting on the game. They'd have to sleep on it and see what was blowing on the wind come tomorrow.

6.15pm, Glenbank Hotel

"BOYS, listen in before ye start eatin'. BOYS!"

The rabble, as ever, took as long to fade to silence as it had when the players had all still been in school.

"Right. Good day? Well, at least ye're still sober, that's somethin', eh Bibs?"

"It's a start, gaffer."

"Anyway, the deal's still the same. Dinner, quick team meetin', then ye're free agents for the evenin' - like Ah said, no curfews, but ye're on trust. It'd be nice if ye were back before midnight, but it's up tae yersels. It'll show at trainin' in the mornin'. On that bus at ten sharp, anybody who isn't doesn't get shouted for an' doesn't figure on Saturday. Fair? Good. We'll be havin' a hard session, the last good runnin' shift before the game. Friday's gonnae be about the ba', about shape. But tomorrow? If anybody's spewin' from the drink or left their legs at the dancin' that's their loss, no' mine. Ah'll be at Hampden whatever happens, aye? Ye know the rules – cheat yersel' if ye like, but don't cheat me. Meetin' at seven, OK? Now, get some scran then go an' have fun. Ah know Ah will."

6.40pm, 16/4, McLean Court, Dundee

IT was a debt collector who found them. He came to the door to chase some guy called Guthrie for a ton he'd borrowed a month ago and which was now sitting at just over three times that. But he was too late.

Whatever Guthrie owed anybody, he'd paid a far higher price than even the most hard-bitten tally man was every going to impose.

The debt collector rapped on the door and it swung ajar at the touch. Whoever had gone in or out of it last hadn't closed it properly. He hesitated for a second in case it was a trap. He called Hello through a crack and into the gloom of the lobby, but there was no sound. He pushed the door a little further open and it bounced back towards him off something. He put his head round to see what the obstruction was.

And threw up.

Lying behind the door, slumped against the wall in a foul, congealed pool of black blood and rancid vomit, was a dead man with a gaping wound in his left leg and half his face missing. The debt collector had slung a few punches, slapped a few late-payers in his time, but he'd never seen anything like this. His stomach heaved a second time and the last of his lunchtime pasta and orange juice came up. He wiped his mouth and took a deep breath. What the hell had happened here? Apart from the obvious, obviously.

He took a look beyond the corpse and, eyes adjusting to the semi-darkness, peered towards the open door of the living room.

And saw more bodies.

Three? Four? There could be any number up there, all in bits. He couldn't be sure from where he was and he wasn't for getting any closer. He put his hand to his inside jacket pocket to take out his moby, then hesitated. If the police were to be informed, someone else could do it. The guy he was collecting for didn't exactly advertise during commercial breaks on the Paramount Comedy Channel. The last thing he needed was to be explaining to Plod why he was there in the first place. He look round the filthy, graffitoed landing. The other three flats were all boarded up. Chances were not a soul had been up here since whenever all this blood was spilled. Fine. He'd leave it that way.

He trotted back downstairs two at a time, emerged into the teatime air, leaned against the wall of the flats until his guts settled, the took out his tally book and wrote off T Guthrie as a bad debt.

Glenbank Hotel

"GOOD stuff last night, boys, really top drawer. Brilliant shift, kept our shape, took the chance when it came, kept them playin' in front of us from then on. Couldn't have asked for more – especially after the build-up we had. Fantastic. Gie us the same again Saturday and nobody'll complain. Bibs?"

"Superb, superb. Williamson never got a sniff, their midfield were goin' backwards all night an' a great finish fae Chopper. The gaffer's right, same again Saturday."

"Anybody any views on anythin'? Any worries after the crash and stuff? No? Good. Couple o' the directors and maself spoke to the police this afty and there's really nothin' more for us to be involved in. They're dealin' wi' a serious armed robbery an' we just happened to be smashed intae by the robbers. Pity they didnae leave us a few bagfuls o' used tenners, eh?"

A weak ripple of laughter went round the room. Blue Eyes clocked the gaffer's brow furrowing and leapt in.

"These guys wouldnae get out o' bed for what was nicked there, gaffer – not wi' the bonus that's up for Saturday. Right, lads?"

"Dunno, what is it?"

"Aye, Blue Eyes, we're a' too focused on the game tae worry about money!"

"Aye, right, Screech – don't push it. No, seriously, gaffer. Everybody's fine. A' just part o' the big adventure. What's the press arrangements tomorrow?"

"Straight after lunch. Open day. Everybody there, no exceptions. Talk it up, get us a' over the papers from now till Saturday – an' before ye start, Willie, no' on the court pages, right? On the back. About fitba'. Tomorrow night's free as well, but Ah don't want anybody leavin' the hotel. We've got movies organised for a private room-."

"Did Screech bring them?"

"Nope."

"Pity."

"Enough. Ye can come an' watch a film or stay in yer rooms or use the leisure club, whatever. Just take it easy, as of Friday we'll start tae feel the pressure – it's unavoidable, no matter how much Ah might babble on about it just bein' another game. It's not. It's the Scottish Cup semi-final against Glasgow City. It's the biggest game of our lives. So enjoy every minute, eh? An' that includes these days leadin' up to it. Remember it a' as part o' that big adventure Blue Eyes was talkin' about. An' keep backin' yersels tae upset the odds."

Blue Eyes breathed a sigh of relief that no one said what he dreaded them saying.

7.10pm, Room 310.

FUD lay on the bed and gingerly poked two fingers into the right side of his groin. It felt like a pair of knitting needles plunging through his flesh. He'd felt the twinges all the way through the game last night, then as soon as they'd stopped running it had started throbbing like a man's groin should only throb in times of happiness.

94

What made it worse was this fuckin' rotten cough he couldn't shift, a tickly, dry job right at the back of his fuckin' throat that shot a pain right down his fuckin' pants every two fuckin' minutes. *Aaarch-aarcch! Oohya bastard! Aaarch-aaaaarrccccchhhh! Ayah!* God almighty, it felt like someone was fondueing his bollocks.

He tried to swing his legs off the bed and walk the pain off, but it shot halfway up into his guts and back down again like a psychotic lift. He collapsed back onto the pillow and the vibration was like being booted in the privates from behind.

This was starting to get worrying.

It was hurting when he jogged, when he sprinted, when he twisted and turned – but, worst of all, when he kicked. The first time it happened in finishing practice this other night he'd made a joke of it and pretended he'd kicked the ground, but how often could he get away with that? Tom was bound to clock it eventually.

At one point, Blue Eyes had come over and asked if he was OK and he'd mumbled something about a bit of cramp. But he knew the skipper wasn't daft. He'd said to him: "Aye, no bother, but if there's a problem see the physio, eh?"

Fud had just nodded back and jogged away kidding on it didn't hurt. Which it did, by fuckin' bastardin' keech it hurt. It hurt so much he couldn't even stretch across the bed to pick up the remote control and turn off that fuckin' awful Aussie Aerobics guff that had come on after the sports headlines.

So there he was, one hand inside his jogging bottoms poking at his bits while 12 blonde gymphettes in slivers of lycra bent across his telly screen – and that's the moment the door flies open and Craw walks in.

If he'd had a trombone, he'd have gone waaap-waaap-waaap-waaaaah!

Except it'd have hurt too much.

"Turn it up, Fud – you havin' a fly thrap to the totty on the box? Ye might have put the Do Not Disturb sign on the door or somethin'. I mean, this is a little more than room-mates are meant to share, pal."

"Shut it, mouthy – and shut the door as well. Ah don't want everyone thinkin' I'm at the nonsense. Which, by the way, Ah'm not."

"So what's all this about then. Because ye have to admit it looks a bit Freddie Starr…"

Fud sighed and withdrew his hand with a groan. "Look, I'll tell ye if ye promise to keep it zipped, right?"

"An inopportune phrase in the circumstances, bud, but Ah get the drift."

"Yeah, yeah, Oscar – you listenin' or what? Right, between you and me, ma groin's fucked big time."

"Ah know."

"What d'ye mean, ye know?"

"Ah mean, Ah know. It's been obvious for a fortnight. The lads have all guessed. They kept schtum in case the gaffer got on your case."

Fud sat up and regretted it as a red-hot poker shot into his upper thigh. "Fuck's sake – is it that obvious?"

"Obvious? It's been sticking out like a … well, like what I thought you had when I came in the room. Ye've been kicking like a girlie, running like Bambi and turnin' like an oil tanker wi' a dodgy rudder."

"Aw shite!"

"Indeed. So how come ye've hidden it this long."

"How come? Let's see … rearrange these words into a well-known phrase or saying – final, cup, semi. Gettit?"

"Sure, ye want to play in the semi. We all do. But this has been going on how long?"

"Two months."

"Two months! Fuck's sake, you could have had something done about it yonks ago. Fizzy would've sorted you, wouldn't he?"

"Aye, mibbes. But at first Ah thought it was just a niggle, so Ah let it go. Then we got to the last eight an' we drew Motherwell an' Ah thought, play this one, we'll probably get beat, then Ah can put ma haun up and have a rest."

"Some faith in yer pals, eh, Judas? D'ye mean ye really didn't think we'd beat that shower?"

"Naw. Did you?"

"Course not. Ah was just thinkin' about the bonus for gettin' there and the Friday night away."

"But we did them, didn't we? And Ah've scored the winner, eh? So how come suddenly everybody's talkin' about me as the main man an' Ah'm in the papers an' … well, when will any of us ever play in a semi-final again?"

"Me? Ah've got years. Probably sort a move to City after this one. Medals all over the shop. Few Scotland caps, coupla years in France, back to the Premiership, Page 3 bird, bijou addiction to something not-too-life-threatening. Few grand selling the dirt about where it all went wrong to the News of the Screws when Ah'm auctioning the medals tae pay the mortgage. Come back home, total new man, settle down wi' nice second wife few years younger than me, player-manager somewhere half-decent, bit o' telly work an' Bob's yer auntie's live-in lover."

"So ye haven't really given the future much thought, then?"

"The odd moment's quiet contemplation, ye know how it is."

"Aye, well Ah'm 29 and I've been here seven years. Ah've got a wife, three kids and a semi…"

"…Ah can see that from here…"

"Arf arf, Alexei. Ye know what Ah mean. This is a job for me, no' a glitterin' career. We're on a grand a man for Saturday – three if we win."

"Though if ye read the papers ye'd think they might as well have made it fifty, eh?"

"Mibbes – but for one, we could well make it 200 grand a man. And for another, this is ma one chance tae DO somethin'. D'ye think Ah'm just gonnae walk away fae it?"

"Or even hobble?"

"Exactly."

"So when we beat Motherwell, ye swallowed a few painkillers, bit the bullet and lied that ye were fine?"

"Right again. There's hee-haw that Fizzy could've done – the only thing for a groin's rest. It needs time and Ah didn't have time. Ah've got the whole summer to put ma feet up once the semi's by wi'."

"Ah take yer point. Ah think Ah'd be the same, son. So how bad is it?"

"Bad enough."

"How bad?"

"Boil the kettle, pour it down yer Ys, then stick a kebab skewer in … well, right … there … *OOYAH!* … y'see?"

"See it? Ah can feel it, pal. Jeez, are ye sure this is worth it – nah, forget Ah asked that. Course it is. But can ye pull it off, as the actress said tae the hingmy?"

"Ah think so. We won't train that hard the next coupla days. Ah'll get there. As long as Ah can run out at Hampden on Saturday Ah'll take any pain it throws at me."

"Fuck me, check out John Wayne – a man's gotta do and a' that, eh?"

"Aye, Craw, a man has gotta do. It's either this man or Willie Walters and this man's no' givin' up the rank outside chance of a cup final shirt for anybody. If Ah cough tae this injury Ah won't even be on the bench. It's shit or bust, pal."

"Well, if there's anythin' Ah can do…"

"Unless ye fancy putting the index and middle fingers of both hands right where the pain is tae keep the lump in ma tackle pushed in, Ah doubt it."

"Ah'll pass, but if ye want Ah'll say to the other boys…"

"Listen, Craw – say nothin' to nobody, please. Once it's out Tom's bound to get a sniff."

"Fud, Ah'd never let Tom get a sniff of that groin."

"As I may have said before, arf arf."

Then Fud coughed and Craw Pants swore he saw his mate levitate two inches off the bed then thud back down again. He backed out of the room and left him fumbling in his tracky bottoms while the TV Sheilas sweated in the Sydney heat.

98

SHYNESS lay back on the bed, reading a copy of the Evening Time from the back to the front. United were big news on the back after all the business the day before and there was a tale about Glasgow City being on £300,000 a man to win the Treble.

He flipped over to Page One. They had a big picture of some bird in a bikini launching a gardening competition. A story about an 87-yearold great-granny being beaten up in her sheltered flat.

He wasn't usually one to bother with the news stuff, which is why his eyes didn't automatically go to the huge main headline. But when they did, they opened wide with shock.

"Gio? You out the shower?"

"Just getting' dried, two ticks, man."

"C'mere!"

"What is it?"

"C'mere!"

Gio came through, fluffy towel round his skinny waist.

"What?"

"Check this out…"

Shyness held up the front page with the banner:

SPUDS LINK TO £250,000 HOLD-UP

"So? They stole the money fae a potato farmer?"

"Naw, half-arse. Spuds, as in Charlie Spuds."

Gio shrugged.

"Charlie Spuds? Top banana of the Glesga underworld?"

"Means hee-haw, pal – Ah'm an Edinburgh boy, mind? We're cultured in the capital, none o' that gangster bollocks for us. So what about him?"

"Dangerous, that's what about him. He's a monster. Mr Respectable on the outside, heavy as an Acme anvil underneath. The story reckons that other heavies are putting it about that Spuds was doing some dodgy deal when he was turned over."

"And that means the money we've just spent belongs tae him..?"

"Sounds like it, old son."

"Do you want tae use the bog first or shall Ah?"

99

TAXI covered his face with the pillow and shouted STOP! over and over again, each time with a bigger exclamation mark at the end. But Althea and Donna's *Uptown Top Rankin'* wouldn't stop, wouldn't leave him alone.

He'd tried letting it sing itself out, but each time it was almost done it kept flipping back to the start. He'd tried singing other songs over the top of it, songs he actually liked, the kind of songs that never played over and over in his brain, but Althea and Donna just sang louder like the annoying brats they were.

He'd got up and switched on the telly, turned the Aussie Aerobics up really loud and everything, then gone to the loo and washed and shaved and tried to do as much as possible to take his mind off such a fuckin' awful song.

But still it kept coming back. And driving him nuts.

All his life he'd has this. Earworms, they called it. A pain in the arse, he called it. The affliction of his head constantly being filled with songs he loathed. The more he tried to drive them out, the louder the volume got. *I Will Survive*, that was a killer. He'd hated that song since the BB discos when he all the birds would gear the deejay put it on and danced with each other to prove some kind of sisterly shit instead of getting their tits out.

He'd told Blue Eyes about his problem once, during a training session when he was being particularly badly tormented by *I Don't Like Mondays* by the Boomtown Rats.

The skipper had asked if he'd seen anyone.

"Seen anyone?" he'd said. "Is it no' bad enough that Ah'm hearin' them?"

Later, though, he'd got what Blue Eyes had meant and it hit him hard. See someone? Like a doctor? A doctor that looked at your napper? A shrink?

Jesus, that had scared Taxi stiff. But he was starting to think it was better that than what he was going through right now.

Except that while he'd been thinking all this, the music had finished. The sound of whining one-hit wonder UK pop-reggae was no more. He stopped shouting and took the pillow off his head and lay holding his breath for a few seconds, like a spinster disturbed by a noise downstairs.

Nothing. There was nothing. No *gimme lickle bass, spill some wine on me waist*, no more love is aal I bring an' Ah'm a car-key boom dang ding. Nothing. Just peace, perfect peace. Althea and Donna had left the building, stopping only to turn sideways and ease their afros through the doorframe.

It was like when a really bad headache disappears, like stopping battering your wedding tackle with a steak tenderiser. A beautiful, beautiful, feeling.

Then, out of nowhere, his head went: *"Wise meen say-ay-ay, onlee fools ru-ush i-in…"*

And he wanted to top himself.

Central Scotland Police, Falkirk

WHETHER McKenzie had really meant what he'd said about wanting the commandos dead, he got his wish shortly after 8pm. After the phone call, he went to see Superintendent Robinson.

"Bob? A minute?"

"In ye come, Andra."

"Just had Tayside on the blower. Our blaggers? Blown away. Or at least if it isn't them, there's another gang of four halfwits in commando gear lying pan bread up a high flat in Dundee."

"Money?"

"Not a penny. If it was Spuds, he'll already have it stashed. If it was just some opportunist who heard there was easy dosh about and ambushed them, it'd have turned up already. You can't keep that much readies quiet in a place like that."

"Not much doubt in your mind it was Spuds?"

"None, Bob, not a sausage. He got rolled, he got the wire on who it was, he got a step ahead of us, he malkied them. If I know him - and you know him even better, eh? - he won't have left so much as a hair in that flat. I'm waiting for forensics, but don't hold your breath."

"Ballistics?"

"No, seriously."

"Ah, the old ones are the best, Andra."

"Sorry. Shotguns lying by each of the four bodies - plus, by the way, there was a fifth victim, the tenant, a junkie - and I'll bet you a fiver they belong to the gang and were used to shoot them. Tayside say all the bodies were in such a position to suggest they'd been made to lie on the floor and beg for their lives."

"Lovely fella, Mr Kerr. Takes the dough back and does them in with their own shooters. Although, hang on - aren't we working on the premise that they used tranquilizer guns? Why would they have proper firearms as well?"

"Belt and braces? Think about it, Bob, they probably knew Spuds would come looking and that they wouldn't get away with doping him a second time. So they were tooled up, but he surprised them, his boys pulled their weapons on them, then prevented us from tracing the job to them by using the shotguns handily scattered around the living room."

"You should take this up for a living, Andra."

Glenbank Hotel

"WHERE to?"

Tom didn't hear the question.

"Excuse me, chief – where to?"

"Destiny," he heard himself mumble.

"What, the clothes shop in Greenock?"

He shook himself out of his own thoughts. "What? No – er, sorry. Glasgow, pal. A restaurant called 78 St Vincent Street."

"No problem. So, what about Saturday, eh? See, Ah'm a Glasgow United man masel' an' Ah think that Dog's over-rated, right – and as for yon Senteanu, well…"

Tom's lapsed back into deafness.

102

BARRY, Garry, their dad Ronald, Lambchop, Chopper, Ginge and Porridge were in the minibus on their way to Kilmarnock to see Glenafton and Kilwinning in the Ayrshire Junior Cup Final. Lambchop had played for Glenafton before going senior and had fixed them up with tickets on the proviso that they shouted for his team.

"Can we not just enjoy the game as neutrals?" Barry had asked. Lambchop had snorted.

"Neutrals? Ah'll neutrals ye! There's nae neutrals at these games. Are there neutrals at an Ancient Firm derby? Naw – and there's nane here. We're in wi' Glenafton fans who ken me an' if ye even breathe a compliment tae the other lot they'll kill you and eat me."

Barry shrugged. He wasn't a competitive person off the pitch. When they played Trivial Pursuit on the bus to away games, he didn't mind who won. Lambchop had to win at everything. The irony that he rarely seemed to win at anything was lost on him.

"See, ma manager at Glenafton was rotten," he'd told them a million times. "The only time we won a cup the swine didnae pick me. Ah was gutted. The fans were ragin' an' it's the same here – they cannae believe Ah don't play a' the time."

Barry rarely got angry, but guff like this drove him nuts. His brother was left-back on merit and Lambchop was out of order. He'd once told him so as forcefully as he'd ever spoken to anyone and Lambchop had looked utterly hurt.

"Ah see," he'd said. "So ye don't like me, then? Is that it? Same as at Glenafton, eh – Ah always get the rough end o' the stick. Well, that's fine, Ah'll show ye."

But he never did. Lambchop was one of those guys who moaned his face off for a game then couldn't hold down a place when the chance came. Faultless in the stand, bad influence in the dressing room, liability on the pitch. He had next to no chance of playing in the semi – Garry had been outstanding for months and even when he'd been injured at the turn of the year Shyness had done well in his place.

103

Lambchop knew in his own heart he probably wouldn't even be on the bench, but he wasn't the kind who could accept his fate and try to gee up the rest of the lads, be part of the team even if he wouldn't be out there with them. Some guys were good reserves, but not him.

His whingeing was one of the main reasons why when Tom named his team on Saturdays he immediately sent all those not included off to train with Bibs. He called them the Huffy Squad, the ones on a downer because they wouldn't be involved. He didn't want them affecting the ones who would, especially quiet lads like the Ronalds.

Now Lambchop was nipping at Barry again. "See, son, you wouldnae last two minutes in the Ayrshire juniors – they eat wee boys like you for breakfast."

"And that's meant to be impressive? I'm here to play football, not rollerball."

"Aye, but see once you've done your apprenticeship in places like this? Everythin' else is a picnic. Look at Blue Eyes – he's an Ayrshire boy and no one messes with him. We're two o' a kind, us."

Porridge was sick of the same old broken record. "So how come if you two are out of the same pod he never talks to you?"

"Aye, well, he's fulla himsel' eh?"

"But isn't that what Ayrshire football's all about, bein' gallus?"

"Aye, right – maybe Ah should've gone tae night school tae keep up wi' you lot."

Lambchop was in a strop now. Best to leave him be. The bus fell silent.

WILLIE had ordered a people carrier for 20 minutes after Tom left. The gaffer was a bombscare for forgetting things and having to turn back to where he'd started, so they gave it enough time to make sure he was well clear for sure. No use risking awkward questions about where they were off to.

They'd been told they could have a couple of beers, but that wasn't for Willie. After the day they'd had, he needed a proper bucket. His head was doing somersaults with the whole betting caper, the excitement mixed with fear and sheer exhaustion from moving and thinking so fast.

His young nephew's band were playing at a boozer in Largs and he'd got a squad up to go and see them. If the gaffer did pull them up, it was an innocent enough cover. He'd already squared off the night porter with a tenner to keep schtum if they came in extra-late.

Gibby was no problem, he wouldn't play on Saturday anyway. Craw was always up for a night out and if he was, Fud usually followed. Jimmy D, Shyness and Giovanni were game for a laugh and young Hairy Bum had said he'd go if the manager agreed. Willie lied that he'd cleared it and Hairy said that was OK, then.

"What's the band's name, then?"

"Special Guests."

"Special Guests?"

"Yes, Great-Uncle Gibby, Special Guests. They thought it'd look good on the posters: Tonight – Special Guests plus Special Guests."

That tickled Jimmy D. "Then someone else could start up a band called Support, so it could read: Tonight – Special Guests plus Special Guests – Support."

"Aye," said Craw, "and there's always a bit under that sayin' Support To Be Announced, so you could have a band called To Be Announced so it went: Tonight – Special Guests plus Special Guests – Support – with Support To Be Announced – To Be Announced."

Jimmy D chuckled again. "An' then they could have-"

"Enough," said Willie.

"OK."

They stuck in a couple of quid each to give the driver a kind of pre-tip-tip, just so he kept it shut as well about who he'd taken where. He said he'd pick them up again at 11, because he'd heard on his radio there was a return booking for Hagen in Glasgow at quarter to. That'd get them safely home before the gaffer and guarantee him another decent bung.

BLUE EYES had decided to stay in. He was quite tired, there was good stuff on the box, he hadn't fancied the junior final – and anyway, a wee waitress he'd met when he came here for a sportsman's dinner a few months earlier had whispered extremely sweet somethings in his ear when she brought his dinner...

"So, you gonnae be a good little athlete tonight?"

"Depends how athletic you mean. And how good."

"Well, we kind of ended things suddenly last time-."

"Not on my part, m'dear!"

"Ye know what Ah mean. Ye were away sharpish that night when Ah thought ye'd hang around."

"Ach, work next day, blahdy blah. Anyway, Ah had no inklin' that you felt that way. Ah'm pretty rubbish at readin' these signals. To be honest, Ah don't have a big success rate wi' the ladies."

It was a killer line every time.

"Well, that's how we like them sometimes. Shy, vulnerable – means we can bring them out their shell, teach them a few tricks."

"You'd be doin' me a favour."

"The pleasure's all mine. So, what's your plan?"

"Early to bed, m'dear. Tucked up by ... what ..?"

"Half nine?"

"Perfect."

OUTSIDE Rugby Park, Lambchop was still in a mood. He told them to wait by the bus and he'd go and pick up the tickets. When he came back, he said they'd let him down and only left two instead of six, so who wanted the spare?

They knew he was at it, he was always like this. They said for him to go himself and they'd do something else. Lambchop shrugged and muttered for them to suit themselves and walked away. Ronald Ronald took out his mobile and punched a number. A minute later he told them they were sorted – the Kilwinning secretary was an old pal and was putting five comps on the door for their end.

Lambchop was going to love this.

GIOVANNI hadn't liked The Old Trout from the moment they walked into its smoky fug. He'd told the rest there was a bad vibe about it. Willie had told him to shut his coupon and get the beers in. Giovanni said he could smell bother a mile off. Willie said with that nose he could probably smell the bins in Calcutta.

The swarthy midfielder harumphed that they better not say he hadn't warned them.

Willie clocked Craw looking round the half-full boozer uneasily. "You got the Gary Glitters about being out as well, then? Or have ye been spooked by Shyness's stuff about the bad man that got robbed?"

"Fuckin' right on that one. Ah've heard o' that Spuds fella – he sounds mental. But Ah suppose whoever's money it is isnae gonnae be a care worker, so we're in the shite anyway."

"That's the spirit…"

"But apart fae that, Ah'm just a bit worried about what happens if we get recognised in here, know? Like, if some City punter has a go or that."

"You? Recognised? Listen, mate, you struggle to get recognised in our hotel. Relax and have a beer, for fuck's sake."

But now they were all getting wobbly. Shyness piped up. "Nah, fair play, Willie – we're a bit public here. We've been in the papers"

"You huvnae-"

"Aye, well you get ma drift – we just better be careful, Craw's right."

"What d'ye mean, Craw's right? It was me that mentioned it."

"Yeah, Gio - but you're just keechin' yersel. Craw IS right, we better watch we don't attract attention tae wursels and get in bother."

107

Willie fondled the sleeve of Jimmy's bright orange and blue Hawaiian shirt. "An' this is your way of stayin' incognito, Mr Donaldson? Damnably cunning, what?"

"Aye, well, Ah'm just sayin', right?"

"Fuck sake, Ah wish Ah hadnae taken you lot out now."

"Taken us oot? You our social worker suddenly, fat boy?"

The argument died as the band came on stage. Willie gave a tall, skinny guitarist with trendy specs and a spiky haircut a pally nod.

"That your Margaret's boy, then?"

"That's him – Kenny Thomas, the next Hendrix."

"Pliss, but who voz the last wun?" said Hairy.

"Jeezo, you really are a teutonic tosspot. Ah suppose you're more into fat men in leather shorts playing the tuba or somethin'? Hendrix was only the greatest guitarist of all time – died tragically young in a typically rock'n'roll accident."

"Tell ye what, Gio, ye make choking on yer own spew sound highly romantic."

"It's better than wearin' it," said Willie, patting Jimmy's shirt again.

8.50pm, The Boston Bar, Springburn, Glasgow.

"SO what next, boss?"

"Ye know what, Rhino? Ah'm not sure."

"No' like ye, boss."

"Aye, Ah know. Any thoughts yerselves, lads?"

"Ah cannae see any other way but gettin' in among the fitba' wankers an' scarin' the money outa them."

"Got tae say Ah'm wi' Tam on that one, boss."

"Aye...aye. Ah'm comin' round to that thought maself."

"Ye don't sound keen, though, if ye don't mind me sayin'."

"Naw, that's fair comment. Ah'm not keen. Don't shout it too loud, but Charlie Kerr's got a sentimental side, boys."

Rhino and Tam didn't know whether to laugh or not. Their boss saw the confusion on their faces and smiled for the first time since they'd been turned over.

"Surprised? Aye, well – that's fitba'. See, they were ma team – well, no' Ochil United, whatever the fuck that's a' about. Ah mean, what have thae tossers that run the game done tae it, eh? What happened tae normal teams fae normal towns, three o'clock on a Saturday and straight out tae buy the evening pink fae a dwarf goin' round the boozers, eh?"

"Dunno, boss."

"Ach, Ah wasn't really askin' anyway. A law unto themsels, these people. Fucked everybody up because they thought they could make things better an' they've only made everythin' fuckin' worse. Pricks. The wrong folk get locked up in this world, honest they fuckin' do. Anyway, Stenny were ma team. Ma granny lived right next tae Ochilview, we could smell the toffee factory soon as ma da's car turned into the street. Loved it there. These things stay wi' ye, know what Ah mean?"

"Ah was a Rangers man masel'."

"Ah never liked fitba'."

"Always thought he was a strange one, eh, Rhino?"

"Aye. Rangers? Whatever happened to them?"

"No Surrender, Rhino ma son."

"Enough, Tam. Don't even joke about that bigotry bollocks when Ah'm around."

"Sorry, boss."

"No worries. Anyway, where was Ah? Aye, Stenny. Ma team. Which kinda makes Ochil stupid fuckin' United ma team. Which kinda means Ah don't feel right about steamin' in and scarin' the shit outa them a few days before the biggest game in their history. Have you any idea what it would've meant tae wee Charlie Kerr tae see his team in a Scottish Cup semi-final at Hampden? Everythin', that's what. How can Ah wreck it for them? For him?"

"But, boss – it's a quarter mill. YOUR quarter mill."

"Ah know, Rhino, Ah know."

"An' we've already had tae malky – whit? – five arseholes tae try and get it back? Ah hope Ah'm no' oversteppin' the mark here, but surely that's bigger than whit team ye support."

Charlie Spuds looked at his minder, all 5ft 7in of him. Width, that was. He was near enough a foot taller than he was wide. And he was the midget of the company security partnership.

"Naw, Rhino, ye've not overstepped the mark. But it's obvious that ye really don't like fitba' or ye'd understand my predicament, son. Ask yerself, what would you do if Tam was turnin' me over?"

"Ah'd do him."

"Right answer. And vice-versa, Tam, Yeah?"

"Course."

"But that's business. And fitba', despite what the smartarses in the blazers might say, isnae a business. It's a passion, it's a love affair. It completely fucks up every notion you ever had about what's right and what's wrong. Listen, Tam, if thae ex-Army dicks had swapped swag bags wi' a busloada nuns, we'd have had Mother Superior tied tae a chair wi' matchsticks under her fingernails 12 hours ago. But fitba's different. You'll no' get it, Tam, but see thae boys that play for Ochil United? Ah envy them. Ah want to be runnin' out at Hampden on Saturday in their place. Ah'd swap everythin' Ah've grafted a' these years for to have played one game for ma boyhood heroes."

Rhino blew his cheeks out. Tam covered his mouth to stifle a grin. His mate just didn't get it – although even he himself, broken-hearted ever since Rangers moved to play in Europe and he was only able to see them on the box, was a tad perturbed about Charlie's sudden fit of softness.

"So what's the plan, then, boss? Just let it go?"

"Fuck off, Tam. Ah might like the smell o' toffee, but Ah've no' got it stuffed between ma ears. No, there's no option but to get in about them. Ah'm just sayin' Ah'm not happy about it. So for once in our lives we have to be menacing but nice."

"What, get the dough back and an autograph?"

"Somethin' like that, Tam. Though half a dozen centre stand briefs would be nice."

"Me and Tam talk nice enough tae them you might even get that game, boss."

9.45pm

LAMBCHOP hadn't spoken all the way back. It was bad enough that Glenafton had lost 2-0, but the rest going on about it non-stop ever since they got on the bus was doing his nut in.

"Brilliant game, brilliant."

"What about that second goal?"

"Topper!"

"And some atmosphere, eh?"

"Superb. Pity about those Glenafton fans fighting wi' the polis near the end, mind."

"Aye – hey, you didn't start that by any chance, Lambchop?"

They smirked behind his back at his silence.

"Nice of that Kilwinning boy to hook us up with the Wilson Pickets, though."

"Main stand? Sweet!"

"Lovely man."

"Got us in for tea and pies at half-time an' everything."

"You get tea and pies behind the goals, Lampchop?"

Not a flicker.

"Still, Lamby, great idea of yours to go," said Garry. "Nice one. 'Preciate it."

Lambchop sat and steamed with bitterness and thought that the cheeky wee twat wouldn't be appreciating life so much in the morning.

AS IT happened, the band were pretty good. Battered out covers of The Clash, U2 and Zep and got a decent hand from a pretty much full house. Craw and Gio were well chuffed that no one had clocked them after all. Until, that is, Willie's nephew gave them a mention and started the barney.

"OK, this next one's for a special guy out there – Willie Walters, star striker of Ochil United. Good luck to him and all the lads playing in the Scottish Cup semis on Saturday. Go for it, big man!"

They still didn't get noticed. Jimmy D was even a bit miffed about that - imagine going to Hampden and no one knowing what you looked like? But as he was worrying about his public image, a roar went up behind them.

"Fuck yer Ochil! 'Mon the City!"

"Aye – sheepshaggin' wankers!"

The United squad kept their heads down and muttered that it was time to move on after all. Then the band burst into Whole Lotta Love and it all calmed down.

"Come on," said Gibby, "let's get these doon us and hit the road. It's nearly ten anyway, we'll grab a pizza then wait for the cab so we're back before Tom."

They were just starting to move for the doors when the music stopped and another shout went up.

"City - wankers! Dirty Muslim bastards – come on the Yiddos."

Then someone shoved someone else and someone shouted about Yiddo twats and the pub revealed itself as half Glasgow United and half Glasgow City.

"Fuck ma old boots, how come they cannae support their local teams?"

"Because, Gio, there's nae excuse for religious genocide wi' Largs Thistle, that's why – now move it."

Craw turned on his heel and gave Willie a shove. Neither of them saw the bottle coming. Neither did Giovanni, mainly because it came from behind him. And smacked him square on the napper. Only Hairy Bum saw their mate drop and he couldn't make himself be heard above the din of fights springing up all around. It was only when the rest got outside and realised they were two men light that Willie said he was going back in.

"We'll all go," said Gibby.

"Naw, it'll look like we're in for a scrap – Ah'll go, you lot leg it an' we'll catch up."

"Naw, we'll wait here."

Willie shrugged, popped his head round the door and saw mayhem. Then he clocked Gio on the deck and Hairy trying to wake him up. He pushed through the crowd and the young German told him what was what. There was no blood, that was a bonus, but Gio was sparko.

"We'll have tae carry him outside an' get an ambulance. There's two chances of getting' help in the middle of a' this."

"Vot are they?"

"Just grab his shoulders, Rommel."

Hairy did what he was told. Willie got the legs. But their way was blocked by a fat bloke knocking lumps out of a guy curled like a foetus on the carpet. Willie bumped the fat bloke to get him to move, but he wasn't having it. He tried to get round him, but there was no way. He let Gio's legs fall and gave the guy a shove.

"Whit's your game?"

"Ah'm tryin' tae get ma mate ootside. He's hurt."

"Aye, well you'll be hurted as well in a minute – fuck right aff."

Willie eyed him for a second. Shrugged. Then nutted him.

And the whole pub seemed to jump on him at once.

Hairy pulled Giovanni out the way, but someone grabbed him from behind and he felt a thump on the temple. He tried to protect himself, but he and Willie and their unconscious mate were being attacked from all sides.

Just then the doors flew open and an army of cops burst in. Someone booted open the fire doors and bodies scrambled into the night. Willie, Gio and Hairy were left on the floor. The young German's ears were ringing. Willie's lip was burst. Gio didn't even know there had been a fight. And now the barman was pointing them out for the cops to huckle.

"Fuck'th thake!" lisped Willie through the swelling. "We're innothent victimth here – ma mate got bottled, the kid there tried tae thave him and Ah wath helpin' them out when thome gorilla noithed us up. What were we meant tae dae – let wur mate lie there unconthious?"

"Save the Two Little Boys speech for the station, Rolf – ye're a' nicked!"

Hairy looked terrified. "But – but how can you arrest a man who is not even conscious?"

"Shut it or you'll find out!"

And so the three footballers were loaded into a meat wagon while their pals watched and wondered what the fuck was going on. Gibby watched the van speed off and shook his head.

"So, who wants the pleasure of tellin' Blue Eyes?"

WHEN the call came, it would be the second time the law had interrupted Francis Albert's plans for a right good night. Just as Gio was being decked, the skipper had been lying in bed, thinking of subtle ways to get the waitress out, dressed and offski so he could go get a decent night's kip.

When out of the blue she came up with one that was about as subtle as 330ml of Budweiser holder to the temple.

"So, m'dear, you'll need tae be up early the morra, eh?"

"No, Ah'm off now till Sunday. No rush night. Unless ye want me out, Francis?"

"Naw, heaven forbid. This cuddlin' up stuff's lovely. Ah suppose Ah was just thinkin' maybe it wouldnae be good for you tae be caught here by yer gaffers."

"No chance, there's hardly anybody on at night. An' anyway, we look after each other here. There's nae gossips. You ARE wantin' rid o' me, eh?"

"Naw, honest. The longer the better. Stay a' night if ye want tae."

"Well, Ah'd need tae draw the line at that. Ma man's in aff the night shift at six."

"Yer man? Ye're married?"

"Aye – an' so are you, don't kid on ye're not. Ah thought we both knew the score."

"Aye, well, like Ah said, I'm no' used tae this kinda thing."

"Sure - once we got up here you were as vulnerable as the Bank of England. Ye're a rascal, so ye are. Look, Ah'll stay a bit then phone a cab. An' then maybe tomorrow night? You could nip round tae mine, he's nights again."

"Mibbes, eh? What's he do anyway – factory or somethin'?"

"Naw, polis."

Blue Eyes felt the will drain away from him in an instant.

"Polis, eh? Great job. Fascinatin'. Total respect for the boys in blue. But, hey, Ah've just remembered – the gaffer's threatenin' tae go round the rooms the night, spot check tae see we're a' behavin'. If we get caught Ah'll be out the team for Saturday. Cannae risk that, eh? Bad for you as well – fitba' players are the biggest sweetie-wives in the world. It'd get back to yer old man before ye can say Sweeney. So, you get yer kit on, Ah'll phone the cab, you take a tenner aff the dresser for the fare an' Ah'll see ye soon. It was lovely, really special."

He was ringing home to tell his missus he loved her before the lift had pinged to take the waitress away.

He'd only just put the phone down again when his moby rang and Gibby was blowing the night for him altogether.

TOM HAGEN had been building up to this moment all night, maybe even all his life. The meal had been lovely, they'd had a couple of bottles of Chianti and the coffee and brandy had just arrived. Across the candlelight, Caroline looked more gorgeous than ever. He wondered what she thought about how he looked.

She'd mentioned about him putting on weight, but he'd taken it as a joke. They'd laughed a lot over the last hour and a half, no ice to be cut or pregnant pauses. It was like they'd taken up again from the point immediately before it had all started going pear-shaped. He'd established as discreetly as possible that there was no one in her life. She was happy enough, earning well, but he got the feeling she had a gap in there and it was shaped like him.

Or was it all just wishful thinking?

For a while during the main course he'd wondered if this marriage business was all just mental, just some hare-brained idea born out of the shock of seeing her again. But the more they talked, the more he remembered how much he loved her and the more it was obvious that they knew each other inside out. They were comfortable together. They fitted.

He decided that if he asked and she said no he'd call it quits, peck her cheek and stay out of her way for the rest of his life. They lived three hours drive apart, after all, so he wouldn't have to face the embarrassment of bumping into her at the shops. And who knew? Mibbes if she did say no she might still suggest they see each other and take it slowly. Win her back in instalments? That might work.

He was just about to pop the most important question of his life when the waiter came across and told him there was a phone call.

Keech! Fuckin', twattin', bastardin' keech!

"Excuse me, Caroline, I just have to-"

She sighed and he knew in that moment all the bad old days had come flooding back to her. Why now? Why him?

"I know, Tom, I know – duty calls."

He barked Hello into the receiver. And then almost dropped it.

"What? Where? When? Is it bad? OK, OK, I'll be there, OK, bye."

He asked the waiter to get him two taxis pronto.

"Where to, sir?"

"One to wherever the lady wants and one to Inverclyde Royal Hospital."

Room 312, Glenbank Hotel

WESTY lay on the bed, hands behind his head, the only person in the room not laughing. Screech was howling. So were the 200 in the *Friends* audience.

"How you doin'? That Joey slays me every time! And how many ways wid ye gie it tae that Rachel? Ah'm sayin' how many ways wid-?"

"Ah've done somethin' mental."

"Ah know, Ah've seen yer night-oot gear."

"Serious, Screech. Ah've done somethin' mental."

Screech flicked the remote and killed the laughter. He swung his powerful little legs off the bed and eyed his best mate. The boy didn't look happy. Come to think of it, he hadn't looked happy all the way back on the train, at dinner or when they'd gone for a game of pool with the others who weren't off out.

"What's up, son? You told somebody about the dosh?"

"Not as such, Screech. But Ah'm worried that somebody else might."

"Westy, ye're talkin' in even mair riddles than one o' the gaffer's pre-matchers. What's happened?"

"Ah got engaged."

"Fuck off!"

"Ah got engaged. Went an' met her when we were in Glasgow, got down on one knee, the full bhoona."

"Whit? An' yer worried ye've done the wrong thing? Nah, son, she's perfect – ye've been goin' out donkeys, eh? She's loyal as that Greyfriars Hingmy. Never dae ye a bad turn. Out the blue, though, eh – Ah didnae even know ye had the ring on ye when we got here. Where d'ye hide – ."

Suddenly Screech was staring right through his pal's eyes and into his soul.

"Aw, fuck me, Westy. Tell me ye didnae?"

"Ah did."

"Aw, Westy, Westy, Westy. Ye blew yer twelve an' a half large on a sparkler for yer bird? Or did ye chuck her an' hook up wi' Liz Taylor?"

"Naw, half on the ring, most o' the other half on two weeks in Barbados. Kept two grand for the legal fees on a new flat."

"Fuckin' hell, Westy. Ah take it she's big schtum about it. At least tell me that?"

"Well-."

"Aw, naw, son!"

"-see, Ah told her to keep it zipped, an' she promised she would an' Ah was sure that would be that. Until about 20 minutes ago when Ah got a text message fae her sister-"

"The one wi' the big paps?"

"-aye, who says congratulations. Says she knows it's all hush-hush but that obviously family were meant to know. Says her lips were sealed."

"No' if Ah ever got the cha-."

"Enough. Thing is, Ah cannae see it, can you? They're women, for Christ sake. They blab. Half Lanarkshire's gonnae know inside half an hour, man!"

"Oh, fuckedy fuck, Westy. What have you done, son?"

Inverclyde Royal Hospital

BLUE EYES was pacing the waiting room when Tom arrived. The manager's glare screamed that he blamed his skipper for whatever had gone wrong that night.

"Can Ah no' leave you schoolweans for two minutes? God almighty, two days before the biggest game o' ma life and it's a' goin' tits up."

"Aye, well –"

"Naw, that's the thing – it isnae well, is it? How the hell can Ah plan for a semi-final when the team's runnin' around like the Dirty Dozen? Or are they auditioning for Death Wish 8? Ah mean, what chance have Ah got when-"

"Giovanni's gonnae be fine, thanks for askin'."

"What?"

"The doctors said there's no serious damage, just some concussion and a bit of a lump. He'll have a bit of a headache in the morning, but it could have been worse. Ah was guessin' you were about tae ask."

"Don't get smart."

"Well, come on, Tom – one of our boys is lyin' in a hospital bed after takin' a bottle tae the napper an' you're thinkin' about tactics."

Tom looked sheepish.

"Aye, well Ah was just gonnae-"

"Aye, Ah know. Ah didnae mean tae be-"

"That's a'right. We're both a bit freaked."

"Aye. You been down the cop shop?"

"Naw. Ah phoned the station an' they said they'd hold them till we got there. But we'll let the diddies sweat, eh? Gio's the one that matters."

"He's got no chance for Saturday, y'know."

"Ye're kiddin'? Ah thought ye said it was only concussion."

"Well, the docs cannae make us leave him out, but the boy Ah spoke tae said they'd recommend ten days rest."

"Fuck it!"

"Ah know. Listen, Ah cannae believe for a minute the boys caused this. Gibby followed the ambulance in a taxi and says they just got caught in the middle o' a United-City barney. Willie-"

"Ah might o' known that trumpet wid be in about it."

"From what Gibby says, Willie was actually the one who went back in tae rescue Gio."

"Willie Don't Be A Hero? Aye, right."

"They getting' charged?"

"Doubt it. The polis reckon the barman's story's got mair holes than a tramp's vest. But that's no' the point, eh? The paper's are gonnae lap it up, eh? Last thing we need. The chairman'll go mental."

"Come on, Tom. Ye gave them the night off, they went tae see a band, got caught in the middle of some numpties fightin' an' had tae defend themsels. We can sell it like that if anybody asks."

"Aye, like any reporter'll write it that way. It'll be Boozed-up United Stars In Pub Brawl – we'll get slaughtered."

"Anyway, there's no point us hangin' round here any longer. They're keepin' Gio in till mornin', so we're as well getting' Willie and Hairy back tae the hotel. Trainin' tae go tae and a' that. Only two sessions left, eh?"

"The way Ah feel we might as well just gie City a bye tae the final."

"Hey, that's no' the Tom Hagen Ah know an' admire. Listen, this could work for us. We should be givin' it the stuff about how Willie helpin' his mates oot in their hour o' need's the way we have tae be on Saturday."

"Nice speech. But even oor lot aren't thick enough tae buy it."

"Jeez, Tom – Ah've never known ye so down. What happened? Were ye on a promise when Ah phoned ye?"

Tom looked into his captain's eyes and for a second thought about spilling his guts, telling him everything about Caroline and the candlelit dinner and the proposal he never got to make. But the moment passed.

"Somethin' like that, Frankie boy."

"Ach, she prob'ly wisnae worth it."

"Prob'ly. Let's get a cab and rescue the Kray Twins."

Room 312, Glenbank Hotel

"IT'S me."

"Mark, honey – are you OK? Ah can't stop thinking about this afternoon. It's all just so excit-."

"Why d'you tell Kim?"

"Ah didn't!"

"Don't come it, she texted me."

"Sorry, Mark, but she's the only one."

"Aye?"

"Well, mum obviously…"

"Oh for fuck-!"

"Don't swear, Mark. How can a girl not tell her mum she's getting married?"

"Because Ah asked ye not to, darlin', that's why. Because it was important."

"Aye, but nobody else knows, nobody that would say anythin'. An' even if they did, who'd care about you an' me getting' engaged? It's not like we're famous…"

THE first edition of the *Daily Record* was running by just after twenty to eleven. The headline above the lead story on Page 5 read:

ROMANCE OF THE CUP
Ochil star splashes £6,000 to win greatest trophy

Then the story:

SCOTTISH CUP giantkiller Mark Weston turned LADYKILLER yesterday — by spending nearly a year's wages on an engagement ring for his childhood sweetheart.

The £150-a-week Ochil United midfielder splashed £6,000 on a 1.5 carat diamond solitaire from a posh Glasgow jeweller to win girlfriend Kirsten Reid's hand.

Weston, 22, sneaked away from the Diddy League club's training HQ for Saturday's fairytale semi-final with superstars Glasgow City to pull the romantic stunt.

Kirsten, a 20-year-old legal secretary, was stunned when Weston went down on one knee in front of cheering shop girls and one pal sighed: "Even if his team lose at Hampden, Mark will always be a winner in Kirsten's eyes."

Beside the story, a picture of Westy in his United kit and a fuzzy one taken of Kirsten as she came out of her office at home time. Everybody had their 15 minutes sometime – though even as the presses rolled, a far bigger story was about to push Westy and Kirsten out of the limelight before their eyes adjusted to the glare.

Largs Police Station

THE street was hoaching with press as the taxi pulled up. Tom cursed under his breath and asked the driver if there was another way in. The driver made some crack about spending most of his life trying not to find out. Tom told him he was as funny as piles.

"Fuck it, just drop us here and wait, pal. We need tae face them sometime, gaffer."

"Bollocks."

The press saw them and bolted over thrusting notebooks and tape machines. Was it true Willie Walters had started a mass brawl by singing anti-City songs? Could they confirm Harri Baum had grabbed the singer's mike and started singing *Deutschland Uber Alles*? Was Giovanni Wilson's coma life-threatening?

Tom suddenly felt very, very tired. He held up his hands to settle them down.

"Listen, Ah don't know what ye've all heard, but it sounds like cobblers. Ah mean, er, infactual. Giovanni isnae in any coma. He has mild concussion and will be back with the lads by lunchtime."

"Will he play on Saturday?"

"Ah won't be namin' the team until an hour before kick-off."

"What about Walters and Baum? Are they being detained overnight?"

"We're about to find out, but as far as we know they were innocent victims in all this. We're horrified that they've been caught up in fighting between a bunch of sectarian thugs and know

122

the boys will be very shaken up by it all, so we just want tae get them back tae the hotel and intae their beds."

"So what about Baum and the German songs?"

"Harri? He's the shyest boy in the world."

"And Walters?"

"Ditto."

The reporters laughed. Even Blue Eyes had a giggle. Tom blushed.

"Aye, OK, Ah'm exaggeratin' a tad - but our information is he actually waded back in among the fightin' tae try and rescue Gio."

"Brilliant - so it's Willie Don't Be A Hero?"

Blue Eyes bit his lip to stop himself laughing out loud. Tom held his hands up again.

"Guys, Ah'm sorry ye've been hangin' about in the cold half the night, but Ah really need to sort this out and get the lads home. Excuse us."

Blue Eyes made a path for them as the flashbulbs went off all around. Tom pushed through the twin swing doors and told the desk sergeant they'd come for Willie Walters and Harri Baum.

Ten minutes later, they were wading through the scrum again with a terrified teenage goalie and a podgy striker whose bottom lip looked like his plastic surgeon had quit halfway through a bee-sting op.

The flashbulbs went again and the questions came like dogs barking in the night, but they kept their heads down, slammed the cab doors and told the boy to give it welly.

No one spoke on the way back, partly so the driver had nothing to flog to the papers, but mostly because Tom was storing it up for a rant at the hotel and Blue Eyes had flashed Willie and Harri a look that said: 'Button it'.

At the hotel, Tom stormed out of the taxi. He'd built himself up into a teacup-smashing, door-booting, paint-stripping, eyebrow-singeing fury and the others knew it. Then the wind got taken out of his sails quicker than a yacht in a vacuum. Fergus Ferry was standing in reception, madder than Tom could ever have hoped to get. The chairman motioned towards the darkened lounge bar.

"In here, now."

"Just give me five minutes, Fergus. I need to speak to the bo-"

"I said now!"

So that'll be now, then. Tom stood in front of his boss and knew in an instant he'd never seen him this angry. He was almost purple. He stood for what seemed like forever, mouth trying to form words but too damn furious to get them out. Finally, he managed a sentence of sorts.

"What the – I mean - what the – the - FUCK is going on?" Tom had never heard the chairman swear before. "Jesus, man, what kind of manager ARE you? Players arrested, players hospitalised, press all over us like a rash – I mean, we're two days from a Scottish Cup semi-final, for God's sake! And you've lost control! I mean, why were they in a seedy pub anyway? This close to a game? It's – it's – DESPICABLE!"

"Chairman, if you'll just let me-"

"Do you know where I was when it all came out? Do you?"

"As a matter of fact, no."

"I was with the Glasgow City directors. They invited our board to the Loch Lomond Plaza for dinner – and right in the middle of the brandy I get a phone call saying half my team are in jail. Do you have ANY idea how that felt?"

No, thought Tom. Do you have any idea how it felt to get a call that ended your love life forever?

"No, chairman, I suppose not. Look, I'm sorry about it all, but it's not as-"

"As bad as it seems? Is that what you're going to fob me off with? Well, let me tell you, Mr Manager – you're right. It's WORSE than it seems. No one involved in this – this – SCANDAL will play on Saturday, d'you hear?"

"What? You want to drop everyone who was in that pub tonight just because they got caught in the middle of a fight? Because that's what happened."

"Or that's what they've told you and you're soft enough to believe them?"

The insult jolted Tom out of head-bowed naughty-schoolboy mode. He'd accept six of the belt for some things, but not for being a pushover.

"Now look here, Fergus – this is a mess, I'll give you that. But I'll tell you two things. First, I treat my players – mine, by the way - like men and they respond to it. That's why I'm fine with some of them being in a pub tonight. They know what's at stake. They know their limits. And second, if they tell me that's what happened, I do believe them. If I can't, that's when I've lost control. But if you think I already have, maybe you should do something about it."

"Like what?"

"You know fine well what – what chairmen always do."

Now the chairman was feeling less like a headmaster on the rampage.

"Look, Tom, let's not you and I over-react here. We're both tired and fractious and hearing bits of stories from excited people. Why don't we get some sleep and regroup in the morning, eh?"

"Might be best."

They both held their territories for a few seconds, looking in opposite directions, cooling off. Then the chairman patted Tom on the shoulder as he made for the door.

"Goodnight, Tom."

"Night, Fergus. It'll be OK, I promise."

"Yes, I know you do."

And then Tom was alone in an unlit bar, gathering his thoughts. Caroline and the proposal-that-wasn't seemed a lifetime ago now. It seemed he was doomed to be unable to concentrate on her and football at the same time.

Pretty soon he might have neither.

When he came out into reception again, it took him a second to remember where the others were. Ah, right, he'd told them to go to Blue Eyes's room so he could deal with them when he'd finished with the chairman. But the mood was off him now. He just wanted his bed. He dialled Blue Eyes from the front desk.

"It's me. Tell those fuckwits to get some sleep and be chapping my door at nine on the button."

"Fair do's, gaffer. You OK?"

"As Ah'm gonnae be. Night"

"Yeah, night."

Blue Eyes put the phone down and turned back to Willie and Harri.

"Right, karate kids, beddy-byes. Gaffer's room, 8.59am. And no smart cracks, right?"

But not even Willie could think of one right then.

Thursday

8.52am, Room 318, Glenbank Hotel

LAMBCHOP had slept angry and he woke angry. He could still hear them ripping it out of him on the bus and it stung – even though at the back of his mind he knew it was himself he should really be angry with, because these situations he got himself into were always, always avoidable.

All it needed was for him not to paint himself into a corner, but he could never resist picking up the brush. He was constantly Van Gogh against the world. One day he'd gnaw his own ear off in frustration.

He should have turned round and joined in when young Garry was baiting him, given him some stick back, been one of the boys. That's how football teams lived and breathed, with the oxygen of abuse. But instead he'd sat there, facing front, as per bloody usual, getting deeper and deeper into a strop until he couldn't have dug himself out with a JCB.

And now, when he should have been forgetting it, he was still raging at Garry. He wanted to go through next door and – and – well? And what, Lambchop? What would you do? Punch his face in for taking the mickey out of you for being a tight-arsed wanker? Because that's what they thought and they were right, most of the time.

They talk about some guys being their own worst enemy and in Lambchop Campbell's case it was actually true, which was saying something in view of the competition. He really, truly hated himself quite a lot of the time. Yet he still felt like taking it out on that young twat Ronald. And to cap it all, Chunky had gone down for breakfast without shouting him. Wee tosser had sneaked out on purpose. They were all the same. He'd show them, one way or another.

HAIRY was already there when Willie sauntered down the corridor. By the nick of the poor boy, he might well have been standing there all night to make sure he wasn't late. Looked like he hadn't slept a wink. Willie hadn't kipped much either, mind. Gibby had kept him awake for hours going over and over and over what had happened earlier…

"Gibby, Ah just want to get some zeds, a'right?"

"Ah just want tae know what went on in there? How d'ye get the bust lip?"

"Hang-glidin'."

"Naw, seriously. We were worried sick out there, man. Next thing we see you three comin' out wi' yer arms up yer backs – well, except for Gio, who's sparko on the stretcher."

"So ye know the script - Gio got banjoed, Ah got a smack, Hairy was keechin' his lederhosen."

"Hey, hey – whit's up? Where's Willie the big man gone? Ah thought you lived for tales like these."

"No' two nights before the semi-final."

"Great for the autobiography, though, eh? Or a nice wad aff the Sunday papers."

"Ye think that makes up for missin' the game? It's a'right for you, you'll no' be playin' anyway."

He'd regretted saying it before it was out. He sat up and put the lamp on.

"Sorry, Gib."

"No sweat."

"But ye know what Ah mean, eh? You're lookin' at this like ye're watching telly, but Ah'm actually on the screen, know' mean?"

"Ye don't think they'll drop ye, dae ye?"

"Ye should've seen Tom in the taxi - he was for severin' our danglies. If the chairy hudnae been waitin' in reception tae cut his aff, we'd have been deid."

"So ye'll get there in the mornin' and he'll have calmed down an' he'll see sense again an' things'll be dandy-o."

"Ye think?"

128

"Aye."

"Ye don't think he'll have had time tae think about the chairy tearin' him tae bits and he'll want tae dae the right thing and maintain the club's family image?"

"Naw."

"Then ye're an idiot. Ferry disnae want us tae win on Saturday, just tae be cuddly bunnies for a day and make a right few bob. Can ye imagine how much a final would cost him in bonuses? And if we got tae Europe..? It'd bankrupt him."

"So you think this is good news for him?"

"Whit? The chairman who put decency before glory? The papers'd love him. He'd be wearin' a top-of-the-range SFA blazer in two minutes flat. Tom'll drap me in a second – Hairy's no' playin' anyway and Gio willnae know if it's Hampden or Hong Kong. Ah'm the fall-guy here."

Ward 12, Inverclyde Royal Hospital

GIO half-opened his eyes to a room full of dried ice. Jesus, he'd had some hangovers, but this was the world's worst ever. How come? He'd only been on the Buds.

Then he remembered. One of the Buds had been on him.

He brought his hands up to check the damage, but couldn't get his head off the pillow. Made it at the third go, tenderly rubbed the bandage covering the lump. It felt like one of those cartoon ones that made Yosemite Sam's cowboy hat sit about six inches above his hair. He tried to open his eyes properly, but the lids were roller blinds held down with ton weights. How had he got back to the hotel? Did the gaffer know about this? And who was the bird talking to him?

Surely to God he hadn't scored when he was unconscious. Even for a magnet that would have been good going.

"Mr Wilson? Mr Wilson? Would you like any breakfast? The doctor'll be round in half an hour, so I could get you some toast if you fancy?"

What? Toast? Doctor? Aw pish, he was in hospital, wasn't he? Yes, he was. And even worse, when he wrenched up the roller blinds the nurse was only a growler, wasn't she?

"Just some water, please."

"No problem. Sleep well?"

"Dunno, I was out for the count. Any ideas what's been happening, m'dear?"

"Well, you came in about ten last night. Someone threw a bottle at you. Nasty lump you had, you needed a couple of stitches too. Your boss came to see you, though, so that's all right."

"Shite..."

"Sorry?"

"I'm saying, that's alright right enough, eh?"

That's all he needed, Hagen on the case. The gaffer thought he was a big enough liability because of injuries without catching concussion three nights before the big game. He'd be raging.

"So what are the docs saying, then?"

"That's for them to tell you, Mr Wilson, but I wouldn't worry. A few days in bed and you'll be fine. Nice rest from work, eh?"

"What? A rest? Ah've got the biggest day of ma life on Saturday!"

"Well, that'll have to wait, I think. I'll get that water for you – back in a tick."

Aye, right. Go fuckin' drown yerself in it, Miss Piggy.

WILLIE'S cloud of pessimism hadn't lifted as he made to chap Tom's door. His hand hovered for a second as if he wasn't sure whether to knock or not. But it didn't matter anyway, because the door opened and he was left looking like he was about to punch his manager.

"Ah thought Ah heard you two breathing out here. Inside."

They shuffled past him, not catching his glare as he held the door. They heard it slam behind them.

130

"Right, you two, Ah don't want tae hear a word, understand? You made all the noise ye were goin' tae last night. It's screamin' at me fae the papers -."

He threw a copy of the *Daily Record* across the room, it fell open at Page 5 and Willie said: "Fuck me – Westy's bought his bird a six grand engagement ring!"

"Not that, ya clown – look at the other headline on the front page."

FISTFIGHT AT THE OCHIL CORRAL, it screamed, then: *Cup Stars Nicked In Pub Brawl Shame*. They had a picture of the manager and Blue Eyes leading Willie and Hairy out of the cop shop. Willie looked at his shoes. Hairy looked like he was about to bubble. Tom tried not to look as if he hadn't realised there was a story inside about one of his own part-time footballers spending Premiership money on his bird.

"Ye know the chairman's ragin'? That he wants ye dropped – no' just you two, but the rest o' yer wee wreckin' crew as well. Gibby? Shyness? Craw? Donaldson? He's for getting' shot o' the lot."

Willie shook his head and looked away.

"Whit? You think that's the wrong decision, Willie?"

Well, he was hung now. Might as well get drawn and quartered as well.

"Naw, gaffer, Ah don't. It might make Fergus Ferry look whiter-than-white, but it wouldnae be fair on the boys, not one bit fair. For a start, we had nothin' tae do wi' the fight. It was-"

"Ah know, United and City knucklescrapers-"

"Right. An' for another thing, Gibby, Shyness and Craw got out right away. Hairy here turned back tae help Gio, who'd been clattered wi' a Bud bottle, which kinda makes the boy a hero."

"An' you?"

"Ah came back in tae help Hairy, some guy wouldnae let us past wi' Gio – OK, so Ah smacked him - an' half Largs bounced on ma heid. Ah suppose Ah was the only one actually involved in the fightin', so if the chairy wants a victim Ah'm his man."

"Big martyr, eh?"

"No' as much as the chairy. He'd rather hang the rest o' us out tae dry than back his ain team. Ah suppose he's threatened ye, gaffer?"

"Listen, son, don't get lippy – Ah run this team, nobody else, remember that. An' that's why, for your information, Ah'll be decidin' who plays on Saturday, no' the chairman."

"Aye, an' surprise, surprise – ye'll decide that Ah'm dropped, right?"

"Wrong, smart guy. As far as Ah'm concerned, you're in ma plans. Same goes for the rest, too. Sit down."

The manager's whole mood was softening. Hairy thought he looked done in.

"Ah'll never forget what every one o' you've done tae get us here. Six months ago we were nothin' - now the whole country's talkin' about us. This club owes you plenty an' no matters what anybody else says, what happened last night doesn't change that. As it happens, Ah believe yer story. As far as Ah'm concerned, this ends here. Me getting' the big stick out won't change anythin', will it? And ye can trust me, whether ye're in or out on Saturday has nothin' to do with any o' this. But for your part, when you go tae trainin' this mornin', Ah want the two o' ye tae act like ye've had the kickin' o' a lifetime fae me."

Hairy was putting on a good act already.

"An' Ah promise – especially you, Willie – that if Ah see one smile or hear one crack, Ah WILL drap ye. Right off the Kingston Bridge. Don't let me down. An' no' a word tae the press this afternoon. One front page in a lifetime is several more than enough, OK?"

"So what about the chairy?"

"If he speaks tae ye, be nice. Tell him ye're the sorriest wee boys in the world. Kiss his Hush Puppies if it helps. Ah don't care, Ah've got a cup final tae reach. Now on yer way an' see if ye can have breakfast without beatin' up the waiters."

Hairy laughed. Tom lasered him with a glare. Willie grabbed the boy's arm and led him to the safety of the corridor.

"Fuck's sake," Willie side when they were well clear, "ye don't make a sound right through the Spanish Inquisition then take a fit o' the giggles."

"Sorry, Willi, but the thing about beating up ze waiters vos funny."

"An' they say you Krauts have nae sense o' humour! Right, let's get some breakfast then hit trainin'. Some of us have got a big game tae play in!"

"Who?"

"Jesus, whoever said you Krauts never had a sense o' humour was dead right. See ye down there in five, Goering."

TOM waited until they were away and punched an internal number.

"Westy? Gaffer. Pop up to ma room if ye've got a minute."

IN ROOMS all along the third floor they were waking each other up or yelling into the bathroom for mates to come and check out Westy's story. It was all there – how much the ring was, the big proposal, the honeymoon, the lot.

Blue Eyes shook his head. How thick could Westy be? OK, so chances were he'd played dumb but that his bird had probably just been dumber and blabbed to the wrong person. However it had ended up in the news, though, it was bad news. Especially when the guy whose money had paid for an idiot midfielder's wedding read it too.

It was time to call in a favour that might just save a few kneecaps.

WESTY tried to look invisible as he walked into the dining room, but only succeeding in turning himself into the World's Most Recognisable Man.

"Fuck me, there she is – Linda Lovebucket, the sex symbol that broke a billion hearts in one moment of fucking stupidity!"

"Shut it, Jimmy."

"Not to mention getting all her pals chopped up by big nasty gangsters!"

"Ah said shut it, Jimmy."

"Congratulations! You've just won Arsehole Of The Year."

"The boy said shut it, Jimmy. So shut it. You OK, Westy?"

"Been better, Blue Eyes."

"Get some scran in ye, son. M'dear? An order for the boy."

"Aye, an' if you bring it nicely he might propose!"

"One mair crack an' Ah'm claimin' you, Donaldson."

"Ah, dry yer eyes, Westy – you're the one who's fucked up here, no us."

Blue Eyes drew his central defensive partner the dirtiest look since coal miners used to take the huff with each other.

"So, what'd the gaffer say, son."

"He congratulated me."

"Aye, right!"

"Seriously, Screech – he congratulated me. Said he had no idea it had been on ma mind, but thought it was great news and asked me to pass his regards on to Kirsten, because she's a great girl."

"Jesus."

"Well think about it, though – he doesnae know about what we know about, does he? Doesnae have a Scooby about the bets nonsense, does he? He just saw me in the paper an' reckoned it was good news."

"What it fuckin' well isnae."

"Thanks for remindin' me, Porridge. Listen guys, Ah'm sorry about this. Ah did a stupid thing – Ah've let ye a' down an' caused us big hassles wi' whoever's money that was."

"So it's OK if we tell the nasty men that it was a' your doin' an' they can cut you up an' leave the rest o' us?"

Enough was enough. Westy leapt across the table and made a grab for JD, who leaned back so sharply he had to grab the tablecloth to stop his chair tipping over. A jug of water went all over the place. Blue Eyes and Porridge lunged from either side to pull Westy back. The waitress coming across with a pad to take Westy's order stopped in her tracks.

"It's OK, darlin', they're just at it. Gie us two ticks, eh? Ta. Right – JD? Fuck up. Westy? Settle. Everybody else, let it go. Ah've made moves tae head this problem off at the pass, so hopefully it'll come to nothin', right?"

"What ye done?"

"Need tae know basis. It's just done, OK? *OK?* Right, not another word. And let's not forget, our pal here has got engaged. I believe congratulations are in order, am Ah wrong?"

"Not tae mention a right good piss up once this is a' ower, chaps!"

"That's the boy, Chunks, priorities right as ever."

10.35am, Greenock Juniors FC

"HEELS up behind for six! Aaand – knees up in front for six – c'mon, high, higher – good! And jog!"

Blue Eyes felt great. He loved training, loved being out there with the boys on a beautiful, warm spring morning like this. Made a nice change – normally United sweated it out on Tuesday and Thursday nights, so from the end of September to the middle of March at least part of the every session was under floodlights.

All season long they warmed up around the edges of the Ochilview pitch, did sprints down rutted red blaes in front of the main stand, piled pressure on their joints playing seven-a-sides on astroturf to save the real grass for matchdays. Sometimes it felt like they were never anything but cold and wet and knackered.

Now, with the sun on their backs, fresh from breakfast at a smart hotel, togged out in the new training maroon and gold gear the kit suppliers had thrown in with the semi-final commemorative strips, everyone was loose and relaxed and happy up for it.

As the skipper shouted for them to walk then stop then stretch, it was almost easy to forget everything that had happened the previous day, 24 of the most bizarre hours any of them would ever live through.

Blue Eyes glanced around the squad as they exercised groins, hammys, calves, shoulders. As they contorted, they were laughing, slaughtering each other – good signs that you were in for a right good session. No one seemed all that tense. Suddenly a Scottish Cup semi didn't seem that much pressure after trying to spend £250,000 of a gangster's money in three hours then getting arrested in a pub fight for an encore.

Willie was at the heart of the wind-ups, as ever, seemingly none the worse for what he'd been through. The others were giving him pelters about Prisoner Cell Block H, changing his name to Old Bill Walters. JD, Shyness and Chunky were the noisiest, as ever. Loved the sound of their own voices. Donaldson, 6ft 3in and built like a stick. McGonigall, fake-tanned and muscular and just under 6ft. Kennedy, five foot five square, crop-haired, bulldog-featured, always moaning, always digging someone up, always willing to fight his mates' battles. A pain in the arse, but you'd rather he was your pain in the arse than the opposition's any day. Fud was grimacing, again. Black hair flopping over his eyes as he put his weight on his left side, his left boot flat on the turf and leaning hard over his left knee. Held it, pushed a little harder, bit his lip in obvious pain. Blue Eyes was getting worried about him. He knew fine well the striker's groin was bothering him – he just didn't know how much. But his guess was that it was bad enough to have the boy shitting himself that he might miss Saturday at Hampden. Blue Eyes wouldn't have wished that on anybody.

Only Craw of the others seemed to notice Fud's problem, but they weren't just strike-partners and room-mates, they were virtually joined at the hip on and off the pitch. The blond, unshaven frontman – shorter and heavier than Fud, bigger in the thigh and the chest – was lying on his back, hands behind head, knees together and bent and flattening left and right to the turf. He stopped and tried to catch Fud's gaze, but it stayed glued to the ground.

Westy seemed miles away as he stretched his hamstrings. Always had problem with his hammys, that kid. Screech, freckled like a life-sized join-the-dots puzzle, short and thick-necked like a weightlifter, was lifting each leg in turn onto the boundary wall, holding his toes and pushing. The Ronalds, identically fair and slim and wiry, had hands on each other's shoulders, pushing away to loosen calf muscles.

Heed Boothroyd and Gibby Johnson stood like twin statues, each with one hand out wide for balance, the other grasping a foot and pulling it up the back of his leg. Chopper McCracken had his right leg up, boot resting in Ginge's cupped palms to make sure his hammys were right. Switched, did the other leg, then returned the favour for his best pal.

Porridge was clutching a ball, gloved hands above his dark, shaggy mop, bending from the hips almost to 45 degrees, then back up, pause, down the other side. He was grinning at the patter flying around him. Harri Baum wasn't. He looked nervous, serious, almost miserable. But that was just him. The young German reserve keeper rarely spoke in training, just did his job and went back to his student digs and studied.

But Lambchop Campbell? He was just genuinely miserable. Stood alone, hands on hips, doing not much more than a half-hearted swivel of the hips as he stared off into the distance. Blue Eyes had heard the crack at breakfast this morning about last night's fallout over the tickets at the junior game. It was typical of the guy, always letting stupid little nothing issues boil up into major fall-outs. Could never just grin and flick them the vicky and get the beers in. Had to be the big martyr.

Well, he wasn't having any huffs this morning, not when the gaffer was in the mood he was in. One long face, one half-arsed performance and they'd all suffer, all be doing press-ups or extra sprints. Tom wasn't the type to bin players for making dicks of themselves off the park – but he was the type to punish them by having every other guy in the dressing room know exactly why they'd been given such a bleaching out there.

"Lambchop! Get yerself movin'! Put yer back intae it!"

And Lambchop thought, aye, that's it – slaughter me, pick me out, don't bother wi' the rest o' the tossers.

Ward 12, Inverclyde Royal Infirmary

GIO was stretching too. Twisting his neck side to side, trying somehow to shift the pain. Maybe if he tipped his head far enough to the side it'd fall out of his ear. Bollocks, it throbbed. He'd told the doc it wasn't too bad, but it was. It hurt like old fuck.

Another nurse now, younger and prettier. Much more like it. He was all ready with the patter until she put the same record as her ugly pal earlier on.

"Lucky you, eh – couple of days lying about in bed. Wish it was me!"

On another morning, he'd have moved over and patted the mattress. But he couldn't be arsed. Instead, he just about managed a smile and a nod.

"Anything I can do for you, Giovanni?"

But he was so depressed he didn't even chance his arm and ask her.

Greenock Juniors FC

"RIGHT, yer Uncle Davie's put his magic cones out, so ye know what's comin' next. In twos, on the line. Bibs – far cone, eh? Don't let them slack off – ye hear me? NO slackin', or Ah'll add them on at the end! It's up tae you! Right, first two, ready tae rock!"

Blue Eyes and Taxi got set, right feet and left arms forward like a photo finish, ready to push off. Others picked partners who ran at the same pace, but the skipper always went with the quickest man in the squad to give himself a target.

"Three-quarter pace tae start. First two ready to go again from the other end when the last two come through ye, OK?"

Pheep!

Taxi was out the blocks like a genuine sprinter, his three-quarter pace full pelt for most of the others. Blue Eyes tried to relax and stay upright, gets the arms and legs right, but felt himself being dragged into a race from the off. Heard the gaffer tell the next two to wait for the whistle.

Westy and Screech bounced on the line.

Pheep!

Both sharp movers, but both running within themselves this early. Heard the next whistle behind them, knew JD and Shyness were on their way. Then Ginge and Chopper, the twins, Fud and Craw, Willie and Gibby, Chunky and Lambchop, with the two keepers and Heed in a three at the back because the numbers were uneven without Gio.

Group by group they went past Bibs, who told each in turn they had to sharpen up. The gaffer shouted from 60 yards away that it was slack, that they were fannying about. Blue Eyes and Taxi were ready again, Bibs on the whistle this time.

Pheep!

Fud and Craw waited in line, shuffling towards their turn. Craw asked his mate how it was, so quiet that he was almost miming. Fud made a non-committal face.

Pheep!

Pheep!

Pheep!

Group after group hammered past the gaffer. He shouted to them that it was better, better, come on Fud, give it more, that's better, come on. Back in, ready to go again.

Pheep!

139

All the way through the squad again, right to the three at the end. Through Bibs, hearts starting to pump now, first beads of sweat gleaming in the sun. Ready again. Craw looked to Fud again. No reaction.

Pheep!

"And take a walk, guys – well done, good start. Let's keep it goin'!"

They walked round behind the goals in their groups, hands on hips, breathing in hard, shaking it out of their legs. The gaffer shouted Davie Jamieson across and gave him some instructions, all jerky hand gestures and nods. Davie stood, hands behind back, nodded, turned and jogged across to a little metal stand with some more mini-cones hung on it.

The boys knew what was coming. Davie wasn't on the United staff, but he was a permanent part of the set-up. The fitness guru. Or The Bastard, as they affectionately knew him. He was five-eight, 47, not a pick on him. Chartered surveyor by day, long-distance runner in his spare time. And their tormentor with any extra few hours he had lying around.

Pre-season he ran their nuts off, on roads, round parks, up hills – he loved hills like some men love women or cars – back down again and then up some more. At most clubs, once the football started the running pretty much stopped. But not at United. The gaffer believed that at a level where teams were much of a muchness skill-wise, fitness was the casting vote between success and failure. So every Tuesday night, Davie Jamieson ran their nuts off some more.

No hills on Tuesdays, of course – not even Tom was that sadistic – but sprints, lots of them. Sixties, 50s, 40s, 30s, 20s, 10s. Four of each, six, eight, ten, 12, 14, 16. The boys hated it, but by God they were fit. They were sharp. No one outlasted them over 90 minutes. Not even Glasgow City would wear them down and they were rated one of the fittest teams in Europe.

They all knew where The Bastard was going with those cones. He'd take them over the other side of the park, lay two down as a start line then place two more at five yards, two more at ten and two more at 15.

Doggies.

The nightmare.

The killer.

Chunky saw Lambchop's face fall and tried to cheer his room-mate up.

"Try not tae think about it, pal – it might just be a threat."

"Fuck that, it's for real. What does that balloon want – fitba' players or fuckin' marathon men?"

Barry Ronald turned with a grin.

"Doesnae really matter in your two cases, eh? Ye need tae get near the ball to be fitba' players!"

His brother laughed. So did JD and Shyness. Chunky gave the kid the finger and managed a grin. Not Lambchop, though.

"What d'you know about it, son? Ah was trainin' when you were in nappies, so don't fuckin' come it wi' me about fitba'!"

Chunky rolled his eyes, shook his head and signalled to Barry to leave it. Lambchop just refused to learn.

"What?"

"What's the silence for?"

"Ah'm recoverin'."

"Ye're annoyed at me!"

"Aw, fuck off!"

"Naw, but why should Ah take that shi-?"

JD spun in his face, not to have a go but because they were heading back for the next set of runs.

"What?"

"Nothin', shift it!"

"What's up wi' a' you people this mornin'?"

JD never looked back as he said they were all sick of training with a baby.

Lambchop was ready for having one of the bastards.

FOUR more 60s. Breathing hard now, hearts reaching a good rate for work. Then four 50s. Gaffer demanding full pelt every time. Another walk. Back in. Four more 50s, gaffer and Bibs calling for more. Blue Eyes straining to match Taxi, who hardly seemed to be working. The Ronalds like one smooth machine in a mirror. Fud feeling it now with every stride. Six 40s. Walk. Then the option, always the option.

"Right, here's yer choice – we can have six more 40s, a walk, then eight 20s OR we can have eight 40s an' get the ball out for half an hour."

"Eight 40s."

"Aye, get it done."

"Let's kick the ba', gaffer."

He knew they'd say that. They always did – which was fair do's, because the ball was the tool of their trade. He just wanted to make sure they had the strength to use it game after game, month after month.

"OK, back in. First two up – an' let's really up the tempo, eh?"

Yeah, like Ah've been slackin' behind this big-eared freak.

Pheep!

Each blast of the whistle from either end of the ever-shortening track forced them to push again, again, again. It was hard now, but they pushed it, pushed it, pushed it. Only way with this guy in charge. Do it right or you'll keep doing it until you *do* do it right. Cheat yourselves if you like, but don't dare cheat me.

Last one now. Blue Eyes running with sweat, Taxi relaxed as if it was the first jog after brekky.

Pheep!

And one by one they went, from Bibs through to the gaffer, hearing the stereo voices yelling for more, more, one more effort, come on, fuckin' brilliant, fantastic, that's the stuff, train like we play! Take a walk, superb stuff!"

Bibs dragged a big nylon bag full of maybe 20 balls over to the edge of the right-hand penalty box, loosened the cord, poured them out onto the turf. Gaffer had to get a touch right away.

"OK, bet ye a can o' Coke that Ah hit the bar. Many chances dae Ah get?"

Bibs, small and ginger and podgy, a rolling walk on legs slightly bowed from a career plagued by knee injuries, laughed and said Two.

"Right. Watch this."

Chipped the first ball, right-footed, and watched it dip two feet under the bar.

"Getting' the eye in, watch this time."

Pinged the second one, perfect. Bounced off the face of the bar, clean as a whistle, plopped just in front of the penalty spot.

"Never lose it – eh, boys? Eh?"

The boys laughed. There wasn't a more competitive guy at the club, maybe in football. Play head tennis with the gaffer and you simply didn't win. Sure, you might take the 21 points you needed for the set, but you wouldn't win. He'd keep playing until he convinced you he'd won. Then he'd play you again. And again. And keep doing it until he was fed up. And it took a lot to make Tom Hagen fed up with anything to do with a ball, a net and winning. He teed a ball up on the D outside the box.

"Anybody fancy a go? Case o' juice if ye hit the bar wi' one shot. Come on, who's up for it. Screech?"

"Aye, OK."

The barrel-chested midfielder jogged across to the jeers of his mates.

"Confident, son?"

"Course, gaffer."

"Right, let's just make sure we know the rules here. You're gonnae hit that ball – that one there -."

"Aye…"

"Off the bar from within, say, a yard of the 18-yard line. OK?"

"Got it."

"So, this ball, no more than yard from the 18-yard line, off the bar without bouncin', yeah?"

"Yep. Understood."

143

Tom shrugged to Bibs. The little assistant knew what was coming next. So did most of the boys, the only surprise was that Screech was buying it.

"OK, Screech, there you go – hit that bar down there."

The gaffer was pointing the length of the pitch. Screech's jaw dropped. The boys were knotting themselves. Bibs shook his head.

"Don't get drawn in, kid, he'll do ye every time."

"Aw, fuck off, gaffer!"

"Hey, a bet's a bet – case o' juice, that was the deal. One shot. Your bottle away? Guys, should that be TWO cases?"

"Three!

"Four!"

Screech blushed and wandered back to the pack, telling them to get it up the lot of them. Westy put his arm round his pal and kissed his cheek.

"Aw, diddums."

WHILE the gaffer was taking the piss, Fizzy and Jackie had been setting up a set of portable goals on the halfway line. Tom took the keepers out, split the others into a seven and two sixes and said he and Bibs would make the sides up.

"Blue Eyes, your team in red bibs – Westy, yours in yellow – Chunky, yours in green. Reds and yellows on, greens spread round the side. All in on the pitch, one touch at the sides. Five minutes on, five off. Let's make it sharp, eh?"

Tom went with the red, Bibs with the yellows. Chunky and his six dotted themselves around the half pitch as the walls for passes. Whichever side fed them the ball, they had to give the same side it back. It was all about them being alert, ready, constantly aware that they could come into the game. The gaffer's pet hate was someone saying: "Sorry, Ah never expected that."

He booted the ball up in the air. Heed went with Shyness for it. Shyness won, banged a header down to Taxi on the right. He played it to Chunky, patrolling the bye-line. The wee man saw

144

Lambchop in a yellow bib and played him in. Lambchop's shot flew ten yards over Harri's bar. The boys howled. Lambchop's head went down.

He gave Chunky a look that said: "Thanks a lot – some pal you, eh?"

Chunky gave up with him.

"TIME! Right, in ye come, make sure a' the balls are here!"

The boys gathered round the gaffer, energised by the pace of the on-off action.

"Good stuff, lads, much better. Listen, last night wasn't a good one. We a' know what happened, but let's forget it now an' put it down to nerves – and maybe stupidity, eh, Willie?"

"Ah'm yer man for that, gaffer!"

"Aye, Ah'm sayin' nothin'. Anyway, this mornin's been exactly what we needed – a right good crack at it. Good tempo, good effort, decent touch o' the ba'. One more session now, then that's it. Nearly there. Eyes on the prize now, nothin' else matters. Now, we'll get showered back at the hotel an' we'll be on the bus in ten minutes. But first -."

"Aw, fuck!"

"Correct! A wee final game o' runnin'! Let's go, five, ten, 15, back in an' go again. That'll do us. One last batter, come on!"

Lambchop spat on the turf and shook his head. The gaffer saw it and fixed him with a glare.

"Problem, Danny? No' enough runnin'? Ah can make it three doggies if ye like."

"Naw, ye're fine."

"Good. Let's do it, then."

Blue Eyes went past Lambchop and told him to get his arse in gear before they were out there another half hour. Lambchop said fuck off.

Then they were on the line again, in fours this time. Blue Eyes, Taxi, Ginge and Chopper first. Not happy men. Never were when it was doggies.

Pheep!

Up to the five, plant the foot, push off, back to the start, plant the foot, push off, sprint to the ten, plant the foot, push off, back to the start, plant the foot, push off – *Pheep!* – and through to 15 as the next the twins, Chunky and Lambchop headed for the five, planted the foot, pushed off...

Fud was dreading it. Every kick he'd taken in the games had hurt. His right bollock felt like a Spacehopper, a whole chunk of muscle down the line of his pants raw and sore. The four in front were coming back from the ten. He got ready with Craw, JD and Shyness. Just do it, son, suck it up and do it. Think of the mon-.

Pheep!

Fud was away, up to the five, planting the foot, pushing off. Fuck! Back to base, planting the other foot, pushing off. OK this time. Up to ten, planting, sore as fuck, pushing off, burning now, back to base, planting, pushing, desperate to be finished, hearing the next four behind him, stumbling over the line, almost falling, landing in Blue Eyes's arms, heading spinning, right leg trembling, face twisted in pain.

Blue Eyes looked right at him and begged him to see Fizzy.

Fud could only see spots.

12.20pm, outside Glenbank Hotel

"SO what's the Hampden?"

"They're due back any time. Trainin' down at Greenock, comin' back by bus."

"Who d'you say ye were?"

"Reporter."

"Ye look the part, t'be fair."

"That an insult, Rhino?"

"Take it how ye like, son."

"OK, girls, enough. Big game heads on. Ye know the drill?"

"Aye, boss – we sit tight until one of them's on their own, then gie him a tug. How far do we go wi' him?"

"Nae slaps, nae marks. Just scare him shitless. There's no way he'll play hero, he'll tell us where the money is, no sweat."

"Think we should take the car somewhere a bit less visible? If they're holdin' your dosh they must have an idea we could trap at some point."

"Mibbes, Tam, but they'll never expect us to be this up front. They'll never even clock the motor."

"Rhino's right. We sit here. Fuck them. There's a quarter of a million quid of ours in their mitts an' we're getting' it back right now."

"What happened to the wee boy wi' the Stenny scarf, boss?"

"He grew up into a right hard bastard."

CHARLIE SPUDS was right enough. None of the boys even noticed the big blue Jag sitting opposite the bus as it pulled up right outside the wide, stone entrance to the hotel. They were too busy listening to the gaffer.

"Listen up – lunch is in 20 minutes, so get showered and be there. Quick chat after we eat then it's the press open day. Everybody be there – except for Willie, Westy, Shyness, JD, Craw, Gibby and Harry. Last thing we need's pub fights and engagement rings bein' brought up. Anyone else who talks to the press, blank these subjects completely. We'll tell them the ones who aren't there are all getting' treatment."

"Aye, like even reporters are thick enough tae buy that shite."

"Ah heard that, Chunky."

TWO little boys found Billy Andrews in a disused quarry near Milton of Campsie, half an hour from the centre of Glasgow. They didn't know it was Billy Andrews. They just saw a bruised and bloated body lying in a shallow pool of water.

One of them burst into tears. The other ran in terror. He shouted back over his shoulder to his weeping pal to get out of there and they scrambled back up the banking together. They hared through the trees to the road and tried to wave a car down. Three, four, five went hurtling past before one finally stopped. The driver wound his passenger window down and leaned across.

"What's wrong, lads?"

"We've – we've – found a boady, mister !"

"A dead wan, mister!"

"Where?"

"In the quarry – we werenae daein' anythin' bad, mister, just playin', honest!"

"We never killed the guy, mister!"

"OK, boys, OK, have a seat by the side of the road and I'll phone 999."

It was 15 minutes before police and an ambulance arrived. Within another half hour the place was buzzing with activity as an incident room was set up. The wee boys sat in the back of a panda car and watched it all happening. It wasn't exciting, not like on the telly. They were simply traumatised.

Two officers got into the car and asked for their addresses. They said they'd take them home and get statements from them with their parents present. The wee boys asked if they were in bother. The officers smiled and said no, they'd been very helpful. One of the boys managed a weak smile. The other just started crying again.

Neither would sleep that night.

1.30pm, Lambie Suite, Glenbank Hotel

THEY sat in little huddles, earnestly probing and nodding and scribbling as Ochil's bit-part players lapped up their 15 minutes in the spotlight. As he watched from in front of the shuttered bar, Blue Eyes noticed that in each little knot of maybe six or seven reporters, only one or two at the most seemed to be asking anything. The rest were just writing down the answers. He found this odd.

Paul Arthur, on the other hand, found it infuriating. He was, as per bloody usual, one of the few asking the questions and as ever he couldn't fathom what right these other guys had to get the benefit of his knowledge to fill their papers. Why didn't they do their own work?

He knew the answer, of course.

They didn't have a clue who there were interviewing.

Waiting in the lobby, they'd been moaning their faces off about being here at all – I mean, who wanted to know about Ochil fucking United? They were only bit-part players, cannon fodder. It was Arrabiatta and Dog the readers wanted, not Willie Whoever and Jimmy No-mark. Arthur had sat shaking his head – and when that big tube Duncan Collins from *The Star* had actually asked - out loud - who United had beaten to get to the semis, he'd snapped.

"Do any of you guys like your jobs?" he'd said. "Because it doesn't look like it – you're not just employed to write about City and United. It's because of the likes of you that clubs like Ochil are struggling."

"Mince," said Collins. "Nobody's interested. How many do they get on a Saturday? Fifteen hundred? United and City get a HUNDRED thousand between them. That's what sells papers, not these diddies."

"So you think Hampden would be full for City playing nobody on Saturday?"

"City ARE playing nobody on Saturday. Face facts."

"What d'you mean, face facts? Listen, I go and watch these teams. This is real football, not the millionaires poncing about as if they own the place."

"Real football?" the *Express's* whisky-faced veteran Jimmy Simpson had sneered. "Well, give me the kiddy-on stuff any day – I mean, have you been up to Ochil's keech-hole? I got sent up when they played Hearts and they didn't even bring us tea at half-time. I told the desk, no way was I going back."

Arthur rose to the bait, like he always did.

"So is that what it's all about? Getting pampered? I'd expect more from you, Jimmy, you go back way beyond all these boys that don't know any better. Are you telling me when you were young it was all red carpet stuff?"

"No – but football's moved on. Fans want more than leaky roofs and stinky bogs and crappy Bovril. They want comfort, better food, big names."

"You mean all the rich clowns who go on United and City's European trips or still follow Rangers and Celtic want that stuff? The ones you guys are scared to offend? It's all fucking rubbish."

Duncan Collins made a wanker sign at him and said Arthur was welcome to get his shoes dirty at these places, but they'd all be out of business soon anyway.

"And that's the considered opinion of someone who earns their money off the back of football? You talk like you want them to shut down."

"Well, why not – what do they do anyway?"

Arthur was about to bite harder when the doors of the Lambie Suite opened and some Ochil director nobody recognised asked them in. A gaggle of shell-suited players waited inside, desperate to be plucked from the crowd and transformed into a celebrity.

Arthur laughed to himself. Tomorrow they'd go to City's so-called open day and their so-called PR chief would march in one unwilling player who'd act all Billy Big-Time and tell them hee-haw. At least this lot were willing to talk their cobblers off.

"HEADS up – here's one o' them now."

Rhino looked at the wiry, unshaven figure walking down the hotel's front steps, hands thrust in tracksuit bottom pockets, then looked back at his *Daily Record* and back up again.

"And guess what? We've hit the jackpot first time. Look."

"Well, well. It's Mr Romance. Pull him in, Tam."

The giant minder waited until his target had walked beyond the Jag, swung out of the passenger seat and strolled behind him.

"'Scuse me, pal!"

Westy turned. "Me?"

"Aye, Ah was lookin' for someone. Can ye help."

Westy stopped and walked back towards the big bloke in the black leather jacket, open-necked black shirt, black trousers and shiny black shoes.

"Aye, who ye lookin' for?"

"Well, no' so much who as what, son. Get in the fuckin' car."

Westy was quick on his feet. He spun in an instant and made to run. But Tam was quick upstairs. He'd handled enough tossers trying to get away from him to be on his toes for the quick getaway. He lunged forward, grabbed Westy by the tracksuit shoulders and hauled him to the car. Westy tried to shout, but a meaty hand covered his mouth. He gave in and went with the guy. Next thing the hand was off his mouth and pushing his head down to put him in the back seat. He found himself sitting next to a suave, middle-aged guy in a sharp black suit, light blue shirt and pink silk tie. He looked exactly like a TV villain. He even had the TV villain's car and sidekicks. But this wasn't TV. This was real.

"Mark, is it?"

Westy nodded. He couldn't speak.

"Sorry for being a little bit rough with you, but my boy here failed his degree in diplomacy. Hope you've not picked up any injuries in transit."

Westy shrugged.

"Oh, congratulations, by the way. Engaged, eh? Time runnin' out for a young lad about town? The old ball an' chain round the ankle soon? Still, she looks happy enough in the paper. Doesn't she look happy lads? Aye, good on you, son. I like to see boys settling down young."

"Look, Mr-."

"Charlie. Call me Charlie."

"Look, Charlie, whatever you want from me, tell me. Ah'm not goin' tae get in yer way here."

"Aye, well, it appears to me that you might already have got in my way big style. See, I've lost quite a lot of money. And it appears that you and your chums have come into possession of it – or maybe you'll correct me there and tell me you haven't, in which case we'll let you out of this car and say no more about it. You can go with my complete and sincere apologies. I mean that, I really do. But, see, if it turns out that you tell me you haven't when you have – well, put it this way. What foot d'you kick with?"

"Er, left."

"Think you could learn to kick with the right, son? In fact don't answer that, it's a daft question. I mean, how can you kick with the right if when you swing it you fall over because the left's not there any more, eh?"

Westy felt tears well up. Spuds smiled at him.

"Settle down, Mark. I know you won't lie to me. I know you'll tell me exactly what happened, I know I'll understand why daft boys like you lot didn't give me back what was mine and I know most certainly of all that Tam and Rhino here will go with you while you get it and bring it to me in its entirety."

Westy sat there, alone and frightened, realising the full stupidity of what he'd done. JD had been right, he really was going to take the rap on behalf of all of them.

"L-look, Ah can explain the whole thing. See, we just-."

Spuds shushed him with a hand as his car phone rang. He motioned for Rhino to answer it.

"Boss, it's some guy called Craig Williams. Reporter from *The Herald*? You want to speak to him?"

"What's he want?"

Rhino pushed a button on the phone. "Can you tell me what it's regarding? Yeah? U-huh? Right, hold on." He pushed the button again.

"You might want to take this, boss – he says he knows what happened to your money."

Spuds glanced at Westy as he took the phone. "Craig? Long time no speak. What's happenin'? Aye? You sure? Where d'that come from? Really, so it's kushty? Aye? The cheeky bastards! And is this comin' out in the papers? Aye? Hey, cannae be helped. Well, thanks, pal – I owe you. And so does someone sitting very close to me at this very moment. Cheers, see you later. Love to Barbara."

He ended the call and looked for a few seconds at the phone as if it had smacked him in the face. Westy swallowed hard. He thought this might be good news, but couldn't be sure with people like these. Charlie Spuds handed the phone back to Rhino, who clicked it into the handsfree unit.

"Well, Mark, it appears I owe you that sincere apology after all. It appears we were sold something of a dummy when we were told you and your chums had what used to belong to me."

Westy just stopped himself blurting out that, yes, they did have it, honest.

"What's the script, boss?"

"Well may you ask, Rhino, well may you ask. Remember our friends we went to see yesterday? The ones who threw the party for us? Well, they fibbed to us about what happened to our merchandise. Don't suppose it'll do any harm for Mark here to know – it'll be all over the press by tomorrow. Want to know, son?"

Westy nodded. He was utterly confused now.

"Well, we were told by some bad people who stole money from us that they had lost it and you and your chums had found it. But guess what? That was a red herring. Well, you know that already, I suppose, seein' as how you'd probably remember if you'd seen a bag stuffed with used notes, eh? The truth, according to a good friend of mine in the media, is that those bad people actually stole

153

my money – wait for this, boys – to buy off Glasgow City and run a betting coup that Ochil United will win on Saturday."

"What?"

"What?"

"WHAT?!?"

"Well may you express your surprise, gentlemen. The word is that around £200,000 has been wagered all across the West of Scotland on United to beat City at 16/1. My guess is that the other £50,000 has gone to a couple of crucial City players to swing the lead. Goalkeeper? Striker? Captain? Doesn't matter, if someone's taken a bribe, the chances are the whole team's got a wedge going on United and they'll all lie down. And as my associates here know, Mark, I have rather a large lump on City to win. Which means I stand to lose out not once, but twice. And that won't do, will it, Mark?"

"Er ... no?"

"Correct. However, that's not your problem. So let's say no more about this unfortunate misunderstanding, eh? In fact, we should really give you a wee something for your trouble."

"No, honestly, ye're fine-."

"Shush, now, won't hear of it. Never let it be said, etc."

Charlie Spuds snapped his fingers, Rhino reached into the glove compartment and took out a wedge of £20 notes that could have choked a horse. He handed it to his boss, who placed it in Westy's sweating hands.

"There, son, buy the lovely lady a necklace to go with the ring. And not a word, it goes without saying, eh? Right, back to training for you, off to work for us."

And then Tam was opening the door and Westy was outside and Tam was shaking his hand and saying no hard feelings and he was getting back in the front seat and the car was crunching across the gravel and Westy was standing there holding a huge lump of cash and wondering what the fuck that had all been about.

Central Scotland CID, Falkirk

ANDY McKENZIE felt like he'd won the pools when he took the call. A body found face down in a quarry pool an hour or so before turned out to be that of a worker in one of Charlie Spuds's dry cleaners. It didn't need Columbo to work out that this was the missing link, the one who'd ratted Spuds out to the commandos, who'd then been rumbled and dealt with accordingly. This time they'd nail that smug bastard.

Lambie Suite, Glenbank Hotel

THE RONALD TWINS sat amidst a huddle of reporters, gamely trying to think of some funny incidents which had happened to them thanks to their identical appearances. Had a ref ever sent the wrong one off? Sorry, no. Had one ever taking a bollocking from the manager when it was the other one's fault? Er, don't think so. Did they get mistaken for each other in the street? Not really.

Paul Arthur, meanwhile, had collared the director no one else had recognised. He knew him to be Ronald Ronald, father of the twins and club secretary-cum-commercial manager and was getting chapter and verse from him on how seeing his boys run out at Hampden together would made up for the tragedy of how their mother had died a year before to the day.

Once again, a little homework had paid off – and what's more, he'd have it all to himself. The rest would emerge from their little huddles and swap quotes so everyone had exactly the same as everyone else. What was the use of that?

It would save a fortune for all the papers to get together and employ a single agency to cover these things – and Arthur was damn sure that was what the bosses would do one day unless his colleagues got a grip and started thinking for themselves.

Taxi, meanwhile, was talking another group through his two goals in the 3-0 third round win over Fort Knox Bankies at

Ochilview when JD went past and shouted for him to tell them the sponge pudding story.

"What's the sponge pudding story?" said a young, bespectacled lad from the *Daily Mail*.

"Ach, it's nothin' – The Shadow's just at it."

"Am Ah? A'right, lads, when you've finished listenin' to him bummin' about his tap-ins, come an' see me an' Ah'll fill ye in, OK?"

"Aye right, bawbags - an' they get some loada keech just so you get yer name in the papers? Ah'll gie them the truth, ta. You away and oil the hinges on thae neck bolts, eh?"

And so he told them the sponge pudding story and guaranteed himself a two-page spread in every Saturday morning pullout special.

"See, Ah was playin' for Dumbarton an' livin' in a flat by mysel'. So this day we've beaten St Mirren, big turn-up for the books at the time, know 'mean? Ah've got two an' Ah'm flyin', so Ah've said tae the boays we'd have a coupla beers in the players' lounge then meet up again in the toon and gie it yeehah."

The huddle nodded and scribbled.

"Right, so it turns into a good few before we even leave the park and wi' the tiredness'n'at Ah'm a bit creamed by the time Ah'm back at the flat, so Ah run a bath tae get masel' goin' again. Then Ah realise Ah'm Hank Marvin."

"So, you were going to a Stars In Your Eyes-style party that night as the leader of the Shadows?" said an extremely earnest young man from the *Daily Record*.

Taxi wondered if he was taking the piss. "Naw, Ah mean Ah wiz hungry – Hank Marvin, starvin', know 'mean?"

The young man scored something out on his pad and looked suitably sheepish.

"So, where wiz Ah? Aye – so Ah've went in the fridge and it's the Marie Celeste, right? Not a sausage. Cupboards almost as bare an' all – except that Ah spy a strawberry jam sponge puddin', thae wans in a tin, right, an' Ah love them. So that's me sorted – on goes the pan fulla watter, Ah sort ma bath, watter boils, tin goes plop, in Ah sploosh. Lovely biscuits."

By now they're wondering where this guff's going.

"Anyway, Ah musta fell asleep, because next thing Ah've heard this huge BANG!, right? An' Ah've woke up just in time tae see this missile flyin' right at us – the bathroom's at the enda the hall wi' the kitchen aff it – and Ah grab the shampoo an' fling it at the door. Well, it shuts it jist enough so Ah don't get it in coupon, but it sticks right in the door!"

"What? The sponge pudding?"

"Naw – the pan. It's boiled dry an' exploded, innit? So the pan flies out the kitchen and doon the hall an' the hob's burned right oot, knackered."

"So where's the sponge pudding?"

"Well, when Ah get masel' robed up an' go through, Ah cannae see it. Ah'm expectin' it to be on the kitchen walls, but there's nothin', know 'mean? Then Ah turn roon – the lounge is open-plan fae the kitchen, right – and it's everywhere. An' Ah mean everywhere – curtains, telly, ma new leather couch that's no' even paid fur yet, carpet, photies, the lot. It looks like there's been eight sponge puddins and some semtex crammed intae wan tin. Incredible."

"So what did you do?"

"What d'ye think? Ah got dressed, went oot, got bladdered, came hame, fell asleep and hoped that when Ah woke up it's been a bad dream."

"And was it?"

"Funnily enough, pal, naw." Taxi began to wonder if these guys really were at it with him. "Naw, sadly, the flat wiz still plastered with sponge and strawberry jam, the cooker wiz still ruined and there wiz still a burnt-oot pot embedded in the bog door."

"So you must have had some cleaning-up job, then?"

"Ye'd think, eh? But Ah'm smarter than that. A mate workin' on a buildin' site got me a snidey door and a new hob an' Ah – Ahem – improvised wi' the sponge puddin'."

"How?"

"Ah cleaned what Ah could aff the telly an' the couch an' at, binned the curtains, emulsioned the walls and ceilin' and put the flat oan the market."

"And did it sell?"

"Aye – it wiz a nice place, tasteful décor an' that. New hob, new bog door. Lovely. Ah sometimes jist wonder what the new folk musta thought when nasty black fungus started growin' through their nice livin' room ceilin' artex, eh?"

They all laughed. What a good tale. One of them even managed to remember to ask if the couple had ever come back to him about it and where the flat was exactly.

"Aye right – so youse can go up and chin them aboot it? Dae Ah zip up the back?"

So instead they settled for sending a snapper out to buy a sponge pudding and setting up pictures of Taxi with the tin on his head, a pot in one hand and a paintbrush in the other.

WESTY saw Chunky sitting in the foyer and got him to go and bring Blue Eyes out of the press conference. He took the skipper into a quiet corner and told him about being pulled up by Spuds and his heavies.

"Good on ye, Brenda!"

"What?"

"Ye know Ah said this mornin' Ah'd done somethin' to try an' take the heat off us about the bets? Well, it looks like yer old da's been a genius."

"How? What d'ye do?"

"Phoned an ex, Brenda Taylor, reporter at *The Herald*-."

"Anybody in Glesga ye've no turfed?"

"Hey, ye've either got or it ye're getting' it, that's ma motto. Anyway, Ah told this sort that Ah'd had the word fae a bookie pal that there was huge wedges bein' lumped on us tae beat City."

"Which there had been."

"Except that in this version, the word Ah'd heard was that it was comin' fae people wi' big City connections. Mibbes even from within the dressin' room. She's obviously poked around an' that's what the bookies really DO think's been happenin'."

"An' why no'? Ah mean, who's gonnae believe we'd have £250,000 tae spare and that even if we did we'd gamble it on oursels at 16/1 instead o' just spendin' it on goodies?"

"Nobody. And in your case, Marky Mark, they'd have been justified. Remember?"

"Aye. Sorry. But d'ye think that's us aff the hook?"

"Looks like it, judgin' by the lucky escape you just had. Did they say what they were doin' about the money now?"

"Ma guess is, giein' someone at City the same tug Ah just got. But without the happy endin'."

"Sweet."

TOM HAGEN still didn't have a clue about the bets. Until, that is, he sat down with a gaggle of daily newspaper sportswriters and they started asking him about reports that City players were betting against themselves for the big game.

"Sorry? Where did all this come from?"

Duncan Collins of *The Star* piped up. "The word is that around £200,000 has been gambled on your team to win on Saturday. How does that feel?"

"Whose word is this?"

Collins blushed and started to stammer. "Er – well, we hear from-."

"You hear from where? This is serious stuff, son. Big allegations. So who's the alligators?"

"Well, we obviously can't reveal-."

"Then Ah obviously can't comment on somethin' as unsubstantiated, can I?"

Brian Miller, chief sports reporter with The *Scottish Sun* glared at Collins and took over.

"Tom, it's come from the bookies themselves. They've taken huge amounts, £500 at a time, on United to win. They've told us, off the record admittedly, that they think the money has come from people closely connected to City. It looks at this stage as if someone in the City dressing room is up for taking a fall."

"Jesus."

"Is that a quote?"

"Ha, ha. Funny guy. Listen, Ah can't believe any of those City guys would do that. They're too professional – Melvin Law wouldn't stand for it, the fans wouldn't stand for it. Nah, Ah can't buy that one."

"Is THAT a quote?"

"Yeah, if ye like. Ye can quote me as sayin' Ah cannot believe anyone at Glasgow City, from the manager down, would ever bet against themselves. And that's all Ah can say, unless you guys have any more to stand this story up."

"Nope, that's it. City aren't sayin' a word."

"Well, until they do, that's it."

"Can we call you later if anything else breaks?"

"Sure."

"Ta."

Loch Lomond Plaza Hotel

MELVIN LAW was watching the tapes of United for the 17th time when press officer Scott Neil tapped the open office door and popped his head round.

"Gaffer, got a minute?"

"Many of them in a day, Scott, always filled with something. Do you have something more important to fill the next one than me preparing for the game?"

"Yes, I think I do."

"So fire away."

160

"The papers have been on. There's a story doing the rounds that people connected with this club have bet £200,000 on United to beat us on Saturday."

Law took off his round glasses, pinched the bridge of his nose then pushed Pause on the video remote. Ochil United froze in the middle of an attack.

"Who?"

"Don't know, gaffer. The story started at *The Herald* and it's spread like wildfire. The big bookies are all confirming that huge sums have gone on United. The word is that bundles of £500 bets have been placed by people, like I say, connected with us."

"When?"

"Wednesday."

"Well, we were all here on Wednesday. None of the players or management could have placed bets in shops. Any of it done by phone?"

"Nope, all in cash at the counter."

"Sounds like an organised coup. Can you get Bobby Bothwell in here please and find out if the chief executive's around for a chat?"

"No sweat."

"Wrong, Neil. Plenty sweat. This is not good, whether it's true or false. I don't like it, not one bit."

And he pressed Pause again and Ochil United put the ball out for a goal-kick. He hit Rewind and watch them do it another four times. Then rewound the tape right back to the start.

Lambie Suite, Glenbank Hotel

"BLUE EYES! Don't disappear, Ah want a word!"

"Gaffer?"

"C'mere."

Blue Eyes followed Tom into the loos and watched the manager go down on all fours to check that all three cubicles were empty.

"Blue Eyes, how much d'you know about betting?"

161

The skipper's heart sunk.

"Ach, ye know, a bit. Ah like a punt now and then."

"Would you put money on us to win this game on Saturday?"

"Bettin' on yer own game's against the rules, is it no'?"

"Aye, well. Some people don't like rules, do they?"

"Ah don't follow."

But he was afraid he was following all too well.

"There's £200,000-odd been put on us to beat City. All in the one afternoon. The bookies are jumpin' up an' down."

"Fuck me, big dosh."

"An' ye know what's worse?"

Here we go.

"What's that?"

"They're sayin' it was City players who put it on – either that or people who know for certain City are gonnae lose. Is that no' the most sickenin' thing you ever heard? Those bastards takin' a dive?"

"D'ye believe it?"

"Not at first. But the more Ah think, the less Ah can think o' another explanation. Ah mean, pro gamblers wouldnae back against odds-on favourites unless they had inside info. An' let's face it, our guys are hardly gonnae get a few hundred grand together to back themsels, eh? No' unless they robbed a bank!"

Blue Eyes managed a weak laugh.

"Maybe some of the lads have been savin' up their pocket money, eh gaffer?"

Tom laughed out loud. "The way some o' them behave they don't deserve pocket money. But Ah tell ye what they also don't deserve – an' that's to go intae the cup final wi' the world thinkin' the other team let them through. If we're goin' tae crack it here Ah want us tae do it on merit."

"City wouldnae throw the game, would they?"

"Give me another scenario, then."

"Somebody wi' more money than sense who reckons we're got a chance?"

"A *sane* scenario, Francis."

Silence.

"Nah, didn't think so. I'm afraid Melvin Law has rats on board his ship. Horrible thought, innit?"

"Horrible."

Except that to Blue Eyes, no thought had ever been happier.

Loch Lomond Plaza Hotel

MELVIN LAW switched off the TV and video and looked across the desk at Bobby Bothwell and Duncan Driscoll.

The chief executive asked what the problem was. He didn't like Law, he didn't like being called in for meetings with him and most of all he didn't like having to interrupt his afternoon dictation session in his bedroom with his secretary.

"So what's up, Melvin?"

"Duncan, Bobby, we have a problem. More than £200,000 in bets have been placed on us to lose on Saturday – and the story doing the rounds is that the money has been staked on behalf of people within the club."

"Fuck off!"

Bothwell blushed a little, as if he'd sworn in front of his parents.

"Bobby?"

"Sorry, gaffer – but that sounds like the players are gettin' the rap for this. An' there's nae way on this earth that we'd-."

"Bobby, I don't believe it about any of you either. But that's the word on the street, as the saying goes. The bookies have no explanation for such sums being stacked on a 16/1 outsider other than the 10/1 on favourites being crooked."

"And you have to admit there's a certain haphazard logic to the argument."

Bothwell didn't like Driscoll any more than Driscoll liked Law.

"Listen, Mr Driscoll, Ah hope Ah'm no' speakin' out of turn here, but if Ah hear that repeated outside these four walls Ah'll be askin' away fae this club."

163

"Bit dramatic, Bobby. I just mean, can you be 101 per cent sure none of your mates would bet against themselves? They've got enough money to finance it."

"Aye, an' they want tae keep earnin' it. If we throw a game we're finished – no' just the ones that did it, but everybody, everybody this scandal touches. We'd never be trusted again. The fans'd lynch us. But you might not get that, Mr Driscoll, seein' as how you're no'-."

"Bobby, whether the chief executive is or isn't a City fan isn't the issue here-."

Law knew for a fact Driscoll was a Glasgow United diehard and for that among many other reasons he hated him more than he hated anyone else in the world.

"-no, the issue is that we have to deflect this bad publicity in some way and prove to the world that our hands are clean. Bobby, I want you and I to sit together at a press conference tonight and answer all questions honestly and openly. OK?"

"No problem. Ah've nothin' to hide. Just let me have a team meetin' first, eh?"

"To check if your trust in the lads is misplaced?"

Driscoll said "the lads" with an undisguised sneer.

"Now you listen-."

"Duncan, Bobby trusts those players with his life. As do I. If you don't, you obviously don't know them as well as you might. I've asked Scott to get the press here at six, so feel free to be on the platform with us when the press arrive. But perhaps your attitude in this meeting suggests that might not be helpful."

"Sadly, I'm unable to attend in any case."

"How ever will we cope?"

Loch Lomond Plaza, 4.45pm

EVERY single City player told their skipper the same thing - that they knew nothing about any betting coup. The very thought seemed to leave them anything from shocked to utterly confused. Us? Throw a game? Why?

Bobby Bothwell hadn't expected anything else. He just hadn't wanted that tosser Driscoll to be running about saying I Told You So if one of the lads somehow got caught out. The prick would have loved that. He stood up and gave it a big apologetic shrug.

"Sorry tae drag ye into this, boys, but ye know the deal. Somebody's tryin' tae do us in an' Ah've told the gaffer there's nae way we're takin' it. Ah'll front up the press wi' him an' hopefully that'll be that."

"Just one thing, Bobby."

Everyone turned to look at England international right-back Eric Thompson.

"What?"

"Out of interest, how much would we have made if we had put this 200-odd grand on ourselves to lose?"

"Four million, give or take a coupla quid."

"So 200 grand each? Pretty much what we'll get if we do the Treble anyway?"

"Exactly."

"Hardly worth the hassle."

"That's what Ah told them."

Room 312, Glenbank Hotel

WESTY put the wedge of notes in front of him on the bed and counted it out once, twice, three times. Seven grand. Fuckin' hell. He heard Screech's key in the door. His mate came in and gave him the kind of look mothers reserve for sons they've caught playing with themselves.

"Westy, Westy - what's this now? You been screwin' piggy banks?"

The boy looked genuinely hurt. For the second time that afternoon, he felt tears welling up inside him.

"What?"

"Nothin'."

"Westy, what is it? Where'd the money come fae?"

"The same place the bagful came fae."

And he told Screech the same story he'd told Blue Eyes half an hour earlier. Screech listened with wide eyes and bottom lip hanging like a pissed pelican.

"Jesus, son. You OK? ye must have been shittin' yersel!"

"Nae kiddin', man. Ah thought Ah was losin' ma knees. Ah had visions of bein' marched up here, the room gettin' turned over an' them leavin' me in a pool o' blood."

"An' instead they gave ye a wedge? Su-fuckin'-perb! So what ye daein' wi' it? Down-payment on Rod tae sing at the weddin'?"

"Weekend away."

"For you an' Kirsten? What a charmer!"

"Naw, for us. The squad. Reckon we'll get flights off the web tae Dublin, coupla nights in a decent hotel an' the first few rounds outa this lot."

Screech walked over, put his hands on Westy's shoulders, bent over and kissed him on the top of the head.

"You're a bigger diamond than the one in that ring, son."

Loch Lomond Plaza

BOBBY BOTHWELL was walking back across from the lodges where the players were staying to the main hotel for the press conference when he heard his name being shouted. He didn't recognise the voice, nor the face when he turned round. But he didn't like the sound or look of either.

Thing was, though, there were some City fans you didn't ignore. Every big club attracts self-made heavies whose financial muscle lets them through the barrier skint punters can never cross. They always seemed to be around hotels before big games, home or abroad. Best thing to do with them was smile, get your fingers crushed with a handshake and say yes to requests for autographs, tickets or a go at your missus. He heard himself ask the guy how he was doing.

"No' bad. Got a minute?"

"Sure, anythin'."

"It's just that ma gaffer fancied meetin' ye."

Fuck sake. This must be one top-flight self-made heavy fan if he was sending minders out to request an audience with the players.

"No sweat. Bring him intae the hotel."

"Actually, if ye didnae mind, could ye come intae the car? He's shy."

Bothwell was liking this less by the second. But he went with it. The minder opened the back door of a classic powder-blue Jag and motioned for him to get in. He hesitated for a second, then wandered across. Next thing he was stooping to get into the back seat - and coming face to face with the last face you ever want to be face to face with.

Charlie Spuds.

Charlie fuckin' Spuds.

"Bobby, thanks for givin' me your time. I know it's precious. I also take it you know who I am."

Spuds loved using the polite voice when he was putting the arm on people. Reckoned it made him more chilling. To Bobby Bothwell, it couldn't have sounded more chilling if Spuds had been sitting in an ice bucket.

"Mr Kerr, how's it goin'?"

"Been better, son. Got myself a little problem you could mibbes help me solve."

Bothwell was bright enough to know the problem must have something to do with the betting business. He just didn't have a fucking Scooby what it was. So he just smiled and shrugged.

"Glad you're happy, Bobby. Because I'm definitely not."

"Naw, Mr Kerr, Ah'm no' happy either. Ah just-."

167

"Why you not happy, son? Preparations for the big game not goin' well? Or have you just realised the full stupidity of tryin' to turn me over?"

"But - but Ah haven't tried tae-."

"Come on, Bobby. We're all adults here, so let's behave like it, eh? Listen, I'll make this simple. I had a large sum of money stolen from me a couple of days ago. An almost identical sum was bet yesterday on Ochil United to beat Glasgow City. The bookies believe that money was placed by people very close to Glasgow City. Do I need to get the tactics board out to make you see the big picture? Some naughty people stole my money to buy you off - maybe not you personally, Bobby, but you as a team - and feel confident enough to lump the rest on the greatest giantkilling in history. Am I warm?"

"Honest, Mr Kerr, Ah've heard about these bets. We're havin' a press conference any minute now tae deny we've anythin' tae dae wi' it. An' obviously Ah've heard about the big robbery the other day. But Ah had nae idea it was you that had been robbed an' Ah'd nae idea the money had been stolen tae finance somethin' like this. Our guys widnae have anythin' tae dae wi' bribes, Mr Kerr. Ah mean, it's no' like we need the money, is it?"

"Dunno, is it? What's enough money, son? H'much you earn a week?"

"Well, Ah mean-."

"C'mon, don't be shy, you're among friends."

The irony was heavy enough to flatten buildings.

"Thirty-one grand a week."

"All in?"

"Basic. Three grand appearance, two grand a win. Plus top-ups for trophies."

Can you spend it all?"

"Well, no."

"So why ask for it? Didn't you have enough before? What was your last wage?"

"Seventeen. Signed a new five-year about nine months ago."

168

"And you couldn't live on seventeen grand a week? Big outgoings, kid."

"It's no' like that, though, is it Mr Kerr?"

"Isn't it? You just said it's not like you need the money. But did you need it nine months ago when you got a two grand a day rise? Don't answer that, son, it's obvious. Too much is never enough, Bobby. That's why somebody - one guy, two, maybe the whole 11 - have taken a bung to sell this game. And it's MY money you're getting, that's what messes me up. You understand that."

"Ah would, Mr Kerr, but it's no'-."

That gentle, horrible shushing gesture again.

"Bobby, maybe you're naive. Maybe you're just not in with the in crowd. Maybe you're telling the truth and you haven't a clue about the rest taking a fall. But they ARE, son. They are. Say what you like at your press conference, but Glasgow City have taken a wedge to take a fall. So here's what you're going to do for me."

Bobby's head was swimming now. His trousers wouldn't be far behind.

"Mr Kerr, listen-."

"Adults speaking now, little boy. Reply when asked to, not before. Or tongues get damaged, OK? Good. So, here's what you do. You can put whatever public face on it you like. But privately, you'll make sure Glasgow City win on Saturday. You'll do this for two reasons. One, because I've got a tidy whack on it - and two, because I'm not having some wankers stealing my two fifty and turning it into - what? - four mill? No way, Bobby, no fucking way on God's green earth. Which brings us to the second part of our deal, son. Which is that you've got until 10am on Monday to return my money. Do it quietly, do it anonymously, send it as a singing fucking telegram. Just get it there. It's on your head. Because if it's not there-."

"Where, Mr Kerr, where?"

Bothwell was desperate now.

"Where I work, son. Look it up. I'm in the Yellow Pages under B for Bad Bastards. So, 10am, Monday. Or-."

He looked at Bothwell, who realised the two monsters in the front seats, who up to now had been minding their own business, had turned to look straight at him. He got the message like a Mitre in the bollocks on a freezing day.

"Jesus, Mr Kerr - Ah havnae done anyth-."

Shush, shush.

"And I don't give a monkey's, Bobby. You just happen to be the one we caught up with. You got unlucky. But not half as unlucky as you'll get if City lose and that money's not back with me when I told you. Oh, and tell anyone about this conversation and we'll have another meeting, regardless. Now fuck off."

Charlie Spuds turned away and looked out the window. Rhino started the engine. Tam drummed his fingers on the dash impatiently. Bobby Bothwell opened the door and got out just as the car moved off. He tumbled onto the tarmac, grazing his right elbow. He sat up and couldn't help what happened next.

He started to bubble.

Inverclyde Royal Hospital

FIZZY picked Giovanni up in a taxi and shook his hand.

"OK, gorgeous?"

"Delightful."

"Ye missed a right pumpin' this mornin'."

"Don't worry about me, Ah was bed-bathed out ma nut by some blonde 19-year-old sort."

"Nice boy was he?"

"Dishy. How's the gaffer?"

"Worried about ye."

"Sweet. But how's his mood?"

"Willie got the worst of it. He's calmed down now that he knows the full tale. The bigger story now is that apparently City have taken bribes tae lose the game an' some big punters have put £200,000-odd on us tae win."

For a second Gio wondered if he dreamed what happened yesterday afternoon and that now his mind was playing some bizarre fast-forward trick on him.

"Aye? Where d'that come from?"

"Papers. They hit the gaffer wi' it just before Ah left. He's outraged."

"Me too – Ah've got fifty notes on City tae do us 4-0 at 11/1!"

Fizzy looked genuinely shocked.

"Kiddin', Fizz, kiddin'."

"Just as well for you. Anyway, you gonnae be OK, ye know, watchin' the build-up an' the game?"

"How d'ye mean?"

"Well, wi' you bein' out an' everythin'?"

"Out? How?"

"Head knock. Docs won't have it. Won't let ye play or train for ten days."

"Fuck them!"

"That your considered opinion?"

"Naw, it's ma decision. Ah feel fine, bit o' a headache, but that's fitba'. As far as Ah'm concerned, Ah'm tellin' the gaffer Ah'm fine."

"An' Ah'm tellin' him that the docs say ye're no'."

"Serious?"

"Deadly. Listen, big game or no', Ah can't let you risk yer long-term health. That might no' be a big brain, but it still keeps the rest o' ye movin'."

"An' there was me thinkin' the gaffer did it wi' remote control. Listen, Fizz, Ah cannae miss this. Ah've waited a' ma career for it. Gie's a break, please!"

"Sorry, no can do. That's what Ah'm tellin' him."

Gio looked out of the window and said nothing.

TWENTY minutes later, Bothwell had pulled himself together enough to sit beside Melvin Law at the press conference. He poured a large glass of water and glugged it in one. Cameras clicked and flashed every time he moved, wringing every perceived shred of emotion from the simple act of quenching his thirst.

He wished they'd all fuck off.

More than that, he wished he could fuck off, not just out of the room but way back in time. He wanted to be a wee boy coming in from a kickabout in the park to have his tea with his folks.

He heard Scott Neill call for quiet and announce that Mr Law would make a short statement before both he and Bobby Bothwell took questions. Reporters came awkwardly forward and laid dictaphones on the table. Law adjusted his glasses and picked up a typed sheet of A4.

"Following speculation about a suspected betting coup on Saturday's semi-final against Ochil United, I wish to make it clear that I have held an investigation involving our management, administrators and players and am totally satisfied that no one employed by Glasgow City has any involvement in or knowledge of improper gambling on Saturday's game. My captain will express his own feelings, but I can safely say neither of us has ever known a more upstanding squad and that not a single one would contemplate cheating his team-mates. Glasgow City will do everything in our power to win Saturday's game and continue on our quest for the domestic Treble. This is our only aim at this time. Thank you."

The reporters who'd put their dictaphones on the table finished scribbling notes on pads. Belt and braces, they were always taught. Then Scott Neill asked if there were any questions. Hands shot up. Bobby Bothwell noticed that he didn't recognise many faces. Few of the usual sportswriters – the heavy news mob had been sent in for this one. Either that or the sports guys who were there were too scared to ask difficult questions and have the gaffer fall out with them.

"Melvin, how can you be so sure that your players are innocent here?"

"Well, for one thing, no one's on trial. Bookmakers are theorising that the bets have been placed by people with City connections. From that, people are taking that they mean players. Because of that, I've investigated. But no one's actually being accused of anything."

"OK, so how can you be sure that if people with City connections HAVE mounted this coup, that none of your players are involved?"

"Because I've looked Bobby in the eye and he's given me his word and he's looked them in the eye and they've given him their word and frankly, without that kind of trust there is no team, certainly not one run by me."

"Same question, Bobby? How can you be sure your mates aren't involved?"

"Because they're not."

"That simple?"

"What bit of 'they're not involved' don't ye get? We havnae done anythin'. We're not cheats. We don't take dives. We'll win that game on Saturday, a'right?"

Another one jumped in.

"Bobby, is there a major gambling culture in modern football, what with the amount of spare cash sloshing about?"

"Guys like a punt - same as some o' you guys do. But if ye're wantin' me to give ye some sort of quote tae say that it's a problem, forget it. Like the gaffer says, we're not on trial here and Ah don't want to be dragged into it lookin' like that."

"Are you not being a little defensive for someone with nothing to hide."

Bothwell shot a look to his right to see who'd asked the question. He didn't recognise the guy and didn't like him from the off. Smug twat. Probably one of the posh papers.

"Defensive? How?"

"Well, that answer, for a start."

"Why am Ah gettin' this here? The facts are simple. Somebody's tried to involve me an' the boys in some gamblin' coup when the truth is we're NOT involved. So why suddenly am Ah bein' put on the spot? The gaffer only organised this so we could set the record straight. Can ye not just accept what we're sayin'?"

Law put a hand gently on the captain's arm and said he'd take it from here.

"Bobby's right, gentlemen. Glasgow City are NOT involved in whatever has been going on with these bookies. Whether my players like to bet or not is not the issue and neither is my captain's annoyance at having his preparations for a big game interrupted by nonsense like this. The issue is that we have said our piece and that's all there is to it. So if the questions are all in the same vein, we might as well stop here and now."

Silence. Then a figure stood up at the back. Big bloke, really big, in a black leather jacket. Bobby hadn't noticed him. He introduced himself as Neil McAllister of some website no one had heard of. He was the first one who'd bothered to identify himself to Law or Bothwell.

"Melvin, Bobby, are you aware that as well as being allegedly gambled by people with City connections - and I accept your version of that - it is also being strongly linked with a £250,000 armed robbery carried out on Thursday? And that the rumour is that the victim was Glasgow underworld figure Charlie Kerr? If so, are either of you worried he might cause trouble? Melvin?"

"Well, it appears to me that every part of that statement you just made and the question at the end of it is pretty much speculation and, as you admit, rumour and therefore I don't really feel it would be right to comment."

"And Bobby?"

Bothwell was chalk white. He reached for another glass of water. The cameras clicked furiously once more.

"Bobby?"

"You OK, Bobby?"

"Aye, gaffer, it's just a bit warm in here. But to, er, answer the gentleman, as we've nothing to do with any of this, we've nothing to worry about."

It was a brave effort. Neil McAllister - and it wasn't a made-up name, everybody in his life always just called him Rhino - even said thank you for Bobby's frankness. But as their eyes locked across the room, the City skipper knew he had more to worry about than at any time in his young life.

These heavies were serious enough to come and put the frighteners on him in a very public place. Yet he couldn't say a word, they'd left him in no doubt about that. He didn't even want to leave the room, because if Charlie Spuds' minder was in here, Charlie Spuds was waiting outside. Maybe in the lobby. In Bobby's very room, for fuck's sake.

He waited until the suite was empty but for a couple of hotel dogsbodies clearing seats, went to the loo, locked himself in a cubicle and vomited.

Central Scotland CID, Falkirk

THE thrill of the pools win didn't last long. Suddenly, DI Andy McKenzie realised the coupon was still lying on his kitchen table. Forensics reports about the death of Billy Andrews had landed back with CID in Glasgow, who'd kept their promise to stay in touch the minute they got them – but McKenzie was left wishing they hadn't bothered.

"So just run that past me again to make sure it's not a wind-up, Tony."

"Like Ah said, Andy, his injuries are consistent with having been raped, then strangled and thrown into the quarry pool from a height of about 20 feet."

"So not the work of Spuds or his goons, then?"

"Not unless they've jumped on the wrong bus overnight. Slashing, stabbing, shooting, burning, garrotting, crucifying – they've done it all in their time. But murder by buggery? Not in their repertoire. And, yes, we've been to the guy's local and his work and everyone we've asked confirms that, yes, Billy Andrews was a poof who liked it dangerous. He's not in the loop for your case, pal. Sorry."

"Fuck me, talk about a pain in the arse!"

"For you or him? Later, Andy."

"For me, funny man," McKenzie said to a dead phone line.

8.30pm, Room 304, Glenbank Hotel

BLUE EYES dialled home for the fourth time in an hour. Still no answer. Still no Claire on her mobile either. He'd called her mother, who said she hadn't seen her. He was starting to worry. This wasn't like her, she was always there.

He'd give it another 15 minutes and try again.

9.45pm, Boston Bar, Springburn

SPUDS got the call he'd waited all night for from his man on the inside at Strathclyde Police. Billy Andrews had been the victim of a gay murder. No one would be coming to call asking awkward questions to do with the robbery.

He put the phone down and laughed out loud. He'd have to give big Tam extra luncheon vouchers in the morning for coming up with that little work of art.

10.04pm, Room 201, Loch Lomond Plaza

MELVIN LAW carefully turned back the corner of his duvet and smoothed down his crisply-starched pyjamas. He had double-creases. He'd speak to Amanda.

He checked the bedside table. Water glass exactly ? full, clock lined up perfectly with the pad and pen he always kept handy in case he had any brilliant tactical ideas in his sleep.

The alarm was set for 13 minutes past five.

In two minutes, no more nor less, he'd be out for the count and into the seven hours of his schedule, no more nor less, he put aside for recharging his batteries. Never called it rest, because rest was for people who couldn't cope. Law could have coped for Britain. Never got in a flap, never panicked, never saw problems, only challenges. This was how it was when you were the best.

He stood, eyes closed, easing his muscles from neck to feet, telling them that it was time to warm down for the night. Even the body had to know its place. He wiggled his toes. Everything was in order. Then he eased himself under the covers and felt the squidginess on his backside. Non-copers would have jumped out of their skin at such an unpleasant sensation. Not Law. Instead, he rationalised and knew immediately what the problem was.

Dog was the problem.

Dog. His talisman, yet the bane of his life. His dream player, yet his nightmare. The one human being who came close to making Melvin Law not cope. The one person who could break his stride. Even when he was in a linesman's face, yelling and yelling and pointing and making less clever people believe he was losing it, Law was always actually in control. It was all designed to unsettle and intimidate and ensure the next decision went his way whether it should or not.

He believed in handling victory and defeat the same way, with an acceptance that if things had gone well he'd done his job and if they hadn't someone else was to blame. This was the logical response and Melvin Law was so logical if he went to the annual conference of the European Guild of Logical People the delegates would ask who the irritatingly logical git was. This was how he knew what it was that had made his sheets squidgy.

Dog had obviously soaked some brown paper and squeezed it into a soggy paste to give the impression of being the dropping of some animal; possibly, by the size and shape, a cow. This was Dog's idea of a joke. Law allowed him this misconception, because Law understood what made non-copers tick and Dog was as non-coping a non-coper as Law could imagine.

Not that Law ever imagined much, because he was too busy with reality.

He pulled back the covers to discover that he was, naturally, correct in his assumption of what had disrupted his sleep. He went to the bathroom, took a small refuse sack from the dispenser he always carried, went back, placed the soggy brown paper in it and tied the handles in a neat bow. He placed it in the bin under the dresser and placed the bin outside in the corridor. Then he phoned housekeeping to come and change his bed, took off his pyjamas and removed a fresh, more accurately ironed pair from a hanger in his wardrobe.

He had been going to change them anyway.

Eight minutes later, he opened the door to a chambermaid whose hat was squint. He paid no notice to the look of distaste she gave him as she saw the brown stain and began to strip the bed. Law didn't entertain for a moment the thought that she thought he had soiled his sheets, because he hadn't, so it wasn't logical. He stood over the chambermaid while she did her job, hands behind his back, observing her technique, then thanked her and suggested she straighten her hat.

When she was gone, he stripped the bed and re-made it properly.

He wouldn't mention the incident in the morning. Attention was what Dog craved, so attention was what Law starved him of. He re-set the alarm clock for 5.31 and at 10.31 precisely was asleep, hands by his side and body in a perfectly straight line. He dreamed of absolutely nothing.

Room 304, Glenbank Hotel

STILL no answer. He called her mother again, asked if she was worried too. She said no. Blue Eyes asked why. She said there was nothing to worry about. Blue Eyes said what if Claire and the kids were stuck in a broken down car or – or – worse. She said not to be so dramatic. He convinced himself she was right.

He'd try her again in ten.

Room 245, Loch Lomond Plaza

DOG couldn't sleep. He rarely could. And even when he did it was a mental time, filled with weird images of giant galloping animals and people falling off skyscrapers and frantic, breathless chases that made him toss and turn and thrash around until his feet were on the pillow and the blood rushed to his head as it hung limply off the edge of the bed. And he always woke up within two hours, always with the telly blaring. Then he'd start his mayhem all over again.

Every day in Dog's life was a whirlwind, always somewhere to be, someone to meet, something to do. Training, personal appearances, visiting sick kids in hospital. Occasionally he stopped to eat something so unbelievably unhealthy – two double-double cheeseburgers and a chocolate shake or a fish supper with a single black pudding thrown in – that even Americans feared for his cholesterol levels, but within an hour his tornado metabolism would have burned it all off and more as he ploughed down the endless list of things he had to do. And in between all the things he was meant to do, he grouted the cracks with things he wasn't.

Dog was always scheming, planning. He never listened to anyone or anything. He'd be introduced to someone and forget their name within seconds because he was too busy checking them for oddities he could slag them about.

When his gaffer gave team talks, he got about as far as "So, here's how we'll play it…" before his manic mind would shrapnel off in a hundred different directions at once. Suddenly he'd be thinking about where he had to be later or who he'd forgotten to call or who he was trying to avoid; that or he'd be working out new wind-ups to play.

Jamming bananas up exhaust pipes, setting off fire alarms, sawing through chair legs so they collapsed when his victim sat down; Dog had done them and fallen about at the thought of them and was constantly seeking to top them.

179

None of his nonsense served any purpose but to keep him from getting bored. OK, so it also drove everyone around him daft, but they never really got really, really angry with him, because he was just too loveable. He was like a big daft kid - mad as a jar of wasps, as an old England manager had famously called him.

Next day, he'd turned up to training with a jar of wasps. While his mates had been having breakfast or their morning walk, he'd spent two hours collecting enough of them to fill the jar for ten seconds of fun.

He could still see them all running about mental when he took the lid off in the team meeting, but they'd still laughed about it after the stings went down – even Robbie Clark, who'd taken an allergic reaction and missed both halves of the World Cup qualifying double-header against Spain and Albania.

No one ever fell out with Dog and that thought kept him going, because he refused to contemplate the possibility that anyone might not like him. Dog loved to be loved – no, needed to be loved. If he ever thought he was capable of hurting anyone ... how man, it didn't bear thinking about.

The papers were just trying to do him in with their stories about how he'd put two team-mates in hospital by spiking their cornflakes with Pernod, caused £2million of damage to a French hotel after piling furniture up outside the physio's door and setting fire to it, blown up the team bus during his spell in Italy.

Couldn't they see the joke, see what he was all about? Dog was the life and soul, the madman every dressing room needed. He was harmless. Why couldn't they get that?

He'd been Dog since he was about eight on the mean streets of Newcastle. His real name was Alan Brown, so he became Al Brown, which became Broon Al and as in Byker a bottle of Broon Ale as a bottle of Dog, it stuck.

Today, kicking 30, he was simply Dog – and not just within football. He'd been debated in parliament, slapped over front pages from London to Lisbon and back. The judge in a divorce case he'd been named in – not as a co-respondent, but as the friend who'd painted the outside of the marital home with HE'S SHAGGIN' YER SISTER in huge red letters for a laugh – had asked: "And who is this Dog?"

Dog's grinning face, usually with his fingers up his nose in his trademark pose, had been on every satirical news-based TV quiz show that week.

He'd cut more toes out of more socks than a team of Arctic paramedics, put more Wintergreen down more pants than some people had had hot dinners. Dog was unstoppable. Dog was an one-off. Dog was a laugh-a-minute, never-know-what-he'll-do-next maniac. Dog was alone in his hotel room, not knowing what to do next.

He was alone because no one would share with him, not with the risk of fake poo in their beds or tabasco in their bath water or simply the guy bouncing round the room like a one-man Goon Show all night every night. He grabbed the phone, got an outside line and hit a dozen numbers at random. He loved this. He waited a few seconds, a far-off phone rang twice and a man picked up. The bloke sounded Aussie. Dog put on his poshest Eton.

"Yars, to whom am I speaking?"

"Lance Ramsay. Who's this?"

"My name is Malcolm McDonald-Shearer and ay hem calling from the top London legal firm of Martin, Barton and Wharton."

"G'day, mate – what can I do y'for?"

"It's more what I can do for you, Mr Ramsay – you see, I act for the descendants of one, er, Lionel Ramsay, deported to Australia as a criminal in 1878. Said descendants have discovered evidence that he buried more than five million pounds sterling of bullion and jewellery on a beach near Perth."

"And what's this got to do with me, mate?"

"Simple - it is our understanding that you too may be a relative of said Lionel Ramsay and would therefore be entitled to one-fifth of all recovered proceeds – to wit, one million pounds sterling - if you can prove your lineage and are willing to organise excavation works on said beach."

181

"Too bloody right I would!"

"Excellent – now if you would care to take down the following number and call our claims department, they will be able to furnish you with more details. Ask for Mr C. Lyon."

He read out the number he'd looked up in the directory during the conversation, the number for Glasgow Zoo, then said. "One last thing, sir – would you mind finding out in which direction water goes down the plughole in your bathroom?"

"Sure - one minute, mate!"

As he heard the receiver drop onto a table 12,000 miles away, Dog hung up and rolled on his bed laughing until he coughed his lungs up. He really had to cut down to 20 a day.

When the laughter and the coughing fit subsided, he wiped the tears and lay back on his bed. It'd been a good night – he'd set the tablecloth alight during the card school, had a couple of whiskies on the fly, channel-hopped in the TV lounge until his eyes swam and played two great jokes. Life was good.

Room 304, Glenbank Hotel

BLUE EYES had his hand on the receiver when the phone rang. It startled him so much it took him a second to realise what was what. Then he answered.

"Francis? It's me?"

"Claire, thank God. I've been worried sick, darlin'."

"Why?"

"Because you haven't answered all day. What's up?"

"What d'you mean, I haven't answered. The phone's never rung. I was getting worried something had happened to you."

"Hasn't rung? It's rung non-stop. Every 15 minutes. And your moby's off."

"My battery's flat and I can't find the charger."

"But what about the house phone? Have you switched the ringer off by accident?"

182

"No, don't think so, let me check – nope, it's on. There must just be a fault. I'll report it in the morning. So, how's the training?"

"Fine. How come if you were worried about me you never called?"

"You know I don't like disturbing you at work."

"But I'm here all week. You know you can phone the room and leave a message. Is somethin' up?"

"No."

"You sure?"

"Yes."

"Claire, somethin's up, what is it?"

"Nothing."

"Claire!"

"What!"

"Tell me!"

"No, I'm just fed up being here myself, me and the kids."

"Aw, come on, this is the first time in my life the football's taken me away this long. It's not like Ah'm jettin' round the world non-stop."

"No, but if it's not this it's work and if it's not work it's your pals and I feel totally left out. But this isn't the time to talk. I need my bed."

"Report the phone – and call me in the morning when you're up."

"Yah."

And the line went dead.

As did something inside Blue Eyes.

Loch Lomond Plaza

AT 12 minutes and 11 seconds past midnight, Melvin Law's eyes flashed open, He reached his arm out at right angles for his pad and pen and wrote:

Move Van Hoffen inside by two yards when possession is conceded to minimise threat of ball beyond midfield and in between Arrabiatta and Senteanu.

183

Then he replaced the pen and paper precisely where he'd taken them from and returned to recharging his batteries.

3.15am, Room 316, Glenbank Hotel

"WHAT if Flipper had an evil twin?"

"Whu-who-whu?"

"Ah said, what if Flipper had had an evil twin? How cool would that have been?"

Gibby rolled over and saw his mate propped up, hands behind his head and a Spike Milligan book open on his chest.

"Ah take it you cannae sleep, ya halfwit."

"Aye, well, sort of - but Ah was just thinkin', y'know-"

"What if Flipper had an evil twin?"

"Aye."

Gibby sat up and rubbed his eyes.

"OK, Ah'll buy it. So what if Flipper DID have an evil twin?"

"Well, he'd have to look like Flipper-"

"Natch-"

"Yeah, but he'd also have to have an immediately-recognisable evil trademark."

"Ye mean like a t-shirt wi' I'M EVIL on the front?"

"Naw - a five o'clock shadow or a pencil moustache, somethin' like that."

"Or a scar."

"Brilliant!" Willie sat up and clapped his hands. "Mars Bars are top evil trademarks. So where?"

"His dorsal fin?"

"Be serious."

"Be serious, he says at 3.17am the day before the Scottish Cup Final when we're lyin' awake discussin' the possibility of a pretendy TV dolphin havin' an identical brother whose sole purpose in life was to spread naughtiness."

"Porpoise."

"Whit?"

184

"Sole porpoise in life. Arf, arf!"

"You're a fuckpig. Where did all this come from anyway?"

"Dunno - Ah was just lyin' here thinkin' about Scooby Doo and how much Ah hated it when they brought in that wee pain in the erchie Scrappy Doo - Ah mean, whit was that a' about? A talkin' puppy? Did the gang need that?"

"Mibbes they were goin' stale."

"Fred? Daphne? Velma? Stale? Talk sense, man - they were geniuses."

"So how come they needed the mutt wi' the speech impediment and the gingey hippy tae solve every mystery?"

"That was contractual - Shaggy had a shark of an agent."

"No' a porpoise or a dolphin?"

"Naw - anyway, Ah was thinkin' aboot the Scoobster - did Ah tell ye Ah met him at Disney two years ago? Onea the best momentsa ma life, by the way - and Flipper came intae ma heid."

"Ah never liked Flipper."

"What about Skippy?"

"Make a dozen good pairsa fitba bits."

"Agreed. Live action animal series jist don't work. Lassie, the Littlest Hobo-"

"Mibbes the morra, Ah'll be homeward bound-"

"Shut it, ye're pittin' me aff. Aye, live action animal heroes. Hopeless. That's why Flipper needed an evil twin before he'd have become interestin'."

"Called?"

"Throbber."

"Throbber?"

"Throbber. 'Tache, scar down the right cheek, ability tae raise wan eyebrow evilly."

"Dae dolphins have eyebrows?"

"Course they do. Everybody's got eyebrows."

"That MP wummin doesnae, Theresa Gorman."

"How no'?"

185

"She had them plucked when she wis young and - wait for this - tattooed back on."

"How come?"

"Dunno, mental probably."

"So, Throbber's got eyebrows, right. And he raises wan at a time, like Roger Moore."

"But wi' better actin' ability."

"Goes without. Anyway, every time Flipper's on the case tae save a trapped wean or avert an environmental disaster-"

"-Throbber tries tae thwart him."

"Exactamundo! He'd be like, watchin' Flipper swim aff intae the distance and he's givin' it: 'Ah've lined up a surprise for you, baby brother'."

"Like what?"

"Like, tae get tae the trapped wean, Flipper's got tae get through an Evo-Stik slick pollutin' the lake. Or Throbber gets his henchmen-"

"Dolphin Lungren, big guys like that?"

"Now ye're getting' it - so he gets them tae capture Flipper and lower him slowly intae a crocodile-infested pool."

"How no' jist put him in quick-style?"

"Dramatic effect. D'ye never watch James Bond?"

"Aye, and Austin Powers, where Mike Myers cleverly exposed the rookie errors of successive Bond villains in trying to kill the hero. Wan dopey guard and a room wi' walls contracting jist slowly enough for hero and busty sort tae escape."

"Well, dae ye want Flipper killed in Episode Wan?"

"Mibbes, if Throbber's gonnae gie us a mair excitin' show - Ah hate it when ye know the good guy's gonnae win nae matter how huge the odds."

"That's evil."

"But you hate Flipper."

"Aye, but that disnae mean Ah'd top him – he's got tae get away fae his nemesis wi' panache an' a bit rapier wit."

"Like neek-neek-neek? That's as witty as dolphins get, innit?"

"Willin' suspension of disbelief, pal. Throbber gets ready to chuck Flipper ower a waterfall and Flipper says: 'Dae ye expect me tae swim, big brother?' an' Throbber says: 'Naw - Ah expect ye tae DIE!'"

"Or Wanker says: 'The night, Flipper, ye sleep wi' the fishes!'"

"An' Flipper says: 'But Ah sleep wi' the fishes every night.'"

"So Throbber says: "Ah - mibbes Ah shoulda thought that wan out a bit better, eh?'"

"Now ye're really gettin' it."

"OK, so what if Flipper had a kinda Scrappy Doo comedy relative - Flippy Doink or somethin'?"

"Whit, the mini-superhero that only did the emergencies in the shallow end? Divin' tae the rescue in armbands?"

"Aye, or takin' telephone messages and mibbes suggestin' solutions without actually incurring a call-out charge?"

"Yeah - they could expand that and have a Superhero Hotline. Call 0990 blahdy blah and speak to the Good Guy of yer choice. Press wan if ye need Spiderman, two if ye need Captain Scarlet-."

"An' three for specky Joe 90, the superhero who answers yer Internet problems."

"Go tae sleep, Gibby."

"You started this guff!"

"Aye, well Ah'm knackered now. Night, night."

"Bollocks - Ah'm wide awake now."

"So count dolphins…"

Room 301

TOM made it back to the restaurant just in time to see Caroline getting into her taxi. He called her name. She turned round and smiled. Then she leaned into the taxi, handed the driver some money and sent him away. She stood on the pavement, hands on hips, mock scorn on her beautiful face. Tom made a petted lip and bowed his head like a naughty schoolboy. Then they both laughed and he walked towards her and held her.

The hug seemed to last forever. Tom felt they had melted into one. He nuzzled her hair and it smelled like summer flowers. She clung to him like she never wanted to let go again.

Then he pulled away and looked deep into his eyes and swallowed hard and went down on one knee. He reached into his jacket pocket and took out the box. He opened it and a solitaire diamond dazzled under the streetlight. He looked up and her asked if she would do him the honour of marrying him. And she said, "What – again?"

For a few seconds, he felt sure she was going to laugh out loud. At very best he was utterly certain she would say no, at worst knee him right in the teeth. Then she cried.

And said yes.

Tom felt his head slump forward in utter relief. He remembered he should put the ring on her finger. It fitted perfectly. She helped him up, knees of his trousers wet from the rain-slicked pavement, and they hugged again and swayed together then danced around like daft kids. Tom rolled over in bed and luxuriated in the warmth of his dream. For a little while, his life was perfect.

Room 316

"WILLIE, you awake?"

"Naw, this is a recordin'."

"Naw, seriously – you awake?"

"Dear God, Gibby, whit it is now? It's quarter past fuckin' four!"

"Listen, Ah've been thinkin'-."

"Don't worry, the first time's always the hardest-."

"-and you know what Ah'd like?"

"A smack in the puss?"

"Ah want a picture o' me that never ends."

"Whit?"

"A picture o' me that never ends."

188

Now it was Willie's turn to drag himself up and listen to nonsense.

He chuckled. "Ah had a burd like that once – remember Liz McAlpine? Her arse had its ain weather system."

"Naw, Ah mean like in Airplane, the film, know 'mean?"

"Whit?"

"Right, there was this scene when Lloyd Bridges stares into space and the music goes dat-dat-daaaa! and he lights a fag and behind him on the wa' there's this picture o' him starin' intae space an' lightin' a fag and on the wa' behind him in it there's a picture o' him starin' intae space an' -."

"Ah'm kinda getting' the general point. But whit's it got tae dae wi' you?"

"Ah want that."

"Tae be in a remake o' Airplane?"

"Naw, Ah want a picture like that – me standin' wi' ma airms folded, one foot on a ba', standin' in front o' a picture o' me wi' ma airms folded an' one foot on a ba', standin' in front o' a pic-."

"OK, OK, Ah get it. Tell ye whit, if ye go back tae sleep right now Ah'll get ye wan, a'right?"

"Aye, but that's the thing – how? How did they dae it?"

"Whit d'ye mean how did they dae it? They took a picture o' him standin' in front o' a picture o' himself standing in front o' a picture o' himself et fuckin' cetera. Simple!"

"Simple? SIMPLE? Think about it, man – where wid ye start takin' the pictures? Whit wid be the first wan?"

"Wan o' him standin' in front o' wan o' him - Ah, Ah get ye. Hey, that's a belter. Will we ca' Fud, he's quite a clever boaby, eh? He'll know."

"Willie, it's twenty tae six, man – he'd gut us. Anyway, he's the heaviest sleeper in the world."

"Aye, unless ye've shared a bed wi' Liz McAlpine an' she rolls over quick."

"Naw, we need tae sort this out alone."

"Well, can it wait till brekky? Ah think better on a full stomach."

"So you should be on University Challenge, porky. Anyway, Ah cannae sleep wi' this on ma mind. Ah need tae know. Gie's that pencil and pad aff yer table, Ah'll draw it."

Willie watched his mate scribble, tongue poking from the corner of his mouth. Now and again he'd stop and look puzzled and scratch his head, then nod frantically and start scribbling again. Finally, he put the pencil down, looked off into space. And frisbeed the pad across the room.

"Bollocks, Ah cannae work it out. They musta done it wi' computers."

"Ah well, never mind, Einstein. Ah'll buy ye a puppy instead. Nighty-night!"

4.35am, Room 245, Loch Lomond Plaza Hotel

DOG lay on the floor, staring into the dark with the telly flickering in the corner, his breathing flattening out as he collected his thoughts for the next move. No thought came. Dog closed his eyes and took a deep breath. Something would come. It always did. It had to.

It didn't.

Dog began to panic, because when his mind wasn't active with nonsense it got active with his life and life was the last thing he wanted to be thinking about.

"Come on, man like man," he said quietly into the darkness, "come up wi' summat. Dee summat. Anythin'. How man, Dog, think."

But it was too late. Reality was climbing the corrugated iron fence which surrounded the junkyard of his brain and running rampage. He saw flashing images of Karen, of little Wayne and Kiara, all running, running, running, with him unable to catch them. He saw his knee mangled and his frightened face and a

190

surgeon with a huge, whirring drill and manic grin. He saw himself waking up in a pool of sick on some pavement somewhere.

And the tears came for real.

For the second time in two minutes, Dog rolled about his bed, even further out of control than usual. He sobbed and blubbed and snottered and caught great clumps of air in his throat like a toddler in a tantrum. He felt like he always did when he'd lost it, the way a drowning man must feel.

He fought to keep his head above the black waters of loneliness, despair, misery. His head swirled as he churned the bedclothes into a porridge around him. Eventually, he ended up on the floor with a thump, limbs tangled in the duvet. The fall brought him to his senses.

He gasped for breath, blinked his stinging eyes, rubbed them with the heels of his shaking hands, heard the squelching noise as he rubbed too hard and too long. Never could do anything in moderation. He wrestled free of the duvet, flung it back on the bed and grabbed a holdall from a corner of the room. There he was, tucked under a pair of tracky bottoms. His best pal in times of trouble. Jack Daniels.

Dog drank himself to sleep.

THROUGH the wall, Bobby Bothwell heard the murmuring and the creaking stop at last and knew the bevvy had seen his midfield partner off at last.

He himself couldn't have dropped off if you'd hooked him to a Drambuie drip.

Friday

THE headline leapt straight at Melvin Law from page one of *The Scottish Sun*:

WE'RE NOT BENT
City stars deny Cup bribes claim

They had denied everything – quite rightly, as they'd done nothing wrong. He was convinced of that. And yet even a denial story read like they were guilty as sin.

The way they'd written it – them and every other morning paper lying in front of him on the bed – suggested that there was no smoke without fire, that it was impossible for highly-paid footballers to be anywhere near dodgy money and a betting coup and not be tempted.

You could almost smell the innuendo coming off the front pages as they announced that all betting on the result of the match had been suspended. The insinuation was that if City had punted against themselves, they wouldn't get to pick their ill-gotten gains up if they did the dirty on their fans and lost deliberately.

Law was horrified at the very thought. It didn't matter to these press vultures that his team had fathers in it, church-goers, university graduates, decent men who visited sick kids in hospital beds and gave endless hours of their time to charity.

Gambling + football + a big match 24 hours away = a scoop.

"Why let the facts get in the way, eh?"

Melvin Law didn't like it when he talked to himself. It wasn't logical, didn't make sense. It wasn't him.

"Get a grip, man."

See? He was at it again.

Glenbank Hotel

UNITED'S players had also read the papers and didn't know whether to laugh or cry.

On the plus side, the heat was off them as far as Charlie Spuds was concerned. Somehow, City were in the frame now, the poor bastards.

But on the very, very negative side, it looked like they'd just pissed £250,000 up against a big, high wall.

"Mornin' lads, an' a beautiful one it is too!"

"Take it ye've no' read the *Record* then, Screech?"

"Naw, how?"

Porridge threw it to him. His freckled brow furrowed and his lips moved slowly as he read the news. Then he threw it back at the keeper.

"So – no one gets murdered but no one gets rich either."

"That's about the size of it, son."

"Ach, hey ho."

"What a philosopher you are, Screechy boy."

"Ta, Willie. You well this mornin'? An' how's Gio – the man who headers a Bud bottle further than Jimmy D headers Mitres."

"Awright, Screech?"

Chopper piped up. "Hey, The Herald says there's a chance the bets will be back on if City lose but the bookies are satisfied it was on the level. So we might get the dosh yet."

"Aye, man – a' we need tae do is make sure we win purely on the basis of our tactical and physical superiority, ya fud."

"OK, Chunks, OK. Just tryin' tae lift the spirits a wee bit."

Somebody threw a roll at Chopper. He ducked and it hit Jimmy, who sprayed a mouthful of tea in shock. Somebody else shouted the gaffer's favourite phrase about how they should never be taken by surprise. Jimmy give them all the Vs.

Blue Eyes saw how bright they all were and felt himself relax. Ginge had been right all along, the whole betting thing was a mistake. Probably best that they didn't have the pressure of making themselves fortunes hanging over them on Saturday. Now they could just be up for the cup for its own sake. He still hadn't heard from Claire this morning, but sod her. Whatever game she was playing, she wasn't going to screw things up for him, not now, not when things were this big.

The gaffer was coming over. The babble died.

"Suppose you've all seen the papers? Well, ignore them. Ah don't buy this crap about City floggin' the game and Ah don't expect you to. As far as Ah'm concerned this bettin' coup's down to people wi' more money than sense. As far as you're concerned, Glasgow City will be out to batter your melts in at Hampden. OK? Nothin' changes. Game heads on. See ye on the bus in half an hour."

They waited until Tom and Bibs were well clear, then they were all babbling again.

Loch Lomond Plaza

MELVIN LAW had been expecting a visit from the police and it came right after breakfast. A DI Andy McKenzie and DS Des Bradley spoke to him, to Bobby Bothwell, to the chairman and to Driscoll, knocking the manager's training plans back a good half hour.

"Officers, I know you have a job to do, but so do I – we've a big game tomorrow and we're due to have our last training session, so if there's any chance we could-."

McKenzie fixed Law with a glare that was at odds with the smile he wore.

"I appreciate your dilemma, sir, but hopefully you'll also appreciate mine. See, while you have the tactics of a game of football to work out, I'm in charge of a team which started out dealing with a £250,000 armed robbery but which has since taken on the investigation of six murders and an alleged gambling coup. In rock-paper-scissors terms, I'd say we've got you beat here."

Law folded his arms and bit his lip. "OK, I take the point."

194

"Very public-spirited of you, sir. Now, as it happen, I don't believe for a minute your players are involved here. In my experience, people with as much money as top footballers tend to bet on account. This wedge has been placed in cash, in small amounts at a whole host of bookmakers right across the Glasgow area. The hotel have confirmed that your players did not leave here at the time when we know the bets were placed, so unless they used friends to do it their involvement is unlikely. Plus, even if my theory is wrong and they *are* involved, they or someone connected with them will have to pick up the winnings soon enough, at which time we'll simply pick them up and start asking difficult questions."

"So why are you here, if you don't mind me asking?"

"Well, Mr Law, what interests us is the TV footage of last night's press conference. See, one of the questions was asked by a certain Neil McAllister, right? Right. Now, whatever section of the media he claimed to be from, he was lying. Neil McAllister is actually a sidekick of one Charles Kerr, aka Charlie Spuds, also pretty certainly the, ahem, businessman who had the £250,000 stolen from him in the first place. Now, what I want to know is: Why was he there? What did he have to gain showing out like that? It was almost as if he wanted someone to know he was around. Someone who knew who he was. Maybe someone he had a hold on. And maybe I'm way off beam, but Mr Bothwell here seemed to react pretty badly when this Mr McAllister stood up and said his piece. Mr Bothwell?"

"I felt sick. In fact, straight after the conference I *was* sick. As a dog."

"Something you ate? Or something hard to swallow?"

Law wagged a finger at the detective. "Now look here, what are you accusing my captain-?"

"No accusations, sir. Just a question. Bobby?"

"My stomach was dodgy all day. I think the worry of these accusations just made me feel worse and the room was roasting. I don't have a clue who this McAllister guy is."

McKenzie looked straight into the City star's eyes. Bothwell refused to be stared out. McKenzie shrugged and said fair enough, that was that. They'd let themselves out.

Melvin Law looked at his captain and said he looked pale. Bothwell shrugged that he was still feeling a bit dicky. The manager offered him the chance to skip training. Bothwell thought a second and said, yes, he could do with a lie down.

Preferably, he thought, on a beach in Tahiti.

10.35am, Greenock Juniors FC

LAMBCHOP knew Tom was talking in the background but he hadn't heard a word. None of it mattered much of a monkey's anyway. It was only for the ones who'd be playing and he wasn't likely to be one of them unless the 16 guys in front got smallpox.

And anyway, even if he'd been first pick he still wouldn't have heard. He had his gaze fixed on the back of Garry fucking Ronald's fucking head. He was staring so hard he got that blurry thing where the head was in soft focus.

He was losing it. He knew he was. But trying to stop was like telling yourself not to scratch when you had an itch. Even while he was telling himself not to stare, he was staring harder until his eyes started to screw up and hurt. He gave himself a shake so sudden and violent Shyness, standing right behind him, jumped back in fright. Tom stopped in mid-lecture about the lot of them having to get more switched on.

"McGonigall, what's your problem? You havin' a fit?"

"Sorry, Tom – a wasp was at us. Sorry. It's away now."

"Jesus God, can we get on wi' it? Listen, this is our last session an' we're a shambles – you lot should be bouncin' around the place, but there's no' one o' ye doesnae look like keech. Did any o' ye get any sleep last night? Fud? Chunky? Screech? It's like a zombie convention, for fuck's sake. Now, listen, Bibs'll take ye for the warm-up, then we'll work on some set-pieces for and against,

do some six-by-four and finish off with a right good nine-a-side –
plenty energy, let's see ye going' for it."

Bibs clapped his hands. "Right, lads, fix bayonets an' over the
top! Let's have ye!"

Three laps in, plus breaks for stretching, Lambchop still hadn't
said a word to Chunky. He stared straight ahead, just doing
enough as usual, showing not a spark of enthusiasm. Chunky was
well used to it – they roomed together because they were the two
biggest moaners at the club and no one else could put up with
them for long – but couldn't handle the foul mood that went with
it this morning.

"What's eatin' you, son?"

"Don't call me son. Ye know Ah hate you callin' me son."

Touch left!

"So what's wrong with you sir."

"You fucked off for breakfast again an' never woke me."

Touch right!

"And that's it? That's what the huff of the century's a' about, is
it?"

"Aye."

"Not the fact that ye're still carryin' on this shite about what
happened on Wednesday night? Ye think the boys weren't talking
about it this mornin', about how easy it is tae wind you right up?
You really are a dimwit, Lambchop."

"Aye right, take their side, ya midget twat."

Touch both!

"Well, if you're going to soft-soap me..."

"Nah, ye know what Ah mean – no one ever asks ma side
o'things, it's always just: An argument? That'll be Lambchop's
fault! Does ma heid in."

*And turn! And turn! And turn! And back men hit the front on the
whistle!*

"And your moods do mine in, ya miserable git. Jesus Christ,
we're out in the fresh air at a five-star hotel, the day before we get

197

the chance tae make the Scottish Cup Final. Like I said to ma pet horse, why the long face?"

"How are we gettin' a chance tae make the cup final? Ah've nae chance o' playin'."

Touch both! Up! Touch right! Touch left!

"As much as me, Ah'd say – but am Ah greetin'? Naw. Well, no in public anyroad. Anyway, how many players get tae be this close? Have ye thought about that or are ye too busy feeling sorry for yersel'?"

"What are you, Harry Secombe on Highway? Every cloud's got a silver lining? We'd be as well watchin' it on the telly for a' the good we'll be."

"Jesus, you really get me down – how many guys in this game do you know who've been in the Hampden dressin' rooms on a day like this? Gone out in their new suits tae test the pitch? Had the big party at night? You're that close, ya dickhead – and, hey, there might be a whole stack of injuries before Saturday – now let's sprint!

Lambchop false-started as the idea hit him. Bibs yelled at him to move his arse. He went off at three-quarters pace, more trotting than sprinting. Craw nearly clipped his heels as he hared up behind him in the next pair.

"Watch it, Lambsy – people could get hurt like that."

Lambchop mumbled sorry and fell back into step with Chunky, his stride suddenly more purposeful, his back straighter. His room-mate was well chuffed to have helped buck the boy's ideas up.

PORRIDGE'S hands stung. Ten minutes solid of shooting, the boys going in a loop, playing one-twos with the gaffer and cracking them in from 18 yards. Willie had just caught one like he personally hated Mitre. The keeper threw himself up and left as the latest one fizzed in from Westy, got his right glove across and into it, but his wrist bent and he came down with a grunt as the net rustled.

"Fuck it!"

"And in ye come, boys – good stuff."

Porridge had spent every second counting down to a breather, yet now he was getting one he wanted to get back up and be chucking himself about again to prove he was unbeatable. He dusted his tracky bottoms down and joined the semi-circle of bodies around Tom.

"Great stuff, boys, really sharp – this is much more like it. Give this effort on Saturday an' we'll no' let ourselves down. Jimmy, Blue Eyes – big and strong in there, big shouts, get out when Porridge tells you. Midfield – good passin', get it wide to Taxi or Westy quick as you can. Fud? Willie? Craw? Lookin' the part."

Fud's groin tightened and he wanted to tell his gaffer he didn't feel the part. Craw saw his mate wince and made a you OK? face. Fud ignored it.

Lambchop wondered if his gaffer had even noticed he was at training.

Maybe it was time he made him.

"Anyway, no lettin' up now, boys. We'll go nine-a-side across the width o' the pitch for half-an-hour tae finish – three-touch, real quick stuff, finishes have to be first time, OK? Ah'll be shoutin' one or two o' ye out at a time for a word – so let's go. Bibs's got the vests an' knows the sides, so let's see ye."

"Right boys, over the top one last time! Vests are – Porridge, Ginge, Jimmy, Barry, Chunky, Screech, Craw, Taxi and me tae make up the numbers. Bounce ba' tae start. Go!"

Craw went for it with Blue Eyes. It wasn't an even fight. The balding sweeper came away with the ball and found Westy with his third touch. Westy controlled, but his second touch was poor and as he stretched for a third Taxi had it off his toes. He didn't need a third touch, pinging one left to right for Fud. It ran under the striker's foot and out beyond the cones that marked the touchlines. Tom thought Fud's wince was down to frustration and shouted Next Time from the side. Fud blanked him.

Craw ran past his pal and asked if he was all right. Fud said aye, fine, let it go. Craw told him to take it easy. Now Ginge's red

199

head was bobbing as he picked a pass inside to Jimmy, who went route one to Craw. One touch and he was hammering with his right foot beyond Harri's clawing hands and high into the net.

The orange vests whooped and cheered. Blue Eyes clapped his hands together and yelled at his team to pick it up, get closer. He had the ball again, found Shyness, who dodged around Taxi and one-twoed with Willie. One touch for balance, second for a sighter and – BANG! – straight into Porridge's guts.

Porridge threw out overarm, Jimmy went long again, Craw brought it down on his thigh, but as he pulled the trigger Heed came through him like a snowplough. Craw yelled and instinctively grasped his ankle as he landed. Heed didn't look his way as he got up and demanded the ball back from Garry Ronald.

Blue Eyes liked that. Train like you play, that was the motto. He watched the black sweatshirt with MW on it pass sideways to MB, who went forward to RMcG, to SMcC, who was closed down, turned back and found MW again. Westy hit one down the line to Chopper, who turned nimbly away from Craw's clumsy challenge and switched play to the sweatshirt with GR on it. Lambchop followed the pass and closed down.

Fud was there before him, pushing his right leg towards the ball. The sweatshirt with GG on it knocked the ball one way and dodged the other. Only one touch left, make it a good one. Looked up, saw Willie running and pulled its right foot back to pass.

Tom shouted into the play. "Barry, Rob, when you're ready, over here."

The sweatshirt with GR on it seemed to lose concentration, just for an instant. Lambchop saw his chance. The ball was loose. He slid, then at the last gasp his trailing right foot seemed to go from under him. His left came up, studs showing, straight into the standing foot of his bibbed opponent. The standing leg buckled. The air was torn by a scream.

Lambchop put his hands up as he landed in a tangle with the boy in the bib, saying a sorry he didn't mean.

"Garry, son, my foot went – Ah didnae mean tae-"

200

"BARRY!"

Lambchop spun and saw the figure haring away from the gaffer and over towards him. "What d'ye mean, Barry? That's Garry – you're Barry!"

The one with the orange bib was standing over the one with GR on his sweatshirt now.

"Naw, it's Barry. Ah'm Garry. Look at me! We – we got asked by the press yesterday if we ever swapped identities to play jokes and we realised we never had. So this mornin' we thought we'd give it a go, for a laugh."

Lambchop felt the colour drain from his face.

Thing is, his trailing leg really *had* gone from under him. It had propelled him into the boy quicker than he'd meant to, higher than he'd meant to, sent the six studs of his left boot into the side of the boy's knee. He'd felt the ligaments give way as the weight of his body followed in.

He'd only meant to go over the ball, catch his ankle, maybe make him struggle for Saturday, maybe give himself some tiny, outside chance of playing left-back in the biggest game of his life. Or even getting on the bench. It'd been a stupid idea, a ridiculous concept that he might profit from injuring one of his own team. Anyway, the bench was as close as he'd have got on Saturday, because Shyness would have been first choice to replace Garry – so what was he going to do next, break his leg?

And in any case, he'd cocked it up big time, as per fuckin' usual. He hadn't even got the right twin. They were crowded round Barry now, making him bite on a towel to stop him screaming while they waited for the ambulance. Fizzy was strapping his legs together, trying to make him comfortable.

Garry was kneeling down at his brother's head, crying.

Lambchop felt like the biggest keech that ever fouled a park.

Blue Eyes happened to turn and saw him standing, grey-faced and wide-eyed. He came over and put a hand on his shoulder.

"Hey, son, don't blame yourself – it could have happened to anyone. Tom wanted us to go full pelt, you went in hard and

201

slipped. It could have been him on you – you could be lying there just as easily."

"Sure."

"Look, it happens. It's a man's game. Let's all get behind young Barry now and help him through this. It's no one's fault."

"Cheers."

But Lambchop knew it was someone's fault. The blame was right on one guy's slumped shoulders.

Garry Ronald was to blame.

If he hadn't – if that stupid wee twat hadn't – hadn't wound him up so much, got him so angry – then if he hadn't played that stupid joke of swapping bibs – I mean, what kind of fuckwit does that before a big game? How juvenile is he? How – how – how could I have been so fuckin' stupid?

Lambchop rubbed his right hand across his face to wipe his tears away.

Central Scotland Police, Falkirk

DCI BOB ROBINSON was on his way out when DI McKenzie and DS Bradley arrived back, so he about-turned and invited them back to his office for a rundown. They told the him about their meeting with the City people, then about a subsequent chat they'd had with Neil "Rhino" McAllister, who'd told them he'd gone into the press conference as a bet with a mate who didn't think he'd have the bottle. He said Charlie Spuds had been raging when he saw it on the telly and had bollocked him.

"So what do you believe and what don't you?"

"Honestly, chief? None of it. It's all so much shite. I've absolutely no doubt Bothwell's either up to his arse in a match-fixing scam or that Spuds believes he is and is leanin' on him and that Rhino went in there to frighten the keech out of him. Because let's face it, there aren't many heavies around as good as shit-frightening as those belonging to Charlie Spuds."

"And?"

"And to be honest? It's getting to the stage where I don't much give a toss."

Even Bradley was startled by that comment. Bob Robinson leaned forward and give his DI a hard look.

"Listen, Andy, as much as this is a tough case and as much as I know it's bugging the life out of all of us, we've a duty to-."

"Actually, Bob, that's where we maybe are at a tangent on things. I mean, what do we have? A pile of corpses which are linked to Spuds but which give absolutely no clues to any guilt on his part. A missing pile of cash that may or may not be his, but which if it is his he hasn't felt the need to report missing. Now, we thought the money would be back with him by now as the ones who nicked it are now deceased. But it appears that Spuds believes it has in fact been re-routed into a betting coup against Glasgow City. If that's true and City lose, we'll be able to pick up those who placed the bets, or at least those who pick up the winnings, easy-peasy. But the truth is that we now have half our manpower out trying to solve a crime on behalf of who? A victim who hasn't even reported it? My feelings right now are that until we see who wins this game, there's nowhere to go. Tayside might turn something up on the five bodies in the high flat and the sixth corpse definitely worked for Spuds but died in what appears to have been a rather nasty gay rape snuff attack. The best we'll get is something on the match-fixing if that's what it turns out to be, in which case it'll be taken off our mitts by the fraud mob anyway. As for the drugs that Spuds was meant to have traded for the 250K? If by some miracle they get traced back we can maybe do him, but that's for another time and it's a whole other situation. This situation, if you don't mind me speaking my mind, is a hopeless one. And I just feel we could be getting back to dealing with other outstanding jobs instead of chasing our tails on behalf of an undiluted arsehole like Charlie Kerr."

Robinson kept glaring for a second or two. Then he laughed. "Hadn't thought of it that way, Andrew – but you make a persuasive case. You're right, I suppose. Where do we go until we

203

find out if the game was fixed? Nowhere. So, OK, we pull back, but be prepared to flood the necessary bookies with bodies if United upset the odds and someone, whoever it is, gets rich quick. But before you move onto anything else, Andy boy, you can write me up a full and frank report of every move you and your esteemed team have made since the moment those idiot commandos smashed up their getaway car. Every move. Not an i left undotted or a t uncrossed. No room for anyone to dig us up, OK?"

McKenzie said that was no problem, thanked his boss and nodded for Bradley to follow him out of the office. He held the door for his sergeant, closed it behind him, then put a friendly arm on Bradley's broad shoulder.

"Well, Des – looks like this case is officially closed. So in your role as my trusted first lieutenant, I'm giving you the privilege of getting that full and frank report done up like the man says. Meanwhile, as the guv'nor, I'm going to enjoy the privilege of an early lunch."

And the case of the missing £250,000 was pretty much over.

Greenock Juniors FC

WHEN the ambulance had bounced around the track and they'd loaded Barry on and it had driven away, Tom called them together and asked if they wanted to carry on with the game. No one really had the heart.

"OK, we'll do some crossing and finishing then call it quits. Let's put some effort into it – Lambchop, you all right? You want to sit it out?"

Lambchop suddenly felt like he looked guilty as an elephant sitting next to a squashed monkey.

"Me? Naw, er, Ah mean, aye – Ah'm fine, gaffer. It's the two boys Ah'm worried about."

"They'll be fine. Garry'll stay with him at the hospital an' Fizzy'll ring us when he knows the score. Just you concentrate on

204

hittin' the target – this squad's shrinkin' fast an' we need everyone up for the cup."

"No sweat, gaffer."

But there was plenty sweat on Lambchop now. He felt clammy all over and he just knew they could see it, like Tony Blair at that party conference when he took his jacket off. Like one big stain. He stood in line while they took turns to hit crosses from Taxi on the right and Shyness on the left. There were four in front of him. He could still see Barry's anguished face. What the fuck had he done? Three in front now. He heard a cheer as the net bulged. Two in front now. What couldn't he just admit he wasn't good enough? What was his problem? Now it was just Fud. His shot bounced hard in front of Porridge, who kept his eye on it and caught it high above his head. Lambchop noticed Fud seemed to be limping. Taxi was already teeing another ball up to cross. It dipped just inside the box, ideal for a left-foot volley. But suddenly Lambchop wasn't sure. Should he adjust and hit it with his right? Should he let it drop and hit it on the up? He felt like he was wearing diving boots. He swung his left, but couldn't get it off the deck. The ball bounced past him and as he tried to get round it to hit it a second time before the bounce died he stumbled and fell into JD. The rest hooted. He wanted to run away and hide. As JD held onto him playfully, he pushed him away and swore. JD told him to cool it. He told JD he'd give him cool. Blue Eyes stepped in and told them both to cool it.

Lambchop told Blue Eyes to fuck right off.

Tom shouted to Lambchop to step across to the touchline. Lambchop said, what? You want to have a go because it was me who caught the boy? You think Ah meant it? What kinda wanker dae ye take me for?

Blue Eyes told him, hey, you're upset, go and see the gaffer and take five. No one's blamin' ye. Ye're just wound up about it. Ye'll be fine.

Lambchop said fuck you. Blue Eyes shook his head and turned away. Craw shouted to Shyness that he couldnae hang about a' day waitin' for crosses. Shyness asked him what the hurry was to put one over the bar. They all did a big, camp *ooooohhhhhh*. The crack had lightened the mood.

Except inside Lambchop's head.

He walked towards Tom, who held an arm out as if waiting for his player's shoulder to fit into it. Lambchop walked straight past him, never looked in his direction, straight off the pitch and through the gate by the corner flag and out of the ground to the bus.

It was locked.

He stood and held onto the handle, feeling their eyes burn into the back of his head. He couldn't go back now, though it could hardly have made him look any more of a plank. Where the fuck was that driver? What a time to go for a pee. What the fuck was he goin' tae do now? He put his forehead against the door and cried. He felt so lonely, stupid, hopeless.

Blue Eyes went across to Tom and said he should maybe go and talk to the boy. Tom said fuck him, he's lost it. Let him sweat, he'd go and see him later. He'd speak to Chunky first and see what the script was. Right then, though, Chunky was telling the boys he didn't have a clue what was going on in his room-mate's head. World of his own, that clown. But did he think he'd done Barry on purpose? No way. Never. Not a chance.

Surely not?

Nah, couldn't have.

They looked across at him and he seemed to be rhythmically nutting the bus door. The boy had problems big time.

Chunky watched Shyness's cross come in and hammered a half-volley low past Porridge's diving right hand.

"Wey-hey! Pick it out, bawbag!"

Lambchop heard the laughter and knew it was aimed at him. Fuck the lot of them.

206

12.40pm, Inverclyde Royal Hospital

FIZZY came through the double doors with his head down. Garry threw down last September's copy of *Women's Realm* and leapt out of his seat.

"Well? What did they say?"

"Have a seat, pal."

"Never mind have a seat, Ah've been sittin' for an hour an' a half. What did they say?"

He looked into the physio's eyes and knew what was coming and part of him didn't want to hear it, but he needed to.

"Garry, it's bad. His cruciate's away, plus one of his medials. There's cartilage damage, the kneecap's off line – it's like a road accident, they said."

Garry slumped back down.

"No, no, it cannae be – they've got tae be-"

"Wrong? Nope, kid, they're right. As soon as I saw it I was pretty sure. I've seen one similar, when I was up at Perth. Remember wee Danny Waddell?"

"Midfield boy?"

"Yep. Took six one Saturday and was hanging all over the place. Out for 18 months – to start with."

"Where's he now?"

Fizzy lowered his eyes. Garry threw his head back and sighed.

"Hey, it's not always like that. He was a slow healer – and he tried too hard. You have to plan a comeback from this stuff properly. I'd left by the time he was doing rehab and he got bad advice."

"But Barry might not-"

"Garry, Garry, he's only just come in. They won't operate until tomorrow, earliest, when the swelling's down. We won't have a clue until after that. But the chances are-"

"Oh my God, he could be finished. Ah cannae play in this game now."

207

Fizzy went down on his haunches and put both hands on Garry's arms. "Kid, it happens. It's a tough game. Nobody went out to hurt your brother. It could have been you just as easy – would you have expected Barry to pull out of the game? Course not. So you go out there and play for both of you."

"Sure, Flanders."

"I mean it – if you go in and see him after that op he'll tell you the same. And when we beat them-"

"If-"

"When we beat them he'll be there at the final and when we win it you can hand it to him personally. It'll be like it it'd all been for him."

"But not *by* him. That's what counts. D'you know what day Saturday is?"

"What d'you mean? It's the semi."

"Apart from that – it's a year to the day since our mum died. Remember how cut up Barry was when it happened?"

"Sure, we felt for you all at the funeral. A terrible tragedy."

"Yeah, but Barry had something special with mum that me and Mhairi never had – an' the last day she was alive he told her he'd make a success of himself for her. Y'see? This was him keepin' that promise – an' now it's been taken away."

"So you do it for her instead – for Barry, your mum, dad, Mhairi. You'll be the Ronald family out there."

"It won't be the same."

"Nothing's the same as it is in our heads. When Barry told your mum that stuff, did either of you think you'd be in a Scottish Cup semi-final a year later? No way! But you are – and you might never get the chance again. So don't chuck it away – go for it twice as hard."

"Ah want to see Barry."

"He's still a bit groggy, they had to sedate him."

"Ah want tae see him."

"It might freak you right out."

"Ah want tae-"

"OK, OK, let's go. Just don't say you weren't warned."

208

1.15pm, Glenbank Hotel

CRAW did the press while Blue Eyes looked on from behind the pack, shooting him daggers if he even looked like he was contemplating mentioning Barry Ronald, Lambchop, Giovanni, Willie, Hairy or the chairman.

Oh, or having £250,000 on themselves to win at 16/1.

They'd put him up because he had a tale to tell. Eight years ago, as a 17-year-old Ipswich trainee, he'd totalled his car coming home from training and had to be cut from the wreckage. He'd been in intensive care for five days and when he came round they told him he'd lost his spleen and part of his left big toe. They reckoned he'd never kick a ball again, but after being freed he came home and played junior and then got a trial with United. He scored two in a reserve game and they offered him a two-year deal. He'd proved the docs wrong.

"So did you ever think you'd see the day you'd play in a Scottish Cup semi-final," asked Jack Keith from the *Daily Mail*, winning that day's Most Blindingly Obvious Question contest.

Yes, when I was lying in that hospital bed I thought, one day I'll play in a Scottish Cup semi-final.

"No, don't be daft, that was beyond my wildest dreams – I was more worried about whether I'd ever walk again."

They liked that.

"So was there a chance you'd be in a wheelchair, Crawford?"

"Er-" Craw saw Blue Eyes nod slowly. "-yes, the doctors feared I'd be a cripple. But luckily, erm, God was with me and saw me through."

"So you're a Christian then, Crawford?"

Blue Eyes nodded again. Craw's heart sank.

"Yes, yes I am. I believe in the Almighty and – and – go to church every Sunday, if not oftener."

"So does that mean when you go out there at Hampden on Saturday it'll be, well, some kind of miracle."

Now Blue Eyes wasn't nodding. He was smiling. Bawbag.

"Absolutely – I am a walking miracle. I could have died in that car crash and the fact that I didn't made me see the light. Now I want to win the cup for the Lord – and those doctors who saved me, of course."

"Brilliant , Crawford – er, just one more question."

"Yeah?"

"Where exactly is your spleen?"

"Dunno – a jar in Ipswich Royal Infirmary, prob'ly."

"Magic – tragic God-fearing miracle man Crawford Brown cracks jokes about the horror smash that almost killed him."

THE pack went into a huddle after Craw and Blue Eyes left, deciding what line they'd all take. This stuff had been quite literally heaven-sent. They'd needed a line big time after the guff served up at the City conference two hours earlier.

Melvin Law had barked at them for three minutes and 30 seconds exactly. He refused to speak any more about the betting coup and dodged a question about why Bobby Bothwell hadn't trained, before getting up in the middle of a rambling question from *The Herald*'s feisty female writer Britney Butler and walking out with a curt nod.

Five minutes later, Romanian defender Darius Senteanu had entered the room wearing the expression of a man who had a bomb in his pants with someone outside the room holding the remote control in case he didn't do what he was told.

So, was he looking forward to Saturday.

Yes, yes he was.

How many other cup semi-finals had he played in?

Eleven.

Er, which ones?

Seven in Romania, three in Spain and one last year here in Scotland.

And how had he got on?

He was sure it was all in the record books.

Okkaaaayy – but did he have a favourite?

All games that he won felt good.

And which had he won?

It's all in the-

- record books, yep. So, preparations going well for this one?

Very well, they were always very well prepared.

Was he fit and raring to go?

Of course, without fitness and mental strength there would be no point being here.

And did he know much about Ochil United?

No.

Was he surprised to see them in a cup semi-final?

In football, all things were possible.

Had he ever been the victim of a giantkilling?

No, he did not believe in giants.

Er, ha-ha, what they'd meant was, had he ever been part of a big team beaten by a smaller team such as Ochil United?

Not that he could remember.

Would it be a disaster if City lost this game?

No, disasters are earthquakes and plane crashes. In any case, we do not think about losing. I go now to sleep for the afternoon, so thank you.

No - thank *you*. For hee-haw.

PAUL ARTHUR had sat at the back of the room, watching the rest hit their heads off a brick wall of obtuseness, his piece for tomorrow formulating as every banal question was blocked by an even more banal answer.

He would write that City deserved to lose because of their arrogance, their obnoxious attitude to the public and their obvious air of being offended at having to play against such underlings.

He would say that if they gave out cups for being aloof, City wouldn't be able to build a trophy cabinet big enough.

He would give them a right good kicking, then follow it up on matchday with his big state-of-the-nation piece. He would weave a magical, romantic spell on his readers, making them not just want United to upset all the odds, but to believe they could.

He would visualise them defending like heroes, tackling like tigers all over the pitch and then, from somewhere deep inside, someplace they didn't even know existed, conjuring the move that created the game's only goal.

He would be the only one who wrote anything different, because even though the rest in that overlit hotel function room were fuming mad at United too, they wouldn't turn against them in print. They knew where their bread was buttered.

Paul Arthur could take his dry.

Ooh, he liked that phrase. He'd file it away and use it soon.

THERE was only one song Taxi hated more than *I Will Survive* and that was *Africa* by Toto. Perm-haired, spandex-trousered, middle-American, early-80s shit rock. Truly appalling and music made even more horrible by the inclusion of the worst two lines ever to spurt from a pen:

I know that I must do what's right,
Sure as Kilimanjaro rises like an empress above the Serengeti.

And what made those lyrics worser than worse this afternoon was that they kept repeating over and over and over in Taxi's head. It was bursting him. He thought he was finally going insane.

He was also going to kill the skipper. The bastard had waited till Taxi dozed off on the bed with *Never Mind The Bollocks* on his Walkman and replaced it with *The Best Of Toto*.

FUD was crying. He didn't know if it was pain, the disappointment, the frustration or what. But the tears were rolling down his face as he lay staring at the ceiling.

In the other bed, Craw was snoring. Loved his afternoon kip, Craw. He'd wake up in about 20 minutes, fresh as a daisy and hungry as a horse. You could read the boy like a book, he was never up nor down. Never seemed to get sick or injured, never seemed to have a care in the world.

Right now, Fud envied him more than anyone else in the world.

BLUE EYES tried getting through to Claire from a phone booth in the lobby. Fourth time today. It rang and rang, but no answer. Called the operator, asked if there was a fault reported for that number. Operator said no. Rang home again. Nothing.

Tried her mother again. Yes, she'd been there, but she'd gone. The kids were here if he wanted to speak to them. He did. He asked how they were, told them all about the hotel, said he couldn't wait to see them at Hampden and asked where mummy was. Both said they didn't know.

She was starting to piss him off big time.

4.30pm, Room 243, Loch Lomond Plaza

BOBBY BOTHWELL'S room was in total darkness. Reception had been told to put no calls through. His mobile was switched off.

Officially, he had a migraine. That was why he'd missed breakfast, skipped training, dodged the press conference and why Johnny McAndrew had been bumming around the pool, the snooker room and the TV lounge since lunchtime.

The truth was, he was simply shit scared – of Spuds turning up again, of one of his hoods grabbing him, of reporters, of the gaffer, of his own fucking shadow. Yesterday had freaked him so badly he didn't know if he could play tomorrow.

He knew he hadn't taken a bribe. He was damn sure the gaffer hadn't. And he believed his mates when they said they hadn't. There should be nothing to worry about. Except that the guy whose money appeared to have been used to bet against City was certain Bobby personally and the rest generally were involved and nothing would change his mind.

213

The only thing that would stop him causing Bobby serious GBH was a City win.

Oh, and a bag with £250,000 in it, on his doorstep – wherever the fuck that was – by ten on Monday morning.

The first bit Bobby was sure he could deliver. The second? If it came down to it, he could find the money. But how would he ever explain it to Mags, to the bank, to anybody? Anyway, he'd be admitting to Charlie Spuds that he DID have something to do with it all – and who knew if in that case he'd walk away without a hiding?

This was a living, walking, kneecap-knackering nightmare.

5.15pm, Balornock, Glasgow

A MAN responsible for the deaths of six people in the past two days as well as a failed £250,000 drug deal and for putting the frighteners on two young footballers straightened his tie and knocked the door.

His hands moved to smooth his hair as he heard footsteps in the hall. He checked his breath as the handle turned.

"Och, it's you, son. Come away in – yer tea's on."

"Hiya, mum – here, orchids for ye. Yer favourite."

"Aw, you're a lovely boy. C'mon, it's stovies."

"Ma favourite. Ye're a star, mum. Ah love ma Friday nights, Ah really do."

5.30pm, Glenbank Hotel

THEY giggled like schoolkids as they waited for the film show to start, making farty noises and kicking the chair of the guy in front. Tom needed three goes to shush them, finally clapping his hands and shouting.

"Right, children! Now, before we start, Fizzy's been on the blower an' I'm afraid it's not good news for young Barry. His knee's pretty bad and he'll be operated on as soon as possible. No idea how long it'll be, but we're talking the best bit of a year."

"Poor boy."

"Tragic, fuckin' tragic."

"Tragic right enough – so remember, when young Garry gets back, we support him. He's still part of this team and he'll be under big P without his brother, so let's stick close and keep his mind off it if we can."

They muttered no problem and we'll look after him.

"Right, eyes down for a full house – video of United's last league game, at home to Hearts. Good day to see them, because they won 4-2, so we see them at their best going forward but also get a peek at some weaknesses. I'll stop it and point out some stuff as we go along, but let's keep questions until the end or we'll be here all day, OK? OK. Bibs, lights."

The lights went down.

"Anybody got popcorn?"

"Shut up, Willie."

"Any nudey bits?"

"You too, Craw."

"Aye, you a good Christian tae!"

They settled down as the teams came out and the commentary started up. They knew they had to watch carefully, this was business now.

The team line-up appeared on the screen and commentator Archie Thatcher talked the viewers through it:

"In goals, Austrian internationalist Walter Salz – 17 clean sheets this season. The back four is Eric Thompson, signed this season from Sunderland, Mario Arrabiatta, Darius Senteanu and Ozzie Fish. The two wide men are Johnny McAndrew and Arie Van Hoffen, with young Scotland star Bobby Bothwell and Allan "The Dog" Brown in the centre. Up front today, 24-goal Dane Anders Jensen and £14million Paraguayan sensation Emilio Rozenkrantz.

"On the bench, five international stars worth a combined £54million – and Melvin Law still has six stars coming back from injury. Glasgow City are truly coming good at the right time of the season."

Tom sensed a depression settling over the room. "Hey, boys – they've only got two arms an' one dangly bit like youse have."

"Aye, but have ye heard about that Arrabiatta's dangly bit?"

They all howled at Willie's patter. Tom shushed them again.

He didn't have to. The re-run of a game many of them had already watched soon had them in awed silence.

City ran Hearts ragged, getting it wide and doing them for pace, playing neat little triangles around the box, hitting huge diagonal balls from the back to take out four and five opponents at a time.

Bothwell was magnificent, breaking up attacks and starting United going forward, linking everything. Even with nine men back, he threaded passes to his frontmen at will. Inside five minutes, he opened Wanderers up for Rozenkrantz to take a touch and slide a shot beyond the flailing keeper.

Ten minutes later, Jensen made a brilliant decoy run that took two men out of position and The Dog barrelled though to hit a shot that rattled the bar and gave Jensen a simple tap-in.

For the next 20 minutes, as they watched Hearts chase shadows, the United squad wondered if it was worth turning up at Hampden. They told Porridge they hoped he was watching as the visiting keeper made save after save to keep the score down. It was a massacre.

But then they got a lift.

Eight minutes from half-time, Arrabiatta brought the ball out of defence, was closed down by a striker, turned inside him, lost control, was robbed by a second striker and Hearts broke through to score.

Then, three minutes later, New Zealand-born left-back Fish was beaten for pace down the United left and when the cross came in, Salz slapped it to an onrushing striker's head. Two-two.

Tom stood up and told Bibs to put the sound down and the lights up. While the game went on across his chest, he addressed his troops.

"See – that's where they're weak. Give Arrabiatta space and he'll carry the ball 50, 60 yards. Ah've seen him go a' the way an' shoot – an' he can hit them, mind. But shut him down and ye see

216

what can happen. He overplays. He's too cocky. He gets caught. And the boy Fish? Milk turns quicker. If we get Taxi at him we can make inroads. Plus, the keeper's wee and doesnae like catchin' crosses. That's good."

"Aye, a' we need tae do now's get the fuckin' ba' aff them!"

They all laughed again, even Tom. "Aye, Willie, that's the problem. They're brilliant in possession. All we can do is keep our shape, close them down, don't let the quick players get down the sides – our wide boys have a hell o' a shift tae put in on Saturday."

"Taxi for Allan!"

"So listen, we'll watch the second half and see if anyone gets any hints off it, though the real clues were in what we've seen. Lights, Bibs."

He was right. Hearts stayed with it until the hour, but then their right-back tracked into the box with Jensen, the winger went down, the ref gave a penalty and sent the right-back off. Dog scored and that was that.

"Fuckin' homer, the boy's got tae be a Moslem."

"They always get the penalty when they need it."

Ten minutes from time, with the stadium already half-emptied of fans who'd seen enough and were off home to beat the traffic not realising they were the traffic, Rozenkrantz went through a stretched defence to dink his second over the keeper. He barely raised an arm to celebrate.

"Miserable wankers, eh? Ye'd think they'd be singin' and dancin' at bein' that good."

"Nah, they're spoiled. Too used tae it. That's why the punters are offski halfway through the second half every week."

"Let's hope they're away hame fed up on Saturday."

"How, you gonnae let them hear yer patter?"

"Fuck off."

Tom stood up and the lights went on. "Right, dinner's at half six. Ye can watch telly in the lounge till ten if ye want, but bed after

217

that. Good night's kip, lads, then the big one tomorrow. Getting close now, don't waste a minute of it."

Blue Eyes stood up and banged his hands together. "An' if ye can't get that through yer heads, just think o' young Barry in that hospital bed."

Lambchop hadn't thought of anything else for a single second all afternoon.

GARRY didn't speak all the way back. It had really shaken him up to see his brother lying there, too out of it on pills to realise the damage to his kicking leg. He'd cried again as soon as he walked into the room...

"Hey, it's me that's meant to be upset. See? The leg?"

"Sorry. Is it bad?"

"What?"

"Ye know what?"

"They won't know till the swellin' goes down."

"That means it's bad."

"They won't know till later."

"Ah know it is. Ah remember when he hit me. Who was it again? Craw?"

"Lambchop."

"Prick."

"It was an accident."

"Course it was. Nobody would be that stupid. Ah just remember the rippin' noise an' the burnin' – an' what about the ambulance driver? Was he collectin' potholes? It was a nightmare. Where are we?"

"Greenock."

"Is it rainin'?"

"Is Lambchop a halfwit?"

"Think Ah'll play again?"

"The piano? No bother."

"Seriously."

"Sure."

"Give it pelters for mum on Saturday."

"Don't, Ah'll bubble."

"Just remember, eh?"

"They gettin' ye a telly?"

"Don't know if Ah could watch."

"Don't be daft, it's us in the cup semi."

"You."

"Us. Ah'll wear your shinnies, so you'll feel it when Ah get kicked."

"Ah love you, pal."

"What've they given you? Morphine or E?"

"Dunno, there's a dodgy striplight in the corridor and it made me feel like dancin'."

"Ye'll need tae hop."

"You better go."

Garry leaned over and hugged him.

"Poof."

"Ah know, they want me to play on one leg, but Ah'm too soft."

When the door shut, they'd cried on either side of it.

Now, as they drove back to base, Fizzy broke the silence.

"You'll have to get that head up. There's nothing you can do now."

"That's what's guttin' me."

"No, Garry, you have to get that head up. The boys need it. You're a main man in this team, they don't need to be another man short. Gio's out, Barry's out, we need everyone else strong."

"Easy for you tae say."

"Listen, I've seen it a million times over. People get hurt. It's sad, but the rest have to get on with it. It's harder because he's your brother, but it still isn't you. It won't help anyone if your chin's on the carpet."

"Ah hear ye."

"Do you?"

"Yes, Ah promise."

"Don't promise me, promise Barry."

"Ah already have."

"Good boy."

Loch Lomond Plaza

SCOTT NEILL rang Melvin Law's room for the fourth time that afternoon to tell him that yet another reporter had been on sniffing about Bobby Bothwell's fitness.

"Who's feeding them this stuff?"

"Come on, boss, nobody has to feed them it. They knew he wasn't training because we let the cameras in for 15 minutes. Then at the press conference you hummed and hawed about him – so they go away and think about the whole betting thing and the edgy way he was last night and put two and two together."

"And making five and a half, Scott, that's the thing!"

"Yeah, maybe, but as far as they're concerned, the captain of the team alleged to be involved in a plot to throw the Scottish Cup semi goes AWOL out of the blue and no one's saying anything about it. Now, I'll keep fobbing them off all night if you like, but you know how it'll look in the morning."

"What have you told them so far?"

"That he has a slight temperature and was kept away from the boys as a precaution. End of story. Except that I don't know the story, Melvin, and that doesn't help me sound all that plausible."

"Sorry, Scott - but to be honest, I'm not sure I know it myself. Stall them for now, I'll phone you back soon."

Enough of this nonsense was enough.

Balornock, Glasgow

"BEAUTIFUL stovies, mum, ye've outdone yersel' the night."

"Only the best for ma baby. There's apple crumble an' custard for afters, that OK?"

"Mum, ye're an angel."

"Thae flowers are lovely, just lovely, ye spoil me."

"Behave, ma, Ah don't do half enough. Sorry Ah've no' phoned this week."

"Och, ye're busy, Charlie. Seems like ye never stop. Sometimes Ah think ye'll put yersel' in an early grave."

Charlie nearly choked on a lump of lamb.

"What's funny, son?"

"Aw, just a joke Ah remembered – but no' one Ah'd tell ma mother, that's for sure!"

"Ye're an awfy boy! So, what's yer week been like, then?"

Charlie Spuds chewed on another piece of meat as he re-ran the memory of Billy Andrews realising he was about to die, of Ian Cowan and his merry idiots the moment they *did* die and the terrified faces of Mark Weston and Bobby Bothwell. He swallowed, then smiled at his white-haired, pale-eyed, 77-year-old widowed mother, a woman who'd never asked any more from life than she was due and who'd rarely got it until her son started earning a few bob.

Even then, Charlie would never have been so cocky as to chuck cash at her – some others in his circle moved their folks into big houses, gave them personal drivers, sent them on flash holidays. But all that did was attract attention from the polis.

And apart from anything else, Cathie Kerr wouldn't have thanked you for it. Bearsden? Benidorm? Double-glazing and big-screen tellies? What did all that have to do with the likes of her?

No, she was happy to keep her wee flat nice and to see her only son every Friday teatime and for him to bring her flowers or maybe a wee box of chocs. She'd lived there when Charlie senior was alive and saw no need to move, even if the area had gone downhill a bit.

Not that her tenement had.

Not a letter of graffiti, not a scrap of rubbish in the tiny front yard, no winos or junkies hanging around. And *definitely* no break-ins. Not at Cathie Kerr's, not at Isa's next door, not at any of the six flats in the block. Not with Charlie Spuds to answer to.

Cathie Kerr didn't realise it, but she and her neighbours were the safest people in Glasgow.

"Ach, ye know, ma – bit o' this, bit o' that. Makin' a bob or two, losin' a bob or two."

"Ye look done in, son. Ye should relax a bit more, believe me."

Charlie Spuds laughed as he remembered lying outside his warehouse with a tranquilliser dart in his arse.

"Na, mum – lyin' down on the job's when you start losin' more than a bob or two – an' then who'd buy ye thae orchids?"

Room 243, Loch Lomond Plaza

BOBBY BOTHWELL ignored the rap on his door. And the second one. When the third became more insistent, he shouted to Johnny to give him peace.

"It's not Johnny, it's Melvin."

Bobby swore quietly as he swung his legs off the bed for the first time since – to be honest, he wasn't sure how long he'd be lying there, but it felt like days. He opened the door and motioned his boss in.

"Sorry. Johnny's been back and forward a' afternoon an' Ah've been asleep."

"Have you? Doesn't look like it."

"How?"

"The bed's made, Bobby."

"Aye. Right, well Ah was just dozin', really."

"Bobby, come on. I've covered for you all day. I've let your story about a migraine or a temperature or whatever it's meant to be filter out to keep the wolves away. But people are starting to ask questions – not least the chief exec, which is the last thing either of us need, eh?"

"Sure."

"So?"

Bobby sat down on the edge of his bed and held his head in his hands. He had to tell someone – and if there was one person in the world who he could trust with what it was he had to tell, it was Melvin Law.

"Gaffer, Ah'm in trouble."

"Trouble? What trouble?"

And so he poured out the whole story of his meeting with Charlie Spuds. By the end of it, his face was greyer and his eyes redder than a man with a genuine migraine.

"Good God, son, why keep this to yourself so long?"

"Did ye no' just hear the story, gaffer? They'll do me if Ah breathe a word!"

"Bobby, that's just playground bully stuff – tell teacher and I'll get you at four o'clock. Surely you must see we have to tell the police, get this handled officially?"

Bobby Bothwell actually managed a laugh, even if it was drier than July in Addis Ababa.

"Gaffer, surely you can see that it's no' as simple as that? Think about it – there's a £250,000 armed robbery earlier this week, right? But nobody reports anythin' stolen. What does that tell ye? That whoever got robbed deals wi' things without shoutin' for The Sweeney. If we phone the polis and try and sell them a story that Charlie Spuds is puttin' the arm on me because that £250,000 was stolen from him and he thinks Ah've got hold o' it to spend at William Hill's, they'll pull him an' he'll laugh in their faces. An' then he'll come round and mark mine."

"But-."

"No buts, gaffer. This isn't *The Bill*, this is real life – not your real life and thankfully not mine, but the way these kind o' halfwits live it. Doin' me in means nothin' tae them. Ah'm nothin'. He'd pay somebody to say Ah'd fell out a windae drunk or drugged oot ma tits. An' the polis'll buy it, because somewhere in their ranks there'll be somebody that he's got somethin' on an' they'll file the inquiry under B for Bin. Naw, gaffer, there's only one way round this."

"You want to pull out of the game? Because in the circumstances it's no prob-."

"Naw, NAW! Ah NEED tae play, can ye no' see that? If Ah'm no' there that's the first clue that we're on the bung. Look, us winnin' this game's the easy bit. Let me out there an' Ah'll take them on single-handed if Ah need tae. They're pish, let's be honest."

"Well, it'd be silly to underestim-."

"Look, gaffer, it's me ye're talkin' tae here. If we don't beat them we should a' get the bullet fae City – which'll mean Ah get it twice, eh? So, naw, Ah play. We win. No arguments."

"So what's the hard bit?"

"Gettin' the £250,000 back tae the maniac."

"Look, Bobby, I can talk to the chairman. You know he used to be a director at the National Allied Bank. He could sort something. We can arrange it."

"Aye? An' who pays it back? The club? That'd look tops on the balance sheets, eh? Or are you offerin'? Naw, it's down tae me. An' there's only one way."

"Bobby, don't sell your house. Don't do it to your family."

"Ma house? Don't be daft, gaffer – Ah'm bettin' on masel' for first goal."

"You're WHAT?"

"Bettin' on masel' tae score the first goal. Ah'm 9/1. Ah can get ma brother tae put thirty grand on credit wi' a bookie we know, nae problem. That's £270,000, plus ma stake back – Ah'd even end up 20 grand ahead on the deal!"

Law thought his captain was getting hysterical.

"Bobby, calm down. This is madness, son - £30,000 of your own money on yourself to score the first goal? It's a hell of a gamble - what if you lose?"

"Then Ah get the team bus tae drop me at the Clydeside an' Ah hoof masel' into the water. Listen, gaffer, Ah'll take every free-kick, any penalties, shoot on sight, Ah'll try an' score direct fae corners – surely it's worth it tae get this lunatic aff ma back?"

"Well, I can't say I-."

"Gaffer!"

"OK, Bobby, OK. You place your bet. I'll forget you ever told me. I'll go and tell the press you're feeling fine after a good rest and will definitely play tomorrow, OK? Good. Now, you do what you have to do then get downstairs and see your team-mates and act like the captain of Glasgow City instead of some bloke on a witness protection programme, eh? We're watching a video of Ochil United at seven. I want you there."

"No sweat, Ah could dae wi' a laugh."

6.15pm, Room 316, Glenbank Hotel

WILLIE WALTERS sang nonsense lyrics as he wandered the room drying himself.

"Don't you want some gravy – gonnae score a go-o-o-ole – doobedoobe baby – or Ah'll be on the do-o-o-ole..."

"Willie?"

"What? You got a request?"

"Aye, fuck up."

"Ooooohhhh..."

"What you gonnae dae wi' the dosh an' the bookies pay out after a'?"

"If? IF? It's a stick-on, me old sausage!"

"Seriously..."

"Ye think they will pay out?"

"Aye, if it's obvious that we've won fair an' square, that City havenae thrown it. They cannae no' honour the bets, can they?"

"So a' we need tae dae is overpower the mighty Glasgow City on merit an' hope that along the way they make absolutely no comic-cuts errors that could be construed as deliberate? Sounds reasonable."

Gibby was lying on his bed, staring at the ceiling, shaggy eyebrows knitted together in a frown like mating caterpillars.

"Seriously, Willie. What if we win an' we get rich overnight. How ye gonnae handle the dosh?"

"Serious? Ah don't know, Gib, Ah really don't. Thought about a' the usual stuff – flash motor, big holiday, pay the mortgage aff. But how d'ye explain it tae the wife or the neighbours or the bank manager, for that matter?"

"Ah know."

"An' it's not like the bank's gonnae treat me droppin' 200 grand intae the deposit account like an everyday occurrence, is it?"

"They'd think ye were an Irish hold-up merchant."

"Precisely. So Ah'm at a loss. Never thought that'd happen if Ah was gonnae get rich overnight, did you?"

"Nope. Think Ah'd go for the mortgage option, square the overdraft, set up two or three smaller building society accounts, spread it about a bit."

"Wee bit Johnny Sensible, innit?"

"Better that than giein' it Sammy Big-Baws an' endin' up caught. Ah mean, look what happened tae Westy wi' a daft wee engagement ring. Listen, when'll we ever get another chance tae get oursels secure for our old age?"

"Aye, assumin' we reach old age seein' as that mobster bloke's still kickin' about."

"Har bastard har."

Room 243, Loch Lomond Plaza

"BOAB??"

"Stevie! Did he take it?"

"Boab, what's this a' about?"

"Did he take it?"

"Aye, aye. Took some convincin' mind – he's havin' to run about layin' it aff just in case you dae the business."

"Who d'you say was puttin' the money on?"

"Me an' the boys. We just fancy you big time for a goal an' the odds are too good tae miss."

"Great. Ah owe ye."

"Boab, what's goin' on? You sound mingin'."

"Ah'm fine, been a bit dicky the day, that's a' - in an' oot the bog non-stop. Tired, havnae eaten since last night. Ah'll be up for it the morra, no worries."

"Well, ye'd better be. Ah know you drap thirty grand runnin' for a bus, but Ah'm shittin' bricks already."

"Trust me."

"It's no' you, it's thae fannies ye play wi'!"

"Night, night, bro'."

"Keep it in yer trousers."

The Lambie Suite, Glenbank Hotel

THIS was the bit Blue Eyes had been waiting for all week. Fun time. His time.

Karaoke time.

He'd got the hotel to hire in all the gear, but he'd brought a pile of his own discs just to make sure there was plenty of choice.

Blue Eyes lived for karaoke. If they gave out awards for the guy who threw the best karaoke parties, he'd win hands down every year. Give him a machine and a mike and he could make an empty room rock.

Of course, this would be a karaoke night with a difference. Just for once, the boys would have to get up and sing sober – but hey, the abuse they'd throw at each other would get them charged up every bit as much as the bevvy.

Not that Blue Eyes missed having a drink. He never touched it. Didn't need it to be hyper, just needed the boys to bounce crack off, a few sorts to flirt with. And, of course, a bit of Sinatra to warble.

His folks used to say he was singing Sinatra before he could talk. Mum used to listen to his records non-stop when she was pregnant. And when Mr and Mrs Albert were blessed with a son, there was no argument that he'd be called Francis.

When the other kids were into Duran Duran and George Michael, Blue Eyes could rattle off any Sinatra number you could mention. Listened to mum and dad's albums until he knew every syllable off by heart.

227

He'd cried for two days when the man died. Part of his childhood died with him. But now, here, was where he kept the memory alive. Karaoke.

"Right, girls, it's the big one – Hampden tomorrow, Glasgow City, the cup final just round the corner. Nervous? You should be, Porridge, you're a shite keeper. An' don't you laugh, Craw, that Arrabiatta's gonnae boot your arse. Anyway, what better way tae relax than a wee singedy-song? I've thrown the door open to our fellow residents and the lovely waitresses once they come off duty, just tae be sociable, like. So – who's gonnae be first up."

"We know who's first up. We always know who's first up. You'll be first up, bawbag!"

"Well, Gio, who am Ah to flaunt tradition?"

He fiddled with a knob or two, then pressed a button. The video screen went pink and, as the intro drifted out of the speakers, up came the title I've Got You Under My Skin.

And he was off. No longer skipper of a part-time football team, but the reincarnation of Francis Albert Sinatra. Young Blue Eyes was back.

The boys wound him up rotten about his obsession – but they had to admit he was good. As he threw himself into it, fingers clicking and head swaying, they whistled and clapped and shouted gaun yersel'.

A middle-aged couple popped their heads round the door leading from the bar. Blue Eyes never missed a beat as he broke away from the lyrics and called for them to join the party. They nodded at each other and brought their drinks with them. Two girls in their twenties hung around the door nervously and immediately got the treatment.

"Lay-deez! Come in an' grab a lap! We've been waitin' for you!"

They giggled, shrugged and grabbed a seat at a table beside Fud, Craw, Jimmy and Gio, who turned on their collective charm like floodlights.

When Blue Eyes finished, the room roared and clapped. He winked at his audience, pressed another button and eased seamlessly into Leroy Brown. It was going to be a top night – especially as his wee waitress pal had just sneaked in at the back of the room with three tasty mates.

TOM wasn't joining in the fun. Didn't feel like it. Didn't feel like hellish much right then, except maybe throwing himself off a very high bridge.

The conversation kept running over and over in his head.

"Listen, Tom, you and I have something special. We always will. You're the only man I'll ever truly, truly love. But it never worked first time and it sure as hell wouldn't work all these years later. I think Wednesday night proved that."

"Caroline, I'm really sorry about that – but what could I do? It was the worst possible time for an interruption, but-."

"No, Tom, you're wrong – it was the best possible time. It was reality slapping me round the face just as fantasy was taking me over. The food, the wine, the memories, the thought of how it used to be – another ten minutes and you'd have had me."

He wanted to be sick when she said that.

"So why let something stupid like that ruin it all? Why not concentrate on all the other stuff?"

"Because reality's what I'd be left with 23 hours of the day. The reality that you'll never be able to give your job any less than 110 per cent no matter what the cost to your personal life. That's how it was last time, and that's how it'd be this time."

"But-."

"No, Tom, no buts. There would always be something. And don't tell em you could change – when you did that before you were miserable as sin. Face facts, you might love me-."

"Oh God, Caroline, I do."

"-but the truth is that only football makes you truly happy."

"So are you telling me we can't be together?"

"Do you think you can be? I mean, were you planning to propose or something the other night."

Silence.

"Oh God, Tom – you were, weren't you? Oh Tom, I'm so sorry. You poor-."

"No sympathy, Caroline. I'd not a poor anything, I'm just an idiot."

"No, Tom, no – you're not. I'm so flattered, so touched. I never thought you'd ever feel like that again. Why didn't you say?"

"Because something got in the way. Like you said, something always does. So is this it, then?"

"Look Tom, let's not rush into saying anything we'd regret. You've got a huge match tomorrow, concentrate on that for now. We'll sleep on it and speak when it's out of the way, eh?"

"Sure. I'll phone you. Goodnight, Caroline."

"Goodnight, Tom. And good luck."

He didn't know if she meant tomorrow or forever. But either way it didn't really bother him much. He couldn't see himself phoning her, that was for sure.

"SO who's up next? Fudster? Givin' us yer world-infamous Elvis?"

"Later, skip."

"Poof. Porridge? Westy? Don't make me pick someone and make an example of them in front of all these lovely people, now."

"Right, Bluey, Disc 12, track 9. An' gie's that mike!"

"All right! Lay-deez and gennelmen – I give you the one, the only, the enormous, the legend – Willie "Fats Domino's Pizza" Waaaaaaalllllters!!"

"OK, folks, join in if ye know it – a-one-two-three – *I've got sunshy-ee-ine, on a clou-ee-oudy day-ay...*"

Taxi Allan clapped along with the rest of the room and knew it was almost time to face his demons once and for all.

MELVIN LAW was content for the first time all week. No more fretting about tactics, about the opposition, about the lack of effort

230

he sensed from his players. Not even a worry about whether or not his squad were as honest as he'd told the world they were.

He'd made a decision. And it had taken him aback just how happy it made him.

He'd been fed up with so much about football for so long now – the spiralling wages, the religious bigotry, the press intrusion, the lack of goals, the poor refereeing, the shocking language from the stands and from the pitch, the desperate grubbing for money that had turned it from The People's Game into a share dealer's plaything.

But this business with the betting coup was the straw that had broken the camel's back. Whatever happened tomorrow, his club's image was tarnished. If they won, they'd get no credit. If they lost? No one would believe they hadn't thrown it – and that would be unbelievably unfair on Ochil United. The greatest giantkilling of all time, dismissed as a cheat's victory? The prospect was truly, truly awful.

Too awful for a man of honour like Melvin Law to handle.

Which was why tomorrow's Scottish Cup semi-final would be his final game.

He had already written the letter. It was addressed to the chairman – quite deliberately so, even though his own direct boss was the chief executive. He wasn't giving that idiot Driscoll the pleasure of reading it first.

As soon as his mind was made up, a change seemed to come over him. His body relaxed. His head cleared. His breathing, his heart, his pulse all slowed. He put the TV on and laughed at an old episode of *Blackadder*. He even poured himself a glass of wine from the minibar while he was watching it.

Then he phoned Amanda, told her how much he loved her, apologised for neglecting her all these years, asked to speak to the children and told them daddy was taking them to Disneyland.

He'd find out later that when he hung up, they started crying and told mummy that daddy had finally gone mad.

"WHAT about that, people – the wonderful Frankie "Fud" O'Donnell with *A Little Less Conversation*. And if you've ever spent time in the boy's company, you'll know that's a brilliant idea. So, who's next on The Golden Shot?"

"Me."

"Sensational – Taxi Allan, ladies and gentlemen – old big ears is back! So, what's your song, wee man."

The winger handed his captain a scrap of paper. He looked nervous as a teenager making his first-team debut. Blue Eyes looked at the paper and back at his pal.

"You sure, son?"

"Abso-bastard-lutely."

"Okey-doke. Just let me get the disc – and in we go – press the buttons – aaaand - take it away, Dumbo!"

The arpeggio running up and down the piano keyboard sent a chill through the wee man. This was horrible. But he had to do it if he was finally to beat his curse. The piano reached a mini-crescendo and he took a deep breath.

"At first Ah was afraid – Ah was petrified..."

And the crowd cheered.

GIOVANNI was having a ball, particularly since the blonde one of the pair from the bar had started rubbing his thigh under the table. He pretended not to notice as they bawled along with *I Will Survive*, but that only seemed to egg her on.

He only had one worry. He could see two Taxis up on stage. One of the big-eared twats was enough, but his twin? That was taking the piss.

Either some tosser has spiked his drink. Or he had concussion.

He prayed some tosser had spiked his drink.

HE was into the instrumental bit now – and loving every note of it. He boogied across the little raised stage, rubbing up against

Blue Eyes, twirling the mike by its flex, playing to the crowd big time. And they came right back at him.

To think all these years he'd loathed this song. And now it was making him a star.

"*Ohhhhhhhhh...*"

And they all went *Ohhhhhhhhhh...*

"*Oooh now go, walk out the door, just turn around now, you're not welcome a-nee-more...*"

AMIDST the singing and the cheering, Jimmy D whispered in the blonde's ear that they could slip upstairs if she fancied.

She slid her hand another inch higher on Gio's leg and whispered back to Jimmy to go play with himself.

"THANK YOU – thank you very much – you're bee-yoo-riful – I'm here till Thursday, don't forget to tip yer waitress!"

Taxi milked the thunderous applause, the whistles and the thumping on tables for all he was worth. Blue Eyes came across and hugged him.

"Wee man, ye're a ledge!"

"Ach, yer arse – here, ye've no' got that *Africa* by Toto in among thae CDs..?"

Room 201, Loch Lomond Plaza

MELVIN LAW was onto his second bottle of Chianti when he decided to make the call. He picked up the receiver, punched four numbers and tried not to giggle.

"Aye?"

"Mr Brown? Mr Alan Brown?"

"Aye, who wants t'knur, like?"

Law had on his gruffest Scottish accent.

"The name's Ronnie McHenry from the *News of the World*. We're running a story this Sunday that you've been havin' a gay affair wi' yon Noel Edmonds aff the television. Is there anythin' ye'd like tae say before we print?"

"What? No – Ah mean – Ah nevva – Ah'm not – listen, me lawyas'll be reet onto yee lot the morra, mind – Ah'll tek yee fu every penny, how, man, like, man!"

"I'll take that as a quote then, Mr Brown. Goodnight!"

Law put the phone down and burst out laughing.

Dog hit himself on the forehead with the receiver and swore out loud. How the bollocks had they found that out?

11.50pm, Room 322, Glenbank Hotel

GIO was seeing double again, though this time he wasn't worried in the least.

The blonde and her mate back for afters?

Winning the semi, the cup and the UEFA bloody Cup wouldn't beat this for a result.

12.45am, Room 243, Loch Lomond Plaza Hotel

JOHNNY McANDREW got the phone.

"Hello? Who's this?"

"Is Bobby there, please?"

"Haud on. Bobby, wake up – phone for you."

"Fuckin' hell, what time is it? Gie's it here."

The City skipper rubbed his eyes and tried to focus in the dark.

"Hello? It's Bobby?"

"A'right, son? Just a wee call tae say good luck in the big game. Yer pals are rootin' for ye, remember that. See ye!"

Click. Brrrr.

Bobby Bothwell's stomach churned.

"Who was it?"

"Whit?"

234

"Who was on the phone!"

"Och, some wanker at the nonsense. Ah'll leave it aff the hook. Now get some fuckin' sleep, we've got a game tae win!"

Saturday

8.22am

TOM saw the sun stream through his curtains and wished it was still dead of night. This was a morning he didn't want to come, not yet, not today.

The greatest few hours of his life? What a joke. He'd been patched by the woman he loved, his chairman was on his case because half his team were either on bail or on crutches – and now even his lifelong dream of leading a team to the Scottish Cup Final was tarnished, because if he did nobody would believe the other team hadn't been on the take.

No matchday morning ever felt so grey.

FUD stirred and waited for the first stab in the privates, but there was nothing. No nagging, no burning, no knitting needles. He lay still and breathed out long and hard, thinking that maybe everything was going to be all right after all.

Maybe it'd just been a pull that needed rest. Maybe it'd sorted itself out during the night. Maybe it'd all been in his stupid mind, just nerves showing themselves in some weird way. The phone on the table between their beds rang. He reached out to pick it up before it woke Craw. He yelled in agony , startling his mate out of sleep and making him shoot bolt upright.

His groin was worse than ever. And it was a fuckpigging wrong number.

236

TAXI took a few bars to tune into his wake-up request. Then he started catching lyrics. A distinctive voice, a little nasal, loaded with emotional and laced with put-on Southern drawl.

"Ah sat on the roof ... and kicked off the maw-aw-aw-awsss..."

It was ... hey, it was *Your Song*.

Bloody hell, it was only his all-time favourite, no-better-one-ever-made record. Lee Allan was actually hearing a song in his head that he fuckin' liked.

Last night's trauma therapy session downstairs had worked.

Today really was going to be the best day of his entire life.

8.29 am and 59 seconds, Loch Lomond Plaza

MELVIN LAW woke a split-second before the alarm buzzed and reached for the Off button. He never understood why some people let it buzz. What was the point of an alarm buzzing if you were already awake? It was illogical.

He didn't rub his eyes or scratch his bits or turn over for another sneaky five minutes in the sack. He didn't have to wonder where he was or what day it was. He was in bed and it was time to get up, so that was what he did.

Why would people have a time to get up and then try to get back to sleep for another five minutes? There was no point. And why scratch out of sheer habit if you were not itchy? He took off his pyjamas, folded them, packed them in his Used Clothes case, showered, shaved, dressed and went for breakfast.

He looked at his watch. Seventeen minutes to nine. Perfect. He would be sitting at his table at exactly quarter to. He would have cereal and toast and scrambled eggs and coffee and be finished by five past, have a walk in the grounds until 18 minutes past, be in his room for 20 past, read the newspapers for nine minutes, tidy them away by half past, at precisely which time his assistant Dennis Farrell and coach Stan Roberts would knock his door for their regular-as-clockwork tactics meeting.

At 10.30 he would send them off, pack his belongings, have the hotel come and take them to the bus, then phone his wife, his mother and his girlfriend in that order, completing his calls at 10.58 and going downstairs to begin the team meeting at 11am on the dot.

Any player even one second late would be fined £100. More than one minute late and it doubled. Five minutes and they would not play that day – cup final or no cup final. He'd left McAndrew out of an Ancient Firm derby for being late for the morning team meeting. It hadn't mattered that he'd been stuck between floors in a broken lift. A Melvin Law player thought ahead for every eventuality.

From that day on, McAndrew had always taken the stairs.

DOG felt sleepy. He didn't know why, he'd had his normal night-before-a-game supper - two party-size boxes of Smarties and nine double vodkas and Red Bull.

He'd been absolutely sure he'd stay awake when the door had gone and it'd been Bobby the kitman with a big pot of decaf for him. He'd said the gaffer had sent it as a little treat for his favourite player.

It'd been good stuff, too – especially when he tipped in three miniatures of Baileys. But on his third cup, he'd got woozy. He was watching Terminator VI on his personal DVD player, but suddenly the robots went all wibbly and he could understand Arnie. Something was definitely wro-zzzzzzzzzzzz.

Dog didn't know Melvin Law knew the only way to stop his man-child talisman going on a pre-match hyperactive frenzy was to slip him six valium.

Even logical men could be devious when they had to.

Dog had felt like this once before, when the England gaffer had sent him up a cheesecake the night before the European Championship game with Italy and he'd fallen asleep with two-thirds of it left. He'd wakened up with it on his face and had had to eat his way out.

He'd felt odd that morning too, listless, tired. Normal? Yeah, that was it – normal. Dog on six valium was like an ordinary bloke wired to the moon on caffeine. There was only one thing to do, the same as he'd done that time with England.

He reached out of bed, into his bag, pulled out a giant bar of tablet. He lay in bed with the cartoons on and ate the lot before going for breakfast. A plate of bacon and eggs and he'd be cutting up socks again in no time.

GIBBY and Willie were watching telly, flicking through the mound of papers they'd ordered the night before and arguing about whether to go down for breakfast or shout it in. Willie fancied room service, mainly because he fancied the wee lassie who delivered it. Gibby wanted to go down and see who was kicking about.

"I mean, it's the big game. We should take it all in."

"Aye, right, Blackie Gray. Let's never forget a single moment of the day we couldnae get a game at Hampden, eh?"

"Fuck's sake, Wulls, whit's up wi' you? Ye're as miserable as Tuesday night in Renfrew. Get yerself motivated – Ah mean, check out the *Record*."

He held up its back page, with the giant headline:

MIR-OCHIL MEN!
Minnows vow to make cup history

Willie was reading the *Scottish Sun*, which had gone with:

BETCHA WE CAN BEAT THE ODDS

Gibby had chucked his paper down and picked up the *Scotsman*, whose back page read:

Part-time outsiders confident of ability to upset apple cart with spirited show against runaway cup favourites

"Jesus, ye see this lot, Walters? This is the only game in town, ma son. How can ye NO' lap it up?"

"Because Ah've got as much chancea playin' this afty as Ah have of havin' a good Tuesday night oot in Renfrew."

"But ye always knew that. How come ye're suddenly on suicide watch?"

"Because, ma happily moronic pal, Ah'm tryin' like fuck not tae let it get tae me. Until yesterday Ah thought Ah had a chance. Tom even told me he wouldnae drop me because o' the pub fight business. Then he pits Fud up front wi' Craw in trainin' yesterday. An' Ah'm left thinkin' that if Ah act like Ah don't care that Ah'm no' oot there for the biggest game in history, maybe Ah'll start tae really no care, know' mean?"

"No' really."

"Gibby, if Ah don't play the day Ah'll regret it forever. The guys oot there might see me as some dopey gink who disnae care about nothin', but Ah love fitba and Ah've never wanted anythin' oota the game like Ah've wanted tae play in a cup final. THE cup final. An' it's no' gonnae happen, so Ah'm tryin' tae affect this façade of no' giein' a monkey's."

"Ahhh..."

"Except, braindead, Ah've now blown ma cover by tellin' you that it's a big front. So you're gonnae have tae kid on ye don't know."

"Don't know what?"

"That Ah don't care."

"Ah was bein' ironic."

"Well, don't. Just order ma breakfast. An' don't spare the tottie scones."

MARIO ARRABIATTA stretched at the window, tall and chiselled and utterly naked. Two chambermaids carrying towels from the main building to the chalets across by the lake looked up and gawped and he pretended not to see them, just like he always did when he was standing naked at a window for attention.

He flexed his pecs one last time then strolled back across the room to check himself in the mirror. Dio mio, he looked good. Then it struck him.

"Are you in the shower?"

"Yes? What?"

"Nothing, I speak to you when you finished."

He heard the water shut off, then Uruguayan striker Emilio Rozenkrantz came out, a towel round his waist and another rubbing at his long, black hair.

"What?"

"Do you remember the name of this team we're playing today?"

BLUE EYES woke up unhappy because he'd phoned home last night and a bloke had answered. He'd put the phone down and called back and this time got Claire.

He'd asked who the guy was.

What guy, she'd said. He must have dialled the wrong number.

He'd said no, he'd hit redial on his moby.

She'd said there must be a crossed line somewhere.

He'd said aye, between us.

She'd told him he was being stupid.

He'd said if he found out she was-.

She'd said, what, doing the same as you? Having a wee bit fun on the side?

He'd said she'd better be kidding.

She'd said nothing.

He'd asked to speak to the kids.

She'd said they were staying at her mother's.

241

He'd said, so it's just you an' Harry Handsome?

She'd told him he was a lunatic and hung up.

He'd phoned back. The machine had clicked in. He'd phoned back. Same again. Five times. Eventually she'd picked up and told him she'd see him at the hotel when the wives were brought in for their own pre-match lunch.

He'd said not to bother. Then he'd hung up.

She hadn't rung back.

CRAW had wakened up unhappy because the phone had gone at ten to five and Fud hadn't heard it, so he'd got up and answered and it had been that wanker Gibby wanting to know some guff about never-ending pictures.

GIO had wakened up as excited as a kid on Christmas morning. Then he remembered that he'd been a bad little boy and Santa wasn't coming to him this year. He put his hand to the back of his head and felt the lump. It was nothing, didn't even hurt any more. But it was still enough to keep him out of the biggest game of his life.

He swore so loudly Shyness ran dripping from the shower to make sure his mate hadn't just had a terrible accident.

"You a'right, son?"

"Fucking magic, Shyness, just fucking magic."

CHOPPER was unhappy because late last night he'd asked Ginge if he was excited about hearing the team for Saturday and had been told that no, Ginge couldn't care less. Chopper had slaughtered him, because with Barry out Ginge had a real chance of playing, but his pal had tut-tutted and said what was the point of getting uptight about daft football?

Chopper had said he'd be climbing the walls if he had a chance of playing and Ginge had said that was the difference between them.

Yet Ginge had also wakened up unhappy, because the truth was that if he wasn't in that team now it would kill him.

GARRY RONALD turned over, saw his twin's empty bed and started to cry again. All he'd ever wanted was for the two of them to share a day like this – not to have the day for himself, but for them both. For dad, for Mhairi. Most of all, for mum. And now it had all been taken away.

He felt his own knee throb. He'd been getting it since yesterday, some kind of sympathy pain. Stupid? Course it was, he couldn't cry off with an imaginary injury, but he wished he was hurt for real. He wondered what Barry was doing and thinking right then.

BARRY RONALD, of course, was thinking and doing exactly the same things in his hospital bed, right down to the tears.

TAXI felt magic. He'd slept great, had a top breakfast, the weather was brilliant as he'd taken his walk with Craw, Gio and Porridge. For the first time in ages, his head was clear of guff.

"Where's Fud."

"Watchin' telly, Ah think."

"Thought you two were joined at the hip."

"Listen smouty, they'd need tae join you at the hip tae a sausage dug."

"Wooo..."

"Hey, you two – rap it. Ye're blowin' ma cup final mornin' high."

"You been at Screech's dope stash, Porridge?"

"Nah, just right up for it. It's some feelin' eh – in a few hours we'll be there, Hampden, takin' on some o' the most famous players in the business. What a rush, man, eh?"

Taxi and Craw could only nod and picture it in their own heads. Then all three realised at the same time how Gio must be feeling.

"Sorry, pal."

"Don't worry. What can ye do? Ah'm out, so Ah'm out."

"Are ye definitely, definitely sure ye're out, though? Ah mean, there's nae medical rule that says ye've got to be left out, is there?"

"Nah, but Tom's no' gonnae take a chance wi' a head knock, no' wi' the way the chairman's been about the whole pub fight bollocks. His heid's on the block."

"Fuck the chairman, that's what Ah'd say. Pick the best team for the game."

"So that's you fucked, Taxi."

"Get it up ye! Listen, Gio's been outstandin' – how should he miss out because o' this? Ah mean, if he got a whack on the napper in trainin' he wouldnae be left out, would he?"

"True."

"Never thought o' that."

"Ah, well, let's just wait an' see, eh? If the gaffer wants me, Ah'm his man. But Ah've got masel' psyched for no' playin'. Anythin' else is a bonus. Ah think Ah'm just jinxed for semi-finals anyway."

"How?"

"When Ah was at the Bankies – before they fucked aff tae America, like – we made the semis, mind? We got the Hibees at Motherwell. What a chance we had."

"Ah'll never work out how ye lost it that year."

"Tell me about it. Gerry Brogan missed a sitter at 0-0 wi' 20 minutes left. Four yards out, hit the keeper. They broke away, we got caught, two in on me, Ah commit, ba' knocked across me, other guy taps in. Ah never felt so low."

"What d'ye say tae Brogan?"

244

"Nothin' - naebody spoke tae him. It was horrible, man. Naebody even looked at him. He was still sittin' there when we were a' in the bath. Ah got changed an' he was still there, a' muddy. He might still be sittin' there for a' Ah know."

"Hope no' – they knocked doon Fir Park two year ago."

"Good enough for him. He did us right in that day. Ah'll never forget that."

They walked in silence for a few seconds before Taxi spoke.

"Think anybody'll end up like that the day? Know' mean, let us doon?"

"Ah just hope it's no' me."

Porridge's little public prayer never even registered with Craw. All he could think of was Fud and his fuckin' groin.

10.59am, Loch Lomond Plaza

JOHNNY McANDREW was halfway down the stairs with his bags before he realised he'd left the sink running. He stopped and thought about going back for it. Then he remembered the last time he'd been late.

"Fuck it. Prices they charge they can afford the repairs."

MELVIN LAW had decided to have his team-talk before lunch. It wouldn't take long, then they could enjoy their food. He cleared his throat for attention.

"No rules on food today. Order what you like off the menu and, as it's a special occasion, you may have one glass of wine each."

He smiled as they shot each other glances that suggested their boss had gone mad. Alcohol was banned from mid-June to the end of May and they were on stricter diets than a supermodel trying for a pipe-cleaner ad campaign.

"Anyway, the waitresses will be around in a few minutes. I won't keep you long."

Now the players began to wonder if their gaffer had secretly quit and was trying to sabotage them. Usually his pre-match talks lasted at least an hour. He went over and over and over the opposition, the set-pieces for and against, the pitch, the referee, the weather, everything.

But the reason Law had wakened later than usual this morning was that he'd gone to sleep later than usual last night and the reason for that was that he'd been rethinking his plans for this game.

All week he'd told the press how he had the utmost respect for Ochil United, how he'd had them watched repeatedly, how he knew they had players who could cause his team problems if his team were not careful, how in football anything was possible.

Now he'd decided it was time to tell the truth.

"OK, listen. This game's very straightforward for us because we're better than they are. We're better in goals, in defence, in midfield and in attack. If we need them, we have subs who are better than their subs. If things go wrong, I'll change them because I'm a better manager than their manager. We'll go out and get an early goal and once we do we'll get more goals and even if we get sloppy and give them a chance to score we'll score more goals. We can afford to take chances at the back and play tricks in midfield because they'll not be good enough to do anything with the ball even if they take it off us. They need to be at least three or four times over their best to have a chance and even then we have to be ten or twenty times below our best – and that's not going to happen. It's not possible. In football, anything can sometimes happen, but not today. Today, only the obvious can happen. Don't believe all the nonsense about us having everything to lose. We have nothing to lose, we are big and rich and famous and they are small and poor and nobodies. Tomorrow they'll go back to being nobodies, but we will all still be rich and famous and big. That's the truth of it. The team is the same as played last Saturday and the subs will be on the board at Hampden. But don't worry if you don't know if you'll be on the bench, have a good lunch anyway if you

246

wish. It's OK today. It's not serious. We'll win and we will win well. Ochil United shouldn't worry you, because they don't worry me at all. Enjoy your day - and relax. Life's good."

The Lambie Suite, Glenbank Hotel

"BELIEVE ME – they'll be more worried about you than you are about them. They're the ones with everything to lose – we've *nothin'* to lose. Everyone expects us to get a doin' – so let's prove them wrong, eh? Eh? Are you with me, boys?"

Tom didn't really expect them to stand up and yell YEAH!, but he was into his stride and revelling in his own rhetoric.

"OK, ye've seen the video and ye've seen them often enough other times yerselves anyway. Ye a' know they can be outstandin', but Ah want ye tae forget the good stuff. Concentrate on the weaknesses – an' we a' saw them in the video the other night, eh? The keeper's too wee and punches too much – get in about him early – Blue Eyes, Jimmy Ah'm lookin' for you at our corners – an' midfield, be around the box for crumbs. Pressurise that big poser Arrabiatta. If we let him wander he'll go 30, 40, 70 yards and have a field day. Put him under P and he'll wobble. Senteanu's slow as a week in the jail, he'll never react if ye rob his pal. Rattle McAndrew's cage early doors an' he'll no' come back. Jimmy, yon Rozenkrantz's right knee's still dodgy, get it? Good. Midfield, hold ontae the Dog's shorts when ye can – he hates that, he'll have a dig an' end up in bother. Rattle them a' round the pitch. Get in about them. Unsettle them. Ah don't care if we're never on the ba' in the first ten minutes, as long as they're no'. And remember this – ye'd be amazed how often in these games the wee team gets a chance in the opening minutes, when we're fired up an' they're swannin'. Take it when it comes and this could be our day."

He scanned their faces for nerves, for confidence, for fear, for arrogance. He saw what he liked to believe was quiet determination. He felt good.

"OK, here's the moment ye've been waitin' for. Now, one or two will be upset tae be on the bench, some won't be playin' at all – but ye're a' involved. Ye've a' got a role tae play. Even if ye're no' stripped, ye can help in the dressin' room, be supportive, run for tie-ups, anythin'. We're in this together."

Ginge wished he'd just hurry up and put him out of his misery.

"In goals, Porridge – back four, Rowland George-"

Chopper slapped his mate on the back and whispered good on you. Ginge looked sideways at him like somewhere a village was missing its idiot.

"-Francis Albert, Jimmy Donaldson and Garry Ronald. Midfield, Lee Allan, Steven McCracken, Giovanni Wilson-"

Gio nearly fell off his seat.

"-and Mark Weston. Up front-."

Willie prepared himself for the worst moment of his life.

"-Frank O'Donnell and Crawford Brown."

Willie wanted to set fire to the hotel.

"Subs – Harri Baum, Ally McGonigall, Danny Campbell-."

Lambchop never flickered.

"-Gibby Johnson-."

All the tension seemed to come out of Gibby like a burst rubber doll.

"-and Willie Walters."

After that he went into "the rest of you can still play a part" mode, a little pat on the head for those not in the 16. Lambchop should have felt sorry for them, but somehow he actually *envied* the twats.

For the first time in a long time, his expectations had been exceeded. He was actually on the bench for a Scottish Cup semi-final. He had nothing to moan about.

What's more, he might just be put in the position of having to back up all the moaning he'd done before.

He felt ill.

Tom clapped his hands amidst the babble his announcement had caused. "Right, boys, have a cuppa then be on the bus ready tae rock for 12.30. Good luck boys – an' try tae enjoy every minute o' yer day."

It'd gone down well. A few banged on tables and shouted Come On. Backs were slapped as men got up to stretch their legs and check bags. Heed stood and shouted for quiet.

"Listen, you twats – if Ah'm no' good enough to get in that 16 it's mibbes time Ah chucked it. But while me and the other naebodies contemplate our options – like whether tae have two pies or three before Ah go intae the stand – let me just say this. Win this game, eh? Beat the bastards. An' watch over yer shoulders, because there's a few guys here who'll be batterin' the door down tae take yer place in the final. Oh, an' every time you go for a ball, think about wee Barry lyin' in hospital. Win the game for him."

The place exploded into a huge roar, faces contorted with aggression, fists clenched in mates' faces. Then it all died down again and they were left wondering what to do next. So they all checked their bags again.

Shyness closed his eyes and tried to take in the disappointment of being overlooked for right-back. Chunky couldn't believe he wasn't getting stripped at all.

Ginge sidled away to the toilet, locked himself in a cubicle and chucked up his scrambled eggs on toast.

JOHNNY McANDREW nudged Bobby Bothwell awake. Bothwell always slept on the way to games, the fucker could've slept on a clothes line. He grunted and grumbled and rubbed his eyes and swore at his room-mate.

"Boaby!"

"Whit, ya wanker? Ah'm kippin'!"

"Ah know, but Ah left the tap running in the bog at the hotel."

"Whit? In the lounge?"

"Naw, oor room. Ah was late comin' downstairs-"

"-so whit's new?-"

"-an' remembered too late. D'ye think the gaffer'll find out?"

"The mood he's in, d'ye think he'd care?"

"Aye, whit's that a' about? He on a promise or somethin'?"

"Dunno, but long may it last, man. Ah was ready for the full 12" megamix team-talk the day - then he gie's it easy-peasy an' tuck in! Magic!"

"Aye, that was some scran you had - the full fry-up! Ye'll be spewin' yer load, man!"

"Naw sweat - the gaffer's right. This is a piecea piss the day. We spend too much time worryin' aboot other teams. It's time we started keechin' a ' ower them, man. They're mingin' - name me wan player ye'd have."

"Er-."

"Exactly. Now let me get back tae ma zeds..."

McAndrew wondered how his room-mate could be so cool about such a big game. What he didn't know was that Bothwell wasn't sleeping. In fact, he hadn't slept a wink since Charlie Spuds and his monsters paid their visit on Thursday.

He hadn't told a soul what had been threatened, that would only have made him an ever likelier candidate for artificial legs. But now that the whole betting coup thing was out, the world was waiting to see if the great Glasgow City really WERE going to take a fall.

The gaffer was right, there was no reason on earth why they should do anything but hump this mob out of sight. But let's just say it all went tits up. Let's just say there was the giantkilling to end them all. There would be no doubt what people would think. And by people, Bobby Bothwell meant Charlie Spuds and his monsters.

Today would quite literally have to be the game of his life.

"FUCKIN' brilliant, eh? On the bus tae a Scottish Cup semi - us! Ochil fuckin' United! Me an' you, bud! In half an hour we'll be at Hampden, in thae big dressin' rooms, testin' the pitch, wavin' tae the folks. Who you got comin' again? Ah've got Rosalyn, ma maw and da', the brothers and sisters, ma Uncle Andy and some pals fae back hame - near enough a busload. Who you got? Fud? You hearin' a word Ah'm sayin'?"

"Whit?"

"Ah said, d'ye think United'll go wi' a four or a three at the back?"

"Aye, Ah was listenin'. Ah think ye're right. Arrabiatta's a liability."

"Ah was talkin' about Hampden, who's comin' tae watch us. What's up wi' you - that leg botherin' ye?"

"Keep it down, man. Course it is. It was gowpin' when Ah woke up this mornin', then it was OK once Ah stretched a bit, then it went again after Ah sat down for breakfast - Ah'm worried that the minute this bus stops Ah'm gonnae be walkin' aff like John Wayne. The telly cameras'll be there an' everythin'."

"A'right, take it easy. Listen, just before we get tae the park, go down tae the loo, stand in there a bit, stretch off, ye'll be fine."

"Ye think?"

"Listen, you'd know if ye werenae fit. Ye'd only be cheatin' yersel', eh?"

"Sure. Ta."

Then Craw went back to the paper he'd put down and Fud went back to staring out the window and both went back to not believing a word of it.

CHARLIE SPUDS hadn't been kidding when he told his minders he'd give anything to be playing for Ochil United at Hampden. Nothing would have made him happier than to play just one game for his heroes, even to come off the bench for ten minutes when a game was done and dusted. But he'd been hopeless at football and that bugged him more than just about anything in his life.

Truth be told, it was probably why he'd turned into such a bastard. Had he been able to get respect by kicking a ball, he wouldn't have felt the need to get it kicking balls. And even now,

251

as he contemplated ruining the life of one of the most famous men in Scotland, he wished it didn't have to be that way.

Today he wanted not to be Charlie Spuds, gangster, but Charlie Kerr, the ex-internationalist midfielder-turn-wily-manager, leading his team out at Hampden. The nearest he wanted to come to violence was flinging a tea-cup across the dressing room during a half-time rant.

But that wasn't his life. This was, making money was – and dealing with anyone who tried to stop him. Like it or not, Bobby Bothwell was that person right now. And unless he produced the goods today, even though that meant Charlie's own beloved Ochil United being knocked out of the cup, Bobby Bothwell was for the malky.

He pulled a brown suede three-quarter-length jacket on over his beige roll-neck sweater, checked himself in the full-length Rennie Mac mirror in the hallway and shouted that he was off.

Brian came through from the kitchen, drying his hands on a tea-towel. He smiled and told Charlie he looked lovely.

"Any idea when you'll be back?"

"Just watching the game at the pub, then in for – what? – half six? Want me to bring Chinese?"

"Excellent plan. Watch yourself."

And with a quick kiss and a hug, Charlie Spuds the bastard was off to work, leaving Charlie Spuds the frustrated football star on the other side of the mirror.

"AH'M telling ye," Fud was shouting above the rabble, "it's been a trick, mirrors or somethin' – it cannae be done."

"Course it can, Ah saw it. They musta done it wi' real pictures."

"Listen, Gibby, surely ye jist get the camera, rattle aff two shots the same and pit wan in a frame? Easy-peasy?"

"Easier than that, Jimmy - Ah think ye take wan normal picture o' yersel' standin' in frontae a mirror, but wi' another mirror opposite ye so ye get a double reflection."

"Shut up, Porridge, ya boaby!"

"Ah tell ye, Gibby – two shots an' wan in a frame, simple."

"Ye're a' miles aff the mark."

Lambchop? Who gave him a voice for Christmas?

"The way tae dae this is very straightforward, right? Ye get a picture taken o' yersel' standing where ye want tae be, right?"

Silence.

"Right, so then ye take that rolla film tae get developed, get the picture enlarged an' pit in a frame. Right? Then ye pit that framed picture o' yersel' on the wa' behind where ye'd been standin' an' stand there again. Then ye get another picture taken of yersel' wi' the picture of yersel' standin' there on the wa'. Gettin' there?"

On or two started to mumble that he could be right. No one argued.

"So then ye get that film developed, get the picture enlarged and pit it in the frame instead o' the first picture ye got developed, right? Then ye pit it on the wa', stand in frontae it an' get another picture taken. Then ye've got-"

Gibby jumped in without considering the consequences of interrupting a maniac in full flight. "-a picture o' yersel' standin' in frontae a picture o' yersel' standin' in frontae a picture o' yersel'!"

"Correct – and so on. Keep takin' pictures, keep getting' them developed, enlarged and framed and ye can have the final picture goin' back as far as ye like."

"Aye, but it seems an awfy wastae film – how no' just take wan picture after another on the same roll?"

Shyness smacked JD on the side of the head. "Because, dimshit, they'd a' be the same picture. Lambsy's idea – if he doesnae mind me presumin' – is tae create a new picture every time. See?"

"Aye, well, film's are expensive. Ah'm just thinkin' about savin' money."

Craw piped up. "Hey – ye could use an instamatic job, so the picture comes out right away and ye can frame it up before takin' the next wan!"

"Mibbes, but ye cannae enlarge them, Craw, can ye. An' the quality's no' as good as proper Boots jobs, know 'mean?"

They all looked back at Lambchop. "Willie's right – ye've got tae suck up the costa films if ye want a picture that never ends. Now how about ye a' forget about fuckin' fuckin' phaties an' think about fitba'."

Then he went back to his fry-up as if they didn't exist.

"Ah still think ye could dae it wi' two mirrors."

"Shurrup, Porridge!"

THE door swung open and a porter held it open with one hand while pushing a trolley through with the other. There was a portable telly on it.

"There ye go, son – sorted."

Barry Ronald forced a weak smile. "Ta."

"Hey, come on, it might never happen."

"Did you not notice the leg? It already has."

The porter settled the trolley in a corner by the window that opened out onto the hospital car park and leaned back against it, hands in the pockets of his brown overall.

"Must be hard, eh? Missing the game an' everythin'?"

"It's killing me, it really is."

"How'd the op go?"

"Seems to be fine. Sore as hell, mind, but the doc says there's no lasting problems."

"So ye'll play again? Ye'll walk? Ye'll live?"

"Aye, but-."

The porter came closer to Barry and pointed through the other window, the one with the view right down the corridor of the orthopaedic ward.

"See out there, son? People have lost legs. People *willnae* walk again. Know who came in this mornin'? A wee boy, nae mair than ten, run down by a motor. Right leg cut aff at the knee. There's people out there whose lives are ruined. Now, Ah'm no' sayin' you

254

shouldnae feel like keech the day, because Ah wid as well. See if Ah played for City an' somebody had done ma knee in before a big game, Ah'd be spewin'. It's a sickener, nae doubt about that. But ye know what else? Ah'd get ower it, because life's too short no' tae. Yer brother playin' the day? Aye? Well, that's somethin'. You watch that telly, get yer chin up an' shout him through it. Before ye know it ye'll be back an' a' this here'll be a fadin' memory. Trust me, son – Ah might only be a daft porter, but Ah see real life every day. Ye know it makes sense."

Barry sat for a few seconds, looking at the porter's creased, care-worn face, looked down that corridor to where the limbless and the crippled lay, then shrugged.

"If you don't mind me saying, that's cobblers."

THE Ochil United bus turned right into Hampden's driveway, up towards the East Stand then left and into the tunnel that led to the underground parking bay. The players oohed and aahed at the luxury of it all. Then Tom was calling for quiet.

"Lads - this is it. We're here. We've come a fuck of a long way, but we've made it. Now we need to decide if we're happy just to be here or if we want to go further. Are we here to make up the numbers while Glasgow City keech all over us? Or do we want to make a game of it? Ah know which Ah want - Ah don't want tae come back out this tunnel wi' any regrets. This is the biggest day of all our lives. Let's go for it!"

They roared and clapped and slapped each other's backs again as they shuffled off and into the glare of TV cameras and press photographers. Taxi thought about it and felt sick, but The Smiths doing This Charming Man in his head kept his dinner down.

Then they were through the big doors and into the Home dressing room and it stopped them all in their tracks. The place was huge. Floor-to-ceiling fitted lockers, miles of benches, a separate area for the manager and coaches, a physio's room behind frosted glass, showers you could have let the whole crowd wash in.

Their kit was already laid out, Porridge's green top, black shorts and black socks nearest the door round to Gibby's No16 next to the door Tom and Bibs had disappeared through. Willie picked up his No12, maroon and gold stripes with the embroidery below the club crest reading:

Ochil United FC v Glasgow City
Scottish Cup Semi-final
Hampden Park, Saturday April 12

He stared at it for a few seconds like an archaeologist surveying some precious find from a dig, then hung it back on its peg and looked around himself, for once lost for words.

The rest sat down or explored or just stood around with programmes off the pile left on a table. This was the business. Tom was right, they'd arrived.

Finally, Willie spoke for all of them. "Fuck me, tell City the game's aff an' we'll just sit in here an' watch the racin' on that big telly on the wa'!"

Tom heard the laughter from next door and relaxed. Blue Eyes had been right, Willie was the perfect guy to have around at a time like this. He heard him again.

"Hey Jimmy, this is nicer than your hoose - at least it's got a shower, eh?"

"Aye, well, Ah hope yer bench is as comfy while ye're watchin' us real pros play."

"There's better pros up Blythswood Square, pal - an' they've got mair stamina than you, ya tosser."

"No' as much as yer maw, though."

"Ma maw makes mair money than your maw any night."

They were off and running. All the problems of the week seemed to have been forgotten. This was what it was all about.

MELVIN LAW reduced the Away dressing room to silence the second he walked in. He always did, it was logical, he was the boss. They all sat down in front of their white shirts with the pale blue trim, still suited up, looking totally relaxed and confident. The mood felt good.

"Gentlemen, I just wanted to take two minutes before we get started to let you know what a great squad of players you are. You've done everything I could ever have asked of you, even when things haven't gone right. I know I sometimes come across as someone who is never happy-"

"-You can say that again," thought Arrabiatta.

"-and I know you in particular will be thinking that, Mario-"

Arrabiatta looked embarrassed. How *did* he do that?

"-but it's only because I want the best. I have standards. And whatever happens today, tomorrow, for the rest of your lives and careers, I want you to maintain those standards. Never be happy with what you have, with what you have done. Always want more, better, stronger. The best. Now, relax however you like until 2.03 when the goalkeepers will be ready to go out and begin their warm-up and 2.11 when the rest will follow. Thank you."

And he walked past them all again and out of the dressing room, leaving them baffled.

"Flippin'eck!" said Arrabiatta. "What's with heem? Has he lost his lid?"

They shrugged and harumphed and mumbled that maybe he was ill or mad or - or - who knew?

"Mibbes he's in love," said McAndrew.

They threw stuff and told him to fuck up.

FUD felt good. He'd gone to the loo on the bus like Craw had said, stretched as best he could in the cramped space and had felt no pain as he stepped down from the bus. He'd deliberately stayed on his feet in the dressing room, constantly pushing his weight from one hip to the other, loosening all the time.

"Coming out for a look?"

"Cool." He knew Craw had been champing at the bit for this part. He hadn't stopped talking about it all week. He was as happy for his pal as he was for himself.

"Now remember, if you're not chewing gum when we go out, kid on you are. Touch the turf as soon as you set foot on it. Have a look at the sky, feel for the wind. Then turn round and spot someone in the stand–"

"But, Craw, it's only quarter to two. Nobody's even there yet."

"Aye, but the cameras are up where ye're waving tae, no one at home'll know the stand's empty. Just smile and wave and chew and look like a star. Nae use havin' a nice suit on for the first time in yer life an' wastin' it, eh?"

"Whatever you say, fannybaws."

They'd gone out of the dressing room, across the narrow corridor and through the doors to the indoor warm-up area, a full-sized astroturf pitch divided across the halfway line by a huge black curtain. United would have one half, the millionaires the other. Craw poked his head round the curtain to see if any United players were already in. It was deserted.

They went out a side door and found themselves in the tunnel with a couple of stewards, three senior cops and a guy with a BBC mike.

"Frank, buddy?"

"Yeah?"

"Chung Ying, pal. Can we do a quick interview trackside, mate?"

"Me? Now? Is it telly?"

"Yep, chief - just two minutes, ma friend."

He looked at Craw, who was nearly beside himself with excitement. "Go on, Fud, fill yer boots - this is the big time. An' Ah'll be behind ye goin: 'Hello mum!'"

BBC Scotland's all-action, half-Chinese reporter took him into the sunlight of the near-empty stadium and gestured with his mike up to someone in the stand. He moved Fud into the right position for the cameraman, seemed to listen to someone in his headphones then nodded that they were ready to go.

"Yes, Dougal, chum, I'm trackside here with Frank O'Donnell from Ochil United. Frank, pal, you must be very excited."

"Absolutely, Chung. It's the biggest game of my life and it's all a lot to take in."

"Well, mate, I see one of your team-mates behind you there – he's obviously getting into the spirit as well."

Fud turned and saw Craw grinning like a lunatic. "Him? Never seen him before in ma life."

Someone in the gantry laughed in Ying's headphones.

"Yes, it's easy to see that see you guys are in the mood today - so has the manager announced the team, Frank?"

"Er, yes, he told us at lunchtime, but he'll make it public later."

"Good news for you, though, mucker?"

"Ah don't think Ah should say - but whoever plays will give their all."

"Frank, buddy, thanks. Enjoy it."

"No bother."

Craw came scurrying over. "Did ye gie me a mention?"

"Course Ah did. Ye're ma amigo, eh?"

PORRIDGE was halfway through getting stripped in when someone knocked the door. It was Ronald Ronald.

"Sorry to butt in, but is our Garry there? Can I have two minutes?"

"Gaz? It's yer dad - you decent?"

Garry came across, embarrassed at being the centre of attention. "Dad?"

"You OK to come out for a tick?"

"If it's OK with the gaffer, give me a minute."

He went through to the little anteroom and asked if he could nip out. Tom nodded. He said thanks, went and pulled his shorts on and went out.

"Dad?"

Ronald Ronald took his boy into the empty warm-up area. "Son, I just wanted to say - well, just to say how proud I am of you today. And that your mum-"

"Dad, don't-"

"-your mum will be watching and she'll be proud too. I never thought I'd get over last year, but-"

"-Da-ad!"

"-but you and Barry and Mhairi have been wonderful. Mhairi's just bursting to see you, but she knew she'd have bubbled if she came down just now, so-"

"-her and me both-"

"-so she'll see you at the end. Give her a wave when you go out, eh?"

"Course."

"And I went to see Barry earlier on. He says you've to give them pelters. Kick one for him, that's an order."

Garry smiled and put a hand on his dad's arm. His dad looked close to tears. Then he hugged his boy tight and whispered. "Just do your best, son, that's all me and your mum ever asked."

"I know. I will. I need to-"

Ronald saw the boy's eyes glaze over. "Sure, on you go."

THE United fans in the half-full stand away to their right rose as one as Fud came back out in his working gear. He booted a ball towards the penalty box and clapped his hands above his head.

Craw was right behind him, then Jimmy, then Garry and Porridge and Harri. They all acknowledged the punters as they jogged and sprinted and sidestepped across the lush turf.

The United fans around the rest of the ground booed and whistled and made wanker signs. Craw applauded them too.

"Fuckin' magic," he breathed.

BLUE EYES stood by the touchline, stretching and watching United warm up. They didn't look bothered. Half of them weren't even out on the pitch, he'd seen them playing keepy-up games on the artificial indoor surface.

Tom had said in his pep talk in the dressing room that maybe United would take it that little bit easy today. It looked like he might have been right - he'd tell the boys to up it an extra gear from the off in case.

"RIGHT, Chunks, lead the way. Where we goin' for a feed?"

"God knows. Ah've no' been rubber-eared for many semis at Hampden before, Screech."

"Heed?"

"Ah got an invite here through a mate for a Scotland game last season. If we go up these stairs an' intae the main lobby, we can go back down a wee flight and there's a big suite there that the players a' went intae after the game. Got the programme autographed for ma wee nephew."

"Aye, ye were like: 'Just sign it tae Heed, please, Bobby...'"

"Aye, right. D'ye want me tae show ye or no'?"

"OK, OK, lead on, Sherpa."

"Haud on, though – there's the very man. The chairy."

"Mr Ferry! Chairman!"

Fergus Ferry was talking to two blokes in blazers. He half-turned and smiled a smile that Chunky thought made him look like a TV preacher.

"Boys, how are you? Not your day today, eh? Still, we're all in this together. Up there cheering the lads on."

"Sure thing, chairman. We'll get the shirts aff them for the final, know?"

"That's the spirit, Martin."

"Er, chairman, we were just wondering – could you put a word in for us to take a wander intae that suite over there – wee cuppa, sarnie, watch the build-up on the box?"

Ferry looked towards the door, to his blazered friends, back to the three unwanted players. His voice dropped almost to a whisper.

"Boys, I'd love to – I mean, if it was down to me, no problem. But you know them here, it's all ticket this and laminated pass that and we've used up our allocation. I'm sorry, but..."

He shrugged about as sincerely as a traffic warden telling you he was only obeying orders and turned back to his conversation. Screech, Heed and Chunky were left standing there like they'd been knocked back for a dance at the school disco. They looked at each other, turned and headed back towards the dressing rooms.

"Boys!"

Cool, maybe he'd changed his mind and could sort it after all.

"You know if you take that other stair you can get up to the pie stalls?"

"Thanks, chairman – we'll tell them you sent us, eh?"

Fergus Ferry laughed, but his eyes were raging. He'd have a word with Hagen later and warn him never to let his players treat him so disrespectfully again.

TOM was waiting for the boys when they clacked back in just after quarter to three. Good, they'd got a decent sweat on. They looked happy, excited, up for the cup. He let them settle down and grab a drink off the trays of orange or from the big pot of tea, then gave it his last shot.

"Right guys, not a lot left to say now. Blue Eyes an' I have both been watching United and they do look too relaxed. That could work for us. Let's get right at them, eh? I can't stress that enough. Fud? Rob? Right from the off, don't let them settle. Jimmy D? It's your job to get us on the ball early doors, give Blue Eyes, Jimmy and Porridge a touch. Ginge, Garry? Decisive on the ball, get it down the lines, away from our box, that's the important thing. But find a man, don't let it come right back at us. Taxi? Westy? You might spend two-third of the game running backwards, but you've got to keep doing it to cover your full-backs and you've got to be ready to spring when the chance comes. Supply to the front two's got to be early, crosses in from 30 yards out and nearer. Find Fud when you're in trouble – he's always got to be the out-ball. So that's it. We're here. Good luck - and above all, do yerselves justice. Ah'm proud o' every one of you guys just for gettin' here."

Blue Eyes stood up and stamped his studs. "LET'S FUCKIN' GO, BOYS - LET'S DO THEM!"

Yeah, let's do them!

Straight in, fucked in about them!

Nae holdin' back!

Let's WIN this!"

MELVIN LAW didn't give a team talk before they went out. He let them go through their usual final preparations, then walked round each man and shook his hand without saying a word.

Then he stood facing the door and waited for the linesman to come and say it was time.

AND suddenly, after all the waiting and the preparation and the hype, there they were. Glasgow City. Coming out of their dressing room and lining up side-by-side with a shower of brickies and students and office workers.

Porridge shook gloves with the gum-chewing Salz. JD tried to stare out Arrabiatta, who looked at him like he was a lunatic. Somebody at the back of the line shouted that there was nothing to be scared of here, just to get rattled in. Nobody in the City team, white shirts and pale blue shorts and white socks, seemed bothered by the prospect. They laughed and clapped each other on the back or just jogged on the spot. Dog Brown had his head against the tunnel wall, eyes closed, mumbling to himself. Bobby Bothwell emerged last from the dressing room, walked between the teams to the front of the line. Blue Eyes looked at him, but got no response.

263

He held out a hand and said good luck. Bothwell took a second to register then smiled and offered a hand back. He wished Blue Eyes all the best. He meant it even less than he did any other week.

Referee Willie Auld appeared, his two linesmen behind him and the fourth official behind them. He shook hands with both skippers, looked round to see everyone was where they should be, got a thumbs-up from the headphoned TV floor manager standing out on the track, clipboard in hand, and told the teams it was time to go.

At the back of the United line, Rowland George closed his eyes and prayed for a miracle.

BLUE EYES lost the toss. Bothwell said they'd kick towards the United fans. Blue Eyes motioned to Fud and Craw to take kick-off.

A roar came up from somewhere beneath the feet of the fans. Blue Eyes shouted for commitment, for a push from the off. Only those nearest to him heard above the din. Porridge booted his post and touched the bar, making an invisible barrier. Ginge felt his stomach rumble. Garry Ronald blew a kiss to his sister. Jimmy wondered if his shirt looked better in or with the tail out. Craw told Fud everything would be dandy.

Gio wondered if it was just the excitement making him feel dizzy or if delayed concussion was setting in.

Taxi got a blast of Leo Sayer singing Moonlighting in his head and all his confidence drained in an instant.

THE roar was at crescendo now. Referee Willie Auld checked both watches, nodded to both assistants then to the TV floor manager on the touchline. Fud had one foot on the ball, Craw one eye on the ref. The whistle was raised. Auld blew. Fud rolled the ball to Craw, who knocked it back to Blue Eyes, who took a touch and found Jimmy square.

The stopper looked up to go long to Fud, but he was marked. He turned and played wide left to Garry instead. Garry took it, pushed it forward on his left foot, saw Westy raise an arm down the line and pinged one. Westy's first touch wasn't great, Eric Thompson nipped in and slid the ball out for a throw.

The United fans went up like it was full-time and they'd won the cup.

Tom came out and put his palms down, saying take it easy. Garry came forward and threw down the line to Westy. His touch was better this time. Thompson was behind him again. The whistle went for a foul. Westy placed the ball to take it. Auld shouted that it was the other way for backing in. Westy put his hands on his hips and asked if he was having a laugh. Auld grinned and showed him a beat-it thumb.

Walter Salz waved his defenders forward and launched one. Jimmy came through a ruck and won it in the air. Auld blew again. City foul. Jimmy shook his head.

"We're gonnae get fuck all aff this guy the day!"

Bothwell clipped it wide left to McAndrew, who dropped the shoulder and jinked at Ginge. The full-back stood up, showing him the outside. McAndrew pushed the ball ahead and sprinted. Ginge slid, won the ball, put it onto the track.

The United fans went crazy again.

The throw went over Jensen and Blue Eyes met it on the bounce, hoofing one 70 yards, right over Fud and Craw and through to Salz. This time he rolled to Senteanu, who looked for an out-ball, saw nothing on, turned inside and found Arrabiatta. Tom yelled for him to be closed down. Fud sprinted in, then slowed up a yard in front. The Italian looked flustered. He put his foot on the ball, had a glance at Senteanu, but Craw had moved in. Bothwell was marked skin-tight by Gio. Arrabiatta swung his right foot to hit one wide. Fud threw out his left leg, blocked, sent the ball spinning out for a goal kick.

And screamed.

265

He went down like a ton of bricks, clutching his shorts. Craw swore to himself. Fizzy came haring on.

"What is it, Frankie?"

"Ma groin, Fiz, it's away."

Craw was over him now. "Ah told ye, Fud, ye shouldnae have played unless ye were sure."

"What d'you mean?"

"Ignore him, Fiz. It's the other side, Craw. Would you fuckin' believe it, the other side's away. Twat!"

Fizzy made a sign that Fud was finished and then motioned for a stretcher. Tom looked to the skies and shouted for Willie to get ready. The burly striker whipped off his top and had a quick loosen. As he touched his toes, Gibby leaned over him.

"Go on, son - this is for the two of us."

"Fuck me, Gibby, Ah've got enough trouble rememberin' what Ah've got tae dae masel'."

He straightened up, his mate gave him a hug and he bounced to the trackside, tucking his shirt in and fixing his socks. Tom put an arm on his shoulder and told him to close down, chase across, be alert for any chances. Willie nodded, eyes fixed on somewhere far off. He took Fud's outstretched hand as the stretcher went past. Then he was on, clapping and clenching his fist at those around him.

The City fans sang *Who Ate All The Pies?*

CRAW and Willie barely got a touch in the next five minutes. When United had it, they either gave it away or hit balls too long to be caught. It was frantic, which was good. Once City got the tempo down to one that suited them, United were done in.

Dog was on it now, in the centre circle, Chopper on his tail like a hungry flea. Dog had the ball on his left foot, right arm out keeping Chopper away. Chopper remembered the team-talk and caught hold of Dog's shorts. Dog slapped him. The whistle went.

"Good shout, ref!"

266

"City ball - No8? Keep your hands off."

"He slapped me, ref!"

"Hands OFF!"

The free-kick came high into the box. Porridge started to come, but Blue Eyes shouted it was his and headed out wide right. Craw was there first, a quick ball to Taxi and a sharp return. For the first time, space. He made tracks, cutting across the pitch, saw Westy, sent one skimming across the turf. Westy took it well, knocked it past Thompson, ran.

He was clear. The United fans were up again. Tom was screaming for an early cross. Chopper's hand was up near post, Willie's far. Craw was arriving on the edge of the box.

The ball was a beauty. Chopper went up with Arrabiatta. Neither got there. It fell beyond Senteanu. Ozzie Fish wasn't ready for that. Willie was. He hit it first time, right foot, clean as a whistle. Salz dived too early, it hit his chest, bounced out to the right. Chopper swung his left leg as Arrabiatta slid in. The ball flicked off the defender, up and over Salz.

Willie's arms were up. Tom's arms were up. Fergus Ferry's arms, Chopper's arms, every fan's arms, they all went up. The moment seemed to last forever.

The ball hit the bar.

Bounced down.

Willie saw the linesman run back towards halfway. He shouted goal and made for Chopper.

Bounced up.

Salz clawed, knocked it into play. Thompson hoofed away. Willie was still bouncing up and down. Chopper had his hands on his head. Willie Auld was waving play on. The linesman stopped running.

"YOU'RE FUCKIN' KIDDIN', MAN – THAT WAS MILES IN! ASK YER LINESMAN!"

Auld rubber-eared him. McAndrew had the ball on the left, went past Ginge. Blue Eyes came across and halfed him, put man and ball onto the track then got up screaming at the referee.

"Surely that was in - the linesman was runnin' back tae halfway."

"Away! I don't want to bring the book out this early, take a tellin'!"

"But it was in!"

"Away!"

"Fuckin' unbelievable."

"No 5, here, now!"

"What?"

"Listen, calm down. I'm not arguing about decisions. I'm in charge, OK?"

"Aye, whatever."

"Make sure the rest know that, too."

Blue Eyes turned and spat as he jogged away. The groggle had wanker written through it like Blackpool rock.

Tom was at the Fourth Official. "How can that no' be in? That was in. Be honest, it was in."

"Move back to your technical area please, Mr Hagen."

"But it was in!"

"He's right, you know."

They turned and Melvin Law said it again. "He's right. It was in. The ref was wrong. But Tom, that's football. We get on with it, eh?"

"Aye, right." Tom booted a water bottle over as he went back, cursing.

The escape seemed to wake United up. Arrabiatta called for more from them, Bothwell started getting on the ball. Van Hoffen turned and found space just outside the box and shot wide. Their fans cranked up the volume.

Tom checked his watch. Seventeen minutes? Is that all?

GINGE looked for Gio infield but played it too short. Bothwell was in, looking for a pass forward. Both strikers were marked. He stood on the ball and turned and went back to Ozzie Fish. He played it inside to Senteanu. Dog came short and demanded it off him.

Dog made five yards, ten. Gio stood off after getting too close last time. A roar built from the City fans, like it always did when their wizard was on the ball. Now he was over halfway. Jimmy D closed him down. He feinted to pass to his right, Jimmy bought it, he went the other way. The City fans whooped. Charlie came out, shouted to Ginge to come in and cover.

Dog cut inside. Blue Eyes jockeyed. Dog stopped, feinted towards Blue Eyes. The United skipper sold himself. Dog megged him. The City fans roared. Now he was 20 yards out, Gio on his tail again, Dog held him off. Garry came at him. Dog megged him too. The City fans were on their feet now. Porridge was coming, spreading, flailing.

The dink floated over him and dropped gently over the line.

Bounced once.

Bounced twice.

Rolled.

Dog stood, arms aloft, back arched, ready to let them come to him. He loved this moment, lived for it.

Tom Hagen put his hands on his head. Bibs did the same.

Taxi appeared from nowhere, slid like a baseball hitter going for home plate, got the sole of his boot on the ball and pushed it away from goal. Jimmy D got to it first and hoofed for a throw.

The City fans behind Porridge's goal couldn't believe it. United players were all over Taxi, ruffling his hair, hugging him. He told them to fuck off and mark up.

"Get a grip, there's four million fuckin' quid at stake here, ya dicks!"

PORRIDGE grabbed the cross, held the ball to his chest like a baby he'd saved from a blazing building, looked all around himself as the box cleared of bodies. Bounced it once, twice, hoofed downfield.

Arrabiatta headed it back into United's half, but Blue Eyes was onto it, controlling, finding Chopper. He slid it back to Jimmy, who went long for Craw. The blond frontman went down in a heap as Senteanu hit him from the back. Auld blew for a foul.

"Hoo-fuckin'-ray!".

"Right - enough's enough! C'mere – name?"

"Whit for?"

"I've had enough lip. Name?"

"Giovanni Wilson."

"Turn round. Six? Right, on your way."

The sarcastic jeering of the City fans drowned out the boos from the United end.

Blue Eyes teed the ball up and raised a hand to signal that it was going far post. Craw got up, knocked it back across goal. Willie took it, facing away from Salz. Jimmy was screaming on the edge. Willie tried to turn, got it stuck under his feet. Senteanu toed it away, McAndrew hoofed it further. Jimmy yelled that Willie was a greedy fat tosser. Willie gave him the V.

Ginge had it now, pumped it back in. Willie went up with Fish, cursed as his header flicked out for a goal-kick. Except that this time, Auld gave United a break and pointed for a corner. This time City's players were in his face, echoing the abuse coming from three sides of Hampden. Auld waved them away without a word. Blue Eyes asked why they didn't get booked for dissent. Auld shot him a look that said: "Don't push me."

GINGE didn't need to be told to hang back for the corner. He might not have played many first-team games, but he knew the drill by heart; both full-backs and the sitting midfielder balanced out on halfway, marking the strikers left up and the space in front. He was on McAndrew, Garry with Rozenkrantz. Gio prowled in front.

That was how it worked. It wasn't up for negotiation. The gaffer's biggest pet hate of all was being put under pressure from their own set-pieces. The corner could be straight into the side-net, someone could miss an open goal from it, it could break to the edge of the box and someone else could lose possession, but if the opposition broke and bit them on the arse he'd always, always blame the three left at the back to balance it out.

So why Ginge decided to shout to Gio to cover his back while he made a run forward he'd never even know himself.

He just did it.

"G, in here."

"Naw, sit tight."

"Gio, in here - I'm going up."

"Fuckin' sit tight!"

"GINGE! DON'T LEAVE YER MAN! BALANCE IT OUT! GINGE! GET ON HIM!"

Ginge blanked his team-mate and the screams from the touchline and jogged 20 yards up the park. Rozenkrantz and McAndrew looked at each other as if waiting for the other to cover the run. Neither did. Bothwell was on the edge of the City box, one eye on Chopper making a late dash across the line of his defence. He saw Ginge, but didn't go.

Taxi dinked the corner in from the left, aiming for Jimmy D near post. Senteanu came in hard behind, but too late to stop the flick. Craw, Blue Eyes and Willie all attacked it. Salz came through the ruck and punched, two-handed, powerful.

Bothwell watched the clearance loop over his head, saw the flash of red hair as he turned, reacted too late.

Ginge was on it.

Every training session he'd told himself that when the perfect one dropped he'd be ready, that he wouldn't panic. The blood would freeze in his veins, time would stand still for him alone while all around was chaos. And incredibly, that's how he felt now. Mellow. Focussed.

Every pair of eyes in the stadium was on him as the ball fell in slow motion, but he never felt their glare. Everyone was screaming, but he was deaf to it. Never heard the shouts for him to take a touch or knock it wide or put it in the mixer.

Just concentrated and felt every pulse point beat calmly and brought his right shoulder round and got his knee over the shot and connected absolutely perfectly. Later, on the video, he'd see the ball rip through the forest of bodies in front of him, past the startled keeper and into the top left-hand corner in a split-second.

But live and in the flesh he seemed to watch it arc ever so slowly, pick its way ever so slowly in and out of the heads, seemed to see Salz track its flight and try in vain to move his feet and yell a final plea to it not to beat him.

Then, somehow, the whole world went on pause and Ginge had the privilege of his own personal, living photograph of the greatest moment of his whole life.

BOBBY BOTHWELL looked back over his shoulder at Salz falling through the air and the ball bouncing down into the net and his heart sank. He went with it, down to his knees, head lolling forward till his chin was on his chest, an empty feeling in the pit of his stomach.

Had he really been so desperate that he'd put £30,000 on himself to score the first goal in a game where something as bizarre as this could happen? Was he really so arrogant that he thought he only had to run onto a pitch and demand the ball and he could get his own way?

He stayed there - hands on thighs, head down, eyes shut – and thought: "Go on, Spuds, kill me now."

THEN the noise hit Ginge like a medicine ball in the guts. First the noise of the crowd roaring. Then the noise of Gio telling him he was a fuckin' lunatic genius. The noise of every other Ochil United player running to him, thumping into him, their screams all melding into one big, mad word you wouldn't find in any dictionary but which seemed to sum it all up perfectly.

Everything was rushing now, fast forward, double-time, everything that had just happened putting itself in order in his head. He'd scored the goal of his dreams. They were 1-0 up on the best team in the country. They were on their way to the Scottish Cup Final.

They were on their way to doing the bookies for millions.

How much would he..? Jesus, now that it was reality it was..? He was...

He was starting to feel faint is what he was. Head rush, like he'd stood up too quick. Hot flush. Dizzy. Wobbly legs, like he needed sugar. He told himself to breathe slowly, chill out, it was just the excitement. He'd be fine once the game started again.

"Ginge! Man on! Play it!"

"What-?"

Thump. Down he went, robbed. Right on the touchline, under the gaffer's nose. Still couldn't work out where the shouting was coming from, though.

Who were they telling to get up and track back? When had they kicked off? He heard a whistle somewhere. Someone was over him. Fizzy? Fizzy.

"Ginge, you OK? Talk to me?"

"I'm fine. Just took a knock - just - weren't they just about to kick off?"

"They had. We took the ball off them, Jimmy D gave it out to you, but you just stood there like a plank and Dog rag-dolled you. Westy's getting booked for halfing him before he got a shot off. Is your head OK?"

"Bit dizzy. Fine in a minute, must be the shock of the goal, eh?"

"Tell me about - what a dig, you're a fuckin' legend! Right, let's get you up."

He knew he was standing, but couldn't feel his feet. Didn't know where he was. Voices fading in and out. Legs going again...

LAMBCHOP saw Bibs waving for a sub and knew this was it at last. All the worrying, all the aggro, all that beating himself up over Barry's injury - and now he was getting on at last. He'd show them he should have been on from the start. He wasn't the gaffer's third choice at right-back, it'd just taken a long time for them to realise he was the main man.

He got the head down and sprinted round from behind the goals where the United fans were. Heard the cheers as they realised he was getting the shout. At least they knew a player when they saw one.

Got onto the straight. Looked up. Saw Bibs shaking his head and pointing beyond him. To Gibby.

"GIBBY! MOVE IT, YE'RE ON!"

Felt Gibby brush past him, already pulling zip down on his tracky top. Realised the cheers hadn't been for him after all, but for the guy they REALLY wanted to go on. Hated them. All of them.

Wanted to die.

He stood there, alone among 45,000 faces, not knowing what to do next. The City fans in the main stand were laughing at him. He wanted to jump in there and Cantona their fat bastard faces. He couldn't go back round and carry on his warm-up, kid on he'd only been on a wee jog. They knew. They all knew.

They'd all been in on it, as usual. Taking the piss, just like they had at the junior game the other night and at training after Barry got done. Fuck the lot of them.

Wanted them to lose.

Worse.

Wanted them to suffer.

Wanted the gangster to know where his money really was.

Maybe he'd phone him at half-time.

"JESUS CHRIST, Bobby, get yer heid up."

Bothwell looked round to see who was on his case. Then he realised he was shouting at himself.

And he was right. He did have to get his head up. The first goal thing was gone, but the game was still there to be won. Once they got that out of the way, he could think about the money.

"C'mon, City, raise yer game here – back in about it! Mario! Dog! Johnny! Get a shift goin', lift it! Let's get fucked intae this mob!"

And fuck Charlie Spuds as well.

GINGE came round and looked up at a white fluorescent light. Was he watching a video? He knew this scene, but where from?. Got it - opening shots of Carlito's Way, Pacino's eye-view as he's rushed somewhere on a stretcher. Weird feeling. Whose voice is that?

"Welcome back, Senor Carlos."

"Doc? That you? Where am I?"

"Our dressing room. The treatment table. You fainted on the pitch, been out for about ten minutes. We're going to have to do a couple of checks on you. What do you remember?"

"Scoring. All the noise, all the guys. Feeling ... feeling wobbly. Then, not a lot. Don't think I took a crack on the head. Did I?"

"Nope. My guess is nervous exhaustion. It was all just too much, matey. Happened in the 1978 FA Cup Final, actually - remember who scored Ipswich's winner against Arsenal? Not msurprised, nobody does. Roger Osborne, his name was. Bit like you, not a regular, then finds himself a hero. Players all over him, hot afternoon, flakes out. Never recovered, ended up at Colchester, I think. I've seen it a lot in my surgery too, people in stressful jobs, people nursing sick relatives, heavy gamblers-."

Then it all came flooding back. The bet. Jesus. How big was that money looking now?

"Any more scoring?"

"Still one up. As long as the rest of them keep it together better than you, Linda, we'll hopefully see it through to half-time."

"How long?"

"Ten."

"Fuck."

"HOW long?"

"Ten."

"Shite."

"We need tae switch back on. Think the goal came too early?"

"Fuck me, Bibs, Ah'd have taken one at ten tae three and got tae fuck home. Nah they're just toilin' tae handle bein' ahead. They've got tae get back on the ba'. BLUE EYES! GET THEM TOLD! SETTLE IT, PASS IT, GET THE TEMPO BACK UP!"

Blue Eyes gave the gaffer a nod and a thumbs-up, clapped his hands together twice, yelled for more effort, did that thing with his arms to tell them to fill their lungs. No one seemed to pay a blind bit of notice. They were in some fantasy world.

Probably counting money.

CRAW looked up at the giant scoreboard on the roof of the East Stand. Forty-two minutes gone. Nearly at half-time, nearly halfway to paradise. Nearly – bastard, there went the ball. His head was wasted.

"Fuck me, Craw, gie yersel' a shake!"

"Sorry, Willie."

"Fuck me!"

THE Fourth Official was fiddling with his electronic board now. Auld gave him a signal. He nodded and fiddled some more, held up a bright orange 2. Tom sighed, not long now. He stepped towards the touchline and cupped his hands to his mouth.

"Come on, keep it going, keep it like this to the break - one last push."

The ball was up to Willie. His touch was out. Fish came away with it and made 40 yards. Bothwell came looking for a pass. Fish made it and kept running. Bothwell timed the return to perfection, took Gibby and Taxi out of the game.

Fish galloped into the box. Jimmy D came across, went to ground. So did the Kiwi left-back. Jimmy came up with the ball and strode forward. He saw Willie Auld going the other way, pointing.

Penalty!

"Fuck me, ref, what dae we need tae dae for a break here - Ah've got the ba'!"

"You took the man."

"He fell over!"

"You took the man. Go away."

"He's a cheat!"

"Any more and you'll be in the book, son!"

"Fuck's sake, man!"

"You heard, Mr Donaldson!"

Gibby had his hands on his head. Blue Eyes looked like he was going to kill someone. Jimmy stood, hands on his thighs, keeping himself together.

Bothwell took three steps and sent Porridge the wrong way. City's fans went mental.

Tom Hagen put his hands on his hips and bowed his head. So did Bibs.

Bothwell closed his eyes and prayed for another dodgy penalty.

WILLIE to Craw, Craw to Gio, Gio to Blue Eyes, Blue Eyes short of Garry, Rozenkrantz stole it, strode in on goal. Blue Eyes stood up and stood up and put him over his knee. He leaned over the writhing Paraguayan and called him a cheat. Rozenkrantz rolled over another couple of times for luck.

Auld pulled Blue Eyes away by his arm and booked him. Blue Eyes was raging. Tom was happy to hear the whistle seconds later and get inside. Blue Eyes wanted to wait for Rozenkrantz as he hobbled towards the tunnel. City fans were leaning over the barrier, spitting and screaming at him. He motioned as if he was ready to jump in among them. A man calm as you like 23 hours and 59 minutes of every single day had lost it. Police got between him and the crowd.

Jimmy D came across and went forehead-to-forehead with him, put his hands on his shoulders and the out-of-character anger seemed to ebb from United's skipper. They went down the tunnel together, dodging the flying gob.

TOM didn't shout. There was nothing to shout about. He knew they were as angry as he was. The ref had given them nothing. They'd had a perfectly good goal chalked off, scored a sensational one and been pegged back by a shocking penalty. He looked around a sea of bitter, unhappy faces.

"OK, let's lighten up - we've done well. Should be ahead. I know nearlys don't count, but that goal we should have got was exactly the start I wanted. Brilliant, everything we talked about. You can't do anything about a fuckin' biased ref. Just try and keep cool, don't get drawn in. Blue Eyes, Gio - just watch yourselves."

Neither looked up.

"Right, get a drink, cool down, then let's go again. Play the same way and we'll be fine. Get one back early and they'll wobble. Ye've done great, 45 more minutes and ye could be legends, boys, legends."

He went back through to the coaches' room. Someone asked how Ginge and Fud were. Craw went to the physio's room to see his room-mate lying with a massive ice pack on his left thigh.

"Feelin' the heat?"

"Fuckin' unreal, man - a' this week Ah've been up tae there about ma other groin an'-"

"No' fair, pal, no' fair. Great block, though."

"Get tae fuck."

"Ah'll pack immediately. Where's Ginge?"

"In the ambulance room. Concussion or somethin'."

MELVIN LAW went in and gave his team the mother and father of a hiding. They'd been lazy, they'd make that tinpot team look good, they'd got out of jail thanks to refereeing decisions - if he could sub them all, he would. They were a disgrace to the shirt and to every fan who'd come to see them win in style.

He walked out and slammed the door behind him.

Inside, his players breathed a huge collective sigh of relief. The gaffer was back. They'd go on and win it now.

GINGE came to again. The doc asked him if he felt any better, but only got a grunt in return. They'd have to get him to hospital, this was getting worrying. No, wait up, he was trying to say something now.

"Can't believe it...fortunes...can't believe it....one shot and...can't belie-."

And he was gone again.

BOBBY BOTHWELL had slipped into the loo the second Law was out the door. He hit his brother's number on the moby.

"Stevie? Me."

"Jesus, wee man, how you feelin'? You're out a mint!"

"Never mind that, there's nae time. We've got to get another bet on quick style, a'right?"

"Bet? What bet? Ye've already lost 30 grand!"

"Listen, Stevie, it's life or death. An' Ah mean that. So don't argue, right. Just phone the man, ask what the numbers on yellow an' red cards is an' get right back tae me – an' Ah mean right back. Ah've got a game tae play."

"Really? Ye'd never know. Bye."

His idea was simple enough. The spread bet on bookings worked like this – they gave ten points for a yellow card and 25 for a red. Being sent off for two yellows got you 35 points.

279

Before every game, the bookie would estimate how many cards the ref would show. If it was an Ancient Firm derby, they might go for a minimum of seven – or 70 points. If you thought that was too high, you did what they called selling. That meant you bet X pounds that it would be lower and if, say, there were only five yellows you'd be two points up and collect two times your stake.

But if the game went tonto and there were, say, ten yellows and two reds and the points ended up at 150, you'd be 80 points out and lost eight times your stake.

Then again, if the market was set low and in the first ten minutes three guys got booked, the bookie could then readjust the estimate. In that case, you might cut your losses and bet higher. Not easy when you were out in the middle of Hampden, though. So whatever he went for here had to be right.

It was a hell of a risky business to bet on.

Unless, of course, you had the power to influence the numbers.

Bothwell had often wondered if the refs themselves bet on their own games and either kept the cards in their pockets or flashed them like confetti to make dosh. He even thought about having a quiet word with Auld – but as the guy was a lawyer by day, maybe that was a dumb shout.

So he'd decided to do the next best thing.

All he needed was a phone call back to find out the market. Why wasn't the bastardin' phone ringing? C'mon, Stevie, c'mon. He heard someone shouting for him. He said to give him a tick, he was in the bog. They said to hurry up, they were going back out in a minute. He said for them to hold their fuckin' horses.

"C'mon, Stevie, c'm-."

The phone vibrated in his hand. At last.

"Stevie?"

"It's low. Only one bookin' so far, so at ten points a bookin' they've set it at 30. Ah doubt if it'll even get tae that the way this ref's lettin' them aff wi' murder."

"Great. Buy at 40. Put ten grand on it in your name an' another ten in yer pal Rab's."

"Twenty fuckin' grand! You mental?"

"Naw, desperate. Just dae it, eh? Ah've got tae go – just make sure it's on, right?"

"But-!"

"RIGHT?!?"

"Aye, whatever."

He heard them shouting again and made a big deal of flushing before he went back into the dressing room. He was just in time for Willie Auld coming in to tell them to get a move on. He was on the ref's case like a shot.

"Aye, gie us a lecture for takin' the full half-time. Never mind that lot out there for kickin' us up an' down the street, eh?"

"OK, Mr Bothwell, I'll make the decisions."

"Well, start makin' some, then."

Ozzie Fish told his skipper to calm down. Bothwell ignored him. He was too busy working sums out in his head.

THE noise from City's fans swelled to a crescendo as Rozenkrantz and Van Hoffen lined up to take the kick-off. A touch forward, a knock back the way, Bothwell receiving and knocking square to Fish without even looking and they were away.

United couldn't get the ball off them for what felt like forever. Every time they closed one sky blue and white shirt down, the ball popped off to another. They were chasing shadows. All the enthusiasm of the first half was draining. They started to fear the worst.

Bothwell had it again, looked up to pick a pass, threaded one for Rozenkrantz. The striker spun, slipped, went down as Jimmy D came in from the side. Then did what he always did, rolled like he'd been shot. Normally his skipper hated the play-acting. This time he hared up to Donaldson and gave him pelters.

"You, ya big animal – how many times? Haw ref – how many times? Does one o' our boys have tae get a broken leg?"

281

Blue Eyes and Gio stepped in between the City man and their mate and tried to calm things down. Auld told them all to settle. Then he pulled out the book and shouted Jimmy over.

"I warned you right before half-time, son. It's your lookout if you didn't listen. Name?"

"Ref, come on—."

"Don't make it any worse, eh?"

"Jimmy Donaldson, Number 5."

"Thank you. Now, Mr Bothwell, enough. I'll referee this game."

But as Bothwell turned away, he already knew that had ceased to be true. Ten points down, many more to go. And a free-kick to take, just outside the box and to the left of goal. Just where he loved them.

"You hittin' it, skip?"

"Aye."

He placed the ball, took a look at the wall and the keeper, then turned and took three paces back. Turned again. Steadied himself. Walk-jogged forward again, hit it right-footed. Up and over the wall, curling out to the right then back in again.

The keeper was moving for it, but he wasn't getting there in a month of Sundays.

Bothwell's arms were in the air almost before the ball hit the net.

Then the rest hit him, leaping on him from all directions. Three-quarters of Hampden was going mental. Ochil's players and fans played statues. Less than five minutes into the second half and they were behind already.

Who had they been kidding in the first place when they thought they could win?

Blue Eyes read the minds around and cupped his hands to his mouth.

"C'mon, boys – plenty time left, plenty chances. A dodgy pen an' a free-kick. That's a' they've had, nothin' fae open play. Let's take it to them again, let's get the chins up and play."

Behind him, Porridge took up the chant. Then Craw, then Taxi. Behind them, their fans realised the players were still up for it and started to roar. If they were going down, they were going down with a fight.

They kicked off, lost the ball, Dog started running at them. Westy slid in and took the feet from him.

Bobby Bothwell trotted over and went through his act again. Willie Auld didn't buy it this time, but the City skipper trotted away again happy. Not with the way he was behaving, because he wasn't normally the type to try and get opponents booked, but with the stark fact that United were getting ratty and ratty meant cards and cards meant points and points meant prizes.

As in, money in the bank from his spread betting bookie.

And therefore a better chance of saving his kneecaps for another season.

The Boston Bar, Springburn

THE cameras homed in on the City and Scotland star's face, a smile splitting it in two as if he'd just thought of something particularly nice. Which, of course, couldn't have been further from the truth – but it still riled the hell out of Charlie Spuds.

"Go on, son, laugh. Have a good giggle. Let's just see if ye're still in such a good mood come Monday mornin'."

"Don't think he's takin' the situation seriously, boss."

"Doesn't look like it, Tam."

"He could do wi' a wee slap, mibbes."

"Ah, don't worry. He'll get better than that soon enough."

"How?"

"Because, Tam, when yer old dad here pulled a string or two and got a ticket for Rhino, he made sure it was right behind Mr Bothwell's mum, dad, wife and wee boy. So when our Bobby looks up to them in the stand after the game..."

"He'll shite his jockstrap."

"Let's hope so, Tam, let's hope so."

283

TAXI ALLAN was in his stride, maybe for the first time in the entire game. He had The Farm singing *All Together Now* in his head and it gave him a nice rhythm as he ran at Ozzie Fish. Took it up to him, dropped the left shoulder, flicked the ball with the outside of his right boot. Put the Kiwi just off balance enough to dodge round him, knock it on and run.

Still had the pace when he needed it.

Saw Arrabiatta coming out of the corner of his left eye. Hesitated. Saw the slide coming, pushed the ball on a yard further. Jumped. Heard the Italian curse as he slid past him into an ad board. Take a touch and cross now? Nah, why waste it?

He looked up, cut in along the byeline, had another look. Spotted Chopper in the D, arms spread wide, screaming. Slid the pass perfectly. Watched his mate pull the right foot back.

Bang.

Salz flying, right hand over left, clawing for it. Missing it. Senteanu behind him on the line. Ball comes flying out.

Whistle goes.

Penalty?

Fuckin' hell, PENALTY!

United's players went crazy, some running to hug Chopper, some to Taxi. Then a wall of booing, a scrum of City players round the ref.

Senteanu was off. Deliberate handball.

Craw had grabbed the ball and was placing it ever so carefully on the spot. As he turned and paced out his run-up, Blue Eyes came over and put both hands on his shoulder. They went forehead to forehead as if saying some joint prayer. Then they broke and did a high five.

Senteanu was taking his time trudging off, milking the defiant ovation City's fans were giving him. Every one of them was on their feet, cheering and applauding.

On the pitch, Bobby Bothwell clapped too.

Another 25 points.

He was already £20,000 up.

Auld went along the 18-yard line, making sure everyone was back. Then he blew and the booing got even louder than before, a deafening tidal wave of hate aimed at everybody who wasn't City.

Craw stood, hands on hips, looking at the ground. Every single pair of eyes in the stadium was on him and he knew it. He rocked back on his heels, glanced up at the keeper. Rocked forward and pushed off into his run.

One step, two step, three, pitter-patter, one more, little shuffle of the feet...

And...

Left foot, across his body, arms perfectly balanced...

Salz diving to his right...

Looking back over his shoulder as he landed and the ball nestled in the opposite corner.

Craw froze in disbelief. He'd been scoring penalties since he was eight, but never one like that, never one that had taken so long to go in. Or that gave him such a rush of adrenaline. He started to run, straight behind the goal – then realised that was City territory and spun, ran the other way. Right past his own team-mates, who chased him towards the dugout.

Tom was standing, arms outstretched like he was meeting a war hero off a troop train. Craw kept running and leap right into his embrace, legs wrapped round the manager's hips. He looked up and punched the air, yelling something incomprehensible. The rest caught up and joined in the scrum. Somewhere at the back, Bibs and the subs were trying to get in on the act. Even Lambchop was excited. Someone was blowing a whistle somewhere now, strange arms in mustard-yellow trying to break up the party.

"C'mon now, on with the game, lads!"

Auld was trying to usher this huge blob of joy back to the United half. Craw wasn't for letting go, not of the gaffer, but just of the moment. Auld gave it another few seconds.

And pulled out a yellow card.

Craw shook his head and smiled almost pityingly at the referee.

"Sorry, lad, but rules are rules."

"Yeah - and you love them, eh?"

"Enough!"

Bobby Bothwell clapped his hands together and ordered his team to catch a grip. Then he closed his eyes and breathed out gently as he realised he was another £20,000 up.

"HOW long?"

"Half an hour yet, Tom."

"You sure that watch isnae knackered, Bibs?"

"Certain."

"Then stand on the bastard thing, will ye?"

GINGE didn't feel great, but at least now he knew what day it was. They'd put him on a drip and hooked him up to a heart monitor and within half an hour he was back in the land of the living.

The doc was sitting on a plastic seat next to his bed, staring up at the game on the box. Ginge couldn't focus in on the score in the top left corner of the screen.

"How we doing."

"Superb, son. Two each."

"Two-each? What happened? Who scored? How long left?"

"Did ye know Bothwell scored a penalty right before half-time? No? Well he did – and then he got a beautiful free-kick right after. Thought we'd cave then, they did. But what about wee Taxi – he's done them like kippers down the line, Chopper's had a shot, that big Romanian's handled and Craw scored the penalty."

"Senteanu? Did he go off?"

"Yeah, straight red. Then Craw got a yellow for over-celebrating."

"That ref's a chuff."

"That a medical term?"

286

"They said what's up with me?"

"Pretty much like I said, nervous exhaustion. The goal's just been too much for you on top of the whole occasion. Don't think you expected to play, did you?"

"Doc, you had a better chance of starting that game than I did. The whole thing's just knocked me sideways. Well, that and-."

"And what?"

"Nothing, nothing. Just the occasion, the goal, everything. You know."

"Sure. Hey – wait a minute – go on Gio, go on son, GO ON-!"

CITY had backed off and backed off. Gio had carried it at them from halfway and no one had made the tackle. He'd even heard Arrabiatta shout to leave him on the ball.

Cheeky tosser.

Watch this, amico mio.

The swarthy midfielder set himself and let fly. He'd hit it with Arrabiatta right in front of him, so Salz was unsighted. The keeper never moved, except to half-turn and see the ball bend past him.

And in.

ON the United bench, mayhem. Hysteria. No one knew what to do, where to run, who to hug. They'd only just recovered from Craw's penalty five minutes ago – and now this! Jesus, 3-2! They were too shocked, excited, drained to even speak.

Tom spun, looking for someone, something, anything to share the moment with and came eye-to-eye with Melvin Law. The City boss didn't look angry. Or sad. Or even as if his mind was already two moves ahead, planning his tactics for the inevitable blitz to come.

He looked empty. Neutral. Gone.

GIO was flat on his back, like Charlie George at Wembley in '71, head just raised off the turf to see them coming, arms and eyes wide. He looked up at the cloudless skies and thought he could see heaven.

Then Jimmy D's big unshaven mug was right over him, grinning, sweating. Blue Eyes appeared next, then Willie. He felt like a new-born baby being goo-gooed at by awestruck relatives.

They peeled him off the grass, hugged him, picked him up, dropped him again. He felt his legs go for a moment, then got it together again and jogged back to centre, both fists in the air, looking to the main stand for a sight of his folks or his girlfriend Aileen. Or that wee nurse he'd given a ticket to and who he hoped didn't get talking to his girlfriend Aileen.

But the crowd was just a blur. Everything was. The only thing clear in his head was – no, wait, there was nothing clear in his head. Shite. He ran past Rozenkrantz. No, two Rozenkrantzes. Was congratulated by two Gibbys. Lifted two left hands to wipe the sweat from his face. Shite, shite, shite.

BOTHWELL was yelling at his team again, more desperate this time than before, angrier. This was getting serious, so serious his first thought was that they might go out the cup and not that Charlie Spuds might have double the reason to chop him into bite-sized chunks.

"For fuck's sake get intae this mob! Who's the champions here? Who's the fuckin' full-timers? Get a haud o' yer pants, City."

MELVIN LAW was aware of voice somewhere, but didn't realise at first that it was talking to him.

"Boss. BOSS!"

"What?"

"We've got to change things. They're running through us. What d'you want to do?"

"What do you want to do, Dennis?"

"What?"

"I asked, what do you want to do?"

"It's not up to me."

"Why not?"

"Because you're the gaffer."

"So what are you? A trained chimp?"

He still hadn't turned round to look at his No2.

"Jeez, Melvin, what's up? Just tell em what changes you want and I'll make them."

"No. You make them. Take some responsibility for once in your life. You might even find you're good at it."

And the conversation was over.

HAD Gio not just scored, there's no way he'd have confessed to having double vision. But his game could only go downhill from here, especially if his eyes got any worse.

So down he went, an arm up for the ref's attention. City played on at first, their fans booing the part-time twat's blatant time-wasting, but then Fish huffily booted the ball into touch.

Fizzy ran on, crouched down by the boy's side.

"What's up?"

"Double vision. Cannae see straight, Ah'll need t'come off."

"Well, at least that explains the goal."

"Hey, an' now Ah've got Chucklevision as well. Just gie's a Frankie up and let them get on wi' the game, eh?"

Fizzy made the roly-poly sign to the bench for a subby. On the bench, Lambchop didn't even budge this time. He'd long since given up.

"Shyness! Get stripped, ye're on."

The broad-shouldered midfielder pulled his tracky top off and did a few hasty stretches. He heard Tom giving him instructions, but they went in one ear and out the other. Jesus, he was getting on in the semi. With less than 20 minutes left. And United 3-2 up.

He was going to be richer than fucking rich.

AS they waited for the game to start again, that same thought had started creeping into more and more minds. In the rush of the action, the thrill of going ahead, the despair of going behind again then the indescribable high of those two goals rapid, football had been all that mattered. No true pro ever thought about money when the ball was pinging and the tackles crunching.

But now, in this lull, their heads filled with pound signs.

Four million quid between us.

Two hundred grand they'll hand me.

Just hang on and we're made for life.

Christ, Ah can't breathe.

Then there was Jimmy D, wondering how he could have been so stupid, wondering why he didn't have the faith in his own mates to even put a lousy tenner on them at 16s, beating himself up inside for his vanity at lumping the lot on himself for first goal. Who'd be mental enough to do that?

And then there was Lambchop, sulking on the bench, without a single pang of conscience for not having faith in his mates. But beating himself up inside that City were behind with time running out.

BOBBY BOTHWELL looking round the faces of the underdogs and saw the nerves. He wasn't to know the real reason they were tensing up, he just thought they had realised how close they were to creating history and that it was making their stomachs churn.

Win, lose or draw now, he'd exploit that. He had no option.

"HOW long?"

"Christ, Tom, about 90 seconds less than the last time ye asked."

"How *long*?"

"Fourteen, plus whatever."

"Fuck."

DENNIS FARRELL told Robbie Norman, Jens Peters and Adebe Zabongo to get ready. Bollocks to it, if he was being left to make the decisions, he might as well make bold ones.

He sent Bobby the kitman to hand a slip with the changes on them to the fourth official and next time the ball went out up went the board.

Jensen saw his number go up and jogged over, head bowed. Johnny McAndrew shook his and looked well pissed off when 11 was illuminated. Arie Van Hoffen looked personally wounded by being subbed.

The young English striker, the Dutch winger and the Ghanain midfielder were greeted by a mixture of angry boos and encouraging cheers as they came on to try and rescue a horrible situation.

Through it all, Melvin Law never flinched.

Farrell stared at his gaffer's back and thought the changes better work or they'd both be out of a job.

The Boston Bar, Springburn

"YOU want a drink, boss?"

"Glengibbons."

"Large?"

"Nah, clear head required here, Tam."

"Gettin' a bit tight, is it no'?"

"A gnat's arse, Tam, a gnat's arse."

"So what happens if..."

"Don't even think about it. That wee tosser better pull somethin' out of the hat pretty damn sharpish or they'll be pullin' things out of his body for weeks."

"Hang on, there he goes – what a run that is – he's flyin', the boy-."

"Put it away, son, save yerself a whole load o' hassle-."

"HIT it, Bobby, HIT IT!"

The shout came from 30,000-odd throats at once. And they were right, he should have shot. He'd left the last man on his backside and there was only the keeper to go now. He took the ball to the left a little to make him come and try to narrow the angle. All he had to do now was slip a shot past him and they were level.

But he didn't.

He was gambling on getting the goal – eventually – but also making some more cash.

He'd take it right up to the keeper, commit him, make him go to ground, go round him.

Go down.

Get the penalty.

Get him sent off.

Get another 25 points.

Get another £40,000 nearer his target.

Porridge came out, just like Bothwell wanted. Went down, just like Bothwell wanted.

Bothwell pushed the ball past him.

Stuck his right leg against an outstretched arm.

Went down like a ton of bricks.

Screams from 30,000-odd throats again.

Bothwell heard the whistle. Auld was standing over him with the book out.

"Up, Mr Bothwell. That was a blatant dive and I won't have it. Yellow card for you and a goal kick for Ochil United."

Bothwell shook his head and jogged back for the kick. Jimmy D called him a cheatin' shite on the way past. The insult stung, but the guy was right. It was the worst kind of cheating and Bothwell hated himself for it.

But at least it was ten more points, which meant 20 more grand.

PORRIDGE placed the ball, stepped backwards and wiped his right boot on his left sock. Tom Hagen turned to Bibs to ask him the time then thought better of it.

"What a let-off that was, Bibsy boy. Ye know, Ah think we're almost there."

Porridge took three steps and swung at the ball.

"Aye, a' we need now's cool heads and a bit luck."

Porridge slipped, got underneath the ball, spooned it into the air.

Tom swore. So did Bibs.

When the ball bounced, it was still inside the United box. Porridge tried desperately to get up and get to it. Blue Eyes yelled to him not to touch it, he'd get it. Jimmy D was haring in as well. So was Garry Ronald.

But no one got there before Robbie Norman. The Scouser hit the rolling ball just inside the D, inside of his left foot, straight at the empty net. As he did, Jimmy caught him on the right ankle. Norman went down in a heap.

City's fans went up in the air, delirious. They couldn't believe their luck.

Jimmy lay there and held his head. Couldn't believe he hadn't been half a stride quicker.

Porridge battered his fists off the turf, furious at his own rotten boots for letting him down.

Willie Auld pulled Jimmy off the ground just as he had Bobby Bothwell a minute before, pulled out a yellow card then a red and pointed to the tunnel.

"What? What for, man?"

"You've been booked for one earlier, I let you off with another one and this is one too many. Off you go, no more arguing."

Blue Eyes tried to reason with the ref, but there was no use. The rest of them knew it too. They were back to ten-a-side. Even scores, even numbers.

Even more money in the bank, thought Bobby Bothwell.

293

Tom Hagen put his head on Bibs's shoulder.

"Nine to go, gaffer."

CRAW had his foot on the ball, ready to roll the kick-off to Willie. He took a look around the stadium at the sea of faces contorted with every possible emotion. He couldn't have imagined ever being in a game like this, not even in his dreams.

Willie must have been reading his mind.

"This is fuckin' bonkers, innit?"

"Tonto."

"Does it go tae extra-time?"

"An' pens."

"An' does our bet count in extra-time?"

"Nope, 90 minutes only."

"Then gie's the ba' an' let's go score another goal, ma friend!"

"Ye make it sound so easy, Wulls. Here, gaun yersel'."

JIMMY didn't look back as he heard the game restart. It wasn't that he didn't want to see how the guys did without him. It wasn't even as if the steward sent with him to make sure he went straight to the dressing room wouldn't have let him take one last peek at what he was missing.

He simply couldn't look back.

Not without bursting into floods of tears.

He'd felt them coming the second Auld reached into his top pocket. Got a lump in his throat like he'd swallowed the match ball as he realised what it meant. Felt his eyes swim as he started the long walk.

Felt despair mix with humiliation and anger as the mocking jeers rang out from all those City fans.

Felt shame as Tom came into his eyeline. Put his head down and walked straight past.

Felt like topping himself once he was behind closed doors.

But just started howling like a baby instead. Sobbed so hard that Fud even got off the treatment table, clutching an ice pack to his hammy to see what the hell was up.

"Big fella, you OK?"

"Am Ah fuck. Sent off. Second fuckin' yellow, never even touched the tosser. You not watchin' on the box?"

"Cannae. Just been followin' it by the crowd. Four-two City?"

"Fuck off, man! Three-each! They only equalised 'cos Porridge fell on his arse an' booted one straight tae the tosser Ah walloped!"

"Thought ye didn't touch him?"

"Aye, well…"

"Hey, worse things happen at sea, big yin. Least you got 80 minutes out there. Ah'd have been as well no' startin'."

"Yeah, sorry. How is it?"

"Shagged."

"Sorry, man. Fancy puttin' the telly on now ye've got company?"

"Go on, Ah'll watch through ma fingers."

WILLIE actually did try to go it alone from kick-off. Beat the first man, beat the second. Then realised he was running up a blind alley. Turned right to push the ball out to Taxi. Got hammered by Zabongo. Landed on his back, winded.

Gibby yelled at him for giving the ball away.

Chopper flew in at the £5million African and left him in bits. Auld was into his pocket before the City sub was onto his second agonised roll.

Bothwell did a quick sum in his head. One booked before half-time. One at the foul for the goal, Senteanu off at the penalty, one booked for celebrating too much, himself for diving, that big posing dick off for a second yellow – and now this boy.

Ten, 20, 45, 55, 65, 90, 100. He was six whole bookings up. Six times 20 grand. Lovely biscuits. But not lovely enough, not by a long way yet.

And time was running out.

He went up behind United's No7, the little right-winger who kept singing to himself, and clicked his heels. The boy spun and swore at him. Bothwell jumped back, palms up, giving it the big innocent routine.

Auld was in his stride now and fell for it big style.

"C'mere, No7. that's enough. Now, I know it's tense out here, but there's no need for that. Name?"

"Lee Allan."

"OK, Mr Allan, one more and you'll leave your team with nine men."

Taxi turned away and glared at Bothwell, who shrugged apologetically. Taxi called him a wanker, which was pretty much how Bothwell felt about himself right then.

But he'd handle some abuse for another 20 large.

He asked Auld how long there was to go. Six, he said. He asked how many would be added on. Auld cracked a smile for the first time that afternoon and said they could still be out here at midnight.

"That'd do me fine, ref."

"Maybe, Mr Bothwell, but I'm out for dinner with the wife at eight."

"Whose?"

"Smart guy!"

BLUE EYES watched them kidding and joking and wanted to boot furniture. It was always the same, when it came down to the crunch refs always went with the big guns. Easier that way. Just watch, they'd get another big decision before time up and normal service would be resumed. Pat on the head for the plucky minnows and off to the lodge for tea and handshakes.

"Right, United, last push – let's get intae this mob! No slackin'! One more crack!"

Fish knocked the free-kick long into United's box. Blue Eyes shouted to Shyness – now filling the gap left by Jimmy – that it was

296

his, got up and bulleted the header 30 yards, out towards the touchline. Porridge yelled at them to get out, get out of ma house. That was his battle-cry every time, out of ma house.

Out they went, Garry Ronald haring wide to close down Peters. Nicked the ball off his toe and onto the track. United's fans stood as one to applaud the kid's effort. Garry shouted for Willie to get in and double-team on the winger as Eric Thompson looked for someone to throw it to.

He shook his head at the lack of movement and hurled one long down the line, making Garry turn as Norman came out to collect. He took a touch, turned, looked for a pass inside. Blue Eyes was across to fill the gap Garry had left. Norman dropped the shoulder and darted inside him. Garry got across him, put his hip in and blocked the ball with his foot. Norman went flying.

Auld blew for a foul. And motioned for Garry to come over.

"Naw? Surely that's not a bookin', ref? Surely not?"

"Afraid so, young man. Deliberate body-check. Name?"

"Come on, ref – Ah've won the ball!"

"Name!"

"Ronald, Garry. Number 3."

"Ah, right. Course you are. Give my best to your brother, eh?"

"Oh aye, sure.

BIBS checked his watch again. Two minutes and counting. Nearly into extra-time, that would be an achievement in itself. Whether they'd survive it or cave in big time was another question.

But please God, just let us get there.

JIMMY D realised he was clinging onto Fud's arm as United shaped up to defend the free-kick. But he didn't let go and Fud didn't ask him to.

Anything for comfort at a time like this.

GINGE didn't know what to think. He'd already done something so utterly incredible he could hardly believe it. The fact that all this time later his mates were still even in the semi-final was the stuff of fantasy.

Even still, though, he'd be shattered if they lost it now. And he never, ever thought he'd feel that way about football.

CHARLIE SPUDS watched Bobby Bothwell calculating angles as he prepared to bend another free-kick round the United wall. For a man as hard and ruthless as any alive, he suddenly felt a terrible uncertainty building inside.

The businessman in him, the professional gambler, the gangster, wanted City to score because there was a bucketload of cash in it for him. Because those City tossers had bet his money on United to win and he wasn't having them get rich off his back.

But deep inside, a wee boy was fighting to get out. A wee boy brought up on Saturdays at Ochilview, watching Stenny with his grand-dad and the other 300-odd regulars. A wee boy who'd bubble all night if United lost this way.

Maybe a draw was the right result now. City could do what they wanted in extra-time, their bet was only over 90 minutes. And United deserved an encore, by Christ they did.

Bothwell? He'd get what he deserved soon enough.

CITY'S skipper wasn't calculating angles, as it happened. He was calculating spread bet profits again. Another booking, another ten points, another 20 grand in his tail.

One hundred and sixty he was standing at now. Ninety short. And 90 was too much for him to make up himself without attracting attention.

The ref's whistle snapped him out of his daydreams. Time for one last piece of magic, one perfect shot that would complete his hat-trick and complete the comeback. One – no, not one perfect shot. One moment of quick thinking that set him apart from the rabble.

He hadn't heard a shout, hadn't been following any training ground routine. He just knew Dog was making a run from nowhere. He'd known it as soon as he'd taken a look round and spotted the Geordie crouched down in the centre circle, tying his laces. That was his way of escaping a marker, particularly one who was knackered and probably felt relieved that the Great Man was having troubles with his boots.

All Bothwell had to do now was time the pass right, get the weight right and disguise it well enough that United wouldn't react quickly enough. In the first two minutes of the game they'd probably have got half a dozen bodies to charge Dog down. Now, though, they were leg-weary. That was the gamble.

It had been a day crammed with them.

Bothwell shaped to curl the shot left-footed, then at the last second stuttered and flicked the ball sideways with the outside of his left boot. It rose off the turf maybe only six inches, but had enough pace to drop bang into Dog's stride.

He met it just as spot-on, outside of his right boot making it swerve at pace. The wall could only do a collective eyes-right like Royalty was passing. No one closed the shot down in time. Porridge was covering a shot from Bothwell's shot, but Dog, his weight all wrong to re-adjust – and with United a man down, he'd done without anyone on the near post so everyone got picked up.

He could only stare in horror as the winner went in. It was all any of them could do – United men, City men, fans of both sides, those on the bench, already back in the dressing rooms, Barry in one hospital, Ginge and the doc in another.

Dog was off and running, legs and arms going in four different directions, tongue out, head back, yelling at the top of his lungs. They all hared after him, across to the opposite side from the dugouts, right in front of a solid sky blue wall of support. A couple of fans came over the wall and leapt into the celebrations. Stewards came to haul them back. Dog told the stewards to piss off and let the lads have some fun.

Auld and his linesman moved in and broke things up. No one got booked for over-celebrating. Blue Eyes was too flattened to care. It was over. No way back now. No extra-time, no cup final, no immortality.

No untold wealth.

BOBBY BOTHWELL asked Willie Auld again how long to go. One, plus two. He asked if there shouldn't be more injury time than that and Auld looked at him surprised.

"Why, are you a glutton for punishment?"

"Nah, I just thought...never mind."

There was no point digging a hole by explaining. He knew what he had to do now.

UNITED were knocking the ball around themselves now, their fans screaming for action but no one able to summon up the energy to provide it. Blue Eyes took a touch, looked up for Willie and hoofed one. The striker got a dunt in the back from Arrabiatta and went down hard. Foul, 35 yards out, bang in line with Salz.

Shyness shouted that he fancied it. Blue Eyes said fair dos, he might as well have a go. The big fella placed the ball with the word Mitre facing him, seemed to be staring it out. Then he stood up and stepped back, checked out the five-man wall shuffling this way and that as Salz yelled at them, hands cupped to his mouth to make himself heard over the crowd's din.

Craw stood over the ball, back to the wall.

"Listen, big man, if ye don't score at least take wan o' the bastard's out wi' the shot, eh?"

"Ah'll try. Now shift yer arse."

Craw stepped out of the way. Auld blew and the wall came forward. He blew again and pushed them back. Willie elbowed his way in to try and give Shyness a gap to it. Auld moved in as Dog shoved the striker out of the way, settled the nonsense down.

Shyness was chomping at the bit to have a crack. The whistle went again.

This is it, son, this is yer moment.

Four steps. Hit it flush. Willie ducked. Ball didn't go through the gap, though. Smacked Zabongo right in the chest, knocked him back off his feet. The ball bounced back towards Shyness. He lined himself up to smack the rebound.

Bothwell cursed himself for what he going to do next, but there was no other way.

He broke from the wall, haring to close Shyness down. Let the United man get to the ball first, just by a split-second.

Kept coming, slid two-footed. Went right through Shyness's standing foot. Ball deflected of Arrabiatta and flew behind for a corner. Shyness went down in a heap. United bodies flew in at Bothwell, City bodies to protect their skipper. Someone was dragging him to his feet.

Someone else put a hand in his face and shoved him.

Down he went again.

Auld was sick of this now. Came in guns blazing, shouting for them all to catch a grip. One of his linesmen was in there too. Blue Eyes and Ozzie Fish were playing peacemakers, bear-hugging mates and leading them away from trouble.

Then Auld was shouting for Bothwell. And Willie.

Pulled out red and flashed it at each in turn, pointed to the tunnel.

Bothwell hung his head, clasped his hands around his neck. Felt grubby, hated himself. Willie closed his eyes and kicked the turf. Pulled his shirt out of the front of his shorts and started to job off. Glared at Bothwell as he passed him.

"You're a fuckin' prick!"

"Tell me about it. Ah'm sorry."

Willie stopped.

"What? You takin' the piss?"

Bothwell went over and shook his hand.

"No, mate, Ah mean it. Sorry. Ah lost the nut. The boy OK?"

They looked round at Shyness, stamping his right foot and grimacing as Fizzy supported him with an arm round the shoulder. Auld blew his whistle again.

"Ladies – off the pitch, please. There's a game to finish."

Bothwell started jogging. Willie followed. The fourth official waited to usher them into the tunnel. City's fans spat abuse at Willie. Bothwell shouted for them to leave it out. They stood and applauded their captain. He shook his head and ran to the dressing room.

TAXI swung the corner in right-footed. Salz came, punched two-handed. Norman picked the ball up 30 yards out, knocked it wide to Thompson, who curled on down the right touchline for Peters to hare after. The flag was up, offside.

Porridge ran 40 yards from goal to place the ball and belt it forward again. Blue Eyes and the limping Shyness had stayed up, only leaving Garry and Gibby on halfway. Nothing more to lose now, only seconds left.

Porridge checked his studs to make sure he didn't fall on his arse again.

BOTHWELL slammed the door behind himself and saw Senteanu sitting on the bench, still in his kit. The Romanian looked up, floppy black fringe stuck to his forehead by old sweat, dark rings round his saucer eyes.

"You are sent off too, Bobby?"

"Aye, nightmare. You a'right?"

"I had to do it, Bobby, the ball was going in."

Bothwell was sitting down opposite Senteanu, pulling his boots off, peeling socks, pulling his shirt out and taking it off with his sodden vest still caught up in it.

"Course ye did. Best save o' the match, big yin."

"What did you do?"

"Somethin' bad, Darius, somethin' very bad."

"A foul?"

He was down to just his white slip and shinpads now.

"Worse than that."

"But what is-?"

"Long story, pal. Let's just say there's times when a man has tae do what a man has tae do an' it's no' very pleasant."

"I don't understand."

Bothwell stood up, took off his pants and shinpads and started through to the showers.

"Mibbes just as well. The less you know about ma day the better."

PORRIDGE humped it long into the mixer. Blue Eyes went up with Arrabiatta, but the Italian got the header away. Peters had it, started haring into open space. On the sidelines, Dennis Farrell shouted for him to take it into a corner. In the stands, fans yelled for him to go all the way and finish the bastards off.

Garry got out to him, leaving Gibby to back-pedal with Norman and Fish charging at him. Porridge was back in his box. Any of the other United players who still had the legs tried to make up the numbers.

Peters went past Garry on the outside, hammered towards the box. Gibby had his arms spread wide as if somehow it would make a three-on-one less hopeless. It was almost too easy for the Dutch sub now. He could do it himself, play Norman or Fish in – and Zabongo and Thompson were both backing up with only Taxi matching their runs. And sure enough, it was too easy. Whatever he thought he was doing with the ball, he overhit it and Porridge was off his line to boot back downfield.

The game was stretched like piano wire, its shape long since gone, minds and muscles equally exhausted. Even Willie Auld looked like he'd had enough. As Taxi picked up the clearance and went on one last run, the ref shot a look to either linesman, checked the watch on his right wrist and the one on the cord round his neck, turned to face the main stand-.

"Fuck, no, ref – not yet!"

Auld shrugged at Blue Eyes like a kindly uncle, put his whistle to his lips and blew three long blasts.

Taxi flocked the ball up and booted it into the North Stand in frustration. City's fans were going nuts. United's just stood there, frozen in misery. City's players punched the air and hugged each other and ran to their supporters to milk the moment. United's fell to the turf, lay on their backs, covered faces with hands or just stood, hands on hips, dead on their feet and dead inside.

Tom Hagen walked across to Melvin Law, held out his hand and said well done. Law held out both arms and hugged his rival, told him all the credit went to United, apologised for the conduct of his captain. Tom said good luck for the final.

Law said he'd be better saying it to his assistant.

Dennis Farrell heard the comment and asked what his boss meant. Law looked him straight in the eye and told him he was about to see the chairman and quit.

Tom didn't know what to say. He felt like he'd just walked in on a married couple in the instant one told the other they'd been having an affair. He shuffled away and left them to it.

"Gaffer – gaffer!"

"Francis, c'mere son."

"Listen, gaffer, Ah'm sorry we couldn't hold on there-."

"Forget it, kid. Ye were magnificent, every one o' ye. Couldn't have asked for more – especially against 12 men, eh Mr Auld?"

The referee ignored him as he and his assistants waited by the touchline for the last players to say their goodbyes to the crowd and trudge off the stage. Blue Eyes told him to leave it. The gaffer's glare lasered into the back of Auld's head and Auld must have known it.

"C'mon, Blue Eyes, let's go an' gie the punters a wave. Seen yer missus in the stand?"

Blue Eyes looked embarrassed.

"Blue Eyes?"

"Nah, Ah'll catch her afterwards, eh? Ye're right, let's take the boys to the fans before we go, eh? Shyness! Craw! Round the boys up and back over to the punters!"

THE Away dressing room door flew open and smacked against the wall. Senteanu jumped for the second time in five minutes. Bothwell came back through from the showers, towel wrapped round his waist, to see what the noise was.

He ducked as Mario Arrabiatta's right boot flew straight for his head.

"Haw, Sir Alex! Cool yer jets, man!"

"No, I won't. Mario he is raging! That performance was the humiliation for this club!"

Bothwell put his palms up for calm.

"Big yin, we won. We're through. Who cares how we did it?"

"Oh yeah? Says the man who did the diving and got himself sent off? You think that doesn't matter, Bobby?"

"How man, Mario, the lad just cared aboot winnin'. Mebbes if a few more had cared as much, like, we wouldn't have been in aal that shit oot there!"

Ozzie Fish stopped in the middle of undressing and barked at the Geordie.

"Who?"

"Who what?"

"Who didn't give their lot then, Dog?"

"They know themsels, man."

"Well, I don't. So name names."

Dog took a couple of steps towards the Kiwi, who threw down his shirt and told him to come ahead. Arie Van Hoffen stepped between them and said to chill out.

Dog told him to butt out, because he was one of the ones he was talking about.

Van Hoffen said that wasn't fair. Nobody backed him up.

"So, what, you guys think I didn't try? Anyone want to say it out loud?"

"Aye, man, Ah'll say it."

"You, Dog? You who wants everyone else to do twice as much so you get to wander about waiting to do your party pieces?"

"Party pieces? Like the winning goal, Little Dyke Boy?"

Salz stood up and told them all to relax. Arrabiatta told the keeper that if he'd been less relaxed out on the pitch it might not have been such a sweat.

"Yeah, Mario? And what about you, letting the fat boy striker knock you around? Maybe you took the manager too serious at lunchtime and had a few vinos. Eh?"

"You say Mario drink before the game? You want to come outside and say it?"

Everyone was shouting now, pointing fingers and squaring up. Everyone but Bobby Bothwell, leaning in the shower room doorway at one end of the dressing room – and Melvin Law, standing un-noticed in the doorway leading out to the corridor.

Eventually the Welshman coughed loudly and they all stopped like misbehaving schoolboys whose teacher had just walked into class.

"Could you all sit down for a minute, boys? I need a word."

Fish muttered a little too loudly that here came the bollocking.

"No, Ozzie, no bollocking. I won't pretend that I was proud of what I saw today. It's partly my own fault for trusting you all too much, of course. I tried to relax you at lunch and it backfired. Too many of you were not professional enough to realise what I was doing. Or maybe I'm just not as clever as I thought."

Arrabiatta started to say that, no, it was the fault of the players, but Law held up a hand for him to stop.

306

"It's OK, Mario. No explanations necessary. In the end, we're there. It won't go down in history as one of Glasgow City's greatest day, but we're in the cup final. Although, I say we..."

Bothwell didn't like what he thought was coming. Maybe this whole thing was about to blow up in his face and he'd be out. Law had done it before, binned top names for dropping their standards of behaviour.

"...when I should probably say you. "

They all sat up at that one.

"What d'ye mean, boss?"

"I mean, Bobby, that I am no longer the boss. While you lot were letting off steam, I was having a brief meeting with the chairman at which I tendered my resignation with immediate effect. Let me say straight away I have no other job lined up, nor will I be seeking one. I am not just quitting Glasgow City, but football."

No one knew what to say. Most just sat with their heads down, waiting for what was coming next. Dog looked confused and close to tears. Arrabiatta's square jaw was hanging open. Bothwell was staring straight at the man who'd made him captain 18 months before.

"Why, boss?"

"Why, Mario? Well, it's been building up in me for some time, a kind of disillusionment with the game – but this last week has confirmed everything in my head. Certain things happened in the build-up to this game that told me once and for all that I cannot go on being part of this business any more. For a team of mine to be accused of betting against themselves was the final straw. I know it wasn't true, but it's clear from the newspapers over the past two days that there is no smoke without fire in the eyes of the world. That killed my faith in so much I used to hold dear. And so, I quit. Football will go on without me, you will all thrive under a new manager and I will always remember what we achieved together with the greatest happiness and pride."

Dog was crying now. Other were holding back the tears.

307

Bothwell couldn't help what he said next.

"Gaffer, is this anything to do with me and-."

Law jumped in quickly, shot his captain a look that warned him to go no further.

"No, Bobby, your sending off has nothing to do with it. I understand your frustrations and that everyone has a day out of character now and again. I mean, look at me here – illogical or what, captain?"

Some of them even managed a laugh at that one.

"And anyway, Bobby, all I'd say to you is everything will be fine. I promise you. You understand?"

Bothwell nodded. All that hurt him was that the only reason everything would be fine was that he'd behaved like a total arsehole out there.

"So what happens now, boss?"

"Well, Ozzie, I have asked the chairman to speak to the board immediately and arrange for whatever portion of my final two and a half years they wish to pay up to be sorted without delay. I do not wish this matter to drag on beyond tonight. By tomorrow, I want to be out of it for good. Dennis is out talking to the media about the game in my place at the moment, but I'm about to go and break the news of my resignation to them and I know they'll be on my case day and night once I do, but the clamour will die soon enough. Anyway, I'm going to Disneyland on Tuesday, so who cares? Plus, they will find no skeletons in my closet and I will have to take it on trust that none of you will decide to go running to them with stories of my ghastly behaviour as the Saddam Hussein of soccer."

Laughter again.

"Ah cannat see even them reporters bein' thick enough t'buy me tellin' them that you're a bad 'un, man!"

"That I can agree with, Dog. Now, I'm off outside to face the hounds. I may be gone some time. As in, forever. Thank you for everything and may you all go from success to success."

And he was gone, leaving them silent and empty and wondering if the guy was breaking with the habit of a lifetime and taking the piss.

OCHIL UNITED'S dressing room had the mood of one full of winners. They were laughing and joking, winding each other up, everyone telling everyone else how brilliant they'd been or commiserating with those who hadn't gone the distance.

Tom had sat them down and said theirs had been a performance that would live in folklore, that they had gone beyond what anyone could have expected and that with a break here and there would be in the final as of right.

Auld's name was mud with all of them, everyone calling him City's 12th man and a cheating bastard.

"He lost the plot so easy you wonder how he got on the FIFA list."

"He's past it, cannae keep up wi' the game any more. He's shagged out when he gets there, so he makes tired decisions."

"Aye, but surely his linesmen should help him out? They're allowed tae gie fouls, eh?"

"Linesmen are poofs."

"Good point, Vicar."

Blue Eyes stood up and clapped his hands together.

"Gentlemen, I have a suggestion. Let's stop worrying about fat refs and poofy linesmen, let's get washed and changed and go an' get absolutely fucking howling."

Willie applauded and the rest joined in.

"Ye see, Gibby? That is what makes a skipper. The ability to time yer run tae the bar perfectly."

Tom chipped in again.

"One last thing, lads. Ah've spoken to the chairman and they're meetin' tomorrow to decide on a bonus, because everyone agrees ye're due somethin' special for gettin' this close. Ah'd hope to have a decision at trainin' on Monday night. Remember, we've got a game Wednesday, so get it out yer system over the weekend and be in wi' the overalls on ready tae go, eh?"

"No sweat."

"Up for it big time."

"Twenty five grand a man'll be fine."

Shyness's quip hung in the air as Tom left them to it. Twenty five grand a man? They'd have been dropping more running for a bus if they'd held on.

"Can ye just imagine if-."

"Aye, Porridge, we can."

"Seriously, though, Willie – we could've been rollin' in it right now. Imagine that kind o' money for boys like us."

They hadn't even noticed Bibs was still in the room.

"What kind o' money?"

Blue Eyes gave Porridge a look and stepped in.

"Ach, we a' had a wee tickle on oursels at sixteens. Worth a ton each, wasn't it?"

Willie caught on.

"Aye, but once ye've lost a hunner quid seems a lot more than it did before."

Bibs shrugged.

"Well, it's a' done now. Ye'll get a decent bung from the board tae make up for it. They'll probably gie ye more than ye'd have got for winnin' because they're so relieved about no' havin' t'take us away again for the final!"

"Big Jimmy's bar bill must have skint the club."

"Aye, but they'll get it back in fines for thae two tackles."

"Ah never touched the bastards!"

"Jack-a-no-ry!"

"Well, just with the ten studs, eh?"

"Some game, though, boys. Some game."

"Fuck me, what about Ginge's strike? Nae wonder he collapsed. Anybody heard anythin'?"

"Aye, the doc's back and says he's fine. Nervous exhaustion or somethin'. He's on a drip."

"He is a drip, ye mean."

"What about Gio? Was it compulsory that if ye scored fae 30 yards or more ye had tae be carried aff?"

"Well seen you never found it, Shyness – what was the free-kick a' about? Ye nearly took that boy's heid aff!"

"Two inches higher an' it was top corner. Anyway, what about Gio?"

"Doc says he's OK, they're keepin' him in overnight because it's a head thing."

"Think they'll find anythin' in there?"

"Some bird's g-string, likely."

"Some game right enough. C'mon, let's take the man's advice an' get rubbered."

THE Sunday newspaper writers had already been toiling to keep up with everything that happened. They'd come expecting a rout and had ended up with a near-riot. Four off – including the City captain – umpteen booked plus a near-catastrophe for the Greed-Is-Good League champions.

You didn't get many games like these to the pound, that was for sure. And then in walked Melvin Law and tipped the scales right over. As soon as he dropped his bombshell, a football match that had guaranteed itself at least a mention on every front page suddenly sent every news story tumbling into the waste bins.

The up side of working for a Sunday when a story like this broke on a Saturday night was that you got first crack at it. The down was that the Mondays had time to dig beneath the surface and put together the full story behind the story before their next edition hit the streets. They were already thinking of who would spill their guts on the real reasons for Law quitting, about how they could get him to hold a press conference tomorrow to find out how he felt in the cold light of his first day without the drug that had kept him going all his life.

And they hadn't even started getting in the Bobby Bothwell story or mopping up the plucky losers stuff from United's lot. It was going to be a hell of a night and a hell of a weekend.

STEVIE BOTHWELL was waiting for his brother in the Arran Suite. He took him by the arm and led him into as quiet a corner as he could find.

"Fuck sake, Boab. What were ye playin' at? Mum an' dad are mortified."

"*They're* mortified? Have you any idea how long it'll take me tae live this down? But we'll sort that later. When can we pick the dosh up?"

The look on Stevie's face made Bobby's heart sink.

"What? What ye tellin' me? *Please* tell me ye got it on!"

"Aye an' no."

"What?"

"Listen, naebody would take 20 grand. An' Ah couldnae exactly tell them who it was for, could Ah?"

"So..?"

"So the best Ah could get was three bets of a grand each. Still good dosh, thirty-nine biggies back – so ye've covered the first goal loss an' make a wee hingmy or two."

"Shite, shite, shite!"

"Shite? How? You've got too much money, son!"

"If only you knew, Stevie."

"Bobby, Ah think you an' me need a chat. What the fuck's goin' down here?"

"Trust me, ye don't want tae know. Nobody does. It's better that way. But it'll a' be over soon an' everybody'll find out, so leave it till then. Thanks for tryin' wi' the bets, by the way, Ah didnae mean tae shout."

"S'a'right. Ah just wish ye'd tell-."

"Ah cannae. Ah just cannae. Where's Mags?"

"Over the far side wi' the other wives. Does she know what's goin' on?"

"Christ, no. An' she cannae. Please, Stevie, no' a word."

"Whatever. But if you're in trouble, ye know Ah can help."

"No' this time, Stevie. Ye'll understand in a day or two."

THE last person Blue Eyes had expected to see when he walked into the boardroom was Claire. But there she was, dolled up big time, Bacardi and Coke in her mitt, laughing in that mega-flirty way of hers at something one of the directors was telling the company. Then she spotted her husband and it was like someone pulled a mask off her. To reveal a face carved from an iceberg.

"OK, darlin'? God, ye had me worried the way ye were up in the stand. Ye looked miserable, just nerves was it? Some game though, eh? The boys enjoy it? Ah got them shirts, Van Hoffen and Jensen. An' mine, of course, for some reason the City players didn't fancy swaps. Wonder why? So, where are they? Yer mother's? They'll be talkin' the legs off her-."

"Francis, can we go somewhere? We need to have a chat."

TOM had his air hostess smile on - the one where the mouth and the eyes were agreeing with everything he heard but behind them his brain was screaming: "SHUT UP, DICKBRAIN!"

The chairman was holding court, going through the game frame-by-frame, making the changes he'd have made, describing every move the way he saw it; as in, nothing like Tom's view. What was the guy talking about? How could anyone have stopped City's goals? OK, so he might have slaughtered his boys from touchline in the heat of the moment, but he'd watched the video since then and Bothwell and Dog had been class, nothing less than that.

Deep inside himself, Tom would forever believe United could have won. Maybe even should. They'd been ahead and it had been snatched away from them. And, yes, he knew in his heart of hearts

313

there were things he might tinker with if he got to replay the action all over again. But he never would - and the truth was, if he had tinkered, surely Melvin Law would have as well and negated anything the Diddy League part-timers could have hit him with.

So, yes, there would always be what might have beens. But he was buggered if he was going to listen to some know-nothing who ran a fucking textile mill telling the world how he would have put his club in the Scottish Cup Final.

"Bollocks."

Everyone turned so sharply in Tom's direction he actually looked over his own shoulder to see who'd said it. Then he realised it was himself. The chairman was glaring, face flushed with Glenmorangie.

"Sorry, Tom?"

"The defending at the winning goal. Bollocks, worst wall I've ever seen."

"Well, exactly, just what I said at the time. Didn't I say that at the time, David?"

The vice-chairman nodded that, yes, he had indeed.

Tom took a slug of his wine and tried desperately to think of a way to excuse himself before he punched his boss and had to pretend he'd contracted Tourette's Syndrome.

BOBBY BOTHWELL hadn't spoken all the way home in the car. Margaret asked if they were still going out for dinner with Stevie and Isobel. He just shrugged, so she took it as a no and texted them to cancel. She sneaked a glance at her man as he drove, knuckles white on the steering wheel of their 4x4 Merc.

It wasn't that he was in a bad mood, a strop at being sent off. She could live with that, goodness knows she'd seen him upset enough after Ancient Firm derbies.

It was more like he was .. well, depressed.

And that really freaked her.

314

"Bobby, has something happened? I mean, something more than the red card? Are you upset at the manager packing it in? Because there's no way a new guy'll ever get shot of you, not in a million years, darlin'. You're the man there, you know that, eh?"

"It's nothin' tae do wi' that."

"So what is it?"

"Nothin'."

"It can't be nothin', honey. Ah've never seen ye like this. It's like ye're really worried about somethin'. Are ye goin' tae be in trouble about that tackle on the guy? Will they ban ye for a long time?"

"Christ, Mags, that's the least o' ma - ach, forget it. Drop it. Just let me be the now, eh. Sorry, kid, just let me be. Ah'll be fine."

Fuck it. He hated lying to his missus.

"BLUE EYES! Ma man! The skipperoony! Top big-bollocked, baldy, karaoke kingarama-ding-dong-doodly-doo chief type dude! Whit ye wantin'?"

Blue Eyes looked at Willie as if the striker was talking to him in Swahili, which to be fair wasn't far off the mark. Then the words seeped through the fog and he said, fuck being tee-total, he wanted a vodka, large, with bitter lemon.

"Triple voddy an' poof-juice for the man, Mary doll, a gigantabulous Drambuie for me, a blanket for ma pal Gibby sleepin' in the corner there an' wan for yersel'. How's that sound?"

"Shite, as usual."

"Ah, yer a sweet talker, Mary. Ye'll get intae ma pants one day an' Ah'll no' even notice."

"Will Ah notice, though?"

Willie grinned as the barmaid turned away to get the drinks. Then he got that I'm-a-serious-drunk-now face on as he tried to focus on Blue Eyes.

"Big fella, Ah might be pished as a fart here, but even Ah can see you look like keech. Whit's up?"

"Claire just left me."

Willie's mouth opened as if his brain had automatically queued up a wisecrack in response to the news, but then he stood gawping like a guppy as his brain caught up and made his brow furrow like a ploughed field.

And all he could say was: "Fuck."

"That was ma response as well."

Mary plonked the drinks on the bar. Blue Eyes downed his in a oner and asked for the same again, only bigger. Willie asked what the script was. So Blue Eyes shrugged and poured it out, how he'd been at the nonsense for long enough - Willie said, aye, so, your point is? - and that Claire had always seemed unaware, but that now it appeared she'd only been playing dumb and her response had been the same one so many women plump for in the circumstances.

"She stabbed ye?"

"No, Willie - she started shaggin' some guy. But instead o' keepin' it schtum so we were equally as shitey as each other, she used him as a stick to batter me ower the head wi'. Even let the bastard answer ma phone in ma house when Ah phoned tae speak to ma kids the other night, the cow!"

"Was that the night ye were humpin' that wee waitress?"

"No, as it happens - but that's the point, that's what Ah'm sayin'. Ah mean, Ah've never thrown any o' ma birds in her face. It's just a wee, well a wee release, eh? Some guys bevvy, some guys gamble, some guys snort it, some guys go wi' hookers-."

"That's big Jimmy summed up, then-."

"-An' some guys are shaggers. Ah'm a shagger. As far as Ah'm concerned, that's why we rarely have a cross word, because Ah've never got any, well, tension goin' on."

"Ye mean yer baws are always empty?"

"Thank you, Joan fuckin' Burnie. But aye, that's about it. An' Ah've always thought, well, what if Claire was - well, y'know - as well? An' if she was, how would Ah be about it? An' Ah always reckoned Ah'd be fine, as long as Ah didnae know."

316

"But instead, she's got this bloke's kippers under your grill and she's rubbin' yer nose in them?"

"Aye."

"An' just for good measure, she's punted ye out."

"Aye - how come we're that different, us and them? How come we can diddle about here and there and get on wi' life, but as soon as they taste a different flavour o' crisps they never go back tae the old one?"

"Prawn cocktail, in ma experience."

"Arf, arf. Listen, man, Ah'm serious here. Ah thought Ah had our marriage sussed, but she's played me like Nigel Kennedy wi' his favourite Stradivarius. The whole thing's fucked an' it's a' ma fault. Ah've lost her and ma two boys."

"Nah, hold on, early bells. Foot on the ba', son. Listen, what ye dae next is - aw fuck, that arse Gibby's pished his breeks, look - get on the blower, fix up a meet, eat as much jobby pie as need be an' basically do anythin' an' everythin' it takes tae get back in that marital household."

"An' then?"

"Go back tae the way it was-."

"Ah might have known, you'd-."

"An' find the bloke an' boot his chuckies so far up he'll have three Adams apples."

"Have you ever thought about becoming a relationship counsellor?"

"Tried it once, ended up shaggin' a' the wives. Seriously, though, man - the question is, dae ye want tae sort it? Dae ye want her back? Or, as a wise chap once said, is that pain you feel just pride fuckin' with you?"

"Christ knows. But Ah tell ye what, another two o' these big mother voddies an' Mary's gettin' it the night! And by the way, how come you an' pish-features there got so howlin' so quick?"

"Practice, son, practice."

MEANWHILE, Ginge lay in his hospital bed planning what to do with his Sunday. Usually it was a lie in, a big breakfast, the Sunday Times cover to cover and maybe a run across to see the folks.

Tomorrow, though, would be different. Special. Unique. He'd rung Chopper to pick him up after the docs had done their mid-morning rounds and told him to bring handers.

"Handers?"

"Yes, handers. I think that's what you poor people call those brought along to provide help in unusual circumstances, isn't it?"

"No, it isnae. Handers are what you get when somebody naebody else likes is giein' ye a kickin'."

"Ah, it's like being in a Charles Dickens novel, Steven."

"Shut it an' get to the point. Why do we need handers and how many?"

"Two should do. Two guys you can trust, two guys we can take on a rather interesting afternoon out."

"But what the f-."

"Patience, Steven, patience. It'll be all the better for you biding your time. Now, go away."

He smiled so broadly in the darkness he was sure his teeth must have looked like they were under a strobe light.

Sunday

Victoria Infirmary, Glasgow

"SO?"

"What?"

"So, what's with the entourage, J-Lo? You're only getting out after a night in the Vicky, not playing a gig at Knebworth."

"I need a bit of help with a little plan to pass the afternoon."

"What plan?"

"Let's just say I've got the bug for the bookies, old sausage..."

Buchanan Galleries Shopping Centre, Glasgow

MELVIN LAW was also having fun and like Ginge's it was the kind of fun absolutely no one reckoned was in the make-up of a man as predictable as Saturday night on ITV. He'd had fun getting the kids up while Amanda had a lie-in, he'd had fun when they'd all taken her up breakfast in bed together. Then he'd sent them down to start watching the pile of DVDs he'd brought him last night and he and Amanda had the kind of fun they hadn't had for months.

He'd dropped the kids off at a pal's house late morning then let Amanda take him shopping for a whole new wardrobe - with her picking everything, right down to the socks and boxers. They'd gone back to the car loaded down with bags and with six new suits to be collected when they came back from the holiday they were going to book next.

He even got the girl in Gap to dump his dreary grey slacks and black crew-neck sweater and he walked out in putty-coloured chinos and yellow polo shirt with a light blue hooded sweat top tied jauntily round his shoulders.

319

Then they sorted themselves for three weeks in Orlando, a luxurious family-sized suite in a five-star hotel right on the doorstep of the Universal Studios theme park. He'd have brilliant fun telling the kids all about that later.

It was Amanda who first mentioned the two guys following them. Melvin said it was OK, he knew who they were. They were from *The Scottish Sun*.

"Then let's tell them to leave us alone!"

"No, darling - let's string them along. Give them their pictures and a wee story, what does it matter? Better that than have ourselves in the paper tomorrow as Mr & Mrs Grumpy, eh?"

Amanda looked at the man she'd been married to for 17 years and wondered if aliens had taken over his body overnight. He seemed to read her mind.

"It's OK, I'm fine! I've just realised there's more to life than trying to second-guess everybody, trying to keep them all at arm's length. Maybe it'll be short-lived, I don't know. Maybe tomorrow they'll turn me over and try and say I've quit because I'm ill or having an affair or had my hand in the till, but we'll cross that bridge when we come to it. For now, let's go and get the children, have a nice lunch - and then I'll go and sort out a wee surprise for us both."

"What surprise?"

"It wouldn't be a surprise if I told you, now would it?"

Starbucks Coffee House, West Nile Street, Glasgow

CHOPPER just about fainted when Ginge told him what their afternoon out was going to consist of. His brother Andy and their pal Brendan sat in the back seat with their chins at their ankles. Ginge looked round them like he'd just been named World's Smuggest Man for the 18th successive year.

"I don't believe you - you're having a laugh."

"Oh yeah? So why did I faint out there on the pitch - because I'd scored a stupid goal?"

"Jesus, you're something else." He turned round to the other two. "Guys, if you want to back out of this, feel free. I'm stuck with the tube, but you're not."

Andy grinned. "Ye kiddin'? I wouldnae miss this chance for the world. This is one tae tell the grandkids for damn sure."

"Er, it is legal, eh?"

Ginge looked offended. "Course it is, Brendan. I'm the straightest guy you'll ever meet."

Chopper snorted as he started the engine. "Tell that to Charlie Spuds..."

MARGARET BOTHWELL didn't know what to do with Bobby. He just lay there on the couch all day, one hand behind his head, the other clutching his mobile, staring at the ceiling. Didn't want food, didn't want to go out, didn't want anything. And especially not disturbed.

She'd never seen him take football so badly. OK, so he'd been sent off - but that had happened before and he'd been over it by his third Bud on the Saturday night. This was different. He seemed to be weighted down by a black cloud of misery, lost in a world of his own. It was as if ... as if he was waiting for something far worse to happen.

She stood in the hall and wondered if it was worth trying again to bring him out of himself. She decided it was, that she couldn't just give up. If something was wrong it was her duty to try and share it. She popped her head round the TV room door. A re-run of the game was blaring from the huge plasma screen on the far wall, but Bobby didn't even seem aware of it.

"Honey, is there anythin' Ah can get ye? A toastie? Cuppa? A beer? Ye can't go the whole day just lyin' there. Is there somethin' Ah can do?"

"There's nothin' anybody can do, kid."

He never took his gaze off the ceiling as he said the words.

BLUE EYES was on his way to pick the boys up when his moby went. Claire.

"Hiya, pet - look, about last night -."

"Listen, Francis, I'm just callin' to say we're goin' out for the afternoon. Leavin' the place clear for you to pack some stuff. Save a scene."

"But why? Can we not talk?"

"No. I've made my mind up."

"And that's it? Ah'm out, no debate? Don't even get to see the boys?"

"You'll see them plenty other times. I've told them you're workin'."

"Aw, brilliant - so you stop me seein' them and they think Ah've let them down!"

"Ye have. That's why we're in this state."

"Dear pot, yours kettle. Who's the one who's had her bit on the side in their house? MY house?" He paused for a second as it hit him. "Wait a minute - just tell me you're not takin' the kids out wi' HIM while I'M clearin' ma stuff. Just tell me that much!"

"It's nothing to do with you what I do or who I do it with now, Francis."

"It is when my boys are involved."

"Don't get all insecure, you're still their daddy. They don't even know Brian."

"Aye, he'll just happen to turn up wherever you're going?"

"Don't be a baby."

"A baby? My world's fallen to bits overnight! My wife's off with another bloke, my kids are going out for tea with him and meanwhile Ah'm stickin' my kit in a holdall and goin' back to my ma's! An' anyway, while we're at it, who says it's me who should be leavin'?"

"So you want Gary and Mark thrown out on the street?"

"You're a twisted woman, Claire - you know what Ah mean. Why should Ah go and leave you wi' them when you're the one

322

havin' the affair. Why don't YOU go shack up wi' Harry Handsome an' AH'LL have the boys?"

"Hey, I'm only the one *admitting* to the affair. You've been at it for years, we both know that."

"Whatever Ah've done, it's never affected the way your life's been run. You've always been looked after, always had everythin' you want - but now as soon as you fancy a leg-over you cut me dead an' take the lot! Fair or what?"

"I won't take the lot. Just enough to pay the mortgage, run my car and look after the boys."

"Well let that tosser cough up - or are ye happy to let him piss all over both of us?"

"Don't swear!"

"Fuck off!"

And so she did. Click.

The bitch. She'd pay for this.

BY the time Melvin Law got to Edinburgh he had half the Scottish press following him. And he was loving it. He even took them on a detour to Murrayfield, right into the car park by the main door, just so they'd think he was going for talks with the consortium planning that Hearts-Hibs merger.

He sat there for a couple of minutes, made two calls on his mobile - one to the speaking clock, the other to his mother - then drove back out again. And watched them all scramble in his wake.

Five minutes later, he was where he actually wanted to be. The car showroom he'd phoned on his way through. The manager rushed out to shake his hand and Melvin saw camera flashes reflect in the sparkling plate glass of the front window. The manager asked if Mr Law would like the scrum on the pavement cleared. Melvin said no thanks, they were friends of his.

And then he bought a British racing green Jaguar XK8 convertible. For cash. To drive away there and then, with his old BMW to be delivered back to his home address next day.

He stood by his new purchase and examined it lovingly, stroking the gleaming paintwork like it was a beautiful woman's skin, all the while facing the window so the snappers got the shots they wanted. He shook hands with the manager, who got a salesman to move the car into the forecourt. Then he put the top down, stuck on the wrap-round shades Amanda had made him buy that morning, put in the Phil Collins CD he'd bought specially and even though there was no traffic coming, waited for maybe ten or 20 seconds before pulling out onto the main road.

He'd let them follow him back to the house, then invite them all into the back garden for a drink and a chat. That'd throw them.

TOM HAGEN was glued to *Godfather Part II* when the phone rang. He put down his tea, a massive brew in an oversized Starbucks mug, and pressed pause on the video. Then hit fast forward in the movie of his life.

"Hello, lover boy."

"Caroline?"

"Who were you expecting? Your other bird?"

"Aye, as if. How ye doin'?"

"Not bad. Be better if we could sort out the stuff about the other night."

"Sort what out? You said I was wasting me time and you were probably right - you know me, Caroline, talkin' rubbish as usual. Doesn't matter, over an' done with, eh?"

"Is it? Look, Tom, I know I reacted all defensive the next day, but do you blame me? My ex-husband takes me to dinner in a fancy restaurants, gets all glassy-eyed over the brandy then rushes off like a kid who's just had their favourite Christmas prezzie nicked. Then he admits he was about to propose again. I was freaked, really spooked."

"And now..?"

324

"Now I've had time to get my head straightened pit – and the truth is, I'm excited. As much as I'm setting myself up for a hell of a fall, I can't help but think we *should* have another stab at it."

His head swam.

"Tom? You there?"

He said he was. But he wasn't really.

He was in paradise.

BLUE EYES stared at the bed. His bed. Their bed. Well, used to be. Had they shagged in it? He'd kill her if they had. Not the guy, what was he going to do, knock it back? Not when it was so obviously on a plate. No, she was the one at fault here. She'd broken their marriage up.

He was so angry he felt like leaving a jobby under the duvet. But he made do with a note on the pillow telling her he'd pick the boys up on Wednesday night at six and if she didn't have them ready she could whistle for a single penny off him.

MELVIN LAW had only one more loose end to tie up and the number showing up on his mobile as he drove along Great Western Road suggested it was about to be either tied up or not.

"Melvin!"

"Mr Chairman."

"Listen, what you asked me earlier's well out of order, you know that? Especially on a bloody Sunday!"

"Granted, Mr Chairman-."

"And you can stop call me that as of now, it only rubs in what you've done."

"Sorry. Bob. Anyway, what I was about to say was that I appreciate exactly how far out of left field my request came, but I reckoned that a) if one man on this earth could make it happen it was Bob Armstrong and b) that after what I've helped this club achieve it was maybe a favour I could afford to call in."

"You've got more brass neck than Frankenstein, you know that? But you're right, I was able to swing it. It's being dropped off with me at six tonight, I've got a courier collecting it at half past and you should receive it by half seven at the latest."

"A courier? You sure?"

"Listen, the fewer people who know what you're up to here the better. Low-key, that's the deal. And, hey, I don't even know myself what you're up to."

"Call it a good deed, Robert, and leave it at that. Please."

"Need to know basis to the last, Melvin. You sure you know what you're doing here - and I don't just mean with the you-know-what. You sure you've made the right decision? I mean it's so not like you to-."

"And that's the point, Bob. It's *not* like me. And I don't like what *was* like me. Too many guys in football do this big it's-a-drug thing, drive themselves to white hair and heart trouble when the truth is they only stay in the job because they're scared of the alternative. Well, this last week has convinced me that the alternative's better. I might be proved wrong one day, but I can always come back, can't I? Can't do that if I'm lying on a slab."

"Thank you Randolph Scott."

"And goodnight, Mr Chairman. Thanks for this - and for everything."

"Whatever, Melvin, whatever."

BY the time their afternoon in bookieland was done, Ginge and his gang were utterly drained - yet at the same time they were incredibly, unforgettably, orgasmically charged up. Brendan spoke for all of them as they sat in the car in George Square.

"Fuck me, that was sensational."

Ginge grinned. "Told you."

Chopper looked at his mate with a mixture of admiration, amazement and something close to adulation.

326

"Jesus, man, a few days ago you were on the pulpit ranting about the evils of gambling - and now look at you, betting-slipped up to the tits an' back! So is this you, right into it for good, because I've seen too many guys -."

"Save it, Steven. I might be mental, but I'm not daft. This has been my one and only sortie into the sordid world of the turf accountant, I can guarantee with complete sincerity."

Brendan reached over the seat and slapped him on the back.

"Well let me just say, mate, it's been one belter of a sortie..."

BOBBY BOTHWELL finally got off the couch when Sky Sports were onto their second re-run of the full game. Outside, the sun had gone and the kids had gone in for the night. He peered at his watch in the TV room's gloom. Twenty five to nine? Time to settle the tiddlers into bed.

Might never get another chance.

He went upstairs and found Margaret in the bathroom drying Leigh off with a huge fluffy towel. His little girl, two just the week before, beamed at him the way only toddlers can; the only human beings who you can be certain have nothing hidden behind their smiles. He told her he'd give her a big hug when she had her jammies on and went to find Ryan.

His five-year-old was in his room, a shrine to Glasgow City - or, more accurately, to his favourite player. His favourite person. His daddy. He jumped off the bed, ran round it, jumped into Bobby's arms, pumping one fist in the air.

"That's how you did the celly with Dog after the last goal, daddy - I saw you, it was brilliant."

"One day it'll be you, pal, eh? You'll be up there, scorin' the goals, an' your boy'll come and hug you afterwards." He felt himself filling up. "One day, son. You just stick in, do the right things, listen to what people tell you - the right people, mind, no' the numpties. You listenin' to me? Good boy. Now, go an' get those teeth brushed. Ye'll never get the big advertisin' contracts lookin' like a jakey."

Ryan ran off to the bathroom, shouting to his mum that he was going to be a football star like daddy.

Bobby Bothwell sat on the pale blue and white Glasgow City duvet, looked up at the giant poster of himself by the window, and decided he wouldn't wish that ambition on his worst enemy.

CHARLIE SPUDS took the call from the manager of the Boston Bar just after midnight.

"You sure, Sammy? Who was it?"

"Not a clue, Charlie. It was chap-door-run-away. Whoever it was waited till the last punter was gone an' the grill was doon, gave it a rattle an' by the time Ah opened up again - you know the drill, Ah went an' got the old baseball bat just in case, know? - they were offski. But it musta been quick as that, because-."

"-Because there's eyes everywhere on that street, Sammy, Ah know only too well."

"So what dae Ah dae?"

"Come round the now. Ah'll take things fae there. Thanks, man."

He put the phone down, shook his head and told himself he was getting too old for this pish.

Monday

HIS eyes were open and working normally. He wiggled his fingers and toes. Normal. He could hear his own breath, feel his heart beat. He ran his tongue around sticky gums and teeth. He scratched his bollocks, farted. Yep, everything was normal.

So this was how it felt to be a dead man.

No, calm down. He wasn't going to end up dead. was he? Nah, no chance. They wouldn't take a risk like that. Would they? Nah, course not.

But if they bust his legs or drilled his knees ... well, he might as well be six feet under. How would he ever explain why he'd never walk again, never mind play football?

Then again, would they even be that ruthless, that cruel? Maybe they'd just cosh him around the kidneys for half an hour, leave him black and blue where the outside world wouldn't see the damage. You think? Behave, man. That's what these people do to guys that walk on the cracks on the pavement. Nicking a quarter of a million quid off them was a Black'n'Decker offence if there ever was one.

Aye, but hang on - Ah didnae nick their money. Aye? Well we know that, but they don't. An' they're hardly the kind that you reason with over tiny details like guilt and innocence. Even if someone did tell them it was somebody else, they probably fancy a smack at yer lungs with a tomahawk just to build up an appetite for lunch.

"Who you talkin' to, Bobby?"

Bothwell was startled to hear Margaret's voice. He thought she was still fast asleep - plus, he didn't realise he'd been arguing with himself out loud.

"What?"

"Ah said, who ye talkin' to?"

329

"Nobody, pet, when Ah sat up late last night Ah watched a gangster movie an' Ah must have been re-running it in ma head. Didnae realise Ah was talkin' - must be goin' nuts, eh?"

"Aye, ye want yer head looked at."

"Ah might know the very chaps to do just that, m'dear..."

BLUE EYES rolled over to cuddle into Claire and fell out of bed. It was only when he hit the floor that it hit him where he was. The single in his mum's spare room. As he fought to untangle himself from the duvet, she knocked the door.

"Francis? You all right in there, son? I thought there was a noise a minute ago."

"Just me, mum, an elephant first thing in the morning. Hope Ah didn't disturb you."

"Naw, son, been up for hours as usual. Ready for some breakfast? It's ten to eight. You watchin' your time for work?"

"No worries, mum, first appointment's not till half nine. And some cereal's fine for me."

"Nonsense, when you're here you'll eat right. Ah'll stick a few links and some ham on."

"Fine, I'll be down soon."

"There's fresh towels in the bathroom and loads o' hot water for a shower..."

"Fine."

"Or Ah'll run a bath if ye prefer..."

"A shower's great, mum."

"There's two kinds o' soap there, didn't know if yer skin still bothered ye, son."

"It's fine, mum. I'll just be a few minutes."

"Good, Ah'll stick the pan on. A wee egg as well, eh? Set ye up for the day..."

He lay back on the mattress in a heap and didn't know whether to laugh or cry.

GINGE was laughing. He'd kept hearing himself do it ever since yesterday afternoon's adventure, as if he kept remembering some brilliant joke. And in a way, he was.

When the rest of them got wind of this, they'd think he was having a right laugh. Taking the piss big time.

And yet, as he put toothpaste on his brush and gave another little giggle, what he had to tell them was deadly serious. Nine hours till training? He could barely contain himself.

BOBBY BOTHWELL had got up, made Mags some breakfast in bed, got the weans ready, then showered and dressed and got ready for a meeting that definitely had no funny side. His face felt as if it had never smiled, not ever. It felt set in a permanent, depressed scowl.

He knew he'd been an arse to the family since Saturday night. He knew he'd been the same on the park on Saturday. Why hadn't he just gone along with what the gaffer said, let him call the polis in the minute Spuds gave him the tug?

Because, fannybaws, Spuds would have chopped you into little bits by now. At least this way there was a pencil-slim chance that he might decide that a victim who at least kept his mouth shut was one who deserved one fewer ligament severed with a machete.

He gave a little shudder at the thought. He almost believed he could feel the pain in the back of his knees. Ah well, no use putting it off any longer. Might as well get over to Springburn, to the pub where he'd read Spuds hung out most of the day, and face the music.

He went upstairs, gave Mags a kiss and told her he'd drop Leigh at nursery and Ryan at school before training. It was their usual Monday morning, so she wouldn't suspect anything. How she'd take things later was another story. But what could he do? Certainly not tell her.

He pulled the bedroom door shut to let her go back to sleep and headed downstairs, shoulders slumped. Got himself together

331

before he saw the kids, natch. Couldn't let them sense that daddy was upset. But when he dropped each of them off in turn, he couldn't help but give them an extra-long hug and look that bit longer into their bright little eyes.

Ryan was still waving to him, half-turned as he ran across the playground, when his moby rang. Jesus, this was it.

"Bobby?"

"Gaffer?"

"Yeah, didn't you recognise me? Surely I've not been gone that long."

Bothwell laughed. "Nah, sorry. Ah was just expectin' another call, that's all."

"Course you are, course you are. Actually, that's why I'm onto you. Where are you?"

"Just dropped the wee fella off at school, how?"

"Can you meet me back at your house in - what? - 15?"

"Sure, but-."

"Look, got to go. Police behind me. This Jag's going to be a magnet for them, I just know it..."

TOM HAGEN woke up beside Caroline for the first time in - God, was it really that long? Aye, suppose it was. Long, long time without her. Long, long time without that warm skin against his. Long time with no moment when they connected soul deep.

Long time since he'd been kept awake with that snoring, since she'd let rip in the middle of the night, since he'd seen her first thing with no make-up.

Christ almighty, how the fuck was he going to get himself out of this one?

LAW was already parked up outside the house when Bothwell pulled into the cul-de-sac. He pulled up behind his old gaffer, who didn't get out of the car. Instead, he signalled to his old captain to come and join him. Bothwell got out of the 4x4 and nodded admiringly to himself as he inspected the jag before slipping into the passenger seat. Law grinned and held out a hand.

"How you, son. Over Saturday?"

"Doubt if I ever will be, gaffer."

"No? Maybe a wee present behind your seat will help."

Bothwell look puzzled. Then he reached round to the footwell and put his hand on what he thought was a bag. "Where is it? Under your gym stuff?"

"No, it's in the bag. Have a look."

So Bothwell grasped the bag, a black and red Nike rucksack, put it on his lap and pulled back the zip across the top. His eyes nearly popped out of his head.

"What the f-? Where did this come fr-?"

"Long story, Bobby, but call it a going-away present. I know the situation you're in and there was no way I could pick up all the money the club were due me and leave you to face the music for something that's nothing to do with you. Just do me a favour and say nothing to nobody, eh?"

Right then, Bothwell wasn't sure if he'd ever speak again. He tried to force words out, but they wouldn't seem to come. Eventually, he sort of spat a mumbled thanks.

"No sweat, you're a good boy. I don't want anything to happen to you and as you wouldn't let me call the cops in this is the best I could think of."

"I tried to get out of it, I really did. Backed myself huge style for first goal and that gingey twat pulled one out the hat instead. Then I got my brother to hammer on dough on the number of bookings, but he couldn't get it all placed so I only got a fraction of what I needed. I couldn't tell Mags what was going on, so I was about to go and get my knees done in off those maniacs."

Law shook his head sadly, but a smile played across his pale face. "You'd have taken a beating just to protect your wife's feelings? You really are a good lad, Bobby."

"Hey, Ah'm worth more deid than alive!"

"Well, I prefer the alive version - so go see the maniacs and square them off. There's £250,000 in there, bang on. If only the chairman knew why I'd had him begging favours off the bank yesterday, eh?"

"Gaffer, I don't know how I can ever-."

"Shush, just be healthy and successful. And don't ever let me see you put the boot in again like you did on Saturday, understood?"

"Got ye."

And they both got something in their eye, so Law told him to beat it.

Bothwell watched the car turn and swish away. His old gaffer didn't even wave. It was like it had never happened.

He was in such a dream he didn't even hear his phone at first. There was no number on the screen, but whoever it was held no fears for him now.

"Young Bobby? Good mornin'."

"Mr Kerr?"

"Hey, like I said before, call me Charlie. First name terms for good customers. This is just a call to say thank you for the prompt return of my goods. Extra-prompt, in fact. We said nine this morning, but you're obviously shy seeing as you left it at the pub last night. Lucky there's no criminal element up Springburn way, know?"

Bothwell didn't know what to say.

"You there, young Bobby? Look, there's no need to worry about anything. All bets are off, if you'll pardon the expression. Nothing lost. Plus, I came in with a nicer earner thanks to you and yer pal Dog. Pass on my fondest, won't you?"

"Yeah, sure. No problem. Look, Mr Kerr-."

"Charlie, son, Charlie."

"Aye, Charlie. Look, are ye sure everythin's OK, Ah mean wi' the money an' that?"

"Well, it's here. It's counted. It's all present and correct. I just hope you or whichever of your team-mates was behind this unfortunate little scamboli has a wee thinky-poo next time before messing with the wrong chaps, eh?"

"Aye, no problem. Ah'm sorry tae have caused ye-."

"Won't hear of it, Bobby. Just keep me in mind for cup final tickets. That'd be a nice gesture."

"No sweat, many as you like."

But the phone had gone dead. And Bobby Bothwell, from being potentially two cruciate ligaments down, was suddenly left standing outside his house a quarter of a million quid up.

And from somewhere, God knows where, he knew immediately what to do with it.

BLUE EYES tried about 50 times to raise Claire before she finally answered.

"Honey, it's me. Look, can we talk."

"Nope."

"But Claire..."

"But Claire nothing. It's all been said."

"No it hasn't. Did ye read the note?"

"Nope. Binned it."

His heart sank. "What? Why? It was important."

"Not to me, Francis, what was important to me was trust in you and that went long ago."

"Yet you're the one having the affair."

"Aye, the one that's been admitted to."

"For Christ's sake, honey, don't start that..."

"Why? Because the truth hurts? Listen, Francis, I've no time for this. I've things to do."

"Aye, or a guy to do, more like."

"You're a child."

"An' you're a cow. This isn't over, not by a long way."

But she said that oh yes it was. And to prove it, she hung up and took the phone off the hook.

PAUL ARTHUR was just thinking of a fresh way into the Game Of Shame stuff for Tuesday's paper when he got a shout that Bobby Bothwell was looking for him.

"Me? What's the occasion? Ramadan? Stick him over."

He waited while Harry McFadden farted around with the phone, twice transferring the call to the Picture Desk then twice gabbling sorry into the receiver before giving up and getting young Danny to help him out. Finally, Paul heard the voice.

"Hello? Hello? Who am Ah through tae now?"

"The Live Football Phone-In. What's yer point, caller?"

"Paul? That you? It's Bobby Bothwell."

"I know, just taking the piss. How ye doin'?"

"Been better. Listen, Ah need a number if ye've got it."

"Sure, but it'll cost ye."

"Cost me what?"

"The exclusive chat on your 90 minutes of Hampden madness, bladhy bladhy blah."

"Aw come on, it's over and done wi', man."

"Ye think so? Punters are still floodin' us wi' letters and calls about how ye're either a nutjob or the ref's a Yid who had it right in for City. It's the talk o' the steamie, Boab."

"Aye? Well, a'right then. When?"

"Now. On the blower, get it out the way before that PR fud talks ye out of it."

"S'pose. But that number first?"

"Ah'm all yours, big stuff..."

LEONARDO'S was chocca when Bobby Bothwell arrived. He'd never been there before and he wasn't comfortable in strange surroundings at the best of times, but he'd rarely been as ill at ease as he was now - especially when he saw punters looking up at him from their lunches and coffees, nudging each other at who it was. He hoped to fuck his man was already in. One thing he hated was sitting in places on his own like a plank, reading the menu like it

336

was a whodunnit and trying to kid on he didn't notice all the stares.

If he paid attention and gave them a wee nod back, chances were they'd think he was Billy Big-Baws, doing the I-Am number. If he blanked them, they'd think he was a tosser. He couldn't win. Especially in a place like this, full of business-suited wanks who'd love to go back to the office and boast about how they'd seen that Glasgow City guy and what an arse he was.

Thank Christ. There he was, leaning out of a nice wee corner booth, giving him a wave. He kept his head down as he went through the restaurant, chrome and glass bar on his left, high tables with big uncomfy-looking stools on his right, then slid into the booth and shook hands.

"How ye doin'?"

"Fine. You?"

"A'right, harassed, but a'right. Thanks for seein' me."

"No sweat. Just a bit confused about what's up. Don't need me to get you a move tae us, do ye?"

"After Saturday Ah couldnae be sure o' a game, man."

"Aye, right. Was winnin' the game single-handed just an accident, then?"

"Aye, well, talkin' about accidents, listen, Ah really need tae apologise tae your boy for that tackle. What a wank Ah was for that..."

"Glad you said that an' no' me..."

"But Ah was under, like, big-time pressure. Ye've nae idea, honest."

Which was when the guilt hit Blue Eyes right in the guts. He had every idea. He hoped it wasn't written all over his coupon. He cleared his throat nervously.

"How d'ye mean, Bobby?"

"Well, ye know a' that bettin' stuff that came out in the papers? It was bollocks, know 'mean, but what was written was only the half o' it."

"Aye?"

"Aye. See - an' naebody knows this, so keep it zipped, eh? – yer man Charlie Spuds gave me a tug and wouldnae believe it was bollocks. Said he knew for a fact we'd been bought, wouldnae let it lie. An' he held me personally responsible for gettin' his dosh back."

Blue Eyes felt something inside him fall over. He didn't want to hear what was coming next, he really didn't - because whatever it was, it was all his fault for feeding his bird on the paper the line that the money had been nicked to nobble City. He felt sick.

"So, eh, what happened?"

"We won, for a start, which was somethin'. Spuds had buckets on us as well as everythin' else. But Ah still had tae get his £250,000 back, so Ah bet fortunes on masel' for first goal..."

"An' our Ginge goes an' beats ye to it..."

"Pre-fucking-cisely. So at half-time Ah get ma brother tae try and wallop thousands on a spread bet for the number o' cards..."

"Which is why ye spend the second half runnin' round like a mentalist..."

"Right again. But at the end o' it a', wi' me sent aff an' yer mate lyin' in bits, ma brothers tells me he only got a fraction o' the dough on an' Ah realise Ah'm still about 200 grand short."

"Fuck."

"Aye, fuck. An' if Ah don't find the money by this mornin', it's goodbye knees. Which is why we're here."

Blue Eyes stopped halfway through a mouthful of coffee and almost choked.

"Ye don't mean ye want me to help square Spuds aff, Ah hope? Ah mean, if it was a tenner..."

Bothwell laughed. "Naw, ye're a'right..."

And he told him the tale of Melvin Law, the Nike holdall stuffed with cash and the phone call out of the blue from Spuds thanking him for sorting everything out.

Then he put the Nike holdall on the table and told Blue Eyes to take it.

Blue Eyes nearly fainted.

"Bobby, what the fuck's goin' on? Are Charlie Spuds and his heavies goin' to come through the doors and malky me any second? Or worse still, is Jeremy Beadle hangin' around outside?"

"Neither. Listen, Ah've had a fuck of a let-off here. The money's been paid back, fuck knows how, the heat's off an' Ah've realised Ah'm actually 30-odd G up on the deal thanks tae ma mad mental spread bet. Ah cannae keep the manager's redundancy money. An' even if Ah wanted to, Ah don't need it. So Ah think tae masel', who does? Answer? You guys dae. Ah make this much every six weeks if we're winnin'. Ah'm no' wantin' tae sound wanky here, but part-time guys'll never see a quarter of a mill in a lifetime."

For about the fifth time in the conversation, Blue Eyes nearly cracked and blurted out the truth. But although he had a conscience, he wasn't stupid. So instead, he held out his hand, shook Bothwell's and said thanks.

"No problem. Now, put that under the table and act normal. Ah'm offski. Nice tae talk tae ye, man."

And with that, the most famous player in Scottish football walked calmly out of the restaurant with two dozen pairs of eyes on his back. And Francis Albert's on stalks.

"So, to recap," he thought to himself as he watched Bothwell disappear back onto the street. "last Tuesday we were on our way to play Inverclyde Thistle, then we crashed the bus, shat ourselves from armed robbers, got the three points, went to our hotel to prepare for the biggest game in the history of big games and discovered we had inherited £250,000 from an armed hold-up. We then decided not to give it to the cops but to keep it and bet it on ourselves, we sparked a massive panic at the bookies who then suspended all betting on the game until it was over, you yourself dropped Glasgow City - and Bobby Bothwell in particular - in the shite with a ruthless gangster by leaking a porky pie that City were throwing the match, your team were 3-2 up with time running out, chucked away two late goals and blew the chance to be legends. Then Bothwell walks into your life and gives you the £250,000 back. Oh, and yer wife's buggered off wi' some soon-to-be-maimed twat."

"You'd think with his money he'd have picked up that tab."

Blue Eyes snapped out of his daydream and looked up at the flushed, smug face of a businessman who'd had a couple of vinos over lunch.

"Aye, right enough, pal - tight as a gnat's, that Bothwell."

And he laughed to himself as the guy went off desperate to tell the tale of how a £30,000-a-week football star who'd just handed him a quarter of a mill was too mean to buy lunch for a mate.

AMANDA LAW could see something was wrong with her husband. He was jumpy, fidgety, kept looking at his mobile as if waiting for a call. The happy-go-lucky husband and father of yesterday was gone. His lemon polo shirt looked out of place beneath a face that had lost the first flush of colour Amanda had seen in her man for years as quickly as it had found it.

She'd let it lie all morning, but now it was dragging on a bit long. She came through with a tuna salad and a glass of ginger beer for him and gently asked what was up.

"Me? Nothing, honey."

"Come on Melvin, you've been like a cat on hot bricks all day. What's up?"

He took over his wire-rimmed glasses and pinched his nose. He looked tired.

"Ah, it's not much. Just the first day away from it, from the football. You can't be in the routine I was in for all those years and just suddenly forget about it. I woke up this morning thinking about what drills I'd give them today and I was shaving before it hit me that they weren't my responsibility any more. It's a big change in my life, love."

Amanda smiled, ruffled his wiry hair, kissed him on the forehead. "I know, darling, it can't be easy. Sorry if it sounded like I was nagging."

He held her hand for a second and looked into her green eyes. He loved those eyes. He could drown in those eyes. They were what first attracted him to her all those years ago. They'd drawn him like a magnet and he'd never wanted to be drawn by anyone else since. They were wonderfully honest eyes. Which made him feel all the worse for having just lied to them.

It wasn't just that it was his first day without football. It was that he knew already, just a few short hours into his retirement, that he'd made the wrong decision. The last week had told him that he couldn't live with the game any more, not the way it had curdled like old milk. But the horrible truth drumming itself into his brain with every tick of his watch was that living without it would be impossible.

Question was, how the hell was he going to turn it all round now and go back?

Maybe the girls could go to Disney on their own and he'd stay behind and think things through.

BRIAN CALDWELL took a second to register who the guy sitting on the leather couch in reception was. Then it clicked. It was a very angry husband.

He tensed as Claire Albert's man stood up, wondered if he should get Marie on the desk to ring security. The fact that Francis Albert was smiling didn't fool him for a second.

"Brian?"

"Francis, is it?"

"Ah think ye know it is. Want tae go somewhere an' chat?"

"Just on my way out to meet a client, I'm afraid."

"Fine, Ah'll walk with ye. Nice day out there."

So Brian Caldwell went outside with his girlfriend's husband, trying hard to look cool when inside he was churning up.

"So, what is it you want. To punch me?"

"Not really. It's her Ah'm ragin' at. You just took what was laid out for ye, eh?"

341

Caldwell stopped and glared at him. "Now wait a minute, Claire's not that kind -."

Blue Eyes smiled at him, a real crocodile smile. "Don't tell me what ma wife's like, pal. Ah'm the one she's shafted. And you're the one she's shaftin'."

Caldwell looked embarrassed. They starting walking again. "So?"

"So Ah just wanted tae meet ye. Touch base. Put a face tae the voice that answered the phone when Ah called ma house the other night."

"Look, I'm sorry about-."

"Don't be. Like Ah said, it's her Ah'm angry with."

"So why this, then?"

"This? Call it a sort o' handover."

"Sorry?"

Blue Eyes stopped again, looking Caldwell straight in the eye. Smiled.

"Brian, this is me, comin' tae you an' sayin' that as of this very moment, she's yours. Ah assume that's what ye want, eh? Ah assume she's no' just a fly shag, because if she was Ah still love her enough tae land that punch ye've been expectin'."

"No, no – she's not – I mean – I'm not - look, what do you mean, she's mine?"

"Just that. I'm out of it. She's your responsibility now. I mean, you're a lawyer, right? Nice job, nice wedge. You're plainly better for her personally an' there's little doubt ye'd be better financially. So, she's yours. Look after her, eh?"

Caldwell stopped a third time. He looked like he expected the guy to point out a hidden camera at any moment.

"Are you seriously saying that you want to GIVE her to me?"

"Brian, ma son, you TOOK her. All Ah'm sayin' is that ye can keep her. She's made it quite clear that Ah'm out, so as long as Ah get to see ma boys, that's a' Ah need. No' the house, no' her car, nothin'. Take her out for the day - say, next Sunday - an' the rest o' ma gear'll be gone. The way, young Brian, will be clear."

"But-."

"But what? Are ye married? No? Well, what? Listen, ye've unmade ma bed, so go lie in it. Ah assume ye love the lassie"

"Of course. She's brilliant. And the boys are-."

"Leave the boys out of it. If you ever try and be what you're not wi' those boys Ah'll tear your arms off, understood? Good. They're ma settlement outa this mess. They're the only success story from that marriage. OK?"

"OK, OK. Look, they love you to bits. There's no way I could muscle in there even if I wanted to. But listen, don't think I'll be moving in to your place or anything. I'm not ready. It's too soon."

"Actually, that's a point? How long has it been?

"What?"

"What d'ye mean, what? Ye think ah mean yer boaby? How long you been seein' her?"

"Not long. Three months, on and off."

"Three MONTHS? Jesus, what paira dark horses!"

Caldwell had stopped again, outside the office he was due for a meeting in. A meeting he could see far enough after all this.

"Now wait a minute, Claire's told me all about the affairs you've had-."

"Aye? Show me evidence, Mr Lawyer. Tell me one name. Find one woman willing tae stand up in a divorce court an' say I had it away wi' her. Ye won't. But AH have evidence. Ah have you. Ah'll be the one filin' the papers, the one namin' you as co-respondent. You will be legally responsible for the breakdown of my marriage and financially responsible for my wife – unless of course you intend breakin' her heart."

Then he smiled again. And held out his hand.

"Shake?"

Caldwell shook.

"Ah'll take that as an agreement, then. Nice tae meet yer. Hope Ah haven't held ye back. Oh, an' ye will give Claire ma love, won't ye?"

And he turned and walked away, whistling a nonsense tune and mentally ticking off his Things To Do list.

All he had left now was to phone the gaffer and make an excuse about missing training tonight and he'd be ready to get out of this mess for good.

He winked at a passing sort, smiled to himself and realised why the Yanks called moments like these Closure.

BOBBY BOTHWELL sneaked up behind Mags as she hoovered the lounge. Westlife were booming out of the hi-fi and she was bawling along, doing the carpet to the rhythm of the music. He stood and watched her for a moment, then put his arms round her and kissed her neck.

She nearly jumped out of her skin.

"Oh my God! Ah nearly had kittens, Bobby! You could have been anybody!"

"Oh aye? The secrets are out now, m'dear - who d'ye usually have in here when Ah'm out graftin'?"

"Ha, ha. Ye know what Ah mean. Anyway, what's wi' the good mood. Ye've been like a bear wi' a sore hingmy since Saturday."

"Aye, sorry, doll. Ah feel crap about that, so how about yer sis picks the kids up the day an' me an' you go out an' make up for me being a rocket?"

"Where?"

"Dunno - few clothes shops, few beers, nice meal? We could try that new Indian up Sauchiehall Street."

Mags gave him a loving smile. Which then turned to a leer.

"Or, Bobby Bothwell, ma sis could pick the weans up like ye say - but we forget the day out and have a wee afternoon in..."

"See? That's why you're the brains o' this outfit. Get on the phone then get up thae stairs..."

344

6.45pm, Ochilview Park, Stenhousemuir

"AND...walk."

The two lines of players dropped down the gears as they came round in front of the main stand. Jimmy D was fairly battering them through the warm-up and they were glad of the break.

"Come on, keep it sharp, keep loosenin' the legs off."

They walked round behind the goals at the Gladstone Road end and Jimmy told them to stop and take a good stretch. Someone said Thank Christ and asked where Blue Eyes was anyway. Jimmy said the skipper had phoned in sick.

The gaffer and Bibs were still inside, letting the boys do this bit on their own before getting into the session proper.

Ginge knew this was his only chance to say what he had to say.

"Er, guys ... while we're here, can I have a second?"

"What? You gonnae talk us through the wonder goal again, Zinedine?"

"No, Chunky, I'm going to invite you all to a rather special meeting after training. Away from this place if you don't mind - maybe your place, Gio, as you live nearest."

"Aye, sure, Ah've got loads o' nibbly stuff and some rather agreeable Chardonnay in, tosspot."

"Can we or can't we?"

"Aye, course. But what is it?"

"Something good, I promise. But can we leave it till then?"

They nodded and shrugged and told him OK. Chunky said he better not be planning to show the video of the game.

TOM was just locking his office behind him when he heard the moby ring again.

"You hidin' from somebody? That's about four times it's gone in the last ten minutes."

"Nah, Bibs, no sweat. Just some tosser agent tryin' to punt us a player we don't need."

345

"Who?"

"Doesnae matter, it's just a reaction tae us makin' a few bob out the cup. Forget it."

The phone rang off. Then rang again almost immediately.

"Fuckin' hell, Tom, he's keen, eh?"

Tom just grunted and headed down the tunnel. It wasn't an agent. There was no agent. It was Caroline and he'd been dodging her all day. Jesus, he'd made a Roger of this one. But he'd have to face her off some time.

"Give me two minutes, Bibs, Ah'm goin' tae sort that agent out right now. Get them in a circle, two in the middle and one-touch. Ah'll be there in two ticks."

"Good shout. Nae point lettin' these things drag on."

He unlocked the office again just as the phone was ringing. The screen said 121. He wasn't even sure he wanted to hear her voice on a message, but to hell with it. Get it over with. He dialled voicemail and the electronic drone said he had five messages.

The first was Caroline a minute ago, sounding cranky and telling him to phone her as soon as.

The second was Caroline half an hour ago, saying she was pissed off missing him and could he get back to her sharpish.

The third was Caroline two hours before that, saying she hoped he was still talking to her and that everything would be OK, just call her and have a chat.

The fourth was Caroline just before one, crying and saying she didn't know if she'd done the right thing and could he speak to her any time he was free so they could sort things out.

The fifth was Caroline at 11.23am, telling him she felt so guilty about doing this over the phone but she simply couldn't face him. The last few days had been great - but face facts, they were kidding themselves, weren't they? You can't go back. It'd never be the same. So she was sorry, but they had to call a halt before they got in too deep. She loved him and always would, but friends was as far as it should go. Though if they were in the same place at the

346

same time, there was nothing to stop them - well, you know? The odd night? Would that be wrong, Tom?"

He ended the call, raised his arms in the air and gave a yell of delight and relief.

"No, darlin', it wouldn't be wrong. In fact, ye've never been more right."

Of course, he wouldn't say that when he phoned her later. He'd be heartbroken, bitter, let down. No use letting her know she was right. But that was for later. Right now, he couldn't wait to get out there and do what he did beat, run a football team.

He jogged onto the pitch, clapping his hands and bawling for them to sharpen the passing up, stop pissin' about. Bibs wandered over and asked if he still wanted the cones out for the sprints. Tom thought about it for a second, then put an arm round his No.2.

"Nah, bollocks to it. Let's just get the wee goals out and have a game. Headers and fancies only to score and Ah'm playin' up front for the best team. C'mon, let's have a laugh..."

8.20pm, Gio's place.

"ANYBODY that wants a drink, help yerselves. There's beer in the fridge and the kettle's on. Ah'm makin' a pot o' tea. Anybody prefer coffee?"

"Ye'll make somebody a wonderful wife some day, Linda."

"Ah've already made yours, Porridge, ya fud."

"Ah know – cheers, apparently ye made her realise how good Ah was after a'."

"See? Ah'm really a one-man marriage guidance service."

"Ye're a one-man idiot."

"That's gratitude. Just for that ye can make yer own toast, fannybaws. Anyway, enough nonsense - what you brought us a' here for, Ginge-features?"

The right-back tried not to grin, but he couldn't help himself. He felt like an idiot, sitting there with his face beaming and 17 guys staring right at him.

"Well?"

"Aye, what's the script?"

"Tell them, for fuck's sake!"

"Patience, Chopper, patience." He cleared his throat and cracked his knuckles, looked at the carpet then back up at his team-mates. "OK, it's like this. Obviously the big bet went down the toilet on Saturday, right? But I have a confession. I didn't put my 12-and-a-half thou on us to win."

"You ginger tosser, Ah *knew* somebody would turn the rest o' us over..."

"Calm it, Chunky. That's not the case - well, not with me anyway. And if anyone else didn't put theirs on us, what does it matter now? We lost. But-." here he paused for effect, but immediately realised he'd only made himself look a prat, "-I did make a bet and it was sort of on us. As in, it was on me."

There was silence as they tried to take in what he was on about. Screech spoke first.

"On you for what?"

"For first goal."

"First goal? What a wanky bet tha-. Oh, wait a minute, it wisnae, wis it?"

"That's right, Screech. See, I couldn't go through with the immoral act of wagering someone else's money on something that would be determined by the actions of all of us. It was a morally bankrupt plan from the off - tell me that any of you didn't look at someone else who made a mistake, even a stupid little mistake, and curse them for screwing up your chance of making a mint? Thought so. Now look at it further from my point of view. Until the team was read out on Saturday, I had no inkling that I'd be playing, so my dependence on others to look after my investment was even greater than most. In my mind, the only person you can rely on in this game, in this world even, is yourself. So I looked at what you could back yourself to do and it turned out scoring the first goal was my lot. So, even though I knew in my heart I wouldn't play, I put on 25 bets at £500 a time at odds of..."

Again the pause, but this time suitably dramatic.

"Fuck me! Ah saw you on the list when Ah was ... well, Ah saw it. You were a hunner to one! An' Ah thought at the time it was a bit mean."

"Thanks, Jimmy. Actually, I was a wee bit disappointed to be as fancied. But still, 100 times £12,500 became rather an intoxicating prospect. I knew that if I *didn't* play and the money was wasted, at least I only had myself to blame. I could at least peek at myself in the mirror, if not exactly gaze with pride. Then, when Tom named me at right-back, I suddenly thought: 'Oo-er, this might actually happen'. Then I went and vomited. Then it *did* actually happen - and as you all saw, it actually became too much when the ball hit the net. I'm ashamed to say I simply fainted, gentlemen."

And right then they all looked like they were about to do the same. Ginge grinned at their stupid, dumbstruck faces.

"Well? Anyone going to say anything to your benefactor?"

Westy sat gawping with the rest of them, then heard himself squeeze some words out, words he'd been bottling up for days.

"Aye - Ah feel guilty as fuck now. My money went on the engagement ring an' the honeymoon. Ah'm really, really sorry. Ah cocked up. Ah nearly gave the game away."

Craw looked like he was going to punch the boy. "Cocked up? Ya twat, ye could have got us shot!"

"Aye, but Ah didnae - it was ME who got the tug fae Charlie Spuds, me that thought it was curtains. But then the mad bastard got a phone call sayin' we didnae have the money an' it was City who were at the madam. And he gave me this..."

He pulled on envelope from the holdall lying between his feet and slapped it on Gio's glass-topped coffee table.

"Ah wanted tae wait until everythin' died down before Ah showed ye. There's seven grand in there - Ah know it's no' ma whole stake, but Ah want to make things up tae ye a' by takin' us away for a weekend in, say, Dublin. Prague? Millport? Wherever ye fancy, that's it paid for."

349

Craw's face spread into a huge grin. "Ah don't care what anybody says, Westy, Ah always liked you."

BLUE EYES had pulled off the dual carriageway onto the slip round, round the roundabouts and seen the sign for the Long Stay Car Park. He'd stopped at the machine, took a ticket, waited for the barrier to lift, found a space.

He'd switched the engine off, opened the door. Closed it again. All the crazy events of the past few days went round and round in his head for the umpteenth time that day. Sat there for – well, he wasn't sure how long. Could have been a minute, ten, an hour. But however long it was, all he knew was that in that time he'd realised he couldn't go through with it.

Not for *her* sake. Bollocks to *her*. No, this was for his boys.

There he was, ten seconds' walk from the terminal, from the departures board, from picking a flight, buying a ticket and getting the hell out. He was self-employed, he was single, he had nothing to hold him back.

Plus, he was rich enough not to care about anything for a while. The world was his lobster.

So he'd got out, gone to the kiosk, paid 60p and driven out of the car park again.

Gio's flat

WESTY felt better now he'd got that lot off his chest. Jimmy D, meanwhile, didn't cough that he'd also bet himself for the first goal. As for Lambchop? There was no chance on earth that he was going to admit betting on City - and even less of him sharing the profits with these wankers.

Screech looked up from the money spilling across the table and back at Ginge.

"So, ye're a millionaire? What's yer plan?"

350

"Get the hell out of football for a start, get the hell out of bloody Scotland and set myself up in the Caribbean. Buy an ice cream stall or something, catch some rays and live off the winnings. Well, a decent slice of them."

"How d'you mean?"

"Well, last night I took a wander over to Springburn. Lovely part of the world, charming people. And at closing time, I left a bag outside a cocktail lounge called the Boston Bar. In it was £250,000. The Boston Bar belongs to one Charles Kerr, a.k.a. Charlie Spuds. I read in the papers about it being his main hang-out. I imagine he'll have been relieved to collect, don't you?"

They were all still in shock when the doorbell chimed and startled them. Gio answered it, came back in ahead of Blue Eyes.

"Skip! Thought you were dyin'?"

"Just dyin' to see ma boys, Screech, that's a'. So, what's goin' down? What's happenin'? How come yer jaws are a' scrapin' the lino?"

Gio explained what Ginge had just told them all. Blue Eyes closed his eyes and shook his head. So *that* was how Bothwell got off the hook. He walked across the room and kissed Ginge on the top of his curly head.

"You, son, are a life-saver. And Ah mean that quite literally."

"Thank you, Francis. Just being public-spirited. Oh, and there's something else..."

"What?"

He reached down the side of the armchair he'd bagged as soon as they went into the flat, pulled up his kitbag, placed it on the coffee table and opened it.

"This."

"*Fuuu*-ckin' hell!"

"Jesus..."

"How much is in there?"

"Five hundred thousand pounds, chaps. After paying Mr Spuds back, I reckoned we should split the rest 50-50. Half a mill for me, half a mill for you lot. Works out at just over double the

£12,500 you each started out with. It's all in envelopes marked with your names, so dig in. Acceptable?"

Gio slapped him on the back. "Acceptable? It's utterly spiffing, old bean. Money for nothin' an' a trip for free thanks to the Westy boy. If ye ask me, things have worked out pretty dandy-o."

Westy let out an embarrassed cough. "Aye, well, Ah don't think Ah should take ma share. Ah mean-."

"Bollocks, Mark – did I want in on this business in the first place? No. But I went in because we're a team. Sometimes in a team you mess up and your mates have to help you out. For you, this is one of those times. So take your money and give me a kiss."

And he did.

"Chunky? Here's yours."

"Cheers, Westy."

"Gio? Jimmy? Garry? Oh – and there's Barry's, that'll be a nice surprise at visitin' time. Lambchop? Willie.."

"Hang on a minute…"

"What is it, Porridge?"

"It's just hit me. Ginge might have given the money back, but d'ye think that means Charlie Spuds's just gonnae forget about it? Ah mean, the story about the million-pound coup on the first goal's bound tae hit the papers an'-."

"Not a worry, Porridge. I'll just say that myself and a few friends felt flush and had a punt on me to score. Charlie Spuds need never know any better."

"Aye, but let's just say he's no' thick as shite, Ginge. Let's give the man the benefit o' the doubt for a second. What if he puts two an' two together an' comes after you? Havin' his money back's one thing, but havin' his plonker tugged like this is gonnae make him a tad tetchy, ma friend."

"'Not going to happen, Porridge."

They all turned to look at Blue Eyes, sitting casually on the windowsill with his feet on a red and black Nike dufflebag.

"How d'you know?"

"Because Charlie Spuds thinks it was someone from City who gave him the money back. Think about it. He *thought* we had it, but then he learned different, remember?. Now, I happen to *know* that he gave Bobby Bothwell a tug after lettin' Westy go and ordered him to get the two fifty grand back to him by Monday."

"Aye? How d'ye know-."

"Because Ah'm yer skipper an' Ah'm a genius, OK? Just trust me. Spuds thinks that City bet against themselves then shat it and won the game after all and clubbed together to give the money back. As far as he's concerned, it's end of story…"

Silence. He was playing the room like Sinatra in Vegas.

As he looked round the faces of his team-mates, he thought about telling them he had somewhere to be, about getting up and walking out with the bag and going back to the airport after all.

But what would he do? Where would he go? Or, more to the point, what would he do once he was there?

Hide forever?

Meet some bird who'd rip him off for every bean?

One thing was for sure. He'd miss his boys like hell.

So he hopped down from the windowsill and grinned.

"…Except, my boys, that Charlie Spuds is wrong. It *isn't* end of story."

He picked up the red and black Nike dufflebag and placed it on the table beside Ginge's kitbag and Westy's stuffed envelope.

"What's in there?"

"I'll tell you in a few seconds, Gio. But first, let me ask you all a question."

"Go on."

"Anybody know what odds we are to win the league..?"

THE END

353